The SFWA
GRAND MASTERS

VOLUME TWO

Also from Tor Books

The SFWA
GRAND MASTERS

VOLUME TWO

ANDRE NORTON

ARTHUR C. CLARKE

ISAAC ASIMOV

ALFRED BESTER

RAY BRADBURY

EDITED BY
FREDERIK POHL

TOR®

A TOM DOHERTY ASSOCIATES BOOK
NEW YORK

THE SFWA GRAND MASTERS: VOLUME TWO

Copyright © 2000 by Science Fiction and Fantasy Writers of America, Inc.

Edited by David G. Hartwell

A Tor Book
Published by Tom Doherty Associates, LLC
175 Fifth Avenue
New York, NY 10010

www.tor.com

Tor® is a registered trademark of Tom Doherty Associates, LLC.

Design by Lisa Pifher

"SFWA" and "SFWA Grand Master" are trademarks of Science Fiction and Fantasy Writers of America, Inc., and are used with permission.

Library of Congress Cataloging-in-Publication Data

The SFWA grand masters / edited by Frederik Pohl.—1st ed.
    p. cm.
    "A Tom Doherty Associates book."
    Contents: Andre Norton—Arthur C. Clarke—
Isaac Asimov—Alfred Bester—Ray Bradbury
    ISBN 0-312-86879-0 (alk, paper)
    1. Science fiction, American. I. Pohl, Frederik. II. Science
Fiction Writers of America. III. Title: Grand masters.
PS648.S3S44 2000
813'.0876208—dc21
                                         99-21933
                                           CIP

First Edition: April 2000

Printed in the United States of America

0 9 8 7 6 5 4 3 2 1

COPYRIGHT ACKNOWLEDGMENTS

*This book is dedicated to Damon Knight
who, all by himself, created
the Science Fiction Writers of America.*

CONTENTS

INTRODUCTION

Science fiction has been around for a long time. How long, exactly, depends on how charitably one wants to define the term—as far back as the Roman Empire, if you're willing to admit *The Satyricon* of Petronius Arbiter and Lucian of Samosata's voyages to the Moon. Certainly Jonathan Swift wrote a kind of science fiction in *Gulliver's Travels* and so did Mary Wollstonecraft Shelley in *Frankenstein*; even more surely, Jules Verne and H. G. Wells were writing genuine science fiction a hundred years ago and more.

But in April 1926, there was a watershed event in the history of the field. Hugo Gernsback published his first issue of *Amazing Stories* and thus gave science fiction an identity of its own, a home and a name.

Actually the name he gave it wasn't "science fiction." Gernsback was a word-coiner, and he preferred to call it "scientifiction," but no matter. With a dedicated magazine of its own, science fiction became self-aware. The magazine attracted new readers; some new readers became new writers. When Doc Smith saw this new magazine on the stands, he pulled the manuscript of *The Skylark of Space* out of the desk drawer where it had languished since 1917, because he hadn't been able to find a good place to publish it, and at once the whole subgenre of space opera was born. By the early 1930s other magazines appeared, and a whole community of science fiction writers had taken form.

The early 1930s were not a particularly good time to be a writer of science fiction. Of the three existing magazines, two were bimonthly and none paid very much for the stories it bought. I once calculated that the average income for a science fiction writer in those days was not much more than $4 a week, and of academic respect for their work there was none.

By the time World War II had come and gone things had begun to improve for the new science fiction community. There were more of them now—a hundred or more men and women writing science fiction by then—and there were more markets, too. Several dozen additional science fiction magazines had come along (and, mostly, gone away again). Science fiction, which had dealt with rockets and atomic energy and television, began to command a little more respect once these things had appeared in the real world. Anthologies of stories from the Good Old Days began to appear, so did book contracts and offers for radio dramatization of the stories, and now and then similar offers from the science fictiony new medium of TV itself and even, once in a great while, from the movies. And writers who for a generation had been cheerfully (or glumly) signing away all rights in return for their $50 short story checks suddenly became aware that these previously unconsidered "other rights" were worth trying to retain.

The time had come to do something about it.

In unity, the writers reasoned, there ought to be strength. So one evening around 1950, Fletcher Pratt invited fifteen or twenty other science fiction writers to his apartment on West Fifty-eighth Street in New York. The meeting had an agenda. Its purpose was to consider whether it was worth trying to form a science fiction writers' organization.

Nearly everyone present at once agreed that such an organization was worth having. Nearly no one agreed on just what form it should take.

In retrospect, that was inevitable. Science fiction writers were, and are, what science fiction writers were, and are.

What are they, exactly?

Why, it happens that I may be able to answer that for you. Some time ago a team of psychologists asked themselves that very question. To find the answer they embarked on a research project. They prepared a psychological evaluation questionnaire and sent it off to every science fiction writer they could find. From their answers the psychologists prepared a group personality profile and contrasted it with similar profiles from two other kinds of human beings—one a group of writers of another sort, the other not writers at all. They found that the three profiles were pretty similar in most respects. However, in one quality—technically they called it "adventurous versus withdrawn cyclothymia," but it translates to pure stubbornness—the science fiction writers were right off the chart. As a former editor, agent, and president of various science fiction writers' organizations, I can testify that this is a true bill. I think it may be an occupational trait. After all, to do his work a science fiction writer must turn her back on the real world around him and make up a whole new one of her own. To do that requires a considerable independence of mind, which is the "adventurous" part of the cyclothymia.

But whether that is the explanation or not, the phenomenon is real enough. By and large, science fiction writers are the nicest and smartest people you'd ever want to meet, but, boy, are they *stubborn*.

They gave an adequate demonstration of this trait at that meeting at Fletcher Pratt's apartment. After the first hour one writer stalked out because it sounded too much like a trade union to him, and he didn't want to join any confounded trade union. After the second hour another writer left because it didn't look like being *enough* of a trade union. At the end of the evening nothing had been resolved. So it was determined to meet again at some later date, when everybody had had a chance to think the matter through, and everyone went home. And that second meeting never occurred.

Over the next few years there were sporadic efforts to get something going, none of which got very far. Then, in the early 1960s, one writer, Damon Knight, took matters into his own hands. He announced the formation of the Science Fiction Writers of America. The question of exactly what it would do and how it would do it he left open, for the organization to decide for itself once it had come into being. He recruited a few of the writers he knew best, and set about signing up everyone else.

As it happened, I was editing a couple of science fiction magazines at the time. Every time a new issue appeared I would get from Damon a batch of letters addressed to each writer in the issue for me to forward. The letters invited the writer to join up, and, by gosh, a lot of them did.

That was pushing forty years ago, and now the Science Fiction Writers of America—later rechristened the Science Fiction and Fantasy Writers of America—is still going strong.

I can't say that it has ever really settled the question of what it should do. That is still debated constantly, and often vigorously, in its meetings and publications, but SFWA just goes on doing whatever seems necessary, regardless. It gives useful trade information to new writers. It investigates and acts on grievances. It provides an emergency fund to help writers in disastrous situations—actually, it is to benefit this fund with a share of the royalties that this particular series of anthologies was commissioned. It keeps its members informed of developments in their field of interest and gives them a forum to exchange their views.

And, once every year or so, it honors one of the great writers in its field by presenting him or her with what is called the Grand Master Award.

The Grand Master Award is given not for any single story but for a lifetime achievement in the fields of science fiction and fantasy. So far, fewer than twenty of them have ever been given. The first five recipients—Robert A. Heinlein, Jack Williamson, Clifford D. Simak, L. Sprague de Camp, and Fritz Leiber—were honored in the first volume of this series; the second five—Andre Norton, Isaac Asimov, Arthur C. Clarke, Alfred Bester, and Ray Bradbury—are herewith.

Enjoy their stories, please. And remember that this would not have happened if it hadn't been for the determination of that one stubborn individual, Damon Knight.

—Frederik Pohl

ANDRE NORTON

b. 1912

Andre Norton is unique among the winners of the Grand Master Award in two respects: first, in her gender—she is the only woman among the first fifteen Grand Masters—second, in the fact that she is the only one who made a distinguished career in science fiction and fantasy with almost no connection to the magazines. Her first published sf, "The People of the Crater," was for the short-lived *Fantasy Book* in 1947. But after that, with very few exceptions, it was novels all the way.

Alice Mary (now legally "Andre") Norton worked as a librarian in the Cleveland, Ohio, system, writing on the side as time permitted. Between 1934 and 1954 she published four novels that lay outside the sf-fantasy genre without making much of a stir. In 1952, however, she published her first sf novel, *Star Man's Son, 2250 A.D.* It was intended, and marketed, as a juvenile novel. So were many of her earlier novels, though they shared with the juvenile books of that other Grand Master, Robert A. Heinlein, the trait of being read avidly by a large number of adults as well. Like Heinlein's, her protagonists were usually young people, male or female, growing up in a spacefaring environment and conquering it. However, unlike Heinlein—and unlike nearly all of the other Grand Masters—Norton had no particular fondness for technology. Only Ray Bradbury shared with her the distaste for machines that marks Norton's work; when the human race turned to technology, Norton has said, we lost important parts of the living experience.

Perhaps for that reason there had always been strains of heroic fantasy in her science fiction, not unlike C. L. Moore's Jirel of Joiry stories. From about 1970 on, the fantasy elements in her work won out, and she has written little on science fiction themes since.

Norton found her audience with her first science fiction novel, and it has stayed with her ever since. She left her job as a children's librarian in Cleveland and moved to Florida as a full-time writer. Some years later she relocated to Murfreesboro, Tennessee, and there she started a whole new project, this time not of her own writing. She called it "High Halleck."

Like several of the other Grand Masters, Norton felt that she had been fortunate in her life's calling and determined that it was worthwhile to try to give something back. That something is High Halleck—the complete title is High Halleck Genre Writers' Research and Reference Library—Norton's gift to the world of genre writers of all kinds.

Physically, High Halleck is in a large building adjacent to Norton's home in Murfreesboro, filled with reference books of all kinds. Norton's own work reflects the product of a good deal of careful research, and she has contributed to High Halleck the ten-thousand-volume reference library she herself accumulated over the years, along with early works of science fiction contributed by Forrest J. Ackerman; the late Robert Adams's collection of military materials, contributed by his widow; a "quite complete" (as Norton herself describes it) collection of early Gothic novels; along with Wiccan materials provided by an eighth-generation Welsh follower of the Wiccan beliefs . . . and, among much else, a pair of certified authentic witches' broomsticks. One major display is an outstanding assortment of fantasy art, but actually there is another interesting display outside the walls of the library. That is the city of Murfreesboro itself, of which the center section has been restored to what it was in the antebellum year of 1860.

"High Halleck," Norton writes, "is the product of many years of work and hoping." Because many of the materials are rare and sometimes quite fragile they can be consulted only on the premises themselves. But to use the materials, Norton says, any writer in any genre field "has merely to write and ask." (The address is High Halleck, 114 Eventide Drive, Murfreesboro TN 37130.)

Recommended Reading
by Andre Norton

Star Gate
The Beast Master
Secret of the Lost Race
Witch World
The Many Worlds of Andre Norton

MOUSETRAP

R emember that old adage about the man who built a better mousetrap and then could hardly cope with the business which beat a state highway to his door? I saw that happen once—on Mars.

Sam Levatts was politely introduced—for local color—by the tourist guides as a "desert spider." "Drunken bum" would have been the more exact term. He prospected over and through the dry lands out of Terraport and brought in Star Stones, Gormel ore, and like knickknacks to keep him sodden and mostly content. In his highly scented stupors he dreamed dreams and saw visions. At least his muttered description of the "lovely lady" was taken to be a vision, since there are no ladies in the Terraport dives he frequented and the females met there are far from lovely.

But Sam continued a peaceful dreamer until he met Len Collins and Operation Mousetrap began.

Every dumb tourist who steps into a scenic sandmobile at Terraport has heard of the "sand monsters." Those which still remain intact are now all the property of the tourist bureaus. And, brother, they're guarded as if they were a part of that cache of Martian royal jewels Black Spragg stumbled on twenty years ago. Because the monsters, which can withstand the dust storms, the extremes of desert cold and heat, crumble away if so much as a human fingertip is poked into their ribs.

Nowadays you are allowed to get within about twenty feet of the "Spider Man" or the "Armed Frog" and that's all. Try to edge a little closer and you'll get a shock that'll lay you flat on your back with your toes pointing Earthwards.

And, ever since the first monster went drifting off as a puff of dust under someone's hands, the museums back home have been adding to the cash award waiting for the fellow who can cement them for transportation. By the time Len Collins met Sam that award could be quoted in stellar figures.

Of course, all the bright boys in the glue, spray, and plastic business had been taking a crack at the problem for years. The frustrating answer being that when they stepped out of the rocket over here, all steamed up about the stickability of their new product, they had nothing to prove it on. Not one of the known monsters was available for testing purposes. Every one is insured, guarded, and under the personal protection of the Space Marines.

But Len Collins had no intention of trying to reach one of these treasures. Instead he drifted into Sam's favorite lapping ground and set them up for Levatts—three times in succession. At the end of half an hour Sam thought he had discovered the buddy of his heart. And on the fifth round he spilled his wild tale about the lovely lady who lived in the shelter of two red rocks—far away—a vague wave of the hand suggesting the general direction.

Len straightway became a lover of beauty panting to behold this supreme treat. And he stuck to Sam that night closer than a Moonman to his oxy-supply. The next morning they both disappeared from Terraport in a private sandmobile hired by Len.

Two weeks later Collins slunk into town again and booked passage back to New York. He clung to the port hotel, never sticking his head out of the door until it was time to scuttle to the rocket.

Sam showed up in the Flame Bird four nights later. He had a nasty sand burn down his jaw and he could hardly keep his feet for lack of sleep. He was also—for the first time in Martian history—cold and deadly sober. And he sat there all evening drinking nothing stronger than Sparkling Canal Water. Thereby shocking some kindred souls half out of their wits.

What TV guy doesn't smell a story in a quick change like that?

I'd been running the dives every night for a week—trying to pick up some local color for our six o'clock casting. And the most exciting and promising thing I had come across so far was Sam's sudden change of beverage. Strictly off the record—we cater to the family and tourist public mostly—I started to do a little picking and prying. Sam answered most of my feelers with grunts.

Then I hit pay dirt with the casual mention that the Three Planets Travel crowd had picked up another shocked cement dealer near their pet monster, "The Ant King." Sam rolled a mouthful of the Sparkling Water around his tongue, swallowed with a face to frighten all monsters, and asked a question of his own.

"Where do these here science guys think all the monsters come from?"

I shrugged. "No explanation that holds water. They can't examine them closely without destroying them. That's one reason for the big award awaiting any guy who can glue them together so they'll stand handling."

Sam pulled something from under the pocket flap of his spacealls. It was a picture, snapped in none too good a light, but clear enough.

Two large rocks curved toward each other to form an almost perfect archway and in the their protection stood a woman. At least her slender body had the distinctly graceful curves we have come to associate with the stronger half of the race. But she also had wings, outspread in a grand sweep as if she stood on tiptoe almost ready to take off. There were only the hints of features— that gave away the secret of what she really was—because none of the sand monsters ever showed clear features.

"Where—?" I began.

Sam spat. "Nowhere now." He was grim, and his features had tightened up. He looked about ten years younger and a darn sight tougher.

"I found her two years ago. And I kept going back just to look at her. She wasn't a monster like the rest of 'em. She was perfect. Then that—" Sam lapsed into some of the finest space-searing language I have ever been privileged to hear—"that Collins got me drunk enough to show him where she was. He knocked me out, sprayed her with his goo, and tried to load her into the back of the 'mobile. It didn't work. She held together for about five minutes and then—" He snapped his fingers. "Dust just like 'em all!"

I found myself studying the picture for a second time. And I was beginning to wish I had Collins alone for about three minutes or so. Most of the sand images I had seen I could cheerfully do without—they were all nightmare material. But, as Sam had pointed out, this was no monster. And it was the only one of its type I had ever seen or heard about. Maybe there might just be another somewhere—the desert dry lands haven't been one quarter explored.

Sam nodded as if he had caught that thought of mine right out of the smoky air.

"Won't do any harm to look. I've noticed one thing about all of the monsters—they are found only near the rocks. Red rocks like these," he tapped the snapshot, "that have a sort of blue-green moss growin' on 'em." His eyes focused on the wall but I had an idea that he was seeing beyond it, beyond all the sand barrier walls in Terraport, out into the dry lands. And I guessed that he wasn't telling all he knew—or suspected.

I couldn't forget that picture. The next night I was back at the Flame Bird. But Sam didn't show. Instead rumor had it that he had loaded up with about two months' supplies and had gone back to the desert. And that was the last I heard of him for weeks. Only, his winged woman had crept into my dreams and I hated Collins. The picture was something—but I would have given a month's credits—interstellar at that—to have seen the original.

During the next year Sam made three long trips out, keeping quiet about his discoveries, if any. He stopped drinking and he was doing better financially. Actually brought in two green Star Stones, the sale of which covered most of his expenses for the year. And he continued to take an interest in the monsters and the eternal quest for the fixative. Two of the rocket pilots told me that he was sending to Earth regularly for everything published on the subject.

Gossip had already labeled him "sand happy." I almost believed that after I met him going out of town one dawn. He was in his prospector's crawler and strapped up in plain sight on top of his water tanks was one of the damnedest contraptions I'd ever seen—a great big wire cage!

I did a double take at the thing when he slowed down to say good-by. He saw my bug-eyes and answered their protrusion with a grin, a wicked one.

"Gonna bring me back a sand mouse, fella. A smart man can learn a lot from just watchin' a sand mouse, he sure can!"

Martian sand mice may live in the sand—popularly they're supposed to eat and drink the stuff, too—but they are nowhere near like their Terran namesakes. And nobody with any brains meddles with a sand mouse. I almost dismissed Sam as hopeless then and there and wondered what form the final crack-up would take. But when he came back into town a couple of weeks later—minus the cage—he was still grinning. If Sam had held any grudge against me, I wouldn't have cared for that grin—not one bit!

Then Len Collins came back. And he started in right away at his old tricks—hanging around the dives listening to prospectors' talk. Sam had stayed in town and I caught up with them both at the Flame Bird, as thick as thieves over one table, Sam lapping up imported rye as if it were Canal Water and Len giving him cat-at-the-mouse-hole attention.

To my surprise Sam hailed me and pulled out a third stool at the table, insisting that I join them—much to Collins' annoyance. But I'm thick-skinned when I think I'm on the track of a story and I stuck. Stuck to hear Sam spill his big secret. He had discovered a new monster, one which so far surpassed the winged woman that they couldn't be compared. And Collins sat there licking his chops and almost drooling. I tried to shut Sam up—but I might as well have tried to can a dust storm. And in the end he insisted that I come along on their expedition to view this fabulous wonder. Well, I did.

We took a wind plane instead of a sandmobile. Collins was evidently in the chips and wanted speed. Sam piloted us. I noticed then, if Collins didn't, that Sam was a lot less drunk than he had been when he spilled his guts in the Flame Bird. And, noting that, I relaxed some—feeling a bit happier about the whole affair.

The red rocks we were hunting stood out like fangs—a whole row of them—rather nasty looking. From the air there was no sign of any image, but then those were mostly found in the shadow of such rocks and might not be visible from above. Sam landed the plane and we slipped and slid through the shin-deep sand.

Sam was skidding around more than was necessary and he was muttering. Once he sang—in a rather true baritone—just playing the souse again. However, we followed along without question.

Collins dragged with him a small tank which had a hose attachment. And he was so eager that he fairly crowded on Sam's heels all the way. When at last Sam stopped short he slid right into him. But Sam apparently didn't even notice the bump. He was pointing ahead and grinning fatuously.

I looked along the line indicated by his finger, eager to see another winged woman or something as good. But there was nothing even faintly resembling a monster—unless you could count a lump of greenish stuff puffed up out of the sand a foot or so.

"Well, where is it?" Collins had fallen to one knee and had to put down his spray gun while he got up.

"Right there." Sam was still pointing to that greenish lump.

Collins' face had been wind-burned to a tomato red but now it darkened to a dusky purple as he stared at that repulsive hump.

"You fool!" Only he didn't say "fool." He lurched forward and kicked that lump, kicked it good and hard.

At the same time Sam threw himself flat on the ground and, having planted one of his oversize paws between my shoulders, took me with him. I bit into a mouthful of grit and sand and struggled wildly. But Sam's hand held me pinned tightly to the earth—as if I were a laboratory bug on a slide.

There was a sort of muffled exclamation, followed by an odd choking sound, from over by the rocks. But, in spite of my squirming, Sam continued to keep me more or less blindfolded. When he at last released me I was burning mad and came up with my fists ready. Only Sam wasn't there to land on. He was standing over by the rocks, his hands on his hips, surveying something with an open and proud satisfaction.

Because now there *was* a monster in evidence, a featureless anthropoidic figure of reddish stuff. Not as horrible as some I'd seen, but strange enough.

"Now—let's see if his goo does work this time!"

Sam took up the can briskly, pointed the hose tip at the monster, and let fly with a thin stream of pale bluish vapor, washing it all over that half-crouched thing.

"But—" I was still spitting sand between my teeth and only beginning to realize what must have happened. "Is that—that thing—"

"Collins? Yeah. He shouldn't have shown his temper that way. He kicked just once too often. That's what he did to her when she started to crumple, so I counted on him doing it again. Only, disturb one of those puff balls and get the stuff that's inside them on you and—presto—a monster! I got on to it when I was being chased by a sand mouse a couple of months back. The bugger got too close to one of those things—thinking more about dinner than danger, I guess—and whamoo! Hunted me up another mouse and another puff ball—just to be on the safe side. Same thing again. So—here we are! Say, Jim, I think this is going to work!" He had drawn one finger along the monster's outstretched arm and nothing happened. It still stood solid.

"Then all those monsters must once have been alive!" I shivered a little, remembering a few of them.

Sam nodded. "Maybe they weren't all natives of Mars—too many different kinds have been found. Terra was probably not the first to land a rocket here. Certainly the antmen and that big frog never lived together. Some day I'm going to get me a stellar ship and go out to look for the world my lady came from. This thin air could never have supported her wings.

"Now, Jim, if you'll just give me a hand, we'll get this work of art back to Terraport. How many million credits are the science guys offering if one is brought back in one piece?"

He was so businesslike about it that I simply did as he asked. And he collected from the scientists all right—collected enough to buy his stellar ship. He's out there now, prospecting along the Milky Way, hunting his winged lady. And the unique monster is in the Interplanetary Museum to be gaped at by all the tourists. Me—I avoid red rocks, green puff balls, and never, never kick at objects of my displeasure—it's healthier that way.

WERE-WRATH

Krobie meat! Krobie meat!

She who had once been the Lady Thra, and was now a brown bone of a woman as worn as one of the carrion birds she snarled at in a harsh whisper, dug her fist into the muck at the foot of the first forest tree. A sharp stone cut into her palm. She welcomed that pain as she made herself watch the scene in the valley below where a man kicked his way into death's peace.

Rinard, shy, slow spoken, hard of muscle if slightly dull of wit, was one of that fighting tail who had broken out of Lanfort at its taking, riding and fighting at her back. Now he, the last of them all, was gone at the hands of these haughty, cruel northerners who would have no more refugees to threaten their own private raids and wars. She was alone.

A black running hound on a blood-red banner—she would remember that. Oh, aye, she would hold that in mind and some day—her hand closed into a tight lock upon the stone, taking the hurt of it to seal the vow she made—though it was a vow she might have little chance to keep.

The forest was her only chance. They had cut her off from the open lands. It was both dark and thick and there were storm clouds gathering. She rose, settling her sword belt more easily, and shrugged the weight of her pack straight.

There were rumors that some made a living in this place of grim dark trees. But it was evil-mouthed by most. Still, she had seen greater evils caused by men with blood reek and fire, and the dusk ahead seemed to promise shelter. Men were alien to this forest, that she had also heard. Well enough. In her heart she felt alien to her own kind; no beast could present a greater threat.

Her face was sharp featured beneath the shadow of a cap oversewn with metal rings, and she had long forgot the luxury of clean linen. Her present world was a harsh one. But there was a path opening before her, a narrow slot marked here and there by paw or hoof, but with no trace of boot track.

The silence here brought odd thoughts to mind. This was a place in which to hide, aye, but one with a secret life of its own, so that now and then Thra glanced over a shoulder seeking something that she felt lurked and watched. Her uneasiness grew the stronger with every step she took as she listened keenly for sounds of pursuit.

Now the trail widened and, in spite of the clouds and the gloom beneath the trees, more light showed ahead. She came out into a glade where two of the giant trees had crashed and now lay together; the tangled mass of branches of the one twined beyond any freeing with the upturned roots of the other.

Backed against this root-branch maze was a hut rough and yet sturdy, part of it walled with stone, and its roof seeming strong enough for a storm shelter.

To her right a basin had been formed of the same stone and into that poured a gurgle of water, welcome to her dry throat and dusty body.

Screened by bushes, Thra studied the scene before her. There was a crude chimney on the cabin, but neither scent nor sign of smoke. Two dark slits, hardly wider than her own hand, flanked the bark-covered door—she sensed no life here.

A large butterfly spiraled down, its brilliant golden wings banded with sable. Suddenly out of a tangle of small plants sprang a gray beast, but its leap was not quick enough. Not until it landed, baffled of its prey, was Thra able to identify it as a cat.

The beast settled on the fallen trunk of the nearest tree and elevated a hind leg to wash with the meticulous care of one un-interested in butterflies. Thra took an impulsive step into the open. The cat looked well fed; its presence here argued habitation. Paus-ing in its washing the cat eyed her speculatively. Into Thra's mind—

"Two-legs—a new two-legs—" There was critical appraisal in that.

Nor was she completely startled by such an invasion. Since she had entered the forest anything seemed possible. This place had its own life. But—she wet her lips with the tip of her tongue—the thought of addressing this furred creature as she might one of her own kind was difficult to accept.

The cat looked from her to the cabin and back again before she ventured hoarsely:

"Someone lives here?" To her own ears her voice was too loud.

"The den is empty—now."

Thra drew a deep breath. To be answered so! She advanced to the side of the basin, went down on one knee, her right hand still near her sword hilt, as she cupped water into the other, half lapped at its freshness.

The cat continued to watch as she pulled forth her water bag, dumped what remained of its murky contents and filled it anew. Having made sure of that future supply, Thra settled herself cross-legged to face the cat. There was a slumbrous content in this clear-ing which subtly eased both her mind and her body. She was aware of herb scents borne by the rising wind and yawned—to catch herself sharply.

Sorcery wooing her? She had fled too long from danger to trust anything or anyone. Pulling to her feet, she went towards the cabin still keeping eye on the cat.

Its gray body made no hostile move, the ears were not laid back against the skull, no warning hiss sounded. Thra set hand to the door on which no latch string dangled out in welcome. But, at the pressure of her fingers it swung inward, moving easily.

In spite of the storm clouds the light of the clearing reached now within, spreading before her like a carpet. A single room. To her right was the rough fireplace. Boards formed a bunk place. Over that was a shelf. There was also a box or coffer, a section of log hollowed out. More shelves supported an array of mugs and bowls, some of wood, others lopsidedly made of fire-burned clay.

Yet there was another piece of furniture in the room and it was enough to center full attention. All the rest was ill made, without true craft, but this armoire might have come from a high lord's castle. Fashioned of reddish wood, it was carved with the skill of a master artist, following no general pattern, rather having a story deep chiseled in the wood. The carving hid the opening of the door, for she could discern neither crack nor hinge.

Twists of leaf garlands formed frames for squares, each of which embodied an intricate scene. Some of the tiny people so depicted were no taller than her fingernail. Here rode a company of men with hounds in the full cry of a hunt. While that which fled before them—

Thra stooped closer. Even in the cabin's gloom the carven pictures were visible. That which fled hunched its shoulder; the head did not seem altogether human in outline.

She shivered. There were old tales a-plenty in Greer. Men and women—in ancient days they were said to have shared lordship with . . . others. That which fled here, which was partly like unto herself—was also something else. Thra turned quickly to the next picture.

The squares *were* allied. Here that which ran had dropped to all fours, upper limbs had become shaggy, the hands were paws.

What of the upper panels? Thra straightened to look. There was one of a forest glade containing a pool beside which lounged a youth bare of body. He dabbled one hand, leaning over to gaze into the water's mirror. So skillful had been the craftsman who had wrought this that Thra never doubted he had taken for his model a living likeness. The scene was one of peace and content.

However, in the next square the head of the lounger was up as if startled, listening. In the next—the beginning of the hunt. Thra saw so well pictured the baying of hounds she could almost hear their cries—

"Found! Found! And away—!"

So the boy from the pool changed. Still, oddly, as Thra followed the pictured story from one square to the next, she found nothing threatening or wrong in the alteration. Rather her sympathy was all for the pursued. He was the hunted—even as she had been. She found herself scratching with a fingernail at the foremost hound as if to claw it away.

Now she squatted on her heels the better to see the finish, unaware that her heart was beating faster, her breath coming raggedly, as if she too ran that course.

A sharp hiss jerked her attention from the last scene to the open door. The cat stood just within, staring in turn at the armoire. Thra looked back to the cupboard. In the last square the runner had thrown up a desperate forepaw to hook claws about a loop of low hanging vine.

"Two legs," Thra spoke aloud, using the cat's designation, "or four legs?"

"Both—neither—"

The answer was instant but one she could not understand. The cat still watched the armoire.

"Both, yet neither?" Thra shifted to view the right hand side of the armoire. Only there was no continuation of the hunt such as she had expected to find.

Rather she looked at a small, deeply incised scene of a room, as if she were a giantess spying through a window. Here was no hunt, not even a peaceful lounger.

Instead, stretched on a bed was a woman, attendants gathered about her. A maid fed wood to a fire on the hearth over which hung a kettle. Such was the detail of the scene Thra could near hear the bubbling of the water. What she saw was a bold representation of a birthing.

Quickly she sought the next square. Here the babe had safely arrived, held up for the mother to view. Only there were expressions of aversion, horror, on the faces of all those gathered there, even upon that of the mother.

A child so greeted—why? Thra hurriedly went to the next square. A man was now present, by his ornamental robe one of high degree. His face was stern set, and, plainly by his orders, one of the nurses was placing the blanket-wrapped baby in a rush basket.

The fourth scene—another man, a huntsman by his clothing

and gear, was mounted on one of those ponies used for transport of game. This rider stooped to take the basket from the nurse, while the stern-faced man watched.

Now a forest—which suggested by the skill of the carver just such a one as held Thra now—dark and secret. Here was the hunter, leaning sidewise once more in his saddle to drop the basket into a stand of rank growth.

So far the story was plain enough. She had heard, even in the south where life had once been easier, old grim tales. Men did not slay those of their own blood, but a newborn babe conveniently left in a wild place—gone before being presented to the Kin—Yes, that might well have been done. She returned to that earlier scene—horror—truly that had been also in the mother's face. This babe must have been recognized at once as something monstrous.

Left abandoned, then what? Thra traced with her finger the vine wreathing the hunter at his cruel task. Some fault in the wood had here produced a streak of darker hue, and the artist had taken advantage of it to add to the somberness of the picture.

Then—next—from a bush showed a face, or was it a beast's eager muzzle?

Man or animal, or both together? Next, that lurker had come into the open and the mixture was plain. A furred, animal-like head with pricked and large pointed ears, supported on human shoulders giving away to a woman's full breasts.

She who advanced out of hiding appeared more human in the next scene, where she had gathered the babe to her so that a small eager mouth found one of her nipples. There was peace, joy, on the animal woman's near-human face.

In other scenes the baby grew with its foster mother, played, lived seemingly happy and content. Until in the last scene of all, a boy, at that age between youth and manhood, stood staring at a huddled body on the ground, a body from which stood a cruel arrow.

Thus he had been deprived of a mother and then—on the fore of the armoire—himself hunted. Thra was not aware that her jaw had set grimly nor that her hand had gone to sword hilt again. What of the panels on the other side? She hurried to look.

Here were the wreathing vines again, dividing the familiar

squares, but all of those were blank! Except for the very first one, where there were only scratches, perhaps marking out a general sketch of a scene yet to be completed. She squinted closely at those, feeling cheated of the rest of the tale. So much so that she thudded her fist home on the meaningless marks.

As flesh met wood there sounded a sharp sound and the well-concealed door of the armoire began to swing open, folding back.

Light! At first, bemused, Thra thought there must be a torch inside. Then she saw that the radiance issued from wooden walls which had been highly polished. To her nostrils came a clean scent such as she had once known to be used in the laying up of fine clothing.

The color of the inner wood was a clear ivory. There was no hint of mustiness or dust. Nor, on investigation, could she see any hinge or latch.

However, it was what hung within which caught her full attention. Two pegs set at her own shoulder height were there, one on either side. From one depended a sword. The hilt was plain of any gem setting, seemingly made of the same ivory which lined the cabinet. Its pommel was wrought into the head of a beast . . . such as was neither man nor animal. A plain scabbard shielded the blade, and the belt was of white leather studded with small yellow gems.

Against the opposite wall was looped a second belt. This was of sleek black fur, thick and plush, so shiny it might still be a part of the coat of some well-kept cleanly beast. It was near four fingers wide and, though it supported no weapon, there was a large clasp for its fastening made to match the head of the sword pommel. Save that this human-animal countenance was snarling, its open mouth revealing curved tusks ready to rend and tear.

Though the metal of the buckle was dark, other colors played across its surface: red, orange, like flames, icy blue, the gold of the sky at sunset.

Thra put out her hand, then snatched it back, for as her fingers passed within the armoire they tingled and smarted. There was some protection here she could not understand.

Power—the power of a blade which could become awesome when the hilt fitted a hand trained to wield such a weapon. The other—more power she did not understand, from which she shrank.

How long had these hung here waiting? And for whom?

The bare side of the armoire was frustrating. She shivered. It would have been better for her had she never stumbled upon such a mystery, even though the cabin was shelter. Still she was not uneasy enough, as yet, to leave that. There was—

Thra sought the right word—waiting! Aye, that was it! Here hung these waiting—but not for her. Someone else—who?

On impulse she looked to the cat. It no longer lounged at ease. The light from the open door of the cabin had grown less. Was this an early coming of evening or the storm at hand? The animal gazed into the open, the tip of its tail swinging slowly back and forth.

"Four-legs—" she began. Instantly the cat looked to her. "For whom do you wait?"

"Wait?" The cat's head lifted a fraction. "Two legs—four-legs—both pass in their time."

"But you remain?"

"I remain," the shared thought concurred.

There had been no cat picture in all that carving. Still, Thra was sure that the animal before her had some part in the mystery. The cabin looked long deserted—

"Who?" This time her voice sounded unnaturally loud, but not loud enough to drown out a roll of thunder. At least she would remain here until the storm was over. She shucked off her pack.

If she expected any answer to her half-question, she was to be disappointed. The cat withdrew, to face out again into the rain. Thra, used to making the most of any meager comfort, moved swiftly past the crouching animal to pull grass, breaking off small thornless branches to be dumped into the bed place. She would sleep this night in better ease than she had for some time.

There was even a stack of dusty wood lengths by the hearth and these she used for a fire. Honest flames leaping there banished some of the strangeness of the cabin. The roll of thunder grew louder, and there came a crack of lightning so near that the jagged light seemed about to probe inward to her.

Thra pushed the door shut as rain slanted across the floor. The fire provided only a palm-sized light, yet in the dusk the interior of the open armoire gave off a continuous glow.

The cat had not moved. Its head still pointed towards the door. While that feeling that she awaited some portentous happening fed Thra's uneasiness. To steady her thoughts, her shaking hands, she dug the last of her trail rations from her pack. Two journey cakes, now near stone-hard, were there. She hammered a piece from the larger with the pommel of her belt knife. Her other provision was a short stick of hard dried meat that she cut into thin slivers.

One of the clay pots from the shelf gave her a chance to crumble the cake and meat into some water, forming a mess she hoped to find more palatable than it looked. Thra spun out these preparations as long as she could, the cat paying no attention to her actions.

The storm continued to loose its fury. Thra heard a distant sound which must have marked the fall of another of the giant trees. She crowded closer to the fire, holding her sunbrowned hands to the flames, though she shivered more from what she guessed might happen than from any cold.

At last she drew both sword and knife and laid them close to hand, for the cat's doorwise stare added to her disquiet. Also she edged farther around that she, too, might watch that portal. Once she arose and strove to move the armoire itself for a barrier, but its weight was beyond her shifting.

She ate the unappetizing mush with her fingers, finding it no worse than much of the food she had eaten in the immediate past. Putting the bowl to one side she sat waiting, her hands loosely clasped about her knees. Unable to stand her own imaginings any longer she asked aloud:

"Who comes?"

For the first time the cat turned its eyes toward hers. "Long waited, perhaps come at last. Take you that sword, two-legs?" Distinctly it nodded towards the weapon hanging in the armoire.

"I hold by my own steel." She dropped hand to her blade. "What or who comes? Tell me, four-legs!"

The cat had turned its full attention to the armoire.

"There hangs power—"

"Still I hold by what I know!" Thra repeated. To be sitting thus, exchanging thoughts with a cat—had some fell fever fallen on her when she entered this misbegotten woodland, or was she indeed ensorceled? Patience she had learned in a hard school during the past years and patience only might serve her now, until she discovered more.

That feeling of otherness which had been with her since she had come beneath these trees was growing sharper even though the storm seemed to be retreating. The cat showed no fear—perhaps that curiosity which men said was a strong trait in these beasts kept it here to watch her blunder into some web unknown to her.

Thra might not be forest-wise but she had stood sentry too many nights, every sense alert, to be mistaken now. Something was outside. There came a snuffling, faint but unmistakable, as if the nose of some creature swept close along the bottom crack of the door.

She arose, sword in hand, her dark brows a-scowl as she edged over to set her back to the armoire, ready to front whatever might force its way in. The lips in her gaunt face flattened against her teeth as if she could snarl like her furred companion. Yet the cat itself faced the door with no sign of anger or fear.

That snuffling ceased but, as surely as if she could see through the door, Thra believed the other still crouched there. Like the cat, it waited.

"You speak of power," she said. "Is it of claw and fang now out there?"

"Perhaps." To her astonishment the cat leaped straight for the armoire, brushing past her. Its teeth fastened upon the belt of fur, but all its energy could not pull that free from the peg on which it hung.

Hardly knowing whether she was reckless and foolhardy, or doing what was only right, Thra braved the warning prickle in her hand and reached inside to slip the strip free. It seemed to her that the fur arched upwards to meet her touch as might an animal seek a caress.

The belt fell, still held tight by the cat, and that animal backed away from the cupboard dragging it towards the door. Did it seek to deliver that prize to the lurker? With a stride Thra gained the door, her sword pointed at the cat.

"I do not know what game you would play," she said. "But here I am master—"

"You are but one sent." Words near as sharp as her own blade cut into her mind. "There is but one master!"

She could have easily spitted the animal, or kicked it aside. There was no good reason to let it outside to what waited. Save within her, brute force still did not entirely rule. So she slipped along the wall to be sheltered from the door as it opened, and then pushed, to let in a burst of rain-sweet wind.

From without sounded a strange cry, one which sent a chill along her half-crouched back. Thra wanted badly to see what stood there in the storm-dark but she did not move, only gripped her sword the more fiercely.

As if that sound were a summons, the cat, still trailing the belt from its jaws, sprang into the dark. Thra waited tensely. The light from the fire was small help and the edge of the door a screen.

Someone stepped within. She could strike now and make sure. Even as that thought came to her, the cat flashed once more into the full warmth of the fire, shaking itself vigorously.

Wet leather—her nose wrinkled at that acrid scent—also a strange musky odor as if he who wore such garments had lived unclean for a long time. For this was a man, not topping her in height more than an inch or so. He might be facing the cat and the fire, but Thra was sure he was well aware of just where she stood.

Aware but not alarmed. That realization awoke in her a spark of anger. Woman she might be, and wanderer without a following, but she was still a force to be reckoned with—as he would discover!

His arms hung loosely by his sides, there was no sword, not even the gleam of a knife-hilt at his belt. As her own, his clothing was leather but worse worn. On the shoulders tatters had peeled away, as they had also about his legs and thighs. His feet were bare, splotched with mud which he tracked on the floor.

Around his slender waist was the belt—its length of silky fur in contrast to the rest of him. For his hair was a tangle of greasy strings knotted with dried leaves and small twigs—he might have rooted in a thicket for weeks on end.

Thra fought to bring up her sword, aiming its point between those rack-thin shoulders. She had seen before men sunk to this extremity of neglect—many in the south. They could not be trusted, nor could one call them beasts, for beasts were far more clean and merciful than such.

Still, though Thra was sure he knew she menaced him, he did not turn his head, but rather dropped to his bony knees before the hearth, raising both palms to the heat. She had a confused memory of how men had once knelt so in places of worship. Did this outcast then worship fire—or only what it signified—shelter, food, warmth—plunder?

That he continued to ignore her meant one of two things— that he was not alone, but the forerunner of a party of like out-casts—or that he possessed some means of defense which did not depend upon weapons.

Those outstretched hands, was there something odd about the nails—were they not unusually long and sharp? Thra wanted him to turn his head so that she might clearly see his features—hu-man—or strange?

The cat settled on the hearth, its back to the fire, tail curled over four paws. Thra could wait no longer; her voice was unnatu-rally loud in the room.

"Who are you?" She was not sure of her question until she had voiced that demand.

He glanced back over his shoulder at last, showing her three-quarters of his face. She had expected to see a tangle of beard as wild as the crop on his head, but his cheeks were smooth as a boy's, though weather-browned to a dark shade. There was an oddity about his features. Perhaps it lay in the slant-wise set of his brows, the narrow forward thrust of his chin. His frowsy hair grew down-ward in a peak between his eyes to nearly meet the brows.

Those eyes—green or yellow—or a mixture of both? Thra had never seen their like in the face of any man of Greer. While his mouth looked too wide, his lips were very dark red and glistening. Small points of teeth showed against those, almost as if he had fangs sprouting from his jaws.

Yet for all its alienness it was not a face to disgust one, nor did it bear the signs of degradation or idiotic mindlessness which she had expected to see. When he spoke his voice was not only low pitched, but calm, even gentle:

"You have my thanks, Lady of Laniat—"

Her sword quivered in her grip. Who in this northern land could still call her by that name? Was he some other refugee? Had she once met him long ago at some feastings? No. Once met this man could never be forgotten.

"There is no more Laniat—" she returned harshly. "But I have asked—who are you?"

His hands moved in a vague gesture she could not understand. "I do not know—"

Some drifter from a lost battle? She had heard of men head-wounded so they could not remember, but were afterwards like newborn children, having to learn again how to live.

"How came you here?"

At least he should be able to answer that, unless his wits were so disordered that even recent events were lost to him.

"I have always been—" His voice trailed away as he continued to regard her with a kind of eager curiosity. In his clear eyes she could detect nothing of a sleeping mind but rather eager intelligence.

Her sword point touched the pounded earth of the floor. In spite of his foul clothing and wild appearance, he had such a quiet air of certainty that he could be wearing a disguise.

His hands had gone now to his belt where he ran fingers back and forth across the sleek fur as one might caress a beloved animal—or reassure himself that a treasure long denied, long lost, had been safely returned.

"Always been?" Doggedly she kept to her point.

He nodded. An errant lock of hair fell across his face and he brushed it aside. Not soon enough. Thra held her breath for an instant. Just so—her eyes flickered to the door of the armoire and away again. No—this was no refugee from her own land. He was— She moved her shoulders along the wall, setting more of a distance between them.

"*What* are you?" Her voice was a whisper. Still, among the wild thoughts now churning in her mind there was no fear—rather wonder. This surely—grown somewhat older—was the youth of the carving—the one who had fled the hunters.

"Why do you ask that?" It was his voice which rang loud and sharp. "When you already know—if you allow yourself to face the truth." His head inclined the slightest towards the open armoire door.

Thra moistened lips with tongue tip. "I have seen that." She, too, indicated the door. "You are like the hunted one. But—"

He raised hands from his belt, flexed his fingers full in the subdued glow of the fire. Those were claws with wet earth clinging to them, not overlong human nails.

"You have heard of my kind?"

Thra could not answer at once. What were old legends compared with this? Though the forest had such an ill name, her mind refused to connect such tales with this slender young man. Legend suggested that such as he were a dark menace of sorcery, yet in her there was no shrinking. She had met many of her own kind who carried with them a far greater stench of pure evil.

His lips drew back so those fang-sharp teeth showed clearly as he stood there straight and tall, as one facing an enemy about to make an assault on a poorly defended last redoubt.

"I am *were*." He might have been shouting a battle slogan against all the world which she represented.

Silence—so deep that she heard a leaf flutter across the floor inward from the open door. Once more his tongue swept across his lips. He looked almost sly—dangerous. Still within her she felt no menace and she held his gaze locked to hers.

"Do you understand, Lady Thra? Or are our kind not known in the south for the dreaded thrice-damned stock we are? Do you lack cursed forests there?"

Her sword point scratched a half-remembered protective pattern on the well packed earth. But what had such to do with turning aside the possible wrath of one who claimed his blood?

"You put your trust in steel?" Those slanting brows near vanished beneath the fringe of rough hair. "Ah, but steel, no matter how cunningly forged, cannot harm us. Though hounds may chase to pull us down, yet no true arrow nor spear can kill. We can feel pain but not death—save by silver. Silver or," his hands quivered, "fire."

"Still you warm yourself by that," Thra returned. "Is this not your home? Yet you bring your enemy fire into it."

His wide mouth stretched in a wry smile.

"You see me in a guise wherein fire is not master but servant. Ah, Grimclaw," he addressed the cat, "who have you summoned here? A lady who shows no fear, does not tremble nor look upon me as if I differed from those of her own kind, one who walks—"

"Two-legged?" Thra interrupted. "How is it that you greet me by my name, stranger? I am new come into these lands, only this day into your forest." She still held the thought that he might be one who had lost his wits from some battle injury.

"This is my talent—" Even as had the cat before him, he projected his unspoken answer into her mind.

That her thoughts could be so invaded was, to her, a kind of ravishment, such a blow as she had never taken before. She stiffened against showing outwardly her repugnance, but rage rose icily within her.

He no longer even looked in her direction; instead he moved a little closer to the armoire, gazing intently at the sword still hanging there. But if that weapon was his, as the belt seemed to be, he made no attempt to arm himself with it. Perhaps he had run four-legged so long that he clung to fangs and claws as his proper weapons.

"I have to thank you." Though he spoke aloud this time she thought that was a concession on his part. "I have been long afield and there are those to whom I am welcome prey. That you have brought me this much freedom," his fingers once more sought the circlet of fur about him, "is almost more than I had dared hope for. Perhaps there is some meaning in this. We are only the playthings of strange forces. And you chose a poor refuge here. Why, my lady?"

Need he ask, when he could read her mind and she could not shut him out? Thra longed to turn her sword on him—to banish so this—this *thing* who could know her in a way so unnatural. Was her every thought and feeling open to him now?

"I cannot enter where you hate—" His voice was low. "It was when I skulked outside and must know who or what waited here that I did that. We have our own oaths which we do not break!" There was high pride in him, such pride as matched her own and she felt herself responding when she did not want to yield. "Do you wish such an oath from me, lady?"

What did he awaken in her—feelings and beliefs she thought long slain? She shook her head, instead accepting this self-confessed forest monster as she would one of her own rank in the old days.

"So—what brought you here?" He returned to his first question.

"A beast pack which marches under the banner of a running hound—" She spat forth the words and thumped the point of her sword into the earth. "My freedom was hard bought—the last of my liegemen hangs from a tree in the valley. Your lords hunt to ill deaths."

His eyes glowed flame-bright for an instant.

"A running hound—aye!" Once more his lips shaped a snarl which was feral. "Roth is abroad then or—" he scowled "—since time moves differently here within the wood and years sometimes speed by without noting—one of his get. They live with fear as their armor and their weapons, but lately they have not tried the forest ways. Perhaps now the hounds will course again—on *your* trail, lady!"

He showed no signs of uneasiness but rather spoke eagerly as if he looked forward to some contest.

"It might be so." She did not enlarge upon that, wondering if she would also be considered prey by some of the forest dwellers.

"This is a place of fear," he continued. "My brethren lair here, and yet even we do not know all the dark dangers which pad the trails." He weighed her with a bold and fierce gaze but she was not to be eyed down so. Instead she returned her sword to its sheath, showing him hands as bare as his own.

"Devils and dangers I have seen a-many and the worst of them are two-legged and name themselves men." She laughed harshly. "You have made free with my name; how then are you called?"

"I am Farne—and there is another name, only that your throat cannot voice. Grimclaw here is my marshal, the holder of my castle. I have not recently been resident in this part of my domain. Lady Thra, I offer you guest right."

He stooped to catch the lower end of one of the smaller branches half-consumed by the fire, holding it aloft so that flame sprouted from its tip as it might from a wax taper.

"I light you to your chamber," he began formally and then laughed. "I fear you shall have to take us as we are, which is in ill condition. But at least—" Still holding his improvised taper he passed her to the door, to return a moment later swinging a brace of wood fowl by their feet.

"Even Roth might relish these—"

"Roth?" That was the second time he had mentioned that name. "His badge is the running hound? Roth of—" She waited.

"Farne." He had settled on his heels before the fire, drawing from a break between stones a knife with which he set about cleaning the fowl. "What is a name? It can be given to a thing, a place, a woman, a man. Those with the old knowledge claim that a name has power—that it can be used for or against that which bears it. But who truly knows?"

There was so much more she wanted to learn. What of the tale carved on the armoire of the babe abandoned in the wilds, the youth later hunted. Was it his story which was thus portrayed?

"The sword—" She pointed to that which hung in the cupboard. "Is that also of Farne?"

His head turned so suddenly she blinked and dropped hand to knife-hilt. Then he voiced a throaty sound like a growl, while the cat hissed. "What have you heard of Farne?"

"Nothing save your own words," she replied. "I saw the raiders at their work and lost a good friend to them. But yonder does hang a sword and its pommel is a head which is strange. While on two sides of that armoire is carven a tale clearly enough. Therefore I ask—does that blade fit your hand?"

"My heritage? Perhaps, lady, when the time is right. For now I wear that which is closer to me." He touched the furred belt. "That," he nodded to the sword, "has a purpose which will come." He arose from where he had set quarters of the fowls on improvised spits and went to the armoire.

"A purpose into which Farne enters?" Thra prodded him.

His shoulders tensed. She had a momentary feeling that this was all a dream. Then he caught at the door and with a sharp push sent it shut.

"Let it hang! I will not have it yet—perhaps never. There are traps and traps, and those who are hunted learn to sniff them out— or die."

Their meal was sizzling and he divided it fairly, laying it in the bowls from the shelf. Thra licked fingers scorched by hot grease before she began avidly to chew the meat from the bones.

Night had come fully but Farne made no move to close the door. Also he paused now and then as if to listen. Perhaps his ears were better attuned to the normal forest sounds so he could detect the unusual. Thra heard the squalling cry of some furred hunter that had missed its prey, the hooting of an owl. And always there was the drip of moisture and the rustle of branch.

When he had finished Farne went to that crude tree-trunk box against the far wall, pawing through its contents to select an arm-load of fresh clothing. Saying nothing he went out into the night.

Thra licked her fingers well and fed wood to the fire. She was tired and this was shelter. She looked to that bunk she had filled with bedding. The cat was washing its face, though now and then its ears twitched as it picked up some sound.

There would soon be need for more wood if the fire was to burn through the night, but there was no use seeking that in the soaked outer world. Farne. A part of Thra wondered at her own calm acceptance of him. There were the old tales—she had heard more of them as she and Rinard had prowled closer to the forest.

They had been seeking greater knowledge of this very wood, as well as supplies, when they had been trapped in the raided village. Thra had thought Rinard close on her heels, but the poor fool had stood his ground, apparently believing that he served her so, as she had discovered too late. Rinard—forcibly she put him out of her mind now. Had the raiders sighted her, tracked her later?

"Hunters—" Thra was not even aware she said that aloud until the cat answered her.

"Not yet. But a hunt comes, yes. Those others seek always for *him!*"

"Often?" she pressed.

"Often enough. Until he chooses—" But there were no more mind words added to that. Thra felt that in another place a door had closed—firmly. She would learn no more—at least for now.

Those stories of the werefolk were awesome. And Farne might be only one of many. She shifted uneasily as the were appeared to materialize out of the dark. He was dressed in fresh leather as sleek as the belt he still wore. Twigs and mud had been brushed out of his hair, the grime washed from his hands and face. He walked with assurance, and, with that same air of authority, he began to question Thra about the raid upon the village.

"It would seem that Roth, or he who holds the Hound rule now, grows overbold," Farne mused when she had done. "To this shelter—" he gestured with one hand, "you are welcome, rough though it is. But I would advise you not to remain here in the forest." He added that decisively and Thra knew resentment. There he stood fingering that belt of his and looking at her as if she were a green girl who had never heard an alarm bell.

"The forest—" He hesitated. "Oh, yes, there are those who *have* sought refuge here but mainly they are the unwary, the ignorant. Tomorrow I shall show you a trail leading westward out of Roth's way, and so see you free of this land. But tonight I have that which I must do." He turned on his heel and, with no other farewell, was gone again into the dark, the cat bounding after him.

Thra crouched in a dusk which was hardly thinned by the light of the dying fire. Her body ached with fatigue, her eyelids were heavy, yet in this place dared she yield to sleep? Tonight there was no Rinard to share the watch turn about.

She fed the last of the wood to the fire and lay down close to the hearth, drawing both sword and knife, to place them where her hand could fall easily. Thra closed her eyes knowing that, trust or no trust, she could not continue without rest.

However, she dreamed, and in that dream she fled, a hunted thing without any defense against the force on her trail. Yet within her rage flared so hot she felt as if her whole body was aflame. There arose before her a dark wall of vines so much interwoven and the terror of the chase flung her full at that. The vines writhed and wreathed, reached, clutched her in an unbreakable grip. She fought and tore at that growth, her hands rent in turn by thorns. Now she was held fast as the din of the hunt drew nearer and she heard a triumphant blast of horn.

Blast of horn! Thra opened her eyes—not upon a mass of imprisoning greenery, though the dream seemed still real for a second or two and her hands were up and out flailing the air. This was a dim and shadowed room—the only light, wan and limited, came through two narrow slits of windows.

As she pulled herself up, her body slick with sweat beneath her worn garments, she heard it clearly—a horn!

Hunters! On her own trail or merely loose in the forest? She dared not remain where she was lest she be trapped, yet to seek a path through the wood without a guide was also a lost cause.

She stumbled as she stooped for her weapons, and her hand, flung out to balance her, slapped the side of the armoire. For the second time the door swung open.

No furred belt—where was that now—and its wearer? But the sword—Her own blade would be the better for a smith's sharpening and it was well worn. Since Farne had chosen not to take this then why could she not arm herself the better?

Thra listened. The horn sounded once again and she could not deceive herself—its blatant blast was closer. She must be out and away. Slamming her own weapon into its sheath and kicking her pack towards the door, she reached for the armoire sword.

Her flesh tingled almost as if flames licked at her. But she had set the weapon swinging back and forth. Only, when she tried to grab for it her hand had no strength, fingers numb, with that numb- ness spreading up her wrist into her arm. She who had scoffed at tales of sorcery was helpless. Fear pushed her away from the slow swing of that sheathed blade.

A third call of the horn and now it was answered by a clear bay and then a second. Thra shivered. Men she could and had faced when necessity drove her to it, but hounds—with them she would have little chance. She swung around to survey the cabin. One entrance, those narrow slits of windows—it offered defense of a kind save there was no bar for the door and she had nothing to build a barricade. Only to venture out—with hounds ready to trail—

Knife, sword, she had no other weapons, she pushed aside the pack and shut the door. No bolt—it could be easily forced.

Thra fingered her knife. There was a way of escape if it came to a last desperate moment—by her own hand. To wait to be rav- ished by hound or huntsman, was that a coward's choice? How could she—?

A loud baying followed, with a note in that deep belling which startled her. Eagerness, such cry as a hound might give when its prey was in sight. Yet that had not come from just without the cabin as she had expected, rather it was farther away—to the west. It was answered by a chorus of other cries trailing away from her. She hardly dared to believe that the hunt had turned. Now her shoulder grazed the armoire.

She stood before the deep carving of the door. The were who had fled—the hunters who followed. Farne's trail, had it this morning crossed hers, setting a counter scent to draw the hounds? She frowned, breathing a little faster as if, though she had not stirred from the cabin, she had indeed run a quarry's hard pace.

Farne—she did not doubt he had been hunted before. This was his country, he would know every rock, tree, shrub of it—be fully aware of any hole giving refuge. Yes, the sound was lessening—the hunt drew westward—she need only wait until she could hear no more and then head east.

Why had he done this? Had it been by chance? Somehow Thra doubted that as she reached for her pack again. By rights he owed her no favors. True, she had, by chance, opened the armoire and the cat had taken the belt—but was that so great a service—?

So far had her thoughts gone, when she was startled by what was no hound's triumphant bay—rather a deep throated howl. Not one of pain—rather anger and—fear!

It was drowned out almost instantly by the frenzied yapping of dogs and the shouts of men. Something—Farne?—was at bay. The shouting grew louder but she could not distinguish words. With bared sword in one hand she pulled open the cabin door.

Across the clearing leaped a flash of gray. The cat was within the hut before she truly saw it. Rearing up on its hind legs it pawed forcibly at the closed door of the armoire. Its ears were flat to its skull and it was snarling steadily. Now it turned its head a fraction as its eyes sought her.

"Trap!" The word sprang into her mind with the force of a blow.

That howl sounded again from the distance. Thra listened. This quarrel was none of hers. Farne, a were, was an enemy to her kind. That he had not harmed her—had offered the gesture of guesting rights—what difference did that make now? One sword against a hound pack and the men who followed it—what could that avail?

"Nothing—" she said aloud, to answer the pressure rising in her mind, what the cat would force upon her. "This is no ploy for me—"

There was no answer in words. Instead, for a moment which might have been lifted out of real time, she saw—not this hut, the furious cat—but rather another scene.

A net which writhed with the wild struggles of what it contained, a beast with a foam-flecked mouth which strove to snap at the cords which so bound it and who flinched from that weaving. Now she could see that it was no true net, rather hide strips interwoven with linked chains which had a silver glint.

Silver!

Memory stirred as that picture broke. What had Farne said— that silver was the bane of his kind.

"That is so!" She saw no prisoner now, rather the cat still reared against the cupboard, its claws busy striving to rip the wood apart.

Guessing the secret of the armoire from her two former experiences, Thra slapped the uncarven side and the door opened. The cat leaped, attempting to pull down the sword. But it could only set that swinging. Thra thrust the point of her own weapon within and caught the loop of the belt, pulling it towards her.

The sheathed blade slid down and the cat crouched before her snarling. Once free of the armoire the weapon appeared to draw light, and the eyes of the head which formed the pommel glinted as might the eyes of a living beast.

Thra let the weapon slide to the floor. She expected the cat to catch it up as it had the belt, but instead the animal stood guard, gazing straight at her.

"What would you have of me?" she demanded.

No reply flashed into her mind, no picture rose in answer. Once more the din of the hunt swelled—almost as if that was her reply.

"Take it if that is what is needed!" she urged.

The cat did not move. Though no words formed in Thra's mind there was a growing compulsion.

"No! Your Farne is no cup brother of mine, nor liegeman. What have I to do with him? One sword cannot stand against a hound pack and huntsmen. I shall not—"

Yet, even as she made that denial, there was rising in her something which she could not understand. Ensorcelment? She fought in vain but she stooped, utterly against her true will, to take up the sword belt.

The cat arose from its crouch and uttered what was undoubtedly a yowl of promised battle. It held her gaze for a long moment before it headed towards the door.

She turned as if another will possessed her, using her body awkwardly and against every instinct. Thra, her own sword drawn, the belt of the sheathed one in her other hand, followed the cat, at first stumblingly, and then with the even tread of one who goes to face some act of sworn duty.

Grimclaw sped ahead, not taking the faint path which had led her here but rounding one of the fallen trees and heading straight through the brush which filled the small clearing.

The clamor of the hunt had not dwindled. Apparently the hounds and their masters were not on the move. As she went in that direction Thra continued to fight the will—the thing which forced her to serve its purpose. Sweat gathered at the rim of her ring sewn cap, made tracks down her face.

She was one. Before her—how many? If she exhausted her strength in fighting this compulsion what might that cost her later? She abandoned the inner struggle, allowed that which possessed her full rein.

The din of the hounds slacked off but the voices of the men grew clearer. Someone was roaring orders to lower that, fasten this—get on with it.

Grimclaw stopped short to look back at her. Thra dropped to her knees and crawled forward through brush toward another clearing. With all the stealth she had learned during her wandering she covered that ground and used her sword tip to lift a branch of leafy shrub that she might see.

Five men, two of them now occupied with cuffing back the hounds and setting leashes to their collars. He who was doing the roaring stood to one side overlooking the labors of two of his fellows who were awkwardly striving to wind closer a net encompassing a still upright and struggling captive.

Thra recognized with an icy chill of full anger the badges these hunters wore—the running hound. But five of them and four hounds—against her! She had no crossbow even, nothing except her sword—she could not attack these!

"Leave be!" ordered the roarer at last. He approached the captive to inspect the bonds tying the net to a tree. "The beast is well caught and my lord will want to see the rest of it. Jacon, get you to camp, you and Ruff taking those hounds. M'lord will not favor any who care not for *them*. And we do not know how many of such beasts slink hereabouts—"

" 'Twould be better to haul the were with us—" began one of those who had been busy by the tree.

Bull throat laughed. "It is well caught. M'lord truly had the proper secret for that after all these years. Silver they cannot break. See how it twists itself even now so that bare bits touch it not."

The prisoner so enfolded was writhing constantly, and, between the voices of the hounds being cuffed into order and those of the men, Thra caught desperate panting sounds which could only have come from the captive.

"Silver and—fire." There was brutal satisfaction in that strong voice. Aye, it was by *his* order that Rinard had been hung—with men shouting wagers on how long their captive would kick before death was merciful. Thra would have given all she possessed at that moment for a crossbow—he was so good a target standing there with his thumbs hooked in his belt, a grin stretching lips near hidden by a greasy beard. "There will be a handsome fire, perhaps of m'lord's own lighting—and good ale drunk this night!"

The two men he watched stepped back from their captive. In spite of the seeming helplessness of the netted creature, they appeared to have little liking for being near it. Thra started at a cold touch on her hand and was fearful that she might have so betrayed herself. It was Grimclaw.

"Behind—" The word blazed in her mind.

Behind what? It was hard to believe that those restless hounds had not already scented her or the cat. Away—get away before they too were trapped. Part of her mind seemed to scream that, but to no avail.

"Behind!" The cat's order was emphatic. It crouched upon its belly, one paw advanced gingerly to draw it forward and then the other. So it angled away from her and the hounds. Also it was plain that she was expected to follow.

Thra hesitated. As she did so the man who had given the orders slouched across to stand by the netted creature. He leaned down to pick up an end of the rope which clearly showed the silver knotted in it. With evil deliberation he thrust this toward the captive, inserting the end through the mesh of the net.

She both heard and felt—the cry rang in her mind worse than a wound, and a searing pain stroked her left cheek, leaving stinging agony behind. What was aimed at the captive had also touched her.

On hands and knees, using all the skulker's skills she had learned, Thra followed the slinking cat. They moved away from the clearing even as the men led out the leashed hounds, but only so for a short distance before the cat made a deliberate turn to the left. "Behind" was plain now, they were heading to the rear of those trees where the net had been anchored. She had to bite down upon her lower lip, call upon full strength not to betray herself as the transferred torture of the captive continued to scorch her own flesh.

Grimclaw halted. There were no more spurts of pain, perhaps the hound master had tired of his game. She could hear a heavy breathing—perhaps from the prisoner.

Longing to be elsewhere Thra was still bound to obey that other will. Not too far away a twist of brown and silver was looped about an upstanding tree root—surely one of the anchors of the net.

With the blade of her own sword between her teeth, Thra reached for her belt knife. The rope was thick and she feared that, even if she could sever that, the metal within would not break. But as the strands parted, the silver did not seem so hard as she had feared—it must be unusually pure and so more workable. She pried and pulled loose an end, twisting that back and forth until it broke.

As the rope end swung free Grimclaw reached up and caught it between ready jaws, stretching it taut while Thra, with all the caution she could summon, started on the next.

"Two more—but two more!" No invasion of her thoughts by Grimclaw, that had come from the captive. Thra did not resent his message, rather threw open her mind as well as she could for a picture of what must be done.

She followed the rope to her left—there was a second loop to be loosened, then hurriedly knotted about a branch to give the appearance of being untouched. She was sawing at the third when there came a shout in the clearing setting both Thra's hands to tear frenziedly at the bonds.

"Netted, by the Fangs of Rane! Netted as any beast!"

Gloating in that voice—and it was not the bull roar of the hunters' leader. Perhaps this was his lord.

"Were—" The tone of voice made the word an obscenity.

"Kinsman—" That answer was Farne's. She could never have mistaken his voice even though she had already been sure he was the captive.

"Beast—devil begotten—"

"Begotten by your blood, Kinsman—do *you* claim devil's blood?"

Thra laid hand to the last knot of rope and gave a jerk into which she put all the force she could summon. The silver mesh sawed at her fingers cruelly, but she twisted, not caring. As she fought, another voice broke in:

" 'Ware, m'lord. Perhaps there may be more of his breed nearby. On guard you dolts, on guard!"

The cord parted, leaving bleeding gouges in her fingers. She curled hand around sword hilt in spite of the pain. The sword she had dragged with her from the hut lay at her feet. Grimclaw burst from the bushes wild-eyed to stand before her.

"Give me the spell spear!" That was the lord's voice. "And you—stand near the brush on guard against any other devils this one may summon. Give me room for a cast now—"

Thra staggered back as a body swung at her. He who had been hanging in the net was free. And this was not the man who had left her in the hut but a furred, four-footed thing which had no right to run in a sane world.

Without thought Thra aimed a blow at the creature. Its yellow eyes blazed as it skidded to a halt and from the hairy throat came a deep warning growl.

Could it possess her by its will? Thra set her back to the broad trunk of a tree. Between them lay the sword from the armoire. The yellow eyes shifted from her to that. The beast advanced a paw towards the belt and then drew back as if it, as well as silver, carried some malignant spell.

Then the lord of the hunters thrust through the brush, though he came warily, a spear held at ready. Farne, if indeed it was Farne, showed fangs. But the man's eyes flickered on to Thra. She had but a moment to duck sidewise before that spear thudded between her arm and her side. Instantly she scrambled on, seeking to set the tree between them.

"There be another! This one yet unwitched!"

The bushes in the direction Thra had headed tossed and crack-led as someone forced a path through to bring them face to face. Farne moved—was before her again.

She steadied herself against the tree. Better take a spear through her here and now than fall helpless into their hands. She was already damned in their eyes and wanted to die cleanly.

The man now facing her was much younger than the leader of the hunters. Slim and agile, there was that about him which pro-claimed some kinship with Farne when the latter walked two-legged. Only the eyes were different. Beneath the edging of a helm his were as blue and cold as winter ice.

He was also armed with a second spear, but now he pounded the butt of that into the forest muck and whipped out a sword of light colored metal. Was that also forged of silver?

He thought to take her alive then, perhaps for a fate like that promised Farne. Would his liegemen help to net her while she fought their lord?

"So this one does not run on all fours. What does such a devil know of skill with steel?"

"M'lord, watch yourself. These creatures deal in foul witchery—" that was the leader of the hunters. "They can make a man see what is not—"

Thra kept silent. If they believed her were, they would indeed be wary of ensorcelment and in their wariness might lie some small chance for her. Not, she knew grimly, that she would be fortunate to live through this encounter, but it was far better to die on steel.

"Watch *you* well!" ordered the lord. "Since this one would use a blade, so shall I. Mayhap I can thus prove that such are not to be so dreaded as foolish tales would have us believe." He lunged at her with the confidence of one who has yet to meet his match.

Blade rang against blade. Thra saw a shift in those cold eyes. Had he truly thought to bring her down with that simple thrust? Was it ignorant self-confidence past belief, or knowledge that he had won many times before?

Her worn blade shivered with that contact and she feared meeting a second such blow would shatter that too often honed length. That other sword from the armoire, how far away now did it lie? She thought of Grimclaw—could the cat drag it to her? The cat had claimed the weapon from the cupboard yet her own hand had burned when she reached for it. Could one depend upon anything dark with witchery?

Thra fought defensively and kept the tree ever at her back. The point of that other weapon seemed to flicker in her very eyes and there was a sharp pain along her cheek. Where was Farne? She was sure he had been there at the beginning of this duel yet it would seem that the men had not sighted him—No time for that now—this battle was her own.

She fixed the picture of the sword in her mind. If Grimclaw read her thoughts now would he answer her? Then there was a flash of thought which did not seem aimed at her but did come like a third dancing blade to join the battle. Sword—to take the sword—to choose—

It was not her desire, something more powerful even than fear had awakened in her. There was denial, and anger, and yes, a touch of terror. The ancient enemy—the sword—No, rend, tear, take payment for the wrong thus. Fang right, claw right—those were best—always best!

There was no animal cry, but out of the bushes sprang a form which fastened upon one of the watching men. For only a second Thra spared a glance towards that struggle, heard sounds from others in the brush. Payment for that glance came with a blow upon her shoulder, which drove the mail painfully inward, bruising, though it did not cut the rings.

"Thus and thus—" He who fought sent the point again flickering into her face. She countered his stroke and her sword snapped, leaving but a jagged fragment in her hand. He laughed then and moved in for the kill.

"Thus!" he cried for the third time and that was a sentence of death or so she hoped. Instead his blade cut painfully across her fingers so she dropped her hold on her broken weapon.

"What I promise I do. Do you take this one—" he turned his head a fraction to give that order.

Thra's knife came up toward her own throat. She was ready to press the point home when pain shot through her head and she would have fallen had not the tree supported her.

No pain of body—no—this was a deeper, stronger pain, such as her kind had never been meant to bear. She heard a voice cry aloud in torment and despair against a fate which could not be denied—but the voice was not hers.

Nor did Thra appear to suffer alone. The lord who had bested her staggered, his sword fell from his hand as he put both to his head. His mouth twisted in a wordless scream.

From where the brush had been beaten down by Farne's charge someone rose. He flung up his head, sending his hair back from his face, a face which wavered and changed even as they stared at him. Man not beast now, he leaped forward and in his hand was the other sword clear of its sheath, its blade giving off a reddish glow as if it were a shaft of Hell-fire.

There were cries. Men ran but Thra did not try to move and her knife was still ready in her hand.

The lord half-twisted to face the swordsman. He visibly drew a deep breath and stooped to seize again his own weapon as if he had already regained full control of body and mind. Of his followers only one flaccid body remained on the ground.

"Well met, ill met, Kinsman!" Farne smiled slowly. He stood waiting attack even as she had earlier done.

There was a wild rage in the other's eyes. Thra thought that for this lord of the hounds the whole world had suddenly narrowed to confrontation with this single man-beast.

The glow in Farne's blade spread. His fingers, locked about the hilt, reddened, the flush wreathed about his wrist, reached up his arm. In Thra a fire seemed to burn. She caught her breath and choked down a cry of agony. If this was the cost of using the weapon to her who only stood aside, what must it be to Farne himself? For she was certain that what she felt was a reflection of what he now had to bear.

Instead he cried aloud on the edge of human rage yet still with an animal note. If the young lord thought that he faced easy meat he was made speedily aware of his mistake, for the fire blade kept play in a way which Thra with all her knowledge of weapons marveled to see.

Only for seconds she watched and then she remembered the others. What of the men who had gone with the hounds, the rest? No matter how skillful Farne might be he could not hope to stand against four or more of them. Dropping her sword shard she leaped for the body in the brush.

Red ruin above a torn throat, she looked no higher. But she had her hands on a spear haft. Above the clash of weapons behind her she heard a stifled moan.

There was a second man in the bushes. He half lay, stark faced, a mangled arm across his breast, staring at her wild-eyed as she came to him, his good hand awkwardly fumbling with a short hunting sword. She took that from him easily, wrenching it free, for her own arming.

While he spat meaningless words at her she staggered back, still afire, straight into the path of another running to the fight.

"Die, devil!"

She was still not at ready and he was about to cut her down when he shrieked aloud and threw up his hands, the wounded man echoing his cry. This pain in her head—she could hardly see. However on hands and knees Thra scrambled away as a heavy body crashed down. To make certain of his helplessness she brought the heavy pommel of the sword against the nape of his neck as his helm loosened and rolled away.

For a moment she simply crouched, sobbing for breath, hardly daring to believe she yet lived. The pain was now no longer a torment, rather a steady fire which strengthened her in a way she could not understand.

Out of a tangle of tall grass came Grimclaw. As he passed the legs of the man before her a paw aimed a quick blow, claws out.

Thra used the spear to aid her to her feet where those other two still fought with skill and desperation. Thrusting the hunting sword close to hand in the ground she stood with the spear at ready, to hold the lists. Grimclaw stationed himself beside her.

Mastery of steel—Thra knew that she watched two evenly matched fighting men of top skill. And they could almost have been brothers from one birthing. That strange cast of Farne's features had faded away. He was smiling slightly, yellow eyes alight— only the color differing from those of his enemy.

The blaze from his blade now formed a nebulous glow about his whole body, through which the sword moved like a darting tongue. Were they so evenly matched that they might fight forever without giving way? Thra could detect no sign of fatigue, no lightening of the clang of weapons.

She had no more than thought that when the flame wreathed blade appeared to turn of itself in Farne's hand. The weapon might command the man, not the man the weapon. There was a hard clang of sound and the lord's sword spun out of his grip to strike against the trunk of the tree where Thra had sheltered. He stood bare-handed, with no change of expression, as if he now awaited stoically that thrust at throat or breast which would put an end to him.

As the fire blade turned point down Farne caught and held those other chill eyes.

"Blood calls to blood," he said slowly.

The other's mouth contorted. He spat and the spittle flecked the trampled leaves by Farne's boots.

"Beast calls not to true man!" He flung up his head in harsh pride. "Kill if you will but think not that aught between us can ever be altered—runner in the night."

Farne swung the sword, not towards the other but as if he weighed something in his hand and that weight dragged heavy upon him. He shook his head.

"I run no more," he said slowly. "The choice has been forced upon me at last. I may well have lost more than I gain—"

"I do not understand you," broke in the other impatiently. "Kill me—you win nothing, beast—"

Farne, to Thra's surprise, nodded. "Nothing," he agreed. "Did you think I challenged your rulership with this?" Again he waved the sword.

That light which had blazed along it was gone. But the strangeness did not return to his face. Now he stepped back and away from the other.

"This much is true. You live, kinsman, by my leave."

The other scowled and took a step forward as if he wished to drag Farne down by strength alone.

"Also," once more the forest man shifted his grip on the sword, "I have at last come into my inheritance. No, kinsman, do not fear that you shall be dispossessed of your lands, your ill-ruled people— not yet. But the 'beast' you have been pleased to hunt is gone. Try your tricks again at your will, they shall net you naught. Take up your liegemen and get you gone. This forest has an ill name among your kind, that was not lightly earned nor shall it be forgotten."

Deliberately he sheathed the sword and held its belt in one hand. The other he put to the wide buckle of the furred belt.

As Farne's fingers touched that buckle it burst open. The metal over which the strange colors had played flaked away. Fur loosened from scaling hide and shifted through the air, the hide itself slipped and fell from about his body, to lie in bits upon the ground. Then he fastened the sword belt in its place.

The lord watched through narrowed eyes.

"You have given me quarter—I asked it not, nor shall I accept it!" His voice was harsh challenge.

"Accept or not as you wish." Farne shrugged. "You stand on land which I know and which knows me. I have made my choices—yours shall be yours only, and you will answer for them."

He turned his head to look to Thra. What he had just said, she thought, was meant in its latter part as much for her as for the lord.

She swallowed. Life was always choices and somehow she knew she faced a mighty one now. As she settled the sword she had taken into the empty scabbard at her belt she saw on the ground a wisp of dirty fur.

Two belts and a man, there was a meaning she could guess at. But in this forest one need not be surprised at anything. She made her choice.

As Farne moved forward she fell in at his right hand, Grimclaw padding into the shadow of the great trees at his left.

ALL CATS ARE GRAY

Steena of the Spaceways—that sounds just like a corny title for one of the Stellar-Vedo spreads. I ought to know; I've tried my hand at writing enough of them. Only this Steena was no glamorous babe. She was as colorless as a lunar planet—even the hair netted down to her skull had a sort of grayish cast, and I never saw her but once draped in anything but a shapeless and baggy gray spaceall.

Steena was strictly background stuff, and that is where she mostly spent her free hours—in the smelly, smoky, background corners of any stellar-port dive frequented by free spacers. If you really looked for her you could spot her—just sitting there listening to the talk—listening and remembering. She didn't open her own mouth often. But when she did, spacers had learned to listen. And the lucky few who heard her rare spoken words—these will never forget Steena.

She drifted from port to port. Being an expert operator on the big calculators, she found jobs wherever she cared to stay for a time. And she came to be something like the masterminded machines she tended—smooth, gray, without much personality of their own.

But it was Steena who told Bub Nelson about the Jovan moon rites—and her warning saved Bub's life six months later. It was Steena who identified the piece of stone Keene Clark was passing around a table one night, rightly calling it unworked Slitite. That started a rush which made ten fortunes overnight for men who were down to their last jets. And, last of all, she cracked the case of the *Empress of Mars*.

All the boys who had profited by her queer store of knowledge and her photographic memory tried at one time or another to balance the scales. But she wouldn't take so much as a cup of canal water at their expense, let alone the credits they tried to push on her. Bub Nelson was the only one who got around her refusal. It was he who brought her Bat.

About a year after the Jovan affair, he walked into the Free Fall one night and dumped Bat down on her table. Bat looked at Steena and growled. She looked calmly back at him and nodded once. From then on they traveled together—the thin gray woman and the big gray tomcat. Bat learned to know the inside of more stellar bars than even most spacers visit in their lifetimes. He developed a liking for Vernal juice, drank it neat and quick, right out of the glass. And he was always at home on any table where Steena elected to drop him.

This is really the story of Steena, Bat, Cliff Moran, and the *Empress of Mars*, a story which is already a legend of the spaceways. And it's a damn good story, too. I ought to know, having framed the first version of it myself.

For I was there, right in the Rigel Royal, when it all began on the night that Cliff Moran blew in, looking lower than an antman's belly and twice as nasty. He'd had a spell of luck foul enough to twist a man into a slug snake, and we all knew that there was an attachment out for his ship. Cliff had fought his way up from the back courts of Venaport. Lose his ship and he'd slip back there— to rot. He was at the snarling stage that night when he picked out a table for himself and set out to drink away his troubles.

However, just as the first bottle arrived, so did a visitor. Steena came out of her corner, Bat curled around her shoulders stolewise, his favorite mode of travel. She crossed over and dropped down, without invitation, at Cliff's side. That shook him out of his sulks. Because Steena never chose company when she could be alone. If one of the man-stones on Ganymede had come stumping in, it wouldn't have made more of us look out of the corners of our eyes.

She stretched out one long-fingered hand, set aside the bottle he had ordered, and said only one thing. "It's about time for the *Empress of Mars* to appear."

Cliff scowled and bit his lip. He was tough, tough as jet lining—you have to be granite inside and out to struggle up from Venaport to a ship command. But we could guess what was running through his mind at that moment. The *Empress of Mars* was just about the biggest prize a spacer could aim for. But in the fifty years she had been following her queer derelict orbit through space, many men had tried to bring her in—and none had succeeded.

A pleasure ship carrying untold wealth, she had been mysteriously abandoned in space by passengers and crew, none of whom had ever been seen or heard of again. At intervals thereafter she had been sighted, even boarded. Those who ventured into her either vanished or returned swiftly without any believable explanation of what they had seen—wanting only to get away from her as quickly as possible. But the man who could bring her in—or even strip her clean in space—that man would win the jackpot.

"All right!" Cliff slammed his fist on the table. "I'll try even that!"

Steena looked at him, much as she must have looked at Bat that day Bub Nelson brought him to her, and nodded. That was all I saw. The rest of the story came to me in pieces, months later and in another port half the system away.

Cliff took off that night. He was afraid to risk waiting—with a writ out that could pull the ship from under him. And it wasn't until he was in space that he discovered his passengers—Steena and Bat. We'll never know what happened then. I'm betting Steena made no explanation at all. She wouldn't.

It was the first time she had decided to cash in on her own tip and she was there—that was all. Maybe that point weighed with Cliff, maybe he just didn't care. Anyway, the three were together when they sighted the *Empress* riding, her deadlights gleaming, a ghost ship in night space.

She must have been an eerie sight because her other lights were on too, in addition to the red warnings at her nose. She seemed alive, a Flying Dutchman of space. Cliff worked his ship skillfully alongside and had no trouble in snapping magnetic lines to her lock. Some minutes later the three of them passed into her. There was still air in her cabins and corridors, air that bore a faint corrupt taint which set Bat to sniffing greedily and could be picked up even by the less sensitive human nostrils.

Cliff headed straight for the control cabin, but Steena and Bat went prowling. Closed doors were a challenge to both of them and Steena opened each as she passed, taking a quick look at what lay within. The fifth door opened on a room which no woman could leave without further investigation.

I don't know what had been housed there when the *Empress* left port on her last lengthy cruise. Anyone really curious can check back on the old photo-reg cards. But there was a lavish display of silk trailing out of two travel kits on the floor, a dressing table crowded with crystal and jeweled containers, along with other lures for the female which drew Steena in. She was standing in front of the dressing table when she glanced into the mirror—glanced into it and froze.

Over her right shoulder she could see the spider-silk cover on the bed. Right in the middle of that sheer, gossamer expanse was a sparkling heap of gems, the dumped contents of some jewel case. Bat had jumped to the foot of the bed and flattened out as cats will, watching those gems, watching them and—something else!

Steena put out her hand blindly and caught up the nearest bottle. As she unstoppered it, she watched the mirrored bed. A gemmed bracelet rose from the pile, rose in the air and tinkled its siren song. It was as if an idle hand played. . . . Bat spat almost noiselessly. But he did not retreat. Bat had not yet decided his course.

She put down the bottle. Then she did something which perhaps few of the men she had listened to through the years could have done. She moved without hurry or sign of disturbance on a tour about the room. And, although she approached the bed, she did not touch the jewels. She could not force herself to do that. It took her five minutes to play out her innocence and unconcern. Then it was Bat who decided the issue.

He leaped from the bed and escorted something to the door, remaining a careful distance behind. Then he mewed loudly twice. Steena followed him and opened the door wider.

Bat went straight on down the corridor, as intent as a hound on the warmest of scents. Steena strolled behind him, holding her pace to the unhurried gait of an explorer. What sped before them was invisible to her, but Bat was never baffled by it.

They must have gone into the control cabin almost on the heels of the unseen—if the unseen had heels, which there was good reason to doubt—for Bat crouched just within the doorway and refused to move on. Steena looked down the length of the instrument panels and officers' station seats to where Cliff Moran worked. Her boots made no sound on the heavy carpet, and he did not glance up but sat humming through set teeth, as he tested the tardy and reluctant responses to buttons which had not been pushed in years.

To human eyes they were alone in the cabin. But Bat still followed a moving something, which he had at last made up his mind to distrust and dislike. For now he took a step or two forward and spat—his loathing made plain by every raised hair along his spine. And in that same moment Steena saw a flicker—a flicker of vague outline against Cliff's hunched shoulders, as if the invisible one had crossed the space between them.

But why had it been revealed against Cliff and not against the back of one of the seats or against the panels, the walls of the corridor or the cover of the bed where it had reclined and played with its loot? What could Bat see?

The storehouse memory that had served Steena so well through the years clicked open a half-forgotten door. With one swift motion, she tore loose her spaceall and flung the baggy garment across the back of the nearest seat.

Bat was snarling now, emitting the throaty rising cry that was his hunting song. But he was edging back, back towards Steena's feet, shrinking from something he could not fight but which he faced defiantly. If he could draw it after him, past that dangling spaceall . . . He had to—it was their only chance!

"What the . . ." Cliff had come out of his seat and was staring at them.

What he saw must have been weird enough: Steena, bare-armed and bare-shouldered, her usually stiffly-netted hair falling wildly down her back; Steena watching empty space with narrowed eyes and set mouth, calculating a single wild chance. Bat, crouched on his belly, was retreating from thin air step by step and wailing like a demon.

"Toss me your blaster." Steena gave the order calmly—as if they were still at their table in the Rigel Royal.

And as quietly, Cliff obeyed. She caught the small weapon out of the air with a steady hand—caught and leveled it.

"Stay where you are!" she warned. "Back, Bat, bring it back."

With a last throat-splitting screech of rage and hate, Bat twisted to safety between her boots. She pressed with thumb and forefinger, firing at the spaceall. The material turned to powdery flakes of ash—except for certain bits which still flapped from the scorched seat—as if something had protected them from the force of the blast. Bat sprang straight up in the air with a screech that tore their ears.

"What . . . ?" began Cliff again.

Steena made a warning motion with her left hand. *"Wait!"*

She was still tense, still watching Bat. The cat dashed madly around the cabin twice, running crazily with white-ringed eyes and flecks of foam on his muzzle. Then he stopped abruptly in the doorway, stopped and looked back over his shoulder for a long, silent moment. He sniffed delicately.

Steena and Cliff could smell it too now, a thick oily stench which was not the usual odor left by an exploding blaster shell.

Bat came back, treading daintily across the carpet, almost on the tips of his paws. He raised his head as he passed Steena, and then he went confidently beyond to sniff, to sniff and spit twice at the unburned strips of the spaceall. Having thus paid his respects to the late enemy, he sat down calmly and set to washing his fur with deliberation. Steena sighed once and dropped into the navigator's seat.

"Maybe now you'll tell me what in the hell's happened?" Cliff exploded as he took the blaster out of her hand.

"Gray," she said dazedly, "it must have been gray—or I couldn't have seen it like that. I'm color-blind, you see. I can see only shades of gray—my whole world is gray. Like Bat's—his world is gray, too—all gray. But he's been compensated, for he can see above and below our range of color vibrations, and apparently so can I!"

Her voice quavered, and she raised her chin with a new air

Cliff had never seen before—a sort of proud acceptance. She pushed back her wandering hair, but she made no move to imprison it under the heavy net again.

"That is why I saw the thing when it crossed between us. Against your spaceall it was another shade of gray—an outline. So I put out mine and waited for it to show against that—it was our only chance, Cliff.

"It was curious at first, I think, and it knew we couldn't see it—which is why it waited to attack. But when Bat's actions gave it away, it moved. So I waited to see that flicker against the spaceall, and then I let him have it. It's really very simple. . . ."

Cliff laughed a bit shakily. "But what *was* this gray thing? I don't get it."

"I think it was what made the *Empress* a derelict. Something out of space, maybe, or from another world somewhere." She waved her hands. "It's invisible because it's a color beyond our range of sight. It must have stayed in here all these years. And it kills—it must—when its curiosity is satisfied." Swiftly she described the scene, the scene in the cabin, and the strange behavior of the gem pile which had betrayed the creature to her.

Cliff did not return his blaster to its holder. "Any more of them aboard, d'you think?" He didn't look pleased at the prospect.

Steena turned to Bat. He was paying particular attention to the space between two front toes in the process of a complete bath. "I don't think so. But Bat will tell us if there are. He can see them clearly, I believe."

But there weren't any more and two weeks later, Cliff, Steena, and Bat brought the *Empress* into the lunar quarantine station. And that is the end of Steena's story because, as we have been told, happy marriages need no chronicles. Steena had found someone who knew of her gray world and did not find it too hard to share with her—someone besides Bat. It turned out to be a real love match.

The last time I saw her, she was wrapped in a flame-red cloak from the looms of Rigel and wore a fortune in Jovan rubies blazing on her wrists. Cliff was flipping a three figured credit bill to a waiter. And Bat had a row of Vernal juice glasses set up before him. Just a little family party out on the town.

SERPENT'S TOOTH

The haze was thinner than a drifting cloud, moving with the travelers ... there was no rain here to temper the burning of the rough soil under Rentarn's bare and already scarred feet. Modic rode, even in this time and place he held to the dignity of a Seeker, but the trembling legs of the bony horse he bestrode (it was the worst mount of his train) threatened any moment to collapse, spilling rider on the ground. Only the Seeker's will kept the horse going along a wandering seam in the surface of the stones they had chanced upon an hour ago.

In Rentarn coiled and wove the old fears which had been bred in his kind for generations. He had been sure of disaster to come ever since this thin-faced man, with a jaw and nose which had the side view of a sword, had come to the village to demand, with a certainty overriding all other wills, a guide for journey west. Neither had Modic followed the rules of the Betweener village but had stabbed with a gloved forefinger at Rentarn and called for him. Though Sequine, the Speaker, had argued it was not the tall youth's turn.

Modic had only grinned fiercely and shaken his head when the first two drawn properly by lot came to him, saying that Rentarn looked sturdy enough to lead a Traveler into the Questionable Land. At last Sequine had shrugged and nodded. Each of them knew sooner or later a guide found the Gate of Death. Now women and children hid in the mud-brick huts as all had heard of Be-tweeners slain for drunken amusement, or because would-be Seekers had been irritated by some small matter. From the moment Modic had made his choice they knew that it was Rentarn who must go. A half company of riders appearing on the bluff above had been an open warning for the clan village to obey Modic's desires.

"No knife." The Seeker had ridden closer to inspect the guide's equipment which Sequine's own son had brought forth. Modic kicked out as the boy passed him with such skill that the knife, a little loose in the scabbard, flew to strike against a hut wall.

"Leave it, you!" Modic moved his mount again until it stood between the Speaker and the boy. The Seeker said no more, but Rentarn nodded to the Speaker. "Obey . . . for the good of the clan."

In that last moment of boyhood the guide lost belief that truth and right were strong against any evil which might prevail. Now to be separated from his own people had only one meaning . . . this doom-faced warrior had a secret, and surely no one would live to betray its discovery. There were his men beyond; might he be able to get rid of them as easily?

"You pledge yourself . . ." That was no question. More like an order. Rentarn nodded. He could sense the tension seep out of the rest of the villagers. A bargain had been struck and surely this one, who knew so much of their customs, would now leave. It was un-fortunate about Rentarn of course, but he had no kin here closer than a cousin, and between them had been many quarrels. What was the life of one man compared to all the village?

They had set out at the first color of sunrise and had kept plodding on straight into the heart of the vast waste. The now risen sun pressed a blanket of heat down upon them. They all carried water gourds which they had filled at the village spring. Yes, Ren-tarn thought, watching them when he believed Modic no longer checked upon him, these were indeed Seekers. Certainly they used water frugally at the rest stops Modic ordered each time the shadows of the towering stones standing here and there lengthened appre-ciatively. Also they watered their beasts, first giving them to drink out of their helms and washing out the nostrils of each with a damp cloth. For themselves they allowed only what must have been a swallow or two.

Hereabouts the desert land was not still flat for there appeared a way which ran straight as if that had been cut by the force of man's desire for a road. Curiosity awakened in Rentarn. At the third stop he pretended to adjust the webbing which held his water gourd and packet of journey food, while, with his left hand, he stabbed one of his long and narrow fingers into the sand and gravel, far enough to scrape against the webbing of flesh which united all six fingers into a more solid fist. Underneath there was indeed a solid obstruction. Two of his middle fingers met a solid surface with bruising force.

Now he pulled his sun-resisting cloak higher on his shoulders and, through narrowed eyes, surveyed the country. Here stood a third hill, a mount of stone, partly seen there some summer dried shrubs . . . Yes! Rentarn's breath puffed against the edge of his cloak as straightaway he fought a sharp stab of emotion which he must not allow any of those about him to see.

Even the guides knew very little of this dreary world . . . save of the paths to which one or two bolder explorers might add a few new lengths several times in a lifetime. He knew that hill right enough . . . it marked the furthermost of his own rovings in this direction. Now, as he sighted it, he believed that this curious sand-covered cut ran directly towards that, as if the hill was indeed a marker on an ancient road.

It could lead where? Still aware of Modic he turned his head slowly, this time seemingly concentrating on the shoulder strapping of his supply net. He was somehow sure that he was right. They had camped on a portion of a forgotten road which ran straight ahead.

Rentarn's pointed tongue slid over his lower lip as if, like his very distant cousin of the true lizard breed, he could pick up scent impressions cast by man or animal.

One kept away from these roads. Such could be traced easily enough, but they led to the spirit places where the haze, such as they had traveled through earlier, thickened to give shelter to things . . . things which he had heard described, legends of all guide villages. He slid his tongue out between his lips, startled past prudence into a grunt.

Could the Seeker know of this? Was he now aware that such roads led to the death light? A shadow fell across his face as he watched Modic, wondering for a moment of real fear if the man had guessed at his own discovery.

The Seeker dropped to the sand and crossed his legs, his hands playing with the hilt of his sword, drawing the blade out an inch or two from the scabbard and then thrusting it forcefully back again, as if he foresaw a need for its use. Rentarn had regained full control . . . he could hear the snick of the blade, however his narrow gaze was on Modic's face not the Seeker's hands. It was always the eyes into which one must look, Rentarn remembered clearly Sequine's warning. For it is by the changes in a man's eyes one could read the coming of violence.

"So," Modic's voice was hardly above a whisper, certainly it could not reach anyone farther away then Rentarn, "you have found it. Dig!" His lazy tone sharpened into an order, he motioned toward where the guide had been secretly delving. Obeying, Rentarn dug both-handed now. Within a number of breaths, lightly drawn breaths (lest he could take into him some danger of this place), he scooped out parched earth, throwing it to one side. He was right, it required very little in the way of labor to lay bare a section of a road of the waste devils . . . the black surface of it uncorroded by time and as smooth as his own scratched and bleeding skin.

Though Modic leaned more closely forward, Rentarn perceived he did not lose sight of the guide for more than half a breath at a time. "Right." When the Seeker spoke it seemed more to himself than to Rentarn. "The road to Lonscraft . . . at last!"

This time Rentarn's astonishment was rooted in fear. He jerked back his hands from hand contact with the damnable thing. Fighting to remain impassive, knowing within him that Modic was well aware of his inbred fear and was now studying the Betweener closely, a small evil smile about his lips.

"Ah, yes." The Seeker kept his voice low and confidential in tone, as if he and Rentarn shared some secret which was unknown to the others. "This is the way to Lonscraft. Though that was not the name it bore in other days when the world was still all for men and not for sand-dwelling rats!"

He scrabbled inside his outer robe with his left hand, bringing out a small sheet of dull metal, near as thin as the skin of a ripe wavel. Still keeping one finger firmly on the edge of it he pushed the plate a little closer to Rentarn.

"Do you know the reading of maps, Guide, or do you only carry such information in your scaled head?" His slight smile now held no amusement, rather cruel, taunting humor.

So this one did not know of those treasure places located by villages . . . to which the youths went to learn . . . by heart and deep in the mind . . . the ancient roads and more than roads, the dangers and few secrets of the Sand Sea. One quick glance told Rentarn much. That which Modic held must have been graven by a master worker in metal. However only as far as the hillock behind them now did the lines assume any kinship with the records he himself had long ago memorized. This map displayed the warning blue of the Before Time road leading to a city of even darker blue, a color which seemed to pulsate in the light as if a breathing, and perhaps sentient, creature.

"Well, and what have you to say to this, Guide? I needed your steering to that hillock, knowing that what I sought lay beyond." Dry as it was, a droplet of saliva gathered at the corner of the Seeker's mouth, as he no longer gazed at Rentarn . . . rather at his map.

It was the colors which confused the sight, Rentarn decided. Certainly those lines did not really coil or quiver. From which clan had Modic stolen this record . . . one of the forbidden ones used to warn?

"It is true!" There was a sharp note in the man's voice as if Rentarn had openly questioned that fact. "Lonscraft lies awaiting us."

"That is a death place," Rentarn replied evenly. "He who rashly adventures into one of those gathers to him an ill for which there is no treatment. His skin rots upon his body, pain wrings him to death. There is nothing worth such a death . . . all the Betweeners know that."

Modic laughed, "Guide, you and your kind have been content

to exist for years on the border of this demon-haunted land with no reason for it. Every illness runs its course and then disappears. Have you not heard of the burning fever which may strike out of nowhere for a season and then be utterly gone . . . or the Great Cough which has devastated whole cities, such as Quaadad, yet men may live there in comfort now. There is no death which lingers forever . . . especially in a desert city where there is naught to feed its hunger. Long ago Lonscraft must have been deserted even by demons. Yet there still lies within its walls secrets. . . ." The fingers of his hand clenched over the map as if he would pluck what he wished from the surface. "Riches beyond richness. Guide . . . think on it!"

Riches, of course, were what had drawn this Seeker and his following of ragged men (who, nevertheless, carried well-kept arms) into the desert. How many such maps had been shown briefly to the Betweeners in the generations since they had begun their very cautious ventures into the parched land? Rentarn knew that it was not in the inner walls of Lonscraft which he himself feared, but perhaps the fact that he knew too much now. He guessed that Modic, on the threshold of what he thought an exciting and profitable discovery, would not parade and plume himself before his rag-tag crew. No, but he might talk freely before one who was destined never to come out of the Forgotten land. That sword which the Seeker held so tightly would put an end to any chance of another's betrayal. Not that Rentarn would fare better than any one of the men clinging to the shadows about them, seeking for some small answer to the burning of the sun. Murder was the practical move for Modic, and the Betweener already accepted the drastic end before him.

The Seeker would use him (in spite of that map) to follow the ancient way. . . . He might even test the authenticity of legends by dispatching Rentarn alone into the midst of a dead city perhaps as bait to spring a trap.

One slight figure, cloaked against the heat, stood alone here. However, the death blow had not yet been openly delivered. Though every breath Rentarn drew brought him closer to that time of challenge.

Warnings known to his own kind worked in him. With those

a small spark of excitement flashed into life, turning his thoughts in another direction. If this Modic was right and he could win through to return with such knowledge for his own clan . . . ! Their own perilous situation might cease to be. There were other "cities" each reported to the Seeker . . . and the information was shared with two other villages within a three days' walking. No longer would they have to point these arrogant and cruel Seekers to the Dry Land, instead they would venture inward for their own loot and trade their findings openly at the Mus-fair, year's end. As long as Modic made no outward attack Rentarn would serve his own people, forcing into his memory a picture of here in relation to the hill point. However he must also watch for a chance of escape. It would indeed be strange . . . even without belief . . . that one of the guides could be tracked and captured traveling a country he knew well. Though he had kept his advance with Modic to a shambling trot which matched the pace of the bone rack of a horse . . . he could summon the speed of his far, far kin, tailed and going four-footed here. Let him but get Modic thoroughly interested in some-thing other than himself . . . say, a forgotten treasure house . . . and Rentarn could slip away before anyone here could use lance or sword. The one thing he had to fear (bow bolts) was lacking among the troops.

He must play a perilous game. His thought, as well as his body, was intentionally slow.

"You seek a great treasure?" he asked, apparently taking no interest in the Seeker's hand upon the sword hilt.

Modic showed his yellow stained teeth in a wider grin.

"Treasure? Yes, but not perhaps quite as you and those . . ." he gestured to his men with his chin, "would so see it." Then he snapped his jaws shut and scowled at Rentarn and the others with narrow measurement, as if, of a sudden he regretted the revelation of even so little.

"You are a guide." He changed the subject abruptly. "Let us now see that vaunted power of such talent beyond the boundaries. Get me to Lonscraft or within sight of it before that sun is gone. He gave a quick glance over his shoulder as if to measure where in the sky the light-giving ball now rode.

"There are many cities . . ." Rentarn said quietly. "It can well be that this trail," once more he patted the sand about that pocket in which lay the traces of the very ancient way, "could lead somewhere else than Lonscraft."

There came a sharp bark of laughter from the other. "No, it is here!" He had picked up his bit of engraved metal and thrust it back into hiding. "I have been long at this game, Guide, but not so long as to become weary and make such an error. Ten times over have I come across the Between lands . . . and more times than that have I listened to the tales told at Mus-fair. First, that hillock which you have found for us is pointing to Lonscraft."

Rentarn blinked, he had indeed believed that the Seeker was an old hand at the game of invading the uninvadable. But what could keep one of a sane mind so long at searching? It was true that the hill behind them was relatively unknown. He, himself, had chanced upon it only last season . . . it had been his first addition to the clan lore. However there were signs of others who visited there . . . horse dung dried into powder where the wind rolled it here and there, some scrapes on one of the upstanding stones which were too regular to be of natural fashioning and which Modic had studied with care as long as there was light enough to see both last night and again early this morning. Messages?

The clan no longer wrote such notes. He would report again what he had seen so that mention was made of it in the training of the young. Who needed scratches set on rocks when he could summon into memory . . . full and vivid as any picture . . . what he had seen over Modic's hunched shoulder?

The Seeker made no protest against Rentarn's watching. Though when one of his own men came near he had lashed out at him with a barbed tongue and an order which was to be obeyed.

Another reason for Rentarn to nourish his own belief that to find Lonscraft would mean his death. In fact he had wondered why that had not yet come. Modic had his road well ready to follow. What more did he want from Rentarn?

The Seeker swung around to give a hoarse, rallying cry which brought up the heads of his men, summoned their attention. He loped towards them at a curious one-sided, limping walk which was his pace when dismounted, meeting them part way. His own mount stood head hanging as others were saddled and made ready to ride.

Modic still bestrode the poorest of the lot, Rentarn noted, his eyes more than half shaded by wrinkled, greenish lids. Why such a choice, and why was Modic waving his men on that straight line which was the work of the ancients? Why would Modic share a treasure find with those ragged and brutish riders at all? Rentarn did not doubt in the least that Modic could have found some other track for them to follow. Yet he stood there, watching them ride on, as Rentarn rose to his feet behind him. They were indeed swinging into the trail Modic indicated. One, at least, had wit enough to be suspicious. He called out something in one of the complicated river languages, reining back his horse, his closest comrades drawing in about him.

"Na . . . Na . . ." Modic raised bare hands in a gesture meant to reassure, following his denial with a stream of speech, each word gliding close to the one before it so that Rentarn could not begin to pick out the few he knew . . . except one "treasure" . . . perhaps that was akin in meaning in every speech, because it was a universal cry to action. Though for a moment or two it looked as if this one rider was not easily convinced, though those who had gathered about him fell into eager talk with much gesturing of hands and licking of lips. At length he, too, grunted, the bush of filthy hair on his cheeks and chin stretching as he made a spitting motion into the sand. Though it was plain he had no excess liquid to so void.

Modic lingered, fussing with his horse's gear as if making sure all was in good order . . . in the mean time giving quick glances at the men riding, two together, down that defile which marked the road. As the last one passed another dune some distance away, he spoke again to Rentarn.

"What is the threat which keeps you and your kind from such places open for looting? I have seen pieces of ancient metal, gems, and even bits of carvings offered for sale. Yet upon the asking they will always say that such was found in some miserable small ruin. Have you never tried for Pospfer or Wejn or perhaps Slasta?"

Rentarn hoped he controlled his surprise well. Why did this Seeker mark down the three worst cities of the old tales, places where in lay death in waiting?

"Such are cursed," he replied shortly.

"The abodes of demons, eh?" Once again Modic showed his teeth in a grin. "How know you that it is not the dead themselves who rise to defend what they once held? What tales do your Speakers tell of these lands? That they were conquered one by one by a fearsome enemy? If that be so where is that enemy now? No tale of such an invasion has ever been told. Why strike your people at one portion of the land only?"

"These be the riddles all share, Seeker," answered Rentarn. He was on his feet, testing the cord of the net which held his supplies. "Legend says the death rode from the sky on a forked flame and where that touched the ground there was ruin and nothingness. . . . The dead do not live to fight for what was once theirs. But the breath of the dying clings to the cities. A man breathes in that which will shrivel his lungs, and stands against the unseen which will eat the flesh from his bones. Some times even now a reckless far rover dies so."

Modic fingered his bristled chin with two grimy fingers, staring after the disappearing men of his party.

"Breath of death . . ." he repeated slowly. "Then we shall at least prove that right or wrong." From one of his saddle bags he pulled two cloths, the metallic smell of leif about them both. One he tossed to Rentarn who automatically caught it. He watched Modic hang his cap on the saddle horn of his horse, shake out the material to pull it like a bag over his head. There were holes for eyes, and where the mouth would be a slit covered by a mesh woven of shining threads. Somewhat clumsily the guide followed the Seeker's action.

The heavy odor which appeared to waft from the material was so pungent that he began to cough and would have taken off the thing if Modic had not caught him by the wrist.

"Leave be, Betweener. That which you smell is a mighty spell against all which fills the air. I paid a full year of swording caravans to get those . . . and had a heavy argument into the bargain. There only lives one in the river land who makes such now. He works from a very old picture and notes of how it is done . . . and those he will share with none. Still Amers of Klydul, wearing one of these, did ride the streets of Maksheeff and returned alone of his company."

"To die ten days later screaming that a demon within him gnawed at his heart," replied Rentarn. "Yes, we have heard the full of that tale."

"Only his demon was a potion brewed by his own second wife, that she might set hand on what he had brought back but would show to no one, saying that it was worth the war ransom of at least five lords. Also he intended to take it to the Fire of Venex for an auction," Modic returned coolly. "It was not his travels which killed him . . . only his own foolish tongue for he told wide and far just what he had gained."

The last of the riders disappeared around an upstanding rock spur, and now Modic swung into the saddle and flicked his riding lash at Rentarn as a sharp-edged order to move. The guide was well able to match the ambling gait Modic's horse approved, it seemed that the Seeker must still be in quest of landmarks. However he and Rentarn followed the same path as those others.

Yet their rest had lasted longer than even Rentarn had noted. Now shadows crept out from the rocks and the chill of the open night, as the baking sun set, loosing winds which carried cold out of the western unknown. The far mountains were only distant blots against a graying sky. No guide had ever struck as far as to climb those. If ever a Seeker had gone there he had not returned. Rentarn pulled his cloak tidily about him and thought of the Seeker again and the tale which threatened all who were with him.

If Modic had even been to Maksheeff that was on a dream supplied by a night demon. Rentarn padded on tirelessly and thought of demons. During his own few years and his strikes into the Dry Country he had never seen a demon. Nor had anyone in his village back to the first foray accounts of their clan's coming, which Jawser the Blind kept counted in his bundle of remembering knots. Demons were talked of often . . . but they were never seen. Rentarn had come to think that they must be totally invisible. Yet the Speakers who had the freedom of Above and Below had not reported them either. Thus they indeed might . . . if they still existed . . . be able to shelter themselves on more than one level of dream seeing. That such would lurk in the dire, broken cities moldered half away by time was reasonable enough.

He felt a sickness gathering at the back of his mouth, born of the stuff in which his mask was steeped. Now he tried to raise the banding from his throat and spat a glob of greenish phlegm to the rock beside him.

"Keep that mask on, you young fool!" Modic's words were muffled but could be heard. "See where we now stand, and you would give the ill which lies in waiting here a chance to get at you!"

The rock against which he spat he could see now through the dulling light of late afternoon, was not virgin stone but rather a tongue of what might be a buried building, pointed skyward. It was fashioned of small stones fitted together so that the cracks of their joining were difficult to see. On the other side of the road was a second such hill; the width between certainly measured a space of entrance which might once have stood as a gate to a road four or five times as wide as those which were known outside the Dry Land. Some of the sand was disturbed here, moved to show under red earth like unto any field where the keeps had little access to irrigation. Where this appeared it was churned and marked by the horsemen who had proceeded them.

Also they could hear voices from ahead where the piers of stone grew higher and even turned into a wall which ran true for more than just a stride or two. Modic's men were gathered there, all a-horse, gazing about them as if they were not really prepared for this. Ahead of them the walls arose abruptly. While there were cracks in them, they were not tumbled across the road. Those led to taller walls . . . to buildings like unto towers such as Rentarn had seen in ruin all along the border, as if erected hastily to help defend against what might come from the Dry Lands. These were broken here and there, after no regular pattern, by narrow slits which must have been intended to give watch sites for defenders.

Here, too, there was a difference. The sun had gone far enough down its sky trail now to lengthen shadows greatly. Only these were no honest shadows such as a man could trust with his eyes. For from those wall slots leaked a defused blue light, thin, hazelike, not unlike, save in color, to that haze which locked trails in the dawn hours.

The men had stopped where four roads came together and there was an open space centered by an oval which was curbed waist high, perhaps in order that none could fall within its circumference.

From that also curled, in wisps like the lazy curls of a smoking fire, bluish swirls.

One of the troopers had looked back to see the two of them. Now he gestured to the Seeker.

"Ho, Modic." They were not too far away for such a shout to carry, yet this greeting sounded as if it came from the other side of the sprawl of ruins, muddled and fuzzy. "Ho, Modic!"

It was plain to Rentarn that the Seeker was hesitating before, at last, he urged his sorry horse to amble on. Had the man actually sent this motley crew of his ahead to be picked off by any hidden enemy, thus securing his own entrance? Rentarn saw him raise his hand as if to pull off the odorous hood but he did not complete that gesture.

Before they had yet reached the party there shot, from the heart of the ruins, a shaft of light, rippling color . . . first the scarlet of man-blood, then the blue cast by the walls around. It reached up to the heavens, as if to provide a guide to a whole army of men even if they did not have the keen sight of the Betweeners. Having shot heavenwards, it now twisted to the left, whirled just above the roofs of the still standing buildings, moving so fast that it wove a great wheel of light. They might be standing again in full sun, save for the colors that touched them, first blue and then red and then blue again.

Having once established this circumference the haze descended again by sharp jerks until it engulfed the upper floors of the build-ings and yet continued to descend.

Modic swung from his horse, grabbing hastily at his saddle bags and a coil of rope around the horn. The horse had lost its early lethargy. It tossed its head as Modic left the reins hanging and retreated before the next circling of the light as might a man, step by step, keeping its head forward and up, while it whinnied and snorted and than gave a sharp cry such as Rentarn had never heard issued from any mount before. Though he had not long to observe it, for Modic had caught his cloak-muffled arm in a grip which dug painfully into his flesh, and his light body was jerked by that hold into a pile of stone which was still connected to a standing wall on three sides. Then Modic flung himself down, perforce taking the guide with him, so they lay flattened on a stony pavement. The eye holes of the mask so shortened Rentarn's vision that he could see nothing but a piece of wall, now red, now blue, and yet always bright at each viewing.

Perhaps he could not see, but hearing was not denied him. Horses screamed. There were other screams, too. With the sounding of each of those he could feel the pressure of Modic's hand still lying heavy upon him keeping him down. The Seeker was mouthing words in his own tongue in a steady litany. Rentarn recognized the name of one of the river land gods. Was Modic striving to make magic in a place already so ridden by the threat of evil? If so he was the greater fool, magic drew upon magic for feeding power, and somehow Rentarn believed that Modic's spell speaking would only encourage that which was on guard here.

So the guide waited, as they lay together under an overhang of an ancient building which was like a cave, for that which would also seek them out.

There was no more screaming from the horses. Once they heard a clatter of hooves showing that one of the mounts was less panicked, able to flee. There was instead a whimpering which tore at Rentarn's mind with the hurt and fear that it bore. Even that was done in time and yet they lay still. The colors no longer swept over the stone which was all Rentarn could watch. And humming, which he had not been really aware of until then, was gone. It was quiet enough so that he could hear the two deep breaths . . . almost like sobs . . . which Modic uttered as he took away his prisioning hand.

Rentarn edged as far as he could out of range of the Seeker's reach and sat up. There was still light overhead, but that was drawing together into the single beam which had first sent it forth. About them the full night was drawing in.

Modic raised up, not to his feet but instead crawled on hands and knees to an aperture through which he could see to where the men of his party had gathered. There he squatted while Rentarn leaned back against the wall, satisfying what had become a weakening hunger with a portion of journey rations he twisted off the tight cone of the stuff which he carried. He had no desire to view what must have been a battlefield of sorts. Now with his right hand he stroked the empty knife sheath at his belt. If he were to come through this venture . . . alive . . . he would need a weapon of sorts. Perhaps Modic was saving him for a secondary sacrifice . . . Rentarn squared his shoulders back against the wall. The Seeker had now no followers, the guide was sure of that even though he had not looked beyond as Modic was doing. Certainly he had no armament which could stand against a circle of killing light. Modic was but a man without a following, no threat to Rentarn's clan. The guide's hand crept out of his cloak and he began to feel about him in the growing darkness. One finger suddenly smarted and instantly he was feeling along something which had a knife's shape right enough, but lacked the smoothness of metal, even though it was edged, as more delicate touch suggested. He still dared not look at what he had found, but continued to tug the object loose from where it had been planted almost straight up with only a finger's breadth or so of blade already uncovered. Wriggling it with care Rentarn kept his gaze on the Seeker, freeing the find by touch alone.

Modic, in this gloom, resembled a headless body for the bag mask covered his full head. He was breathing noisily . . . as might a man who had been running quite a distance. Then he spoke, in a very low voice, which was so muffled by the bag, Rentarn barely heard.

"The poor devils . . ."

Strange that he would mourn men he had sent to whatever frightening death the whirling colors had cloaked. Rentarn could never understand this man. If one of his own kind made an enemy, and that was seldom, for their barren life was precious to the Be-tweeners, none worked out such elaborate plot as this. Instead either of the two took their quarrel to the Speaker. There they talked, each telling what was in his mind and heart. Sometime it did lead to a battle with the hands and there would be hurts to tend. But death never entered in . . . that was too familiar a visitor on its own to be deliberately summoned.

Now Modic had stripped himself of his main threat, the men who rode in this train. There was certainly that between him and Rentarn which sooner or later would lead to open confrontation. The guide was not afraid but he accepted wariness to be a part of his thinking and planning from this time forth. He had freed the thing in the earth. Glancing up now and then to make sure that

Modic was paying no attention, he brought it forth, holding it under one of the flaps of his cloak to examine it more clearly.

It was, he believed, made of stone . . . but not the same as that which formed the buildings moldering around them. As long as his thin forearm it was a blade with a butt end surely intended for a hilt and a sharp point. The tip of that had been broken off, but the remained possessed a cutting edge. This was a shimmer of color. As the defense of the city had been red and blue interweaving, so this was a gray-white, in the depths of which showed gem beauty, red, golden, green, blue. Those colors moved when one turned the blade from side to side. Had Rentarn seen this cut into gem size, he would have believed he had a fortune in his hand. As it was he shoved it quickly back into full hiding. Hoping to have escaped Modic's eyes he slipped the blade into an inner loop of his cloak. However, as Rentarn dropped his fingers from the hilt, he was still aware of a tingling, a prickling. Modic had not moved. He had thrust head and shoulders as far as he could through the spy hole he had chosen. For a space there was quiet between them. Rentarn viewed the ruins about him, trying to guess what had been the original use of this now vanished building. At the same time, with the patience of a Xole caught waiting to make a heo prey he began a new search with his long prehensile toes trying to discover if any more treasure lay beneath the scum of wind-driven sand. His claws raked across the rock which appeared to be a flooring but each piece of that he so located was firm set and could not be lifted out. If another one of these gem-bladed knives awaited discovery it would take more time and perhaps a lot of extra digging to uncover it.

As Modic moved Rentarn ended such exploration. The Seeker drew back from his hole and untied his bag mask, signaling Rentarn to do likewise.

"There is naught to fear . . . for now!" Sweat had plastered his greasy hair flat to the skull, and small trickles of moisture made their way down, to drip from his square chin.

"You have been here before. . . ." Rentarn spoke aloud the suspicion which had been growing in him ever since the Seeker had waved on his men and taken a slower pace.

"No!" Modic sounded overly emphatic in that. "No!" His hand

went to the breast of his thigh-length overrobe where he had put the map stone for safe keeping. "No . . ."

Rentarn's tongue flicked out from between his jaws and in again. Once it was said that those of his blood could test the very air to sift truth from falsehood. If that gift had been lost they had other small ways of dealing with any double talk from strangers. Oddly enough Rentarn had to believe that Modic was now speaking the truth. Yet he was not ready to allow the Seeker to believe he had satisfied his unwilling companion by so much as that. And perhaps there was a frayed feeling of right within the man which brought out of him an explanation Rentarn was sure he had never meant to give.

Modic once more caressed his chin under the crust of sweat and plaster of sand, studying the guide narrowly. "The Old Ones, those who lived here," he made a gesture indicating the ruins, "had many secrets. Is not that the reason for both Seeker and Guide to come hither?"

Rentarn shook his head. "We wrest no secrets from the dead. . . ."

"The more fools you." Modic got to his feet, stretching arms and legs as if the time he spent at the spy hole had rendered him stiff. "If you seek not for treasures, why do you venture into this sin-damned land year after year? What brings you here?"

Rentarn once more flicked his tongue over his lower lip taking the grit of sand into his mouth. With it there seemed to come that sickening flavor with which the mask was imbued. He plucked that off and shook head and shoulder much as the Seeker had stretched. Then he deliberately wet a forefinger against his lips, used it to gather up some grains of sand from a nearby wall stone and licked that up. A moment later he spewed it forth.

"Now what do you do?" Modic wanted to know.

"There is salt in this earth. . . ." In turn Rentarn got to his feet and looked about the jumble of wall and piles of fallen stone.

"Salt!" Modic hooted with what he must consider laughter, still Rentarn slowly surveyed each standing wall, seeking something which was not there. "I asked you, Guide," the Seeker returned to the question, "what seek you within this desert if you come not to plunder the towns? Do the demons walk only in those so you feel safe in the open . . . ?"

Rentarn's two strides took him even with and then past Modic. Now he needs must kneel to look upon what had so engrossed the Seeker. "We seek," his voice was absent in tone, for what he told was not secret . . . neither was it ever believed, "water."

"Water!" Modic's voice arose to a whoop. "Here in the dead sands you seek water? Be like you follow some old tale where some ancient evil one struck stone and it enclosed your precious water."

Rentarn did not turn his head, he found that he must crouch even lower to look through Modic's vantage point. "You have the truth of it, Seeker," he answered still absently. Then even forgot the man by his side when he looked out to where the horse and men had waited. Sun was gone, shadows were heavy. In his nostrils was the raw, sweet smell of blood, and he saw enough to near bring the scanty contents of his stomach up into his mouth. Bones . . . goblets of torn flesh. But the bones were the worst, for from the way they lay twisted and piled against each other he could believe that something might have stripped their bodies of flesh while yet they lived. There was a head which had rolled closer to his view-point and was exposing bone to chin and cheek and a mass tattered of flesh above. Yet by Hyqur, the Keeper of the Gates of Darkness, the flesh had not been devoured or even carried far. The still drip-ping chunks and strips lay within what once must have been a fountain, pulled into a pile as if laid out for a feast.

Modic's hand fell heavily on his shoulder. "Quiet as the sand when there is no puff of air to give it life." He was crouched beside Rentarn again, his mouth so close to the Betweener's leathery cheek that the foulness of his breath for an instant made Rentarn gag as he had from the mask. "There are those who come to feast at such a table. . . ."

"Yet," Rentarn dropped his own voice and half hissed, half whispered, "you have not been here before. Then how do you know what chances here? Let me guess, Seeker. You had full knowledge of that which killed and took precautions that you should not be among the slain by coming last. Why chose you . . ."

His question was interrupted by a soft sound like a heavy sigh such as a beast of burden might give when loosed of that burden, the need for going on. The darkness was not quite as complete as it would have been outside the ruins. Rentarn was not sure just where the pale light came from, unless it was from the uncovered bones of the city itself. But he was able to see the outline of a horse's head against whitish block a little beyond them.

Modic chuckled. He might not have been viewing a fatal battlefield, but rather was anticipating some coming gift.

"So . . . SOOOO . . . sssoooo . . . Dus," again that whispering voice but he did not address Rentarn this time. The mount's ugly head swung in his direction and the horse took one step and then another as one answering a detested jerk upon dangling reins, edging by as far as it could from the horror about the pool.

"Never judge a mount by looks." Modic dug an elbow into Rentarn's ribs. "Dus has been a-questing before. But he has been thrice blessed by the Voice of Ugan and also endowed at birth with more brains than many a man! Ugly and spare he may look, but he is as fresh at the trail's ends as when he first stepped out. Ah!" Modic's first touch on the guide's arm became a grasp which twisted flesh and brought pain.

"Look you, Betweener! Here comes those to the banquet their protector has laid out for them!"

The horse had managed to reach their crowded hide just as his master spoke. The animal made no sound but his sweat was that of fear and it was rank in their small space. Giving voice to a harsh whinny Dus turned and pulled away. Modic did not appear to notice his going. Rentarn saw a dark shape detach itself from a fraction of wall to scuttle towards the basin of blood and flesh. It was only the first. However Rentarn was not to be turned by such a sight from his need for the truth.

"You know this place." He made a statement out of that, not a question. "Yet you swear you have never been here before."

"Nor have I, Betweener. But I have been to Lyrh and Kenzy. . . ." He spoke with pride in his voice. "Though never within these walls. Yet I saw a Seeker disappear into Lyrh with all his company. And he did not return, nor did any one or thing, save my fool Dus here, when the sun arose the next morning. There were sounds in a plenty during the night and they were not pleasant ones."

"If you were so near, how does it that you were not caught in the same trap?"

Again Modic chuckled. " 'Twas my own thinking which saved me there. I was well behind the Seeker, not a member of his crew, and when the killing light came I was beyond its radius. Also . . ." His hand strayed inside his robe again and Rentarn would swear that what he sought was that map. . . . "Also, I sat at the feet of many story tellers . . . in all the Down Lands. Some had one small bit to spew forth, some had nothing . . . but I listened with patience for more than a year. I even had such brought to tell to me alone. It was one of those, an ancient Speaker of your own kind, Betweener, who gave me the first clue." He settled back into the shadows and sat more at ease with his back against a broken wall. Yet he still spoke in so low a tone that Rentarn had trouble making sure of all the words.

"What do you know of the tale of Lonscraft, Betweener? Or is that legend so old it has dried up in all men's minds, to be blown away in an autumn tempest?"

Truth? Rentarn's tongue tasted the air. There were many foul and dangerous odors about but he could still pick up this Seeker. Modic told the truth, or what he believed to be the truth, or . . . at least a portion of it, destined to hook Rentarn to him.

"Lonscraft." He remembered back to days not so long ago when he had toiled over learning . . . names, places, events which had been the portion of the Betweeners lore for such a long time. "Lonscraft," he repeated, "is a tale. . . ."

"What are the past doings of us all but legends when time speeds further and further away from the event," Modic wanted to know. "Yes, there is the tale of Lonscraft . . . but it is worn ragged by passing through so many tellers, each changing a little to make it suit his or her own ideas of what was exciting, or fitting, or proper. Your people tell dark stories of the cities within this dead land, yet they learn its trails and mark its guide posts as if such acts are a matter of unchangeable law. You do believe yet, deep inside of you . . . there is a faint stirring when one calls the name of a vanished city. You have built up a number of taboos and most of them have truth in them. Your training tells you that death was here . . . and it was. Still you are not aware of what kind of death . . . only of its shadow. But me, Modic," he thumped himself on the chest, "I allow no story to stand alone and be only half believed. Always have I sought for more. I heard of the woman Kasiu, she who was first wife to Amers. Her I hunted out and she was afraid, for there were many in her village who knew how much she hated her husband and who were skeptical of her story of Demons entering him when he came here. I made a bargain with her, that she could travel with my company down to the River towns and that she was grateful for, also she could not guess that more lay in her husband's journey bag upon his return than crumbs of food. But I learned where she had spilled the bag, so I found what I sought for what seems now half my life.

"There was the map and I hardly think truly that it was of his own making . . . it may be generations old. Also there were some guide scratches . . . look for yourself, Betweener."

Modic was holding out an oblong of slate painstakingly ground into a narrow slip. Rentarn accepted it gingerly, then might have gasped had his species been that of the Seeker. It was hot in his hand, not as something which had gathered body warmth from resting against flesh, but with a heat which radiated from it. He could have been holding an actual part of the sun's beam. To the sight in this part-dark it was bare, but when his fingers quested over it, ridges and curves lay plain against his skin. Deep in him was that first flutter of fear known when a thing which is thought to be without truth suddenly throws aside the cloak of falsehood. His lips shaped words which his voice whispered:

"In the ninth month when the Lords of the Three Lands strove together, there came out of the depths of the dead and riven land one who was veiled and lacking in speech. Yet no one raised hand to pull aside the veil and cloak, or spoke. Rather did they draw back away from this one who was not like unto others of the world.

"Then rose up Utyr of Lonscraft who was ever of hasty tongue and impatient hand. He spoke, saying that truth was to be known and if there was a message then let this one speak it forthwith.

"So that one from the dead land turned to Utyr and made certain gestures which no one understood, but which had an ill look to them. Utyr, though he shifted from one foot to the other as a person ill at ease, did not speak again. Nor did he give any orders to his men as that shrouded one turned and walked from him. Those before the walker hunched to either side making a free path for the cloaked one. Thus the stranger came to the first opening of the broad marsh which was then to the gates of Lonscraft, that city being partly built on landing of stone long and deep set in unsteady earth. Going out upon one of the piers of the swift flying marsh boats, the stranger opened wide his cloak, which then hung in the air itself like wings. Although all the company stayed ashore and none could see what the cloak had hidden.

"But a hand flashed forth bearing such a weapon as no man had seen . . . white, and gold, blue, red and green, color followed color across its surface. Then the stranger whistled, a clear, sharp sound like the cry of some sea bird.

"Down one of the aisles of open water which served for the boats came that which those of the land had never seen. It was both a fish and a crawler upon the land for it showed stubbly legs. When it came to a belt of weed it climbed over that growth, not giving way to it.

"As for the staff, this flashed with color, mainly green, but also swirling red, blue, and gold.

"The head of the water one was held high above the surface, and from its mouth issued words which all man could hear but none could answer, for there was no understanding them. Then the voice grew louder, boomed and belled, until it filled the ears of all those in Lonscraft and there was no escaping it. Also it carried in it, even if one could not understand the words, a feeling of coming shadow and ill fortune. So that those waiting by Utyr drew sword or battle knife, even though no challenge had been offered.

"Utyr himself strode forward near enough to the stranger that he might grasp that one's shoulder if he wished; he even put forth his hand as if to do that very thing. Yet he did not complete that gesture for the thing in the water ceased upon an instant its calling and there was a strange and abiding silence which held for five breaths, perhaps more. Then he who stood at the pier's end turned slowly around so that those gathered there could see, that though he walked upright and cloaked as might a man of the city, he was not of their form nor wore any covering known to them. . . ."

"Yes," Modic broke in, "do your tellers of ancient tales say then what manner of creature this stranger was?"

Rentarn's tongue flicked out, he raised the water carrier to his wide mouth and took the smallest of sips, though that was enough to strengthen his voice.

"You have heard the same tale, Seeker . . . what manner of creature was this stranger?" prodded Modic.

Then he laughed. There was a shadow of contempt in his voice: "Go hunt out a quiet pool and look into it, Guide. There shall you see well what you wear . . . for the stranger was of your kin by blood."

What Rentarn might have replied to that was lost, for from the broken walls before them arose a keening cry, and straightway that was stifled in turn by cries and shouts of despair, horror and terror on the verge of madness. If some had escaped the massacre in the open they were now being dragged to their deaths.

So awesome was that chorus that Rentarn put his hands over his ears but found he could not shut out the sound which seemed to enter and pulsate in his body so he rocked a little forward and back as if he was shaken by something a great deal stronger than any sound, no matter how hideous.

A musky-sweet corruption of blood scent arose about him also. Thus he could believe that those scavengers of this ill-omened place gathered again for a feasting. There was movement behind him and he whirled to see something which slid through the black of shadow to advance past the end of a broken wall. From that spread the odor of horse sweat, Dus once more. The fear born in animal broke through the ugly spell which kept both travelers quiet. Modic did not move, but Rentarn stepped forward and caught again that trail of broken rein. By this he drew the bony horse to them.

Behind he heard once again Modic's chuckle as eerie as a madman's.

"Did I not say," Modic asked, "that Dus was one of the best of all that train? The rest stood pinned by fear until they met death, but this one fled, which is often the greater part of any valor, and note its coming does us also a service. For it would not venture to us now again if the way was not clear. Now yield your guideship to me, Betweener, and we shall come out of this . . . but tell me first what sorcery your distant kin worked here which defeated Utyr, and with him many other lords of a land not then dead."

"That the tellers of tales never knew," Rentarn returned sharply.

The moans, screams, and cries of fear and torment had died away as if one by one those who voiced them were being silenced forever.

"And the water thing which came to his call? What was that, Betweener? Why during one day and night did all those who followed Utyr die? What death twisted and wrung their bodies, tore and shredded the very flesh which made them what they were?" Modic advanced a step or two, now facing Rentarn. There was a full moon and, as if he still clung to some ancient fear for all his brave talk, he was fingering the broken rein and standing close enough to the horse that he might be in the saddle and off before Rentarn could move.

The Betweener shrugged. "I know nothing of sorcelment or the plays of warlocks and Mages."

"Ha! And still those of the stranger's kin went out of the city untouched. None of them bore so much as a water bottle with them, bareheaded they went, unpursued and free. *That* is the ending of the tale they chant in the Down Lands. Eh, Guide, how fared them? Death did not claim *them*."

"I know no such ending of the legend," countered Rentarn. "When it is spoken among us death is universal."

Modic grinned evilly. "Do men, or Betweeners, ever really make that clear? Perhaps it is better to forget than to admit one has made some pact with that which should never have been thought of? Do we greet Betweeners with open arms and fair smiles to this day . . . even when they bring us those things we have need of? Why come you in parties of fighters if you are merchants with nothing to fear?"

Rentarn gestured with one hand as if brushing aside something worn threadbare, an action with its reason lost far back in time.

"Why do we stand here," he asked, "and talk of old tales and whether or not there was death of a city, a curse which grew out of Utyr's orders when he went desert raiding. Rather it would be well for us now to be on our way before that guardian returns, to jealously remove us from its present lair."

"True, true. We shall go hence from here." Modic looked about him as if he stood in some noisome place. "But from Lonscraft we go not until . . ." He brought out of the bosom of his robe something which fitted into the hollow of his hand and which he handled as carefully as if he held a palm full of water which he must carry without its draining away. "Give me the map. . . ."

Rentarn handed him that oblong of stone which had the message on it near erased. With this firmly held in his left hand, Modic clapped his right hand about also. Though it looked to be a shard of dull gray, such as lay in the thousands along any trail, Modic was touching it to the map.

It was if he now held a coal, for there sprang up a steady red light in the stone. Modic's features twisted, his lips grimaced as if he did indeed carry a fire's heat against flesh. The fire was answered by a spark on the map, one which glowed as steadily as the Seeker's stone. Modic gave a half-stifled oath, his eyes wide and brightly open so that he would not lose a fraction of what he looked upon.

With the wane of the moon Modic stepped as forward boldly as he would have had it been day. For the lack of anything on which to base a protest, Rentarn followed after, leading the horse which plodded as if it had been sentenced to too heavy a task.

Lonscraft. In Rentarn's mind revolved the name of that ancient death of a city. So far the tale he himself had repeated had been exact . . . yet never had it told what manner of death was spewed forth by the marshes, or why it had not fallen upon those of Betweener blood, just those of Modic's species.

Still, in the many years since that time, perhaps too many to be told over without a knot string to aid, those who ventured into the Great Dry had died . . . one way or another. None had told what they had chanced upon which was so perilous an enemy. Lonscraft itself was the name which had been gasped by one of the earlier venturers as he died, tongue stricken save for that word.

They now angled well away from the open center about the dead pool where the others had died. The memory of the color which arose to slay, or else hold the intruders here until something more subtle had come seeking life and blood, haunted Rentarn. His hand beneath his cloak sought out that piece of fire curling stone which he had found in the ruin. Yes, there was a brilliant swatch of color to match that which had flashed to kill on the rod or knife. With each step he took, he glanced sharply about and then at the blade. The star-dotted sky above the central buildings remained free of lighting or change. Though color still swirled within the pointless blade, it did not even reflect on the hand which held it. Still there was a feeling . . . Rentarn's head jerked as if that sudden thought had been a blow. Why did he come to imagine thus as he followed Modic through these ruins? Never before had he conceived of things which were not of the earth he knew.

Oh, there had been tales a-plenty concerning demons and creatures from other worlds (with hints that the meddling of some man or Betweener had opened forgotten gates), but always such had appeared or had happened to some guide or wanderer from another clan. One far away enough for the report to become muddled and overlaid with all the fears which were a part of their heritage.

He knew well that the men of the lower lands by the rivers had similar ghosts. Nor were there many who even dared to make a short essay into the Dry with or without a guide. Still there was about Modic now a kind of fever which darkened his skin even under the moon's glow, and made his journey one of erratic pauses and swifter advances, as if two desires warred violently within him, now this and now that taking command.

It was the horse who broke through the Seeker's tight absorption. Not uttering any sound, it drew back upon the rein, jerking its head as if to free itself. Bracing its spindly legs within a narrow way between two piles of rubble, it refused to advance.

Modic at once appeared fully awakened from his obsession. He stood dragging with all his force at the reins . . . the horse's head now stretched forward at a painful angle. It was the animal that struck first. It kicked out, though it was not facing Modic, and Rentarn, who had had no part in its pull forward, was the victim of that assault.

There was a keening wail . . . not from either man or beast in their struggle, nor from Rentarn either. The guide threw himself backward, not only to escape the hooves of the animal but in utter surprise . . . for the sound issued from the artifact he had found. Nor did it emit a single note, rather a near scream which was suddenly cut off. Neither the horse nor Modic turned to see what had made that cry. Rather the horse sprung forward, near overrunning the man as it burst out of the narrow way between the two tottering pillars of rubble.

The light from the moon was gone. Clouds built up in the northern sky. Rentarn's instinct told him a storm was on the way. But that was of little importance when compared to this thing he had found. It was emitting a droning beat, broken now and then as if each portion of sound was a word of warning or a threat.

He could have turned in the moment and found his way out of this dead curl of broken walls and mounds of stone. The horse and Modic had vanished around a turn in the debris so that he could not be seen.

It was not curiosity, nor any sense of responsibility toward Modic, which brought him apart from the way where he had taken refuge some moments earlier. Seemingly of its own accord the hand holding the weapon (if weapon it was) shook free from his cloak without his willing it. The colors within were running as if he were turning the stone about in his hand. It was . . .

For a second, perhaps even less, he opened his eyes to their greatest extent. The thing was moving weapon-wise at last, though there was no enemy before him. His muscles responded as they never had to any journey knife or battle staff, thrusting and recovering with a knowledge which he knew he had never learned in any clan drill. His hand and arm might now be possessed by . . .

By the dead? In all the lore taught by his people there was no room for such an idea. One was born, lived, and when the time set had come, one died. Nor had the ken any tales of the walking of the dead, troubling from those who were past all of this world's sorrows, acts, thoughts. The dead spoke not . . . between them and the living there was not even the thinnest crack of a doorway.

It was not the dead suspicioned so to frighten some of the Seeker's people and be a part of the dangers of the Dry as far as they were concerned. The Betweeners hinted of dealing with dark powers. Demons . . . some of his kin, he knew, believed that there were unseen malignant forces at loose in ancient cities. This city . . .

Rentarn stopped short and stared unseeingly at the shard he

held. What of that story Modic had asked of him, a story long current among his own people? The cloaked one from out of the desert who had gone to the marsh pier and thereafter summoned a thing past any man's knowing.

Rentarn, still keeping the broken sliver in his hand under a flap of clothing, strode in the direction Modic and his mount had taken. Rounding a tall heap of debris he came abruptly into the open once more. There was just enough light to see a square ahead and the facades of the buildings forming its sides had apparently suffered less from whatever doom had erased Lonscraft. Directly across from him was a seemingly intact building which bore no signs of ruin at all. The wide doorway was above the level of the square so that a flight of broad steps led to its open doorway. Strangest of all in this desert country, there was a runnel which had cut its way through the steps, to a hole which gaped at ground level. Running water? No, the color was wrong. Each drop of that small flood was as scarlet as newly shed blood. While above its surface, back and forth, danced winged things which skimmed so closely to the small flood that they might have been swallowed up, yet always they coasted to safety beyond.

Modic had lost hold on the broken rein, the horse backed away from the steps and the liquid on them, showing the whites of its eyes, foam dripping from its nostrils to slime its nose and the bony expanse of its chest. It retreated from Modic, from the building. Then it swung half around and cantered awkwardly to Rentarn's left. Modic was pulling on the head-concealing mask that he had worn when they had entered Lonscraft. As he did so he walked as does one who bends his body against the force of a mountain wind, taking one slow step and then another. He gestured forceably with one arm as if to keep off an attack of flies. While in his other hand was that map which now was a fire to light the whole of the stairway. If that spark of light upon it had been fashioned to beckon, now surely it proclaimed to be nearly to the goal.

The smooth running rill was disturbed on the surface, now dimpled as if a shower fell upon it. The flies gathered in the upper air to become a black blot, still over the water but hovering above Modic as he climbed.

Rentarn shivered. He had known fear before, but it had always been caused by things he understood . . . of one of the Vort beasts raiding the herds of the Betweeners . . . of the sickness which was supposed to strike anyone invading the old cities, of the ill will of his own clan should he break their few but skintight taboos (for that would unclan him and make him as one dead walking among the living). Now . . . this was like fronting a cold rage, an ire so great that his kin could not even sense more than a portion of it. Here lay in wait a will, a power, a brutal rule which shook him. Still the time had come . . . or he had come . . . too far past the borders of its control to struggle against it now.

A will, a power . . . he was caught up by sharp command as he came fully into the open passing the horse that now stood with drooping head as if the beast had lost all hope. This horse lived, so did Modic as he climbed from one step of the wide stair to the next. Still, though Rentarn began search with his own heightened guide's sense, he could trace back that bold assault against him to . . . nothing! There was no trace of man, of Betweener, of animal, of life as he knew it, aroused to draw him shivering towards the source. To that highly developed sense, trained to locate life, there came, at last, an answer from a source he had not expected.

From the broken tip of the many-colored blade sped a thin thread of red and blue, entwined one with the other. Those were the same colors as the light which had been thrown across the rubble-lined streets of Lonscraft . . . the fearsome alien weapon. What did Rentarn now hold? An artifact which was a dueling ground for bursts of killing color? By arousing his will, pitting his inner strength against that pull, the guide was able to linger on the second step, even as Modic reeled and wavered far closer to that aperture above which served as an ever open door.

Inch by inch Rentarn edged around to look back over the way he had come. The horse screamed and reared to strike out with its front feet as might a war-trained stallion. Around it ringed a crowd of shadows, curious moving bolts of darkness which never clearly showed themselves. Though there were a number of these remains gathered around the horse, others padded to the foot of the stair to form a double line of dark forms, though they avoided the running rill. Rentarn flicked out his tongue in their direction. Full of viciousness, yes, but these were not a true part of that which waited within. However they now formed a guard wall against any retreat, and that could only mean that Modic and he were being edged towards another and doubtless more powerful enemy.

His foot touched on the next step. There was a crackling, the sound of something rolling back toward the waiting band. Rentarn saw a skull, polished enough to reflect the gleam of this alien light. He no longer watched the hunters, rather studied his footing. That remnant of his own species, or Modic's, was not alone. There lay a scattering of broken bones, some near reduced to powder, along each step.

He heard a thin, half-muffled cry which might have come from Modic, muffled as he was by mask. The Seeker tripped, fell to his knees on the last step, his shoulders shaking, his head turning from side to side as if so he tried to avoid blows. Some strong compulsion drew him on to crawl along the platform above as might a seriously injured animal seeking shelter. There was no cracking of splintering bones now, all sound had been absorbed by a deep hum which hurt Rentarn's ears, throbbed through his body. Two more strides brought the guide beside Modic. He reached down and hooked his fingers in the other's armpit, giving a steady pull, while the Seeker scrambled in the bones and flopped about, seeming unable regain to his feet.

"Up!" He was so near to Modic Rentarn believed that his words were not lost in that ever growing throb. "Up to your feet, Seeker. Would you meet battle on your knees, already so far spent as you seem?"

Modic turned his shaking head to look up at Rentarn dull eyed. Spittle ran from the corner of his mouth and with it a thread of blood from a lip he had bitten though. He showed no understanding, but some part of the guide's urgency must have reached him, as he swung around to clasp both of his sweat slicked hands on Rentarn's arm. Using that hold for leverage as he might a tree or rock pillar, he drew himself up, near oversetting Rentarn in the process, when for a moment or two he hung a dead weight on the other before regaining his feet.

The throbbing grew heavier, more assertive as if something ahead was impatient at their delay. As they moved forward, Modic, still using Rentarn as a support, they were plunged into light . . . a blaze of blue. Modic halted, stopping Rentarn almost in midstride, to jerk at the edge of the mask the guide had worn into the city. "Put on," he croaked hoarsely, his mouth close to the guide's nearest ear.

One-handed, for he could not put aside the gem light he held, the Betweener obediently pulled on the mask once again though he did not like the curtailment of sight which wearing it caused.

Only it was true that once he was again shrouded that blaze of raw light was subdued, and he could see enough to mark the fact they they were indeed in a palace or some incredibly rich shrine. The light might blot out a measure of response from the display of unbelievable wealth about them, but it could not utterly hide what was set in patterns on the walls, and not only on the walls. There were dunes and drifts of precious metals and gem stones across the floor, many of the pieces broken.

As they shuffled on they tramped on a medley of stones and metals of stones and metals such as could not be seen at a fair even if all which had ever changed hands there had been reassembled for one great showing.

There were weapons, too, swords and knives possessing hilts rich in jewels, strange other objects which were certainly not intended for adornment but which, if weapons, Rentarn did not recognize.

Here and there was a rack of bones . . . some draped with chains of office of the adornment of chief wives. Several of these lay broken across the things which Rentarn believed might be weapons.

Before them was still that blast of light which gave no hint of its source or purpose . . . unless that latter was death, which Rentarn could well believe. In his hands the colored spindle of stone quivered past all his endeavors to control it, but so far it had not broken free.

His tongue touched the rough stuff of the mask, the tip of it pointed through the hole which served for the mouth cutting and the opening for breathing. Deliberately he began to try to set the pace for himself, to be quickly forced into the maelstrom of color. It was a battle, and his uncovered skin pricked and stung. Modic had again fallen to hands and knees. Even his head hung low so he did not watch the way ahead, he merely crawled toward the source of the light.

Rentarn was able to slow his advance though he could not tear himself free of the strong pull upon him. Still he quested with tongue tip, thrusting that even farther into the crackling air about. The light must have a source, and having a source it must be set, meant to protect it's own inner sanctum as he had seen its overflow light up the sky in the first coming of their party. Animal, biped, brain . . . thought process which?

His flesh was so seared by assault . . . what awaited him? For the first time . . . his Betweener-born organ for detection brought him no knowledge. There was nothing ahead, that sense insisted, but the light itself, and that was not tended by any living thing.

The way was growing narrower as the great room started to close in about them to form a corridor. Here the treasure was less visible. There were more skeletons, insignias of office mingled with brittle bones, and there were indeed weapons he knew, some lying half into the red flood of the stream from which he edged away as it began to flow widening more and more. The stench rising from it was choking. Rentarn coughed hollowly and leaned with one hand against the wall as he steadied himself against unseen gusts which struck him.

Modic halted. Then he hunched in a crouch, sweeping his hands from side to side about him though without seeming to see what lay there. By chance his fingers curved about one of the rod-like things which Rentarn believed was a weapon. Still not raising his head so that he might look at what he had found, the Seeker allowed the rod to slip through his fingers until a dark band meant for a grip was resting in his hold.

Rentarn was not prepared for what followed. Modic swung around, moving with the speed of a trained hand and foot warrior. The end of that rod pointed unerringly at Rentarn's middle, though the Seeker still did not lift his head.

No! Rentarn's sense had never proved to be deceptive but it had to be so now . . . it had to be! There was life in the other but it had dwindled down as might the last coal of a fire being fast smothered. In its place . . . the guide's tongue tip sent a thrill of pain through his body, kept him pinned to the wall. There was life ending . . . and nothing, nothing gathered beyond to take its place. Yet Modic was on his knees, his head hanging forward nearly resting on his chest.

Not dead . . . possessed! Other evil tales from the wild slipped into memory. The Seeker gave body room and aid to something else. . . . Only, when Rentarn strove to touch that, to discover what had chained the River worlder to such a trap, he could not pick up anything save always the burning of the power.

Rentarn jerked his body to the left as that weapon pointed in his direction. He felt the heat of a ray which burst at him. It was gone as quickly as two breaths, though Modic still held it aimed at the Betweener. Rentarn saw the other's hand tighten about the band on the rod with full strength.

The shining length of his own find was ready. In its heart, flaring from the butt to the broken point, was a rich roll of color. That twisted as if to wrench itself free but Rentarn's six fingers held tight. His whole body jerked as if the artifact from the city ruin was a rope with him imprisoned in a loop. He flailed out with his other arm, striving to keep his balance, and so struck against Modic.

Whether the unexpected contact between their bodies was the reason or not, the Seeker staggered halfway around to bring up the strange weapon. That gesture was never completed, for Modic's rod, touching by chance the broken knife Rentarn unconciously advanced in defense, burst, scattering fragments which melted to drip to the floor. Spots of dull dark blue fell smoking and glowing at their cores. The Seeker lurched forward, his unsteady pace close to a run, shouldering Rentarn aside. The guide went after him at a speed which was nearly equal.

They came upon more skeletons. However the bones were scattered, no rack of them whole. Also they appeared as if they were more recent than those in the hallway. Another Seeker band which had reached this point before falling prey to an enemy they could not sense? Rentarn wondered.

In the center of the large chamber beyond was a bank of chairs, constructed, not of stone, but of some substance which glittered with dancing lights. Before those bubbled a pool from which arose the dread runnel of red they had companied with from without. It appeared to Rentarn that small bursts of flame danced over surface just as had the black insects in the outer world.

At the entrance of the pool crouched something which was surely out of some nightmare of the damned. Rentarn, gazing at it with horror was near overborne. For it might be that one of his kin, larger, mad with blood lust, stared straight into his eyes as if the mask he still wore was transparent. The thing's mouth gaped wide and the pointed fangs within dripped glowing slime into the pool.

It was not dead. His own guide's sense told him rather it had never lived as he knew life. There was nothing at all Rentarn could detect from it. While in the seats . . .

Yes, there sat dead . . . six bodies, not riven and torn, not reduced to racks of bones. . . .

These were not Betweeners, nor Seekers, nor of any race Rentarn had knowledge of. What he could see of their skin (they wore wrappings which covered most of it) was a dark blue. The hands of each were spread out so the withered fingers could lie upon a series of buttons upon lap boards which perhaps kept each in his chair.

From this scene, the pool, and the long dead, there thrust upward a beam of light. Even as Rentarn sighted it that beam pulsed again and again and then vanished. He drew in breath and expelled it again in a hiss which near carried away his mask. The hands of the dead had moved . . . pressing certain of those buttons.

While the thing in the pool dropped its scaled muzzle into the slimy flood and drank—or seemed to do so. Yet that was impossible, Rentarn's senses still told him there was no life here. If there had ever been it was long since gone.

Modic scrambled along the edge of the pool. His head no longer hung down but his features were twisted in such an expression of rage as Rentarn had never seen.

The Seeker's mouth worked as he threw his mask into the pool, his eyes never leaving Rentarn's face. Now he half turned and sprang forward to the nearest of those seats. His hands closed upon the body there and he jerked it out of its perch to the floor, catching and holding the board as the body fell. Now he seated himself where the corpse had been . . . his fingers also spanning the board of buttons.

His whole body shook as he flung up his head and brayed wild laughter, his attention on the thing which had drunk and again raised its head to stare at Rentarn. "The hour is now!" Modic's voice seemed to fill the place. He might have been shouting with the full power of his lungs. "Let that which purifies go forth and . . ." His finger tips played a fluttering game on the board. "This is the hour," he repeated. "Broken was the pattern when these died." He glanced at his dead companions. "Some of their training lives on as was meant. They rule the world. . . ." He leaned forward a little, spittle flicks on his lips, and yet he grinned and the wild exultation was not gone from his eyes. . . .

He nodded toward that thing on opposite bank of the pool. "How go things with you, oh, Farguel? Yes, you are dead and gone but the treasure you gave us still does its duty. See this one of your kin . . . he knows not even now what he has found . . . the root of that which had made a desert of blooming land. Dead!" He pounded his hand on the arm of the chair in which he sat. "We died too soon!" Again his face twisted in that horrifying way, as much of a mask as the one he had flung from him.

"We will it not!" He pulled at his underrobe as if it had begun to choke him. "Dead, we shall take with us a dead world. Come, brothern from the outer stars. We shall move even as we have planned, for that one," he looked to Rentarn, "shall be food for Farguel. So fed life will return . . . is that not so? Have not I, Thebar, returned in the body of this rover . . . little by little he became me . . . first as a whisper of treasure, and, when he had taken that, a stronger vision and a stronger. Until he saw himself a conqueror and a king! And he had heard of this guide who knew the desert so well and would provide him with the means of coming. . . . Ah, brothern, rejoice that I was strong, that though I was what men called dead, I was not, only abiding deep within another body waiting.

"Did I not grow the stronger even as the chosen one began to come nearer? Did I not bid him send those fool beasts who followed him ahead that they might be harvested? Yes, the doing was mine . . . and now I shall be even as he who once wore this body . . . Lord of the world . . . a world!"

Again he screeched with laughter, and now he beckoned to Rentarn "Come here, Betweener . . . look at Farguel who is what our voice called from the swamp!" He gestured to the thing which drank.

"Once all you and your kin were as he. That day shall come again. For it is my will and desire, and only what I wish shall ever more happen here. Look you . . . and die!"

Rentarn had seen men before who came raving from the wasteland. This talk of bodies and of kingdoms yet to come . . . those were only the dreams of a broken-headed man. Yet when he watched the sureness of Modic's fingers on the board he had taken from the dead there was something in the man as well as in this place which no Betweener had ever mentioned, which no legend enshrined from other years. Who were those from the past who Modic called upon? And this thing which had now lifted its head again from the deep red flood and stood, its jaws dripping red? The thing which had no life, or never had had, but which moved even as he watched, teetering a little with its forepaws near into the flood.

Farguel, Modic had named it. There was no such name in Betweener clans nor did any of his kin walk upon all fours. That huge head swung a little toward him, the mouth gaped as if the thing could wish him to it for feasting.

But there was something wrong with that mouth! Great forefangs promised death . . . in the strange light they changed in color with waves of blue, green, yellow, red running up and down. Yes, he could see now . . . one of these was missing. Without conscious thought Rentarn swung up the broken knife he had brought out of the ruins, comparing that to the dread fangs which the creature wore. It was certainly the truth . . . what he had must be a fang . . . but from what jaw had it been taken? This beast? Surely it depended too much on luck for that to be the truth and Rentarn's kind were suspicious of such a thing as luck.

"SSaaa . . ." The sound was a hissing mighty enough to be from the throat of a king serpent himself, another traveler's tale the core of which perhaps to be found here. Rentarn blinked and blinked again.

That thing was changing form before his eyes. In the desert wind devils could raise whole phantom cities to delude a traveler. Yet never had they called her a Betweener. Guides were immune to that troubling of sight.

The legs of the thing were being drawn back into its bloated body. It now rested its belly flat.

"No!" Where Modic had sat voicing insane laughter, he now arose in the chair, clasping the board before him, his fingers thudding home with force on the buttons. "Farguel!" he screamed at the hunched shape of that thing. "Farguel, down with you to the battle even as we set together in thoughts of what must be done. Was it not I, Thebar, who drew you from the swamp to this city, who delivered to you those who were as the beasts, only food to nourish you? Remember, once you fought before and there were those who did not run and scream and strive to hide against that which allowed no hiding. Farguel, this two-legged meat standing here is such a one as those who drove you back, who starved you of food and drink, who made you what you are . . . for I think, Farguel, you are no longer the death hunter you were when we sealed our bargain. Kill this one, Farguel, and prove that you are again great and awesome, so that those sent to bear you down shall themselves die between your fangs. Kill, Farguel!"

Surely this thing, for all its alteration of shape, was not alive as he sensed life! Rentarn watched it coil its serpent shape and lift high that head now losing all resemblance to his own. It opened wide its mouth and a broken line of fangs was fully bared. Not alive, not alive . . . Rentarn held to that thought with all his strength of will.

Yet he could not judge whether it would answer Modic's order or not. His right hand still held in sight the fang, while the fingers of the other moved, writing on the air an unseen pattern. He had believed that such learning was a legend mumbled over by the old ones of the clans, and when he had been set to learning all that finger play he had done so believing it was only a part of his training.

The great head halted in its reach across the flood. Rentarn felt a blow on his shoulder hard enough to numb his arm and near send him sprawling forward into the stream. Modic's board of control lay but inches away on the very lip of the pool.

"Farguel, strike . . . there is no way he can . . ."

Modic was out of the seat, had sunk to his knees as he still held one arm over the chair and was manifestly trying to draw himself up again.

Rentarn watched the creature closely. Its head stretched even higher, supported by a long neck. The open mouth displayed the loss of a front fang.

"Farguel . . ." Modic's voice was harsh but faint as if that of the dead. Rentarn fell back a step as he sensed what was happening to the Seeker. Life was receding. No, now, returned again in a wave with a desperate surge. Was Modic making a supreme effort against another force?

"SSaaa . . ." hissing from the beast. Then a singsong of words from Modic. Only those words were not in any language that the guide could understand, drilled though as he was in the three major languages and numerous dialects of Between and River lands. There was an authority in that chant. Instinctively Rentarn reached for the knife he did not wear. The Seeker huddled again in the chair, his features strangely bloated as if he put on another type of mask.

Whatever he said was addressed, not to Rentarn, but to the thing by the stream. Modic raised his hands jerkily and outspread them again as if the button board still rested on his knees. Then, seeming to understand dimly that that was gone, he voiced a wailing cry, such a sound as Rentarn had never heard before, but the peril of which he could taste with his flickering tongue.

Modic did not face the guide but, at that moment, Rentarn's body throbbed as if that sound reached within him to the very bones, took command of him, flesh and blood. The head of the creature begun to swing again. Rentarn, in spite of his struggle to command himself, moved toward the lip of the pool. Also . . . his feet no longer obeyed his will, instead they carried him forward. Though the Betweeners no longer owned any god or goddess, they still believed in a force for good and one for evil. The Speakers had told of old days when certain strong people, both male and female, reached such heights of control that they could command even stones to move. Those were of yesteryear and few believed their like might even have lived. Rather most Betweeners said inwardly that such were but creatures of legends cast into words by early Speakers to give the clans some fear of the unknown and thus limit their wandering.

"Essar, Roqued, Alsa . . ." To drown out Modic's call or summons without words Rentarn roared full throatedly those names of great bravery and supreme command. He bent his mind toward the battle with raw fear, worked for the control of his body. To that purpose he repeated the roll of Sacred Dead in a battle song. The serpent thing was moving. It drew back its head, tensed muscles, and then . . .

Like a journey staff used as a lance, the head flashed toward Rentarn. By the thickness of a bavard leaf only did it miss seizing upon him.

Modic shrilled that cry a second time. The sound got inside Rentarn's head to cause a new kind of pain. "Essar!" he shouted back, or did he?

Was it true that he was answered, or merely that the tone and pitch of his voice cut through the sound spell Modic was weaving? Rentarn might never know. Anymore than he could tell why and how the warmth in the broken length of colored fang ran up his arm, through him, banishing Modic's influence. Out of the far beginnings of his kind shot a thought that at first was a dim shadow, like a fear in night time, to set him moving.

"Alsa . . ." he said to himself. Modic was being answered by another effort of the serpent creature. Its head launched out a second time across the stream which divided them. The open jaws hung poised above him, ready to seize. Rentarn braced himself. Though the thing was near enough now that it could breathe upon him, there was no breath . . . but a faint odor he had smelled many time before, Lacseed oil such as filled any lamp.

The jaws closed in as Rentarn waited. His hand swung up. He thrust the butt end of the rod he had found into that open hollow in the jaw. It settled there, fastened tightly, now a part of the dreadful set of fangs.

Then . . . there was a flash of orange and green, followed by streams of light. The snakey head rose high. It twisted. Something shaped like a door broken open in its side. One of the weighty feet snapped off.

The scent of oil was throat thickening as the creature threw itself backward, heaving and twisting violently. A shudder and the fearsome head broke loose to fly through the air and smash against one of the chairs of the dead. Bits of wire and small fragments of metal erupted out of the headless body.

That floundered forward into the stream. For a moment or two the water boiled up about it in a mighty sweep of the current. One of the great talons flairing outward caught upon the board of buttons which Modic had fingered. As the mutilated thing dropped, it drew that with it. There followed a flash so bright that Rentarn cupped his hands over smarting eyes, able to see nothing but the scarlet light. But he heard. This was no more wailing encouragement from the Seeker, rather explosions or giant crashs such as might come from the fall of a rock or of a great tree.

Another odor filled the stagnant air. Rentarn pressed the mask dizzly. What he smelled, what his tongue tasted was oil burning, but with that other stenches he could not name. He rubbed his eyes. The second lid there may have saved him from total blindness for he could see, hazily, yet enough to witness what had followed the destruction of the serpent-headed thing.

You could not say it was dead, for his senses still assured him that it had never lived. But the great head had rolled along the edge of the pool. Steam or mist arose from that sickeningly, making him flick his tongue back behind tight lips. A dark smoke rolled along the passage which carried the flood out of the pool. There were flames within that, burning with the same violent colors as had painted the sky when the first of the city's weapons had been launched.

Those flames were not alone. The mummified bodies in the chairs each became a candle set alight by the boards they held. From the heart of each of those pulsed tongues of fire, but these were white.

Modic still huddled in the chair. His body writhed from side to side as if he were caught in a trap and was fighting feebly for freedom. The Seeker's face had changed, it was the countenance of a stranger, a stranger who could not believe in what was happening to him. He screamed a fountain of words, beating upon the arms of the chair with his fists.

The head of the snake thing had rolled to the foot of the first of the chairs. From it still spilled oily liquid which quickly drew sparks of fire. When the head thudded to a stop it was upright and those huge eyes stared at the funeral fire of the dead.

"Farguel!"

There was loss of all sanity in that whimper. Modic leaned forward to the next chair, paying no attention to the smoldering body it still supported.

He spewed forth more words in an erratic pattern which held ghosts of the ritual sounds of a curse or incantation. Then suddenly he stopped—his head shifted and he tried to raise his hands.

"Farguel . . ."

The head with a tangle of molten metal still trailing into the burning stream stared with its round eyes back at him. Modic looked shriveled, empty, as he might have been one of the dead who shared his perch. Rentarn tested the air once again.

That nameless will which he had felt—centering for a while in Modic—was gone. The man was now what he had always been, a Seeker, sly, treacherous, greedy. Only he was rapidly becoming less and less of a man. Flooding out of him, even as the molten metal had flowed from the serpent's head, was that other—that strength which was not his but an unknown other's.

He used the arms of his chair to lever himself to his feet and stood gazing about the whole of this chamber as might a child who had awakened from a dark dream. There was a looseness to his lips, his shoulders hunched as if he was awaiting some punishment. He said, not looking towards Rentarn, but as if he spoke to himself:

"He . . . he is gone." His hands clenched on the chest of his under robe. The edge of it was scorched and there was a small trail of smoke coming from it. "He is . . ." now he shook his head as if to dislodge some insect. For the first time he appeared to recognize Rentarn and there was bemusement on both his face and in the way he staggered as he arose from the seat.

He leaned forward to stare down at the serpent, shivering.

"Farguel . . . there is no way . . . no way! They believe in the demons . . . we cleared the city so . . . and then . . ." He paused, looked at the dying embers which had been the bodies. "What do I say?" Modic drew a hand across his face and let it fall limply to his side. "I am not he . . . but he remains in a little here." Again his hand arose, to touch his head "To be a king . . . more than a king . . . to rule a world. That *he* might have done. . . ." Then Modic lapsed into silence.

For the first time Rentarn spoke, "Who was he, Seeker?"

"He was—one who waited—and waited—from our beginnings they came, all of them." He raised his hand a little to indicate the remains in the other chairs. "They made Farguel." His voice was stronger, as if some small thread of another still curled in his mind. "They would be rulers here and *he* was the greatest among them. But when those they awaited did not come, they put barriers about the cities they had taken and sat to wait. How long did *you* wait?" He addressed the nearest chair as if that still held a living man. "Too long, too long. They said then that they would set up the final guards and sleep as they sometimes did when they traveled among the stars. So it was decided. But not by *him!* He went hunting always, hunting for that which would awaken the rest, take from them dreams of stars that they would learn of this world and what could be done here.

"*He* sent out power to poison the land, to be another barrier behind which he remained to labor. . . ."

Another pause. Modic dug his fists hard against his temples. "Why do I remember, tell me that, Guide? He holds . . . still he holds . . . and he will . . . No." Before Rentarn could move, Modic, his voice shrilling upward, as it had during his frenzy of his possession, threw himself down and out. His body struck against the disintegrating head of the thing he had called Farguel. He did not scream again as he slid on and out into the fire which flowed with the stream.

Rentarn retreated swiftly to the far wall of the hall, then leaped toward the entrance of the corridor. As if the death of Modic was the last fuel, flames flared behind, reaching so that he had to beat the fire from the edge of his cloak. But that other will . . . that power which had measured him so hungrily was gone. There was no life any longer in this place.

The guide reached the outermost part of the great palace or temple. Flames sped in waves along the sluggish stream. Only that light which had touched the sky was gone. Here was only a dry emptiness, an absence of all life within the ruin.

That which Rentarn had sensed as shadows of terror was also gone. He stood, his chest heaving from his run. All the stream was now afire.

He glanced back just once at the palace from which he had escaped. His tongue flicked out . . . all life was not gone. There was a whinny. The horse showed himself within the core of a long gone building, picking his way toward the guide. Rentarn's mind filled with surprise, then content. He and this animal were alive. The flame which destroyed the dead—the last of that was licking at the pool, flickering as what had fueled it was eaten up.

"Come." The guide crossed to the horse who nuzzled at his shoulder and whinneyed louder than before. "Let us get out of this place, brother—for it is of long dead and should be left to them in peace."

He swung up into the saddle. Willingly the horse turned without urging, pacing along that road which had led to the heart of Lonscraft.

Rentarn would never understand all which had happened, but his flickering tongue assured him of safety—here was only tumbled stone, dust, and a sprung trap. The destruction of the creature (he had to think of that as having life even though he could not sense it) and of the will of that other unknown which Modic had brought to half life, had perhaps reversed the poison of this dust-dry land and all it held. However let that be proven at some later time, by those who were born to be Seekers. For himself now, he wanted no more of the Dry. Thus he threaded a way between the masses of stone rubble until he passed beyond the gate of Lonscraft which once was.

ARTHUR C. CLARKE

b. 1917

When Arthur Charles Clarke was a teenager in London, in the years before World War II, his nickname among his fellow science fiction fans was "Ego" Clarke. They didn't mean it as an insult. It was only their way of recognizing the fact that, from childhood on, Clarke had a high opinion of his own abilities. His opinion was right on target, too; it just took a while for the rest of the world to confirm it.

Like many other fans of the period, Clarke wasn't merely interested in reading and writing about the future. He wanted to make it happen, and he wanted it to happen *soon*. There was the matter of space travel, for instance.

It was perfectly obvious to young Arthur Clarke that if you simply built the right kind of rocket it would take you to the Moon—or, if you had a little more time, to pretty nearly anywhere else you wanted to go in the universe. All that was lacking to make this come about was money and a certain amount of engineering, plus the will to make it happen. To help find ways of supplying those needs, Clarke became a member of the brand-new British Interplanetary Society (still well and functioning, more than sixty years later), eventually becoming its secretary. World War II, however, called a recess to that sort of long-range rocket planning—that is, not counting what Werner von Braun was doing on the other side of the Channel.

The war didn't stop Clarke from thinking about space, though, and as it was drawing to a close he single-handedly invented the modern orbiting geosynchronous communications satellite, in a paper published in a technical journal. The article clearly spelled out the technology for what has since become a megabillion-dollar industry. For some years in the sixties and seventies Clarke was wont to muse wistfully over how his fortunes might have fared if he had only thought to patent the idea, instead of giving it away. (Actually, not all that well. Patents have a finite life span. By the time all the ancillary technology to make communications satellites real came along, the patent would have expired anyway; such are the penalties of being ahead of one's time.)

Then Clarke found his true vocation. (One of them, anyway.) For the fun of it he wrote a science fiction story, "Rescue Party." He mailed it off to John Campbell on the chance it might make it into *Astounding*. It did, and the rest is history.

"Rescue Party" was an unusual first story. It was perfectly formed; it would have done credit to any of the best sf writers around, and it made the fans eager for more. Clarke didn't disappoint. Over the next few years he published a good many first-rate stories, culminating with the two novels that confirmed his reputation in science fiction, *Childhood's End* and *Against the Fall of Night*. (Curiously, Clarke wasn't satisfied with *Against the Fall of Night*. Not long afterward he rewrote it substantially and reissued it under the title of *The City and the Stars*. For a time the two different versions of the story were offered for sale side by side in the bookstores.)

Then Clarke's life moved to a new plateau. He had published a nonfiction book on space travel. The manuscript was given to Basil Davenport, powerful editor of the Book-of-the-Month Club and a closet science fiction fan; Davenport loved it, fought for it against considerable opposition from other BOMC editors and judges and managed to get it issued as a main selection of the club. This brought with it a paycheck orders of magnitude higher than any Clarke had seen before; more important, it made Clarke a familiar figure to the host of Book-of-the-Month Club members who had never previously given a thought to any science fiction writer.

Then, a decade or two later, along came Stanley Kubrick.

Kubrick was one of the most adventurous and idiosyncratic of movie moguls. It seemed to Kubrick that there was something that might make a great film somewhere in science fiction, some kind of theme that went beyond the usual crop of quickies and Japanese monster movies. Kubrick didn't, however, know exactly what. More or less at random, he bought film rights on a cluster of four of Clarke's short stories, but the more he thought about them the more he realized that they weren't precisely what he wanted to film.

Then he and Clarke met. They talked about what a truly great science fiction film might be and decided that one of the four stories—"The Sentinel"—contained the germ of a filmable script. Kubrick gave the other three stories back to Clarke, and signed him up to collaborate on a scenario.

I wish I might have been a fly on the wall, to listen in on some of those endless story conferences. These were two men who, though alike in self-confidence and in limited tolerance for being told what to do by others, differed fundamentally in their approach to creation. Clarke's methodology was straightforward: get an idea, start writing, see where it takes you. Kubrick was a tinkerer: shoot a scene, look it over, shoot it again in a different way, or maybe throw it out and shoot something entirely different. When at last a script was agreed on and filmed, and the sets struck and Clarke allowed to go off to begin writing the novel version, Kubrick holed up and created the light show that ends the film all by himself—leaving Clarke with the problem of trying to describe, in comprehensible words, what Kubrick had been getting at with his fuzzy symbolism. (And all this time—years of it—Clarke had been so fully occupied with working with Kubrick that his production of saleable fiction had suffered. Publishers were waiting for the book, with large amounts of money ready to pour into Clarke's coffers—but none of it would pour until the book was finally finished and delivered.)

But then it was all done. The film was *2001: A Space Odyssey*, and Clarke was famous to the largest world yet.

2001 (Clarke said) elevated his financial status from the "rich poor" to the "poor rich." It made it possible for him to pick and choose among the things he might do with his writing time, so that (he also said) he could limit himself to projects which, (1) were worth doing for their own sake, (2) offered worthwhile rewards, and (3) were such that he was the person who could do them better than anyone else. It also made it possible for him to leave chilly

England and move to the sunny, lovely tropical island nation of Sri Lanka, which has been his home ever since.

In the summer of 1970 Arthur and I, with Brian Aldiss, Judith Merril, and a clutch of Soviet science fiction writers, spent a couple of weeks in a sort of Chautauqua tour of Japan, from Tokyo to the vacation resort of Lake Biwa. It was a relaxing trip with a lot of fun things going on between lecture appearances—for example, Arthur Clarke doing a hula for a fascinated audience of Japanese science fiction fans—but he wasn't entirely carefree. The Tamil insurgents were shooting up parts of Sri Lanka in their effort (still ongoing now) to attain independence, and sometimes they were coming close to his home. However, he was in good health and good spirits. The next time I saw him, in New York City a year or so later, not quite so much so.

Arthur had become a convert to the sport and science of scuba diving, for which there is no better place in the world than the waters around Sri Lanka. He dove every chance he got, wrote books on the subject, explored old wrecks and came up with fistsful of ancient silver coins, enjoyed every moment of it . . . but then there was a small sort of diving accident. It triggered some problems left over from childhood illnesses, and in New York he was having some difficulty in getting out of particularly deep chairs. It didn't get better. The problem kept recurring, ultimately putting him in a wheelchair. . . .

But not in the least slowing down his remarkable literary productivity. It turned out there were quite a few projects that met his strictures. The books kept pouring out, and so did such other ventures as Clarke's own syndicated TV series, *Arthur C. Clarke's Mysterious World*. All those activities brought rewards to match. Arthur Clarke became chancellor of Sri Lanka's university, a friend of the nation's president, the person journalists from all over the world called up for a reaction every time there was a news story concerning space or science. And in 1997 came the final accolade. Her Majesty, Queen Elizabeth II, knighted him for his accomplishments.

The only thing that surprised his many admirers was that it had taken so long to occur. But occur it did. The title was formally conferred upon him in person by HRH, the Prince of Wales, and now, and for all time to come, he is to be known as *Sir* Arthur Charles Clarke.

Recommended Reading
by Arthur C. Clarke

2001: A Space Odyssey
Childhood's End
Against the Fall of Night/The City and the Stars
A Meeting with Medusa
Rendezvous with Rama

RESCUE PARTY

W*ho was to blame?* For three days Alveron's thoughts had come back to that question, and still he had found no answer. A creature of a less civilized or a less sensitive race would never have let it torture his mind, and would have satisfied himself with the assurance that no one could be responsible for the working of fate. But Alveron and his kind had been lords of the Universe since the dawn of history, since that far distant age when the Time Barrier had been folded round the cosmos by the unknown powers that lay beyond the Beginning. To them had been given all knowledge—and with infinite knowledge went infinite responsibility. If there were mistakes and errors in the administration of the Galaxy, the fault lay on the heads of Alveron and his people. And this was no mere mistake: it was one of the greatest tragedies in history.

The crew still knew nothing. Even Rugon, his closest friend and the ship's deputy captain, had been told only part of the truth. But now the doomed worlds lay less than a billion miles ahead. In a few hours, they would be landing on the third planet.

Once again Alveron read the message from Base: then, with a flick of a tentacle that no human eye could have followed, he pressed the "General Attention" button. Throughout the mile-long cylinder that was the Galactic Survey Ship S9000, creatures of many races laid down their work to listen to the words of their captain.

"I know you have all been wondering," began Alveron, "why we were ordered to abandon our survey and to proceed at such an acceleration to this region of space. Some of you may realize what this acceleration means. Our ship is on its last voyage: the generators have already been running for sixty hours at Ultimate Overload. We will be very lucky if we return to Base under our own power.

"We are approaching a sun which is about to become a Nova. Detonation will occur in seven hours, with an uncertainty of one hour, leaving us a maximum of only four hours for exploration. There are ten planets in the system about to be destroyed—*and there is a civilization on the third.* That fact was discovered only a few days ago. It is our tragic mission to contact that doomed race, and if possible to save some of its members. I know that there is little we can do in so short a time with this single ship. No other machine can possibly reach the system before detonation occurs."

There was a long pause during which there could have been no sound or movement in the whole of the mighty ship as it sped silently towards the worlds ahead. Alveron knew what his companions were thinking and he tried to answer their unspoken question.

"You will wonder how such a disaster, the greatest of which we have any record, has been allowed to occur. On one point I can reassure you. The fault does not lie with the Survey.

"As you know, with our present fleet of under twelve thousand ships, it is possible to re-examine each of the eight thousand million solar systems in the Galaxy at intervals of about a million years. Most worlds change very little in so short a time as that.

"Less than four hundred thousand years ago, the survey ship S5060 examined the planets of the system we are approaching. It found intelligence on none of them, though the third planet was teeming with animal life and two other worlds had once been inhabited. The usual report was submitted and the system is due for its next examination in six hundred thousand years.

"It now appears that in that incredibly short period since the last survey, intelligent life has appeared in the system. The first intimation of this occurred when unknown radio signals were detected on the planet Kulath in the system X29.35, Y34.76, Z27.93. Bearings were taken on them and they were found to come from the system ahead.

"Kulath is two hundred light-years from here, so those radio waves had been on their way for two centuries. Thus for at least that period of time a civilization has existed on one of these worlds—a civilization that can generate electromagnetic waves and all that that implies.

"An immediate telescopic examination of the system was made and it was then found that the sun was in the unstable prenova stage. Detonation might occur at any moment, and indeed might have done so while the light waves were on their way to Kulath.

"There was a slight delay while the supervelocity scanners on Kulath II were focused on to the system. They showed that the explosion had not yet occurred but was only a few hours away. If Kulath had been a fraction of a light-year further from this sun, we should never have known of its civilization until it had ceased to exist.

"The Administrator of Kulath contacted Sector Base immediately, and I was ordered to proceed to the system at once. Our object is to save what members we can of the doomed race, if indeed there are any left. But we have assumed that a civilization possessing radio could have protected itself against any rise of temperature that may have already occurred.

"This ship and the two tenders will each explore a section of the planet. Commander Torkalee will take Number One, Commander Orostron Number Two. They will have just under four hours in which to explore this world. At the end of that time, they *must* be back in the ship. It will be leaving then, with or without them. I will give the two commanders detailed instructions in the control room immediately.

"That is all. We enter the atmosphere in two hours."

On the world once known as Earth the fires were dying out: there was nothing left to burn. The great forests that had swept across the planet like a tidal wave with the passing of the cities were now no more than glowing charcoal and the smoke of their funeral pyres still stained the sky. But the last hours were still to come, for the surface rocks had not yet begun to flow. The continents were dimly visible through the haze, but their outlines meant nothing to the watchers in the approaching ship. The charts they possessed were out of date by a dozen Ice Ages and more deluges than one.

The S9000 had driven past Jupiter and seen at once that no life could exist in those half-gaseous oceans of compressed hydrocarbons, now erupting furiously under the sun's abnormal heat. Mars and the outer planets they had missed, and Alveron realized that the worlds nearer the sun than Earth would be already melting. It was more than likely, he thought sadly, that the tragedy of this unknown race was already finished. Deep in his heart, he thought it might be better so. The ship could only have carried a few hundred survivors, and the problem of selection had been haunting his mind.

Rugon, Chief of Communications and Deputy Captain, came into the control room. For the last hour he had been striving to detect radiation from Earth, but in vain.

"We're too late," he announced gloomily. "I've monitored the whole spectrum and the ether's dead except for our own stations and some two-hundred-year-old programs from Kulath. Nothing in this system is radiating any more."

He moved towards the giant vision screen with a graceful flowing motion that no mere biped could ever hope to imitate. Alveron said nothing: he had been expecting this news.

One entire wall of the control room was taken up by the screen, a great black rectangle that gave an impression of almost infinite depth. Three of Rugon's slender control tentacles, useless for heavy work but incredibly swift at all manipulation, flickered over the selector dials and the screen lit up with a thousand points of light. The star field flowed swiftly past as Rugon adjusted the controls, bringing the projector to bear upon the sun itself.

No man of Earth would have recognized the monstrous shape that filled the screen. The sun's light was no longer: great violet-blue clouds covered half its surface and from them long streamers of flame were erupting into space. At one point an enormous prominence had reared itself out of the photosphere, far out even into the flickering veils of the corona. It was as though a tree of fire had taken root in the surface of the sun—a tree that stood half a million miles high and whose branches were rivers of flame sweeping through space at hundreds of miles a second.

"I suppose," said Rugon presently, "that you are quite satisfied about the astronomers' calculations. After all—"

"Oh, we're perfectly safe," said Alveron confidently. "I've spoken to Kulath Observatory and they have been making some additional checks through our own instruments. That uncertainty of an hour includes a private safety margin which they won't tell me in case I feel tempted to stay any longer."

He glanced at the instrument board.

"The pilot should have brought us to the atmosphere now. Switch the screen back to the planet, please. Ah, there they go!"

There was a sudden tremor underfoot and a raucous clanging of alarms, instantly stilled. Across the vision screen two slim projectiles dived towards the looming mass of Earth. For a few miles they traveled together: then they separated, one vanishing abruptly as it entered the shadow of the planet.

Slowly the huge mother ship, with its thousand times greater mass, descended after them into the raging storms that already were tearing down the deserted cities of Man.

It was night in the hemisphere over which Orostron drove his tiny command. Like Torkalee, his mission was to photograph and record, and to report progress to the mother ship. The little scout had no room for specimens or passengers. If contact was made with the inhabitants of this world, the S9000 would come at once. There would be no time for parleying. If there was any trouble the rescue would be by force and the explanations could come later.

The ruined land beneath was bathed with an eerie, flickering light, for a great auroral display was raging over half the world. But the image on the vision screen was independent of external light, and it showed clearly a waste of barren rock that seemed never to have known any form of life. Presumably this desert land must come to an end somewhere. Orostron increased his speed to the highest value he dared risk in so dense an atmosphere.

The machine fled on through the storm, and presently the desert of rock began to climb towards the sky. A great mountain range lay ahead, its peaks lost in the smoke-laden clouds. Orostron directed the scanners towards the horizon, and on the vision screen the line of mountains seemed suddenly very close and menacing. He started to climb rapidly. It was difficult to imagine a more unpromising land in which to find civilization and he wondered if it would be wise to change course. He decided against it. Five minutes later, he had his reward.

Miles below lay a decapitated mountain, the whole of its summit sheared away by some tremendous feat of engineering. Rising out of the rock and straddling the artificial plateau was an intricate structure of metal girders, supporting masses of machinery. Orostron brought his ship to a halt and spiraled down towards the mountain.

The slight Doppler blur had now vanished, and the picture on the screen was clear-cut. The lattice-work was supporting some scores of great metal mirrors, pointing skyward at an angle of forty-five degrees to the horizontal. They were slightly concave, and each had some complicated mechanism at its focus. There seemed something impressive and purposeful about the great array; every mirror was aimed at precisely the same spot in the sky—or beyond.

Orostron turned to his colleagues.

"It looks like some kind of observatory to me," he said. "Have you ever seen anything like it before?"

Klarten, a multitentacled, tripedal creature from a globular cluster at the edge of the Milky Way, had a different theory.

"That's communication equipment. Those reflectors are for focusing electromagnetic beams. I've seen the same kind of installation on a hundred worlds before. It may even be the station that Kulath picked up—though that's rather unlikely, for the beams would be very narrow from mirrors that size."

"That would explain why Rugon could detect no radiation before we landed," added Hansur II, one of the twin beings from the planet Thargon.

Orostron did not agree at all.

"If that *is* a radio station, it must be built for interplanetary communication. Look at the way the mirrors are pointed. I don't believe that a race which has only had radio for two centuries can have crossed space. It took my people six thousand years to do it."

"We managed it in three," said Hansur II mildly, speaking a few seconds ahead of his twin. Before the inevitable argument could develop, Klarten began to wave his tentacles with excitement. While the others had been talking, he had started the automatic monitor.

"Here it is! Listen!"

He threw a switch, and the little room was filled with a raucous whining sound, continually changing in pitch but nevertheless retaining certain characteristics that were difficult to define.

The four explorers listened intently for a minute; then Orostron said: "Surely that can't be any form of speech! No creature could produce sounds as quickly as that!"

Hansur I had come to the same conclusion.

"That's a television program. Don't you think so, Klarten?"

The other agreed.

"Yes, and each of those mirrors seems to be radiating a different program. I wonder where they're going? If I'm correct, one of the other planets in the system must lie along those beams. We can soon check that."

Orostron called the S9000 and reported the discovery. Both Rugon and Alveron were greatly excited, and made a quick check of the astronomical records.

The result was surprising—and disappointing. None of the other nine planets lay anywhere near the line of transmission. The great mirrors appeared to be pointing blindly into space.

There seemed only one conclusion to be drawn, and Klarten was the first to voice it.

"They *had* interplanetary communication," he said. "But the station must be deserted now, and the transmitters no longer controlled. They haven't been switched off, and are just pointing where they were left."

"Well, we'll soon find out," said Orostron. "I'm going to land."

He brought the machine slowly down to the level of the great metal mirrors, and past them until it came to rest on the mountain rock. A hundred yards away, a white stone building crouched beneath the maze of steel girders. It was windowless, but there were several doors in the wall facing them.

Orostron watched his companions climb into their protective suits and wished he could follow. But someone had to stay in the machine to keep in touch with the mother ship. Those were Alveron's instructions, and they were very wise. One never knew what would happen on a world that was being explored for the first time, especially under conditions such as these.

Very cautiously, the three explorers stepped out of the air lock and adjusted the antigravity field of their suits. Then, each with the mode of locomotion peculiar to his race, the little party went towards the building, the Hansur twins leading and Klarten following close behind. His gravity control was apparently giving trouble, for he suddenly fell to the ground, rather to the amusement of his colleagues. Orostron saw them pause for a moment at the nearest door—then it opened and they disappeared from sight.

So Orostron waited, with what patience he could, while the storm rose around him and the light of the aurora grew ever brighter in the sky. At the agreed times he called the mother ship and received brief acknowledgements from Rugon. He wondered how Torkalee was faring, halfway round the planet, but he could not contact him through the crash and thunder of solar interference.

It did not take Klarten and the Hansurs long to discover that their theories were largely correct. The building was a radio station, and it was deserted. It consisted of one tremendous room with a few small offices leading from it. In the main chamber, row after row of electrical equipment stretched into the distance; lights flickered and winked on hundreds of control panels, and a dull glow came from the elements in a great avenue of vacuum tubes.

But Klarten was not impressed. The first radio sets his race had built were now fossilized in strata a thousand million years old. Man, who had possessed electrical machines for only a few centuries, could not compete with those who had known them for half the lifetime of the Earth.

Nevertheless, the party kept their recorders running as they explored the building. There was still one problem to be solved. The deserted station was broadcasting programs—but where were they coming from? The central switchboard had been quickly located. It was designed to handle scores of programs simultaneously, but the source of those programs was lost in a maze of cables that vanished underground. Back in the S9000, Rugon was trying to analyze the broadcasts and perhaps his researchers would reveal their origin. It was impossible to trace cables that might lead across continents.

The party wasted little time at the deserted station. There was nothing they could learn from it, and they were seeking life rather than scientific information. A few minutes later the little ship rose swiftly from the plateau and headed towards the plains that must lie beyond the mountains. Less than three hours were still left to them.

As the array of enigmatic mirrors dropped out of sight, Orostron was struck by a sudden thought. Was it imagination, or had they all moved through a small angle while he had been waiting, as if they were still compensating for the rotation of the Earth? He could not be sure, and he dismissed the matter as unimportant. It would only mean that the directing mechanism was still working, after a fashion.

They discovered the city fifteen minutes later. It was a great, sprawling metropolis, built around a river that had disappeared leaving an ugly scar winding its way among the great buildings and beneath bridges that looked very incongruous now.

Even from the air, the city looked deserted. But only two and a half hours were left—there was no time for further exploration. Orostron made his decision, and landed near the largest structure he could see. It seemed reasonable to suppose that some creatures would have sought shelter in the strongest buildings, where they would be safe until the very end.

The deepest coves—the heart of the planet itself—would give no protection when the final cataclysm came. Even if this race had reached the outer planets, its doom would only be delayed by the few hours it would take for the ravening wavefronts to cross the Solar System.

Orostron could not know that the city had been deserted not for a few days or weeks, but for over a century. For the culture of cities, which had outlasted so many civilizations, had been doomed at last when the helicopter brought universal transportation. Within a few generations the great masses of mankind, knowing that they could reach any part of the globe in a matter of hours, had gone back to the fields and forests for which they had always longed. The new civilization had machines and resources of which earlier ages had never dreamed, but it was essentially rural and no longer bound to the steel and concrete warrens that had dominated the centuries before. Such cities that still remained were specialized centers of research, administration or entertainment; the others had been allowed to decay where it was too much trouble to destroy them. The dozen or so greatest of all cities, and the ancient university towns, had scarcely changed and would have lasted for many generations to come. But the cities that had been founded on steam and iron and surface transportation had passed with the industries that had nourished them.

And so while Orostron waited in the tender, his colleagues raced through endless empty corridors and deserted halls, taking innumerable photographs but learning nothing of the creatures who had used these buildings. There were libraries, meeting places, council rooms, thousands of offices—all were empty and deep with dust. If they had not seen the radio station on its mountain eyrie, the explorers could well have believed that this world had known no life for centuries.

Through the long minutes of waiting, Orostron tried to imagine where this race could have vanished. Perhaps they had killed themselves knowing that escape was impossible; perhaps they had built great shelters in the bowels of the planet, and even now were cowering in their millions beneath his feet, waiting for the end. He began to fear that he would never know.

It was almost a relief when at last he had to give the order for the return. Soon he would know if Torkalee's party had been more fortunate. And he was anxious to get back to the mother ship, for as the minutes passed the suspense had become more and more acute. There had always been the thought in his mind: "What if the astronomers of Kulath have made a mistake?" He would begin to feel happy when the walls of the S9000 were around him. He would be happier still when they were out in space and this ominous sun was shrinking far astern.

As soon as his colleagues had entered the air lock, Orostron hurled his tiny machine into the sky and set the controls to home on the S9000. Then he turned to his friends.

"Well, what have you found?" he asked.

Klarten produced a large roll of canvas and spread it out on the floor.

"This is what they were like," he said quietly. "Bipeds, with only two arms. They seem to have managed well, in spite of that handicap. Only two eyes as well, unless there are others in the back. We were lucky to find this; it's about the only thing they left behind."

The ancient oil painting stared stonily back at the three creatures regarding it so intently. By the irony of fate, its complete worthlessness had saved it from oblivion. When the city had been evacuated, no one had bothered to move Alderman John Richards, 1909–1974. For a century and a half he had been gathering dust while far away from the old cities the new civilization had been rising to heights no earlier culture had ever known.

"That was almost all we found," said Klarten. "The city must have been deserted for years. I'm afraid our expedition has been a failure. If there are any living beings on this world, they've hidden themselves too well for us to find them."

His commander was forced to agree.

"It was an almost impossible task," he said. "If we'd had weeks instead of hours we might have succeeded. For all we know, they may even have built shelters under the sea. No one seems to have thought of that."

He glanced quickly at the indicators and corrected the course.

"We'll be there in five minutes. Alveron seems to be moving rather quickly. I wonder if Torkalee has found anything?"

The S9000 was hanging a few miles above the seaboard of a blazing continent when Orostron homed upon it. The danger line was thirty minutes away and there was no time to lose. Skillfully, he maneuvered the little ship into its launching tube and the party stepped out of the air lock.

There was a small crowd waiting for them. That was to be expected, but Orostron could see at once that something more than curiosity had brought his friends here. Even before a word was spoken, he knew that something was wrong.

"Torkalee hasn't returned. He's lost his party and we're going to the rescue. Come along to the control room at once."

•   •   •

From the beginning, Torkalee had been luckier than Orostron. He had followed the zone of twilight, keeping away from the intolerable glare of the sun, until he came to the shores of an inland sea. It was a very recent sea, one of the latest of Man's works, for the land it covered had been desert less than a century before. In a few hours it would be desert again, for the water was boiling and clouds of steam were rising to the skies. But they could not veil the loveliness of the great white city that overlooked the tideless sea.

Flying machines were still parked neatly round the square in which Torkalee landed. They were disappointingly primitive, though beautifully finished, and depended on rotating airfoils for support. Nowhere was there any sign of life, but the place gave the impression that its inhabitants were not very far away. Lights were still shining from some of the windows.

Torkalee's three companions lost no time in leaving the machine. Leader of the party, by seniority of rank and race was T'sinadree, who like Alveron himself had been born on one of the ancient planets of the Central Suns. Next came Alarkane, from a race which was one of the youngest in the Universe and took a perverse pride in the fact. Last came one of the strange beings from the system of Palador. It was nameless, like all its kind, for it possessed no identity of its own, being merely a mobile but still dependent cell in the consciousness of its race. Though it and its fellows had long been scattered over the Galaxy in the exploration of countless worlds, some unknown link still bound them together as inexorably as the living cells in a human body.

When a creature of Palador spoke, the pronoun it used was always "We." There was not, nor could there ever be, any first person singular in the language of Palador.

The great doors of the splendid building baffled the explorers, though any human child would have known their secret. T'sinadree wasted no time on them but called Torkalee on his personal transmitter. Then the three hurried aside while their commander maneuvered his machine into the best position. There was a brief burst of intolerable flame; the massive steelwork flickered once at the edge of the visible spectrum and was gone. The stones were still glowing when the eager party hurried into the building, the beams of their light projectors fanning before them.

The torches were not needed. Before them lay a great hall, glowing with light from lines of tubes along the ceiling. On either side, the hall opened out into long corridors, while straight ahead a massive stairway swept majestically towards the upper floors.

For a moment T'sinadree hesitated. Then, since one way was as good as another, he led his companions down the first corridor.

The feeling that life was near had now become very strong. At any moment, it seemed, they might be confronted by the creatures of this world. If they showed hostility—and they could scarcely be blamed if they did—the paralyzers would be used at once.

The tension was very great as the party entered the first room, and only relaxed when they saw that it held nothing but machines—row after row of them, now stilled and silent. Lining the enormous room were thousands of metal filing cabinets, forming a continuous wall as far as the eye could reach. And that was all; there was no furniture, nothing but the cabinets and the mysterious machines.

Alarkane, always the quickest of the three, was already examining the cabinets. Each held many thousand sheets of tough, thin material, perforated with innumerable holes and slots: The Paladorian appropriated one of the cards and Alarkane recorded the scene together with some close-ups of the machines. Then they left. The great room, which had been one of the marvels of the world, meant nothing to them. No living eye would ever again see that wonderful battery of almost human Hollerith analyzers and the five thousand million punched cards holding all that could be recorded of each man, woman and child on the planet.

It was clear that this building had been used very recently. With growing excitement, the explorers hurried on to the next room. This they found to be an enormous library, for millions of books lay all around them on miles and miles of shelving. Here, though the explorers could not know it, were the records of all the laws that Man had ever passed, and all the speeches that had ever been made in his council chambers.

T'sinadree was deciding his plan of action when Alarkane drew his attention to one of the racks a hundred yards away. It was half empty, unlike all the others. Around it books lay in a tumbled heap on the floor, as if knocked down by someone in frantic haste. The signs were unmistakable. Not long ago, other creatures had been this way. Faint wheel marks were clearly visible on the floor to the acute sense of Alarkane, though the others could see nothing. Alarkane could even detect footprints, but knowing nothing of the creatures that had formed them he could not say which way they led.

The sense of nearness was stronger than ever now, but it was nearness in time, not in space. Alarkane voiced the thoughts of the party.

"Those books must have been valuable, and someone has come to rescue them—rather as an afterthought, I should say. That means there must be a place of refuge, possibly not very far away. Perhaps we may be able to find some other clues that will lead us to it."

T'sinadree agreed, but the Paladorian refused to be enthusiastic.

"That may be so," it said, "but the refuge may be anywhere on the planet, and we have just two hours left. Let us waste no more time if we hope to rescue these people."

The party hurried forward once more, pausing only to collect a few books that might be useful to the scientists at Base—though it was doubtful if they could ever be translated. They soon found that the great building was composed largely of small rooms, all showing signs of recent occupation. Most of them were in a neat and tidy condition, but one or two were very much the reverse. The explorers were particularly puzzled by one room—clearly an office of some kind—that appeared to have been completely wrecked. The floor was littered with papers, the furniture had been smashed, and smoke was pouring through the broken windows from the fires outside.

T'sinadree was rather alarmed.

"Surely no dangerous animal could have got into a place like this!" he exclaimed, fingering his paralyzer nervously.

Alarkane did not answer. He began to make that annoying sound which his race called "laughter." It was several minutes before he would explain what had amused him.

"I don't think any animal has done it," he said. "In fact, the explanation is very simple. Suppose you had been working all your life in this room, dealing with endless papers, year after year. And suddenly, you are told that you will never see it again, that your work is finished, and that you can leave it forever. More than that—no one will come after you. *Everything* is finished. How would you make your exit, T'sinadree?"

The other thought for a moment.

"Well, I suppose I'd just tidy things up and leave. That's what seems to have happened in all the other rooms."

Alarkane laughed again.

"I'm quite sure you would. But some individuals have a different psychology. I think I should have liked the creature that used this room."

He did not explain himself further, and his two colleagues puzzled over his words for quite a while before they gave it up.

It came as something of a shock when Torkalee gave the order to return. They had gathered a great deal of information, but had found no clue that might lead them to the missing inhabitants of this world. That problem was as baffling as ever, and now it seemed that it would never be solved. There were only forty minutes left before the S9000 would be departing.

They were halfway back to the tender when they saw the semi-circular passage leading down into the depths of the building. Its architectural style was quite different from that used elsewhere, and the gently sloping floor was an irresistible attraction to creatures whose many legs had grown weary of the marble staircases which only bipeds could have built in such profusion. T'sinadree had been the worst sufferer, for he normally employed twelve legs and could use twenty when he was in a hurry—though no one had ever seen him perform this feat.

The party stopped dead and looked down the passageway with a single thought. A *tunnel, leading down into the depths of the earth.* At its end, they might yet find the people of this world and rescue some of them from their fate. For there was still time to call the mother ship if the need arose.

T'sinadree signaled to his commander and Torkalee brought the little machine immediately overhead. There might not be time for the party to retrace its footsteps through the maze of passages, so meticulously recorded in the Paladorian mind that there was no possibility of going astray. If speed were necessary, Torkalee could blast his way through the dozen floors above their head. In any case, it should not take long to find what lay at the end of the passage.

It took only thirty seconds. The tunnel ended quite abruptly in a very curious cylindrical room with magnificently padded seats along the walls. There was no way out save that by which they had come and it was several seconds before the purpose of the chamber dawned on Alarkane's mind. It was a pity, he thought, that they would never have time to use this. The thought was suddenly interrupted by a cry from T'sinadree. Alarkane wheeled around, and saw that the entrance had closed silently behind them.

Even in that first moment of panic, Alarkane found himself thinking with some admiration: "Whoever they were, they knew how to build automatic machinery!"

The Paladorian was the first to speak. It waved one of its tendrils towards the seats.

"We think it would be best to be seated," it said. The multiplex mind of Palador had already analyzed the situation and knew what was coming.

They did not have long to wait before a low-pitched hum came from a grille overhead, and for the very last time in history a human, even if lifeless, voice was heard on Earth. The words were meaningless, though the trapped explorers could guess their message clearly enough.

"Choose your stations, please, and be seated."

Simultaneously, a wall panel at one end of the compartment glowed with light. On it was a simple map, consisting of a series of a dozen circles connected by a line. Each of the circles had writing alongside it, and beside the writing were two buttons of different colors.

Alarkane looked questionly at his leader.

"Don't touch them," said T'sinadree. "If we leave the controls alone, the doors may open again."

He was wrong. The engineers who had designed the automatic subway had assumed that anyone who entered it would naturally wish to go somewhere. If they selected no intermediate station, their destination could only be the end of the line.

There was another pause while the relays and thyratrons waited for their orders. In those thirty seconds, if they had known what to do, the party could have opened the doors and left the subway. But they did not know, and the machines geared to a human psychology acted for them.

The surge of acceleration was not very great; the lavish upholstery was a luxury, not a necessity. Only an almost imperceptible vibration told of the speed at which they were traveling through the bowels of the earth, on a journey the duration of which they could not even guess. And in thirty minutes, the S9000 would be leaving the Solar System.

There was a long silence in the speeding machine. T'sinadree and Alarkane were thinking rapidly. So was the Paladorian, though in a different fashion. The conception of personal death was meaningless to it, for the destruction of a single unit meant no more to the group mind than the loss of a nail-paring to a man. But it could, though with great difficulty, appreciate the plight of individual intelligences such as Alarkane and T'sinadree, and it was anxious to help them if it could.

Alarkane had managed to contact Torkalee with his personal transmitter, though the signal was very weak and seemed to be fading quickly. Rapidly he explained the situation, and almost at once the signals became clearer. Torkalee was following the path of the machine, flying above the ground under which they were speeding to their unknown destination. That was the first indication they had of the fact that they were traveling at nearly a thousand miles an hour, and very soon after that Torkalee was able to give the still more disturbing news that they were rapidly approaching the sea. While they were beneath the land, there was a hope, though a slender one, that they might stop the machine and escape. But under the ocean—not all the brains and the machinery in the great mother ship could save them. No one could have devised a more perfect trap.

T'sinadree had been examining the wall map with great attention. Its meaning was obvious, and along the line connecting the circles a tiny spot of light was crawling. It was already halfway to the first of the stations marked.

"I'm going to press one of those buttons," said T'sinadree at last. "It won't do any harm, and we may learn something."

"I agree. Which will you try first?"

"There are only two kinds, and it won't matter if we try the wrong one first. I suppose one is to start the machine and the other is to stop it."

Alarkane was not very hopeful.

"It started without any button pressing," he said. "I think it's completely automatic and we can't control it from here at all."

T'sinadree could not agree.

"These buttons are clearly associated with the stations, and there's no point in having them unless you can use them to stop yourself. The only question is, which is the right one?"

His analysis was perfectly correct. The machine could be stopped at any intermediate station. They had only been on their way ten minutes, and if they could leave now, no harm would have been done. It was just bad luck that T'sinadree's first choice was the wrong button.

The little light on the map crawled slowly through the illuminated circle without checking its speed. And at the same time Torkalee called from the ship overhead.

"You have just passed underneath a city and are heading out to sea. There cannot be another stop for nearly a thousand miles."

Alveron had given up all hope of finding life on this world. The S9000 had roamed over half the planet, never staying long in one place, descending ever and again in an effort to attract attention. There had been no response; Earth seemed utterly dead. If any of its inhabitants were still alive, thought Alveron, they must have hidden themselves in its depths where no help could reach them, though their doom would be none the less certain.

Rugon brought news of the disaster. The great ship ceased its fruitless searching and fled back through the storm to the ocean above which Torkalee's little tender was still following the track of the buried machine.

The scene was truly terrifying. Not since the days when Earth was born had there been such seas as this. Mountains of water were racing before the storm which had now reached velocities of many hundred miles an hour. Even at this distance from the mainland the air was full of flying debris—trees, fragments of houses, sheets of metal, anything that had not been anchored to the ground. No airborne machine could have lived for a moment in such a gale. And ever and again even the roar of the wind was drowned as the vast water-mountains met head-on with a crash that seemed to shake the sky.

Fortunately, there had been no serious earthquakes yet. Far beneath the bed of the ocean, the wonderful piece of engineering which had been the world president's private vacuum-subway was still working perfectly, unaffected by the tumult and destruction above. It would continue to work until the last minute of the Earth's existence, which, if the astronomers were right, was not much more than fifteen minutes away—though precisely how much more, Alveron would have given a great deal to know. It would be nearly an hour before the trapped party could reach land and even the slightest hope of rescue.

Alveron's instructions had been precise, though even without them he would never have dreamed of taking any risks with the great machine that had been intrusted to his care. Had he been human, the decision to abandon the trapped members of his crew would have been desperately hard to make. But he came of a race far more sensitive than Man, a race that so loved the things of the spirit that long ago, and with infinite reluctance, it had taken over control of the Universe since only thus could it be sure that justice was being done. Alveron would need all his superhuman gifts to carry him through the next few hours.

Meanwhile, a mile below the bed of the ocean Alarkane and T'sinadree were very busy indeed with their private communicators. Fifteen minutes is not a long time in which to wind up the affairs of a lifetime. It is indeed, scarcely long enough to dictate more than a few of those farewell messages which at such moments are so much more important than all other matters.

All the while the Paladorian had remained silent and motionless, saying not a word. The other two, resigned to their fate and engrossed in their personal affairs, had given it no thought. They were startled when suddenly it began to address them in its peculiarly passionless voice.

"We perceive that you are making certain arrangements concerning your anticipated destruction. That will probably be unnecessary. Captain Alveron hopes to rescue us if we can stop this machine when we reach land again."

Both T'sinadree and Alarkane were too surprised to say anything for a moment. Then the latter gasped, "How do you know?"

It was a foolish question for he remembered at once that there were several Paladorians—if one could use the phrase—in the S9000, and consequently their companion knew everything that was happening in the mother ship. So he did not wait for an answer but continued: "Alveron can't do that! He daren't take such a risk!"

"There will be no risk," said the Paladorian. "We have told him what to do. It is really very simple."

Alarkane and T'sinadree looked at their companion with something approaching awe, realizing now what must have happened. In moments of crisis, the single units comprising the Paladorian mind could link together in an organization no less close than that of any physical brain. At such moments they formed an intellect more powerful than any other in the Universe. All ordinary problems could be solved by a few hundred or thousand units. Very rarely millions would be needed, and on two historic occasions the billions of cells of the entire Paladorian consciousness had been welded together to deal with emergencies that threatened the race. The mind of Palador was one of the greatest mental resources of the Universe; its full force was seldom required, but the knowledge that it was available was supremely comforting to other races. Alarkane wondered how many cells had co-ordinated to deal with this particular emergency. He also wondered how so trivial an incident had ever come to its attention at all.

To that question he was never to know the answer, though he might have guessed it had he known that the chillingly remote Paladorian mind possessed an almost human streak of vanity. Long ago, Alarkane had written a book trying to prove that eventually all intelligent races would sacrifice individual consciousness and that one day only group minds would remain in the Universe. Palador, he had said, was the first of those ultimate intellects, and the vast, dispersed mind had not been displeased.

They had no time to ask any further questions before Alveron himself began to speak through their communicators.

"Alveron calling! We're staying on this planet until the detonation wave reaches it, so we may be able to rescue you. You're heading towards a city on the coast which you'll reach in forty minutes at your present speed. If you cannot stop yourselves then, we're going to blast the tunnel behind and ahead of you to cut off your power. Then we'll sink a shaft to get you out—the chief engineer says he can do it in five minutes with the main projectors. So you should be safe within an hour, unless the sun blows up before."

"And if that happens, you'll be destroyed as well! You mustn't take such a risk!"

"Don't let that worry you; we're perfectly safe. When the sun detonates, the explosion wave will take several minutes to rise to its maximum. But apart from that, we're on the night side of the planet, behind an eight-thousand-mile screen of rock. When the first warning of the explosion comes, we will accelerate out of the Solar System, keeping in the shadow of the planet. Under our maximum drive, we will reach the velocity of light before leaving the cone of shadow, and the sun cannot harm us then."

T'sinadree was still afraid to hope. Another objection came at once into his mind.

"Yes, but how will you get any warning, here on the night side of the planet?"

"Very easily," replied Alveron. "This world has a moon which is now visible from this hemisphere. We have telescopes trained on it. If it shows any sudden increase in brilliance, our main drive goes on automatically and we'll be thrown out of the system."

The logic was flawless. Alveron, cautious as ever, was taking no chances. It would be many minutes before the eight-thousand-mile shield of rock and metal could be destroyed by the fires of the exploding sun. In that time, the S9000 could have reached the safety of the velocity of light.

Alarkane pressed the second button when they were still several miles from the coast. He did not expect anything to happen then, assuming that the machine could not stop between stations. It seemed too good to be true when, a few minutes later, the machine's slight vibration died away and they came to a halt.

The doors slid silently apart. Even before they were fully open, the three had left the compartment. They were taking no more chances. Before them a long tunnel stretched into the distance rising slowly out of sight. They were starting along it when suddenly Alveron's voice called from the communicators.

"Stay where you are! We're going to blast!"

The ground shuddered once, and far ahead there came the rumble of falling rock. Again the earth shook—and a hundred yards ahead the passageway vanished abruptly. A tremendous vertical shaft had been cut clean through it.

The party hurried forward again until they came to the end of the corridor and stood waiting on its lip. The shaft in which it ended was a full thousand feet across and descended into the earth as far as the torches could throw their beams. Overhead, the storm clouds fled beneath a moon that no man would have recognized, so luridly brilliant was its disk. And, most glorious of all sights, the S9000 floated high above, the great projectors that had drilled this enormous pit still glowing cherry red.

A dark shape detached itself from the mother ship and dropped swiftly towards the ground. Torkalee was returning to collect his friends. A little later, Alveron greeted them in the control room. He waved to the great vision screen and said quietly:

"You see, we were only just in time."

The continent below them was slowly settling beneath the mile-high waves that were attacking its coasts. The last that anyone was ever to see of Earth was a great plain, bathed with the silver light of the abnormally brilliant moon. Across its face the waters were pouring in a glittering flood towards a distant range of mountains. The sea had won its final victory, but its triumph would be short-lived for soon sea and land would be no more. Even as the silent party in the control room watched the destruction below, the infinitely greater catastrophe to which this was only the prelude came swiftly upon them.

It was as though dawn had broken suddenly over this moonlit landscape. But it was not dawn: it was only the moon, shining with the brilliance of a second sun. For perhaps thirty seconds that awesome, unnatural light burnt fiercely on the doomed land beneath. Then there came a sudden flashing of indicator lights across the control board. The main drive was on. For a second Alveron glanced at the indicators and checked their information. When he looked again at the screen, Earth was already gone.

The magnificent, desperately overstrained generators quietly died when the S9000 was passing the orbit of Persephone. It did not matter, the sun could never harm them now, and although the ship was speeding helplessly out into the lonely night of interstellar space, it would only be a matter of days before rescue came.

There was irony in that. A day ago, they had been the rescuers, going to the aid of a race that now no longer existed. Not for the first time Alveron wondered about the world that had just perished. He tried, in vain, to picture it as it had been in its glory, the streets of its cities thronged with life. Primitive though its people had been, they might have offered much to the Universe later in history. If only they could have made contact! Regret was useless: long before their coming, the people of this world must have buried themselves in its iron heart. And now they and their civilization would remain a mystery for the rest of time.

Alveron was glad when his thoughts were interrupted by Rugon's entrance. The chief of communications had been very busy ever since the take-off, trying to analyze the programs radiated by the transmitter Orostron had discovered. The problem was not a difficult one, but it demanded the construction of special equipment, and that had taken time.

"Well, what have you found?" asked Alveron.

"Quit a lot," replied his friend. "There's something mysterious here, and I don't understand it.

"It didn't take long to find how the vision transmissions were built up, and we've been able to convert them to suit our own equipment. It seems that there were cameras all over the planet, surveying points of interest. Some of them were apparently in cities, on the tops of very high buildings. The cameras were rotating continuously to give panoramic views. In the programs we've recorded there are about twenty different scenes.

"In addition, there are a number of transmissions of a different kind, neither sound nor vision. They seem to be purely scientific—possibly instrument readings or something of that sort. All these programs were going out simultaneously on different frequency bands.

"Now there must be a reason for all this. Orostron still thinks that the station simply wasn't switched off when it was deserted. But these aren't the sort of programs such a station would normally radiate at all. It was certainly used for interplanetary relaying—Klarten was quite right there. So these people must have crossed space, since none of the other planets had any life at the time of the last survey. Don't you agree?"

Alveron was following intently.

"Yes, that seems reasonable enough. But it's also certain that the beam was pointing to none of the other planets. I checked that myself."

"I know," said Rugon. "What I want to discover is why a giant interplanetary relay station is busily transmitting pictures of a world about to be destroyed—*pictures that would be of immense interest to scientists and astronomers.* Someone had gone to a lot of trouble to arrange all those panoramic cameras. I am convinced that those beams were going *somewhere.*"

Alveron started up.

"Do you imagine that there might be an outer planet that hasn't been reported?" he asked. "If so, your theory's certainly wrong. The beam wasn't even pointing in the plane of the Solar System. And even if it were—just look at this."

He switched on the vision screen and adjusted the controls. Against the velvet curtain of space was hanging a blue-white sphere, apparently composed of many concentric shells of incandescent gas. Even though its immense distance made all movement invisible, it was clearly expanding at an enormous rate. At its center was a blinding point of light—the white dwarf star that the sun had now become.

"You probably don't realize just how big that sphere is," said Alveron. "Look at this."

He increased the magnification until only the center portion of the nova was visible. Close to its heart were two minute condensations, one on either side of the nucleus.

"Those are the two giant planets of the system. They have still managed to retain their existence—after a fashion. And they were several hundred million miles from the sun.

"The nova is still expanding—but it's already twice the size of the Solar System."

Rugon was silent for a moment.

"Perhaps you're right," he said, rather grudgingly. "You've disposed of my first theory. But you still haven't satisfied me."

He made several swift circuits of the room before speaking again. Alveron waited patiently, he knew the almost intuitive powers of his friend, who could often solve a problem when mere logic seemed insufficient.

Then, rather slowly, Rugon began to speak again.

"What do you think of this?" he said. "Suppose we've completely underestimated this people? Orostron did it once—he thought they could never have crossed space, since they'd only known radio for two centuries. Hansur II told me that. Well, Orostron was quite wrong. Perhaps we're all wrong. I've had a look at the material that Klarten brought back from the transmitter. He wasn't impressed by what he found, but it's a marvelous achievement for so short a time. There were devices in that station that belonged to civilizations thousands of years older. *Alveron, can we follow that beam to see where it leads?*"

Alveron said nothing for a full minute. He had been more than half expecting the question, but it was not an easy one to answer. The main generators had gone completely. There was no point in trying to repair them. But there was still power available, and while there was power, anything could be done in time. It would mean a lot of improvisation, and some difficult maneuvers, for the ship still had its enormous initial velocity. Yes, it could be done, and the activity would keep the crew from becoming further depressed, now that the reaction caused by the mission's failure had started to set in. The news that the nearest heavy repair ship could not reach them for three weeks had also caused a slump in morale.

The engineers, as usual, made a tremendous fuss. Again as usual, they did the job in half the time they had dismissed as being absolutely impossible. Very slowly, over many hours, the great ship began to discard the speed its main drive had given it in as many minutes. In a tremendous curve, millions of miles in radius, the S9000 changed its course and the star fields shifted round it.

The maneuver took three days, but at the end of that time the ship was limping along a course parallel to the beam that had once come from Earth. They were heading out into emptiness, the blazing sphere that had been the sun dwindling slowly behind them. By the standards of interstellar flight, they were almost stationary.

For hours Rugon strained over his instruments, driving his detector beams far ahead into space. There were certainly no planets within many light-years; there was no doubt of that. From time to time Alveron came to see him and always he had to give the same reply: "Nothing to report." About a fifth of the time Rugon's intuition let him down badly; he began to wonder if this were such an occasion.

Not until a week later did the needles of the mass-detectors quiver feebly at the ends of their scales. But Rugon said nothing, not even to his captain. He waited until he was sure, and he went on waiting until even the short-range scanners began to react, and to build up the first faint pictures on the vision screen. Still he waited patiently until he could interpret the images. Then, when he knew that his wildest fancy was even less than the truth, he called his colleagues into the control room.

The picture on the vision screen was the familiar one of endless star fields, sun beyond sun to the very limits of the Universe. Near the center of the screen a distant nebula made a patch of haze that was difficult for the eye to grasp.

Rugon increased the magnification. The stars flowed out of the field; the little nebula expanded until it filled the screen and then— it was a nebula no longer. A simultaneous gasp of amazement came from all the company at the sight that lay before them.

Lying across league after league of space, ranged in a vast three dimensional array of rows and columns with the precision of a marching army, were thousands of tiny pencils of light. They were moving swiftly; the whole immense lattice holding its shape as a single unit. Even as Alveron and his comrades watched, the formation began to drift off the screen and Rugon had to recenter the controls.

After a long pause, Rugon started to speak.

"This is the race," he said softly, "that has only known radio for two centuries—the race that we believed had crept to die in the heart of its planet. I have examined those images under the highest possible magnification.

"That is the greatest fleet of which there has ever been a record. Each of those points of light represents a ship larger than our own. Of course, they are very primitive—what you see on the screen are the jets of their rockets. Yes, they dared to use rockets to bridge interstellar space! You realize what that means. It would take them centuries to reach the nearest star. The whole race must have embarked on this journey in the hope that its descendants would complete it, generations later.

"To measure the extent of their accomplishment, think of the ages it took us to conquer space, and the longer ages still before we attempted to reach the stars. Even if we were threatened with annihilation, could we have done so much in so short a time? Remember, this is the youngest civilization in the Universe. Four hundred thousand years ago it did not even exist. What will it be a million years from now?"

An hour later, Orostron left the crippled mother ship to make contact with the great fleet ahead. As the little torpedo disappeared among the stars, Alveron turned to his friend and made a remark that Rugon was often to remember in the years ahead.

"I wonder what they'll be like?" he mused. "Will they be nothing but wonderful engineers, with no art or philosophy? They're going to have such a surprise when Orostron reaches them—I expect it will be rather a blow to their pride. It's funny how all isolated races think they're the only people in the Universe. But they should be grateful to us—we're going to save them a good many hundred years of travel."

Alveron glanced at the Milky Way, lying like a veil of silver mist across the vision screen. He waved towards it with a sweep of a tentacle that embraced the whole circle of the Galaxy, from the Central Planets to the lonely suns of the Rim.

"You know," he said to Rugon, "I feel rather afraid of these people. Suppose they don't like our little Federation?" He waved once more towards the star-clouds that lay massed across the screen, glowing with the light of their countless suns.

"Something tells me they'll be very determined people," he added. "We had better be polite to them. After all, we only out-number them about a thousand million to one."

Rugon laughed at his captain's little joke.

Twenty years afterwards, the remark didn't seem so funny.

THE SECRET

H enry Cooper had been on the Moon for almost two weeks before he discovered that something was wrong. At first it was only an ill-defined suspicion, the sort of hunch that a hardheaded science reporter would not take too seriously. He had come here, after all, at the United Nations Space Administration's own request. UNSA had always been hot on public relations—especially just before budget time, when an overcrowded world was screaming for more roads and schools and sea farms, and complaining about the billions being poured into space.

So here he was, doing the lunar circuit for the second time, and beaming back two thousand words of copy a day. Although the novelty had worn off, there still remained the wonder and mystery of a world as big as Africa, thoroughly mapped, yet almost completely unexplored. A stone's throw away from the pressure domes, the labs, the spaceports, was a yawning emptiness that would challenge men for centuries to come.

Some parts of the Moon were almost too familiar, of course. Who had not seen that dusty scar in the Mare Imbrium, with its gleaming metal pylon and the plaque that announced in the three official languages of Earth:

ON THIS SPOT

AT 2001 UT

13 SEPTEMBER 1959

THE FIRST MAN-MADE OBJECT REACHED ANOTHER WORLD

Cooper had visited the grave of Lunik II—and the more famous tomb of the men who had come after it. But these things belonged to the past; already, like Columbus and the Wright brothers, they were receding into history. What concerned him now was the future.

When he had landed at Archimedes Spaceport, the Chief Administrator had been obviously glad to see him, and had shown a personal interest in his tour. Transportation, accommodation, and official guide were all arranged. He could go anywhere he liked, ask any questions he pleased. UNSA trusted him, for his stories had always been accurate, his attitude friendly. Yet the tour had gone sour; he did not know why, but he was going to find out.

He reached for the phone and said: "Operator? Please get me the Police Department. I want to speak to the Inspector General."

Presumably Chandra Coomaraswamy possessed a uniform, but Cooper had never seen him wearing it. They met, as arranged, at the entrance to the little park that was Plato City's chief pride and joy. At this time in the morning of the artificial twenty-four-hour "day" it was almost deserted, and they could talk without interruption.

As they walked along the narrow gravel paths, they chatted about old times, the friends they had known at college together, the latest developments in interplanetary politics. They had reached the middle of the park, under the exact center of the great blue-painted dome, when Cooper came to the point.

"You know everything that's happening on the Moon, Chandra," he said. "And you know that I'm here to do a series for UNSA—hope to make a book out of it when I get back to Earth. So why should people be trying to hide things from me?"

It was impossible to hurry Chandra. He always took his time to answer questions, and his few words escaped with difficulty around the stem of his hand-carved Bavarian pipe.

"What people?" he asked at length.

"You've really no idea?"

The Inspector General shook his head.

"Not the faintest," he answered; and Cooper knew that he was telling the truth. Chandra might be silent, but he would not lie.

"I was afraid you'd say that. Well, if you don't know any more than I do, here's the only clue I have—and it frightens me. Medical Research is trying to keep me at arm's length."

"Hmm," replied Chandra, taking his pipe from his mouth and looking at it thoughtfully.

"Is that all you have to say?"

"You haven't given me much to work on. Remember, I'm only a cop; I lack your vivid journalistic imagination."

"All I can tell you is that the higher I get in Medical Research, the colder the atmosphere becomes. Last time I was here, everyone was very friendly, and gave me some fine stories. But now, I can't even meet the Director. He's always too busy, or on the other side of the Moon. Anyway, what sort of man is he?"

"Dr. Hastings? Prickly little character. Very competent, but not easy to work with."

"What could he be trying to hide?"

"Knowing you, I'm sure you have some interesting theories."

"Oh, I thought of narcotics, and fraud, and political conspiracies—but they don't make sense, in these days. So what's left scares the hell out of me."

Chandra's eyebrows signaled a silent question mark.

"Interplanetary plague," said Cooper bluntly.

"I thought that was impossible."

"Yes—I've written articles myself proving that the life forms on other planets have such alien chemistries that they can't react with us, and that all our microbes and bugs took millions of years to adapt to our bodies. But I've always wondered if it was true. Suppose a ship has come back from Mars, say, with something *really* vicious—and the doctors can't cope with it?"

There was a long silence. Then Chandra said: "I'll start investigating. *I* don't like it either, for here's an item you probably don't know. There were three nervous breakdowns in the Medical Division last month—and that's very, very unusual."

He glanced at his watch, then at the false sky, which seemed so distant, yet which was only two hundred feet above their heads.

"We'd better get moving," he said. "The morning shower's due in five minutes."

The call came two weeks later, in the middle of the night—the real lunar night. By Plato City time, it was Sunday morning.

"Henry? Chandra here. Can you meet me in half an hour at air lock five? Good—I'll see you."

This was it, Cooper knew. Air lock five meant that they were going outside the dome. Chandra had found something.

The presence of the police driver restricted conversation as the tractor moved away from the city along the road roughly bulldozed across the ash and pumice. Low in the south, Earth was almost full, casting a brilliant blue-green light over the infernal landscape. However hard one tried, Cooper told himself, it was difficult to make the Moon appear glamorous. But nature guards her greatest secrets well; to such places men must come to find them.

The multiple domes of the city dropped below the sharply curved horizon. Presently, the tractor turned aside from the main road to follow a scarcely visible trail. Ten minutes later, Cooper saw a single glittering hemisphere ahead of them, standing on an isolated ridge of rock. Another vehicle, bearing a red cross, was parked beside the entrance. It seemed that they were not the only visitors.

Nor were they unexpected. As they drew up to the dome, the flexible tube of the air-lock coupling groped out toward them and snapped into place against their tractor's outer hull. There was a brief hissing as pressure equalized. Then Cooper followed Chandra into the building.

The air-lock operator led them along curving corridors and radial passageways toward the center of the dome. Sometimes they caught glimpses of laboratories, scientific instruments, computers—all perfectly ordinary, and all deserted on this Sunday morning. They must have reached the heart of the building, Cooper told himself when their guide ushered them into a large circular chamber and shut the door softly behind them.

It was a small zoo. All around them were cages, tanks, jars containing a wide selection of the fauna and flora of Earth. Waiting at its center was a short, gray-haired man, looking very worried, and very unhappy.

"Dr. Hastings," said Coomaraswamy, "meet Mr. Cooper." The Inspector General turned to his companion and added, "I've convinced the doctor that there's only one way to keep you quiet—and that's to tell you everything."

"Frankly," said Hastings, "I'm not sure if I give a damn any more." His voice was unsteady, barely under control, and Cooper thought, Hello! There's another breakdown on the way.

The scientist wasted no time on such formalities as shaking hands. He walked to one of the cages, took out a small bundle of fur, and held it toward Cooper.

"Do you know what this is?" he asked abruptly.

"Of course. A hamster—the commonest lab animal."

"Yes," said Hastings. "A perfectly ordinary golden hamster. Except that this one is five years old—like all the others in this cage."

"Well? What's odd about that?"

"Oh, nothing, nothing at all . . . except for the trifling fact that hamsters live for only two years. And we have some here that are getting on for ten."

For a moment no one spoke; but the room was not silent. It was full of rustlings and slitherings and scratchings, of faint whimpers and tiny animal cries. Then Cooper whispered: "My God—you've found a way of prolonging life!"

"No," retorted Hastings. "We've not found it. The Moon has given it to us . . . as we might have expected, if we'd looked in front of our noses."

He seemed to have gained control over his emotions—as if he was once more the pure scientist, fascinated by a discovery for its own sake and heedless of its implications.

"On Earth," he said, "we spend our whole lives fighting gravity. It wears down our muscles, pulls our stomachs out of shape. In seventy years, how many tons of blood does the heart lift through how many miles? And all that work, all that strain is reduced to a sixth here on the Moon, where a one-hundred-and-eighty-pound human weighs only thirty pounds."

"I see," said Cooper slowly. "Ten years for a hamster—and how long for a man?"

"It's not a simple law," answered Hastings. "It varies with the size and the species. Even a month ago, we weren't certain. But now we're quite sure of this: on the Moon, the span of human life will be at least two hundred years."

"And you've been trying to keep it secret!"

"You fool! Don't you understand?"

"Take it easy, Doctor—take it easy," said Chandra softly.

With an obvious effort of will, Hastings got control of himself again. He began to speak with such icy calm that his words sank like freezing raindrops into Cooper's mind.

"Think of them up there," he said, pointing to the roof, to the invisible Earth, whose looming presence no one on the Moon could ever forget. "Six billion of them, packing all the continents to the edges—and now crowding over into the sea beds. And here—" he pointed to the ground—"only a hundred thousand of *us*, on an almost empty world. But a world where we need miracles of technology and engineering merely to exist, where a man with an I.Q. of only a hundred and fifty can't even get a job.

"And now we find that we can live for two hundred years. Imagine how they're going to react to *that* news! This is your problem now, Mister Journalist; you've asked for it, and you've got it. Tell me this, please—I'd really be interested to know—*just how are you going to break it to them?*"

He waited, and waited. Cooper opened his mouth, then closed it again, unable to think of anything to say.

In the far corner of the room, a baby monkey started to cry.

REUNION

People of Earth, do not be afraid. We come in peace—and why not? For we are your cousins; we have been here before.

You will recognize us when we meet, a few hours from now. We are approaching the solar system almost as swiftly as this radio message. Already, your sun dominates the sky ahead of us. It is the sun our ancestors and yours shared ten million years ago. We are men, as you are; but you have forgotten your history, while we have remembered ours.

We colonized Earth, in the reign of the great reptiles, who were dying when we came and whom we could not save. Your world was a tropical planet then, and we felt that it would make a fair home for our people. We were wrong. Though we were masters of space, we knew so little about climate, about evolution, about genetics. . . .

For millions of summers—there were no winters in those ancient days—the colony flourished. Isolated though it had to be, in a universe where the journey from one star to the next takes years, it kept in touch with its parent civilization. Three or four times in every century, starships would call and bring news of the galaxy.

But two million years ago, Earth began to change. For ages it had been a tropical paradise; then the temperature fell, and the ice began to creep down from the poles. As the climate altered, so did the colonists. We realize now that it was a natural adaptation to the end of the long summer, but those who had made Earth their home for so many generations believed that they had been attacked by a strange and repulsive disease. A disease that did not kill, that did no physical harm—but merely disfigured.

Yet some were immune; the change spared them and their children. And so, within a few thousand years, the colony had split into two separate groups—almost two separate species—suspicious and jealous of each other.

The division brought envy, discord, and, ultimately, conflict. As the colony disintegrated and the climate steadily worsened, those who could do so withdrew from Earth. The rest sank into barbarism.

We could have kept in touch, but there is so much to do in a universe of a hundred trillion stars. Until a few years ago, we did not know that any of you had survived. Then we picked up your first radio signals, learned your simple languages, and discovered that you had made the long climb back from savagery. We come to greet you, our long-lost relatives—and to help you.

We have discovered much in the eons since we abandoned Earth. If you wish us to bring back the eternal summer that ruled before the Ice Ages, we can do so. Above all, we have a simple remedy for the offensive yet harmless genetic plague that afflicted so many of the colonists.

Perhaps it has run its course—but if not, we have good news for you. People of Earth, you can rejoin the society of the universe without shame, without embarrassment.

If any of you are still white, we can cure you.

THE STAR

It is three thousand light-years to the Vatican. Once, I believed that space could have no power over faith, just as I believed that the heavens declared the glory of God's handiwork. Now I have seen that handiwork, and my faith is sorely troubled. I stare at the crucifix that hangs on the cabin wall above the Mark VI Computer, and for the first time in my life I wonder if it is no more than an empty symbol.

I have told no one yet, but the truth cannot be concealed. The facts are there for all to read, recorded on the countless miles of magnetic tape and the thousands of photographs we are carrying back to Earth. Other scientists can interpret them as easily as I can, and I am not one who would condone that tampering with the truth which often gave my order a bad name in the olden days.

The crew are already sufficiently depressed: I wonder how they will take this ultimate irony. Few of them have any religious faith, yet they will not relish using this final weapon in their campaign against me—that private, good-natured, but fundamentally serious, war which lasted all the way from Earth. It amused them to have a Jesuit as chief astrophysicist: Dr. Chandler, for instance, could never get over it (why are medical men such notorious atheists?). Sometimes he would meet me on the observation deck, where the lights are always low so that the stars shine with undiminished glory. He would come up to me in the gloom and stand staring out of the great oval port, while the heavens crawled slowly around us as the ship turned end over end with the residual spin we had never bothered to correct.

"Well, Father," he would say at last, "it goes on forever and forever, and perhaps *Something* made it. But how you can believe that Something has a special interest in us and our miserable little world—that just beats me." Then the argument would start, while the stars and nebulae would swing around us in silent, endless arcs beyond the flawlessly clear plastic of the observation port.

It was, I think, the apparent incongruity of my position that caused most amusement to the crew. In vain I would point to my three papers in the *Astrophysical Journal*, my five in the *Monthly Notices of the Royal Astronomical Society*. I would remind them that my order has long been famous for its scientific works. We may be few now, but ever since the eighteenth century we have made contributions to astronomy and geophysics out of all proportion to our numbers. Will my report on the Phoenix Nebula end our thousand years of history? It will end, I fear, much more than that.

I do not know who gave the nebula its name, which seems to me a very bad one. If it contains a prophecy, it is one that cannot be verified for several billion years. Even the word nebula is misleading: this is a far smaller object than those stupendous clouds of mist—the stuff of unborn stars—that are scattered throughout the length of the Milky Way. On the cosmic scale, indeed, the Phoenix Nebula is a tiny thing—a tenuous shell of gas surrounding a single star.

Or what is left of a star . . .

The Rubens engraving of Loyola seems to mock me as it hangs there above the spectrophotometer tracings. What would *you*, Father, have made of this knowledge that has come into my keeping, so far from the little world that was all the universe you knew? Would your faith have risen to the challenge, as mine has failed to do?

You gaze into the distance, Father, but I have traveled a distance beyond any that you could have imagined when you founded our order a thousand years ago. No other survey ship has been so far from Earth: we are at the very frontiers of the explored universe.

We set out to reach the Phoenix Nebula, we succeeded, and we are homeward bound with our burden of knowledge. I wish I could lift that burden from my shoulders, but I call to you in vain across the centuries and the light-years that lie between us.

On the book you are holding the words are plain to read. AD MAIOREM DEI GLORIAM, the message runs, but it is a message I can no longer believe. Would you still believe it, if you could see what we have found?

We knew, of course, what the Phoenix Nebula was. Every year, in our galaxy alone, more than a hundred stars explode, blazing for a few hours or days with thousands of times their normal brilliance before they sink back into death and obscurity. Such are the ordinary novae—the commonplace disasters of the universe. I have recorded the spectrograms and light curves of dozens since I started working at the Lunar Observatory.

But three or four times in every thousand years occurs something beside which even a nova pales into total insignificance.

When a star becomes a *supernova*, it may for a little while outshine all the massed suns of the galaxy. The Chinese astronomers watched this happen in A.D. 1054, not knowing what it was they saw. Five centuries later, in 1572, a supernova blazed in Cassiopeia so brilliantly that it was visible in the daylight sky. There have been three more in the thousand years that have passed since then.

Our mission was to visit the remnants of such a catastrophe, to reconstruct the events that led up to it, and, if possible, to learn its cause. We came slowly in through the concentric shells of gas that had been blasted out six thousand years before, yet were expanding still. They were immensely hot, radiating even now with a fierce violet light, but were far too tenuous to do us any damage. When the star had exploded, its outer layers had been driven upward with such speed that they had escaped completely from its gravitational field. Now they formed a hollow shell large enough to engulf a thousand solar systems, and at its center burned the tiny, fantastic object which the star had now become—a White Dwarf, smaller than the Earth, yet weighing a million times as much.

The glowing gas shells were all around us, banishing the normal night of interstellar space. We were flying into the center of a cosmic bomb that had detonated millennia ago and whose incandescent fragments were still hurtling apart. The immense scale of the explosion, and the fact that the debris already covered a volume of space many billions of miles across, robbed the scene of any visible movement. It would take decades before the unaided eye could detect any motion in these tortured wisps and eddies of gas, yet the sense of turbulent expansion was overwhelming.

We had checked our primary drive hours before, and were drifting slowly toward the fierce little star ahead. Once it had been a sun like our own, but it had squandered in a few hours the energy that should have kept it shining for a million years. Now it was a shrunken miser, hoarding its resources as if trying to make amends for its prodigal youth.

No one seriously expected to find planets. If there had been any before the explosion, they would have been boiled into puffs of vapor, and their substance lost in the greater wreckage of the star itself. But we made the automatic search, as we always do when approaching an unknown sun, and presently we found a single small world circling the star at an immense distance. It must have been the Pluto of this vanished solar system, orbiting on the frontiers of the night. Too far from the central sun ever to have known life, its remoteness had saved it from the fate of all its lost companions.

The passing fires had seared its rocks and burned away the mantle of frozen gas that must have covered it in the days before the disaster. We landed, and we found the Vault.

Its builders had made sure that we should. The monolithic marker that stood above the entrance was now a fused stump, but even the first long-range photographs told us that here was the work of intelligence. A little later we detected the continent-wide pattern of radio-activity that had been buried in the rock. Even if the pylon above the Vault had been destroyed, this would have remained, an immovable and all but eternal beacon calling to the stars. Our ship fell toward this gigantic bull's-eye like an arrow into its target.

The pylon must have been a mile high when it was built, but now it looked like a candle that had melted down into a puddle of wax. It took us a week to drill through the fused rock, since we did not have the proper tools for a task like this. We were astronomers, not archaeologists, but we could improvise. Our original purpose was forgotten: this lonely monument, reared with such labor at the greatest possible distance from the doomed sun, could have only one meaning. A civilization that knew it was about to die had made its last bid for immortality.

It will take us generations to examine all the treasures that were placed in the Vault. They had plenty of time to prepare, for their sun must have given its first warnings many years before the final denotation. Everything that they wished to preserve, all the fruit of their genius, they brought here to this distant world in the days before the end, hoping that some other race would find it and that they would not be utterly forgotten. Would we have done as well, or would we have been too lost in our own misery to give thought to a future we could never see or share?

If only they had had a little more time! They could travel freely enough between the planets of their own sun, but they had not yet learned to cross the interstellar gulfs, and the nearest solar system was a hundred light-years away. Yet even had they possessed the secret of the Transfinite Drive, no more than a few millions could have been saved. Perhaps it was better thus.

Even if they had not been so disturbingly human as their sculpture shows, we could not have helped admiring them and grieving for their fate. They left thousands of visual records and the machines for projecting them, together with elaborate pictorial instructions from which it will not be difficult to learn their written language. We have examined many of these records, and brought to life for the first time in six thousand years the warmth and beauty of a civilization that in many ways must have been superior to our own. Perhaps they only showed us the best, and one can hardly blame them. But their worlds were very lovely, and their cities were built with a grace that matches anything of man's. We have watched them at work and play, and listened to their musical speech sounding across the centuries. One scene is still before my eyes—a group of children on a beach of strange blue sand, playing in the waves as children play on Earth. Curious whiplike trees line the shore, and some very large animal is wading in the shadows yet attracting no attention at all.

And sinking into the sea, still warm and friendly and life-giving, is the sun that will soon turn traitor and obliterate all this innocent happiness.

Perhaps if we had not been so far from home and so vulnerable to loneliness, we should not have been so deeply moved. Many of us had seen the ruins of ancient civilizations on other worlds, but they had never affected us so profoundly. This tragedy was unique. It is one thing for a race to fail and die, as nations and cultures have done on Earth. But to be destroyed so completely in the full flower of its achievement, leaving no survivors—how could that be reconciled with the mercy of God?

My colleagues have asked me that, and I have given what answers I can. Perhaps you could have done better, Father Loyola, but I have found nothing in the *Exercitia Spiritualia* that helps me here. They were not an evil people: I do not know what gods they worshiped, if indeed they worshiped any. But I have looked back at them across the centuries, and have watched while the loveliness they used their last strength to preserve was brought forth again into the light of their shrunken sun. They could have taught us much: why were they destroyed?

I know the answers that my colleagues will give when they get back to Earth. They will say that the universe has no purpose and no plan, that since a hundred suns explode every year in our galaxy, at this very moment some race is dying in the depths of space. Whether that race has done good or evil during its lifetime will make no difference in the end: there is no divine justice, for there is no God.

Yet, of course, what we have seen proves nothing of the sort. Anyone who argues thus is being swayed by emotion, not logic. God has no need to justify His actions to man. He who built the universe can destroy it when He chooses. It is arrogance—it is perilously near blasphemy—for us to say what He may or may not do.

This I could have accepted, hard though it is to look upon whole worlds and peoples thrown into the furnace. But there comes a point when even the deepest faith must falter, and now, as I look at the calculations lying before me, I know I have reached that point at last.

We could not tell, before we reached the nebula, how long ago the explosion took place. Now, from the astronomical evidence and the record in the rocks of that one surviving planet, I have been able to date it very exactly. I know in what year the light of this colossal conflagration reached our Earth. I know how brilliantly the supernova whose corpse now dwindles behind our speeding ship once shone in terrestrial skies. I know how it must have blazed low in the east before sunrise, like a beacon in that oriental dawn.

There can be no reasonable doubt: the ancient mystery is solved at last. Yet, oh God, there were so many stars you could have used. What was the need to give these people to the fire, that the symbol of their passing might shine above Bethlehem?

A MEETING WITH MEDUSA

1. A Day to Remember

The *Queen Elizabeth* was over three miles above the Grand Canyon, dawdling along at a comfortable hundred and eighty, when Howard Falcon spotted the camera platform closing in from the right. He had been expecting it—nothing else was cleared to fly at this altitude—but he was not too happy to have company. Although he welcomed any signs of public interest, he also wanted as much empty sky as he could get. After all, he was the first man in history to navigate a ship three-tenths of a mile long. . . .

So far, this first test flight had gone perfectly; ironically enough, the only problem had been the century-old aircraft carrier *Chairman Mao*, borrowed from the San Diego Naval Museum for support operations. Only one of *Mao's* four nuclear reactors was still operating, and the old battlewagon's top speed was barely thirty knots. Luckily, wind speed at sea level had been less than half this, so it had not been too difficult to maintain still air on the flight deck. Though there had been a few anxious moments during gusts, when the mooring lines had been dropped, the great dirigible had risen smoothly, straight up into the sky, as if on an invisible elevator. If all went well, *Queen Elizabeth IV* would not meet *Chairman Mao* again for another week.

Everything was under control; all test instruments gave normal readings. Commander Falcon decided to go upstairs and watch the rendezvous. He handed over to his second officer, and walked out into the transparent tubeway that led through the heart of the ship. There, as always, he was overwhelmed by the spectacle of the largest single space ever enclosed by man.

The ten spherical gas cells, each more than a hundred feet across, were ranged one behind the other like a line of gigantic soap bubbles. The tough plastic was so clear that he could see through the whole length of the array, and make out details of the elevator mechanism, more than a third of a mile from his vantage point. All around him, like a three-dimensional maze, was the structural framework of the ship—the great longitudinal girders running from nose to tail, the fifteen hoops that were the circular ribs of this sky-borne colossus, and whose varying sizes defined its graceful, stream-lined profile.

At this low speed, there was little sound—merely the soft rush of wind over the envelope and an occasional creak of metal as the pattern of stresses changed. The shadowless light from the rows of lamps far overhead gave the whole scene a curiously submarine quality, and to Falcon this was enhanced by the spectacle of the translucent gasbags. He had once encountered a squadron of large but harmless jellyfish, pulsing their mindless way above a shallow tropical reef, and the plastic bubbles that gave Queen Elizabeth her lift often reminded him of these—especially when changing pressures made them crinkle and scatter new patterns of reflected light.

He walked down the axis of the ship until he came to the forward elevator, between gas cells one and two. Riding up to the Observation Deck, he noticed that it was uncomfortably hot; and dictated a brief memo to himself on his pocket recorder. The Queen obtained almost a quarter of her buoyancy from the unlimited amounts of waste heat produced by her fusion power plant. On this lightly loaded flight, indeed, only six of ten gas cells contained helium; the remaining four were full of air. Yet she still carried two hundred tons of water as ballast. However, running the cells at high temperatures did produce problems in refrigerating the access ways; it was obvious that a little more work would have to be done there.

A refreshing blast of cooler air hit him in the face when he stepped out onto the Observation Deck and into the dazzling sun-light streaming through the plexiglass roof. Half a dozen workmen, with an equal number of superchimp assistants, were busily laying the partly completed dance floor, while others were installing elec-tric wiring and fixing furniture. It was a scene of controlled chaos, and Falcon found it hard to believe that everything would be ready for the maiden voyage, only four weeks ahead. Well, that was not *his* problem, thank goodness. He was merely the Captain, not the Cruise Director.

The human workers waved to him, and the "simps" flashed toothy smiles, as he walked through the confusion, into the already completed Skylounge. This was his favorite place in the whole ship, and he knew that once she was operating he would never again have it all to himself. He would allow himself just five minutes of private enjoyment.

He called the bridge, checked that everything was still in order, and relaxed into one of the comfortable swivel chairs. Below, in a curve that delighted the eye, was the unbroken silver sweep of the ship's envelope. He was perched at the highest point, surveying the whole immensity of the largest vehicle ever built. And when he had tired of that—all the way out to the horizon was the fantastic wilderness carved by the Colorado River in half a billion years of time.

Apart from the camera platform (it had now fallen back and was filming from amidships) he had the sky to himself. It was blue and empty, clear down to the horizon. In his grandfather's day, Falcon knew, it would have been streaked with vapor trails and stained with smoke. Both had gone: the aerial garbage had vanished with the primitive technologies that spawned it, and the long-distance transportation of this age arced too far beyond the strat-osphere for any sight or sound of it to reach Earth. Once again, the lower atmosphere belonged to the birds and the clouds—and now to *Queen Elizabeth IV*.

It was true, as the old pioneers had said at the beginning of the twentieth century: this was the only way to travel—in silence and luxury, breathing the air around you and not cut off from it, near enough to the surface to watch the everchanging beauty of land and sea. The subsonic jets of the 1980s, packed with hundreds of passengers seated ten abreast, could not even begin to match such comfort and spaciousness.

Of course, the *Queen* would never be an economic proposition, and even if her projected sister ships were built, only a few of the world's quarter of a billion inhabitants would ever enjoy this silent gliding through the sky. But a secure and prosperous global society could afford such follies and indeed needed them for their novelty and entertainment. There were at least a million men on Earth whose discretionary income exceeded a thousand new dollars a year, so the *Queen* would not lack for passengers.

Falcon's pocket communicator beeped. The copilot was calling from the bridge.

"O.K. for rendezvous, Captain? We've got all the data we need from this run, and the TV people are getting impatient."

Falcon glanced at the camera platform, now matching his speed a tenth of a mile away.

"O.K.," he replied. "Proceed as arranged. I'll watch from here."

He walked back through the busy chaos of the Observation Deck so that he could have a better view amidships. As he did so, he could feel the change of vibration underfoot; by the time he had reached the rear of the lounge, the ship had come to rest. Using his master key, he let himself out onto the small external platform flaring from the end of the deck; half a dozen people could stand here, with only low guardrails separating them from the vast sweep of the envelope—and from the ground, thousands of feet below. It was an exciting place to be, and perfectly safe even when the ship was traveling at speed, for it was in the dead air behind the huge dorsal blister of the Observation Deck. Nevertheless, it was not intended that the passengers would have access to it; the view was a little too vertiginous.

The covers of the forward cargo hatch had already opened like giant trap doors, and the camera platform was hovering above them, preparing to descend. Along this route, in the years to come, would travel thousands of passengers and tons of supplies. Only on rare occasions would the *Queen* drop down to sea level and dock with her floating base.

A sudden gust of cross wind slapped Falcon's cheek, and he tightened his grip on the guardrail. The Grand Canyon was a bad place for turbulence, though he did not expect much at this altitude. Without any real anxiety, he focused his attention on the descending platform, now about a hundred and fifty feet above the ship. He knew that the highly skilled operator who was flying the remotely controlled vehicle had performed this simple maneuver a dozen times already; it was inconceivable that he would have any difficulties.

Yet he seemed to be reacting rather sluggishly. That last gust had drifted the platform almost to the edge of the open hatchway. Surely the pilot could have corrected before this. . . . Did he have a control problem? It was very unlikely; these remotes had multiple-redundancy, fail-safe takeovers, and any number of backup systems. Accidents were almost unheard of.

But there he went again, off to the left. Could the pilot be *drunk?* Improbable though that seemed, Falcon considered it seriously for a moment. Then he reached for his microphone switch.

Once again, without warning, he was slapped violently in the face. He hardly felt it, for he was staring in horror at the camera platform. The distant operator was fighting for control, trying to balance the craft on its jets—but he was only making matters worse. The oscillations increased—twenty degrees, forty, sixty, ninety. . . .

"Switch to automatic, you fool!" Falcon shouted uselessly into his microphone. "Your manual control's not working!"

The platform flipped over on its back. The jets no longer supported it, but drove it swiftly downward. They had suddenly become allies of the gravity they had fought until this moment.

Falcon never heard the crash, though he felt it; he was already inside the Observation Deck, racing for the elevator that would take him down to the bridge. Workmen shouted at him anxiously, asking what had happened. It would be many months before he knew the answer to that question.

Just as he was stepping into the elevator cage, he changed his mind. What if there was a power failure? Better be on the safe side, even if it took longer and time was the essence. He began to run down the spiral stairway enclosing the shaft.

Halfway down he paused for a second to inspect the damage. That damned platform had gone clear through the ship, rupturing two of the gas cells as it did so. They were still collapsing slowly, in great falling veils of plastic. He was not worried about the loss of lift—the ballast could easily take care of that, as long as eight cells remained intact. Far more serious was the possibility of structural damage. Already he could hear the great latticework around him groaning and protesting under its abnormal loads. It was not enough to have sufficient lift; unless it was properly distributed, the ship would break her back.

He was just resuming his descent when a superchimp, shrieking with fright, came racing down the elevator shaft, moving with incredible speed, hand over hand, along the *outside* of the latticework. In its terror, the poor beast had torn off its company uniform, perhaps in an unconscious attempt to regain the freedom of its ancestors.

Falcon, still descending as swiftly as he could, watched its approach with some alarm. A distraught simp was a powerful and potentially dangerous animal, especially if fear overcame its conditioning. As it overtook him, it started to call out a string of words, but they were all jumbled together, and the only one he could recognize was a plaintive, frequently repeated "boss." Even now, Falcon realized, it looked toward humans for guidance. He felt sorry for the creature, involved in a manmade disaster beyond its comprehension, and for which it bore no responsibility.

It stopped opposite him, on the other side of the lattice; there was nothing to prevent it from coming through the open framework if it wished. Now its face was only inches from his, and he was looking straight into the terrified eyes. Never before had he been so close to a simp, and able to study its features in such detail. He felt that strange mingling of kinship and discomfort that all men experience when they gaze thus into the mirror of time.

His presence seemed to have calmed the creature. Falcon pointed up the shaft, back toward the Observation Deck, and said very clearly and precisely: "Boss—boss—go." To his relief, the simp understood; it gave him a grimace that might have been a smile, and at once started to race back the way it had come. Falcon had given it the best advice he could. If any safety remained aboard the *Queen*, it was in that direction. But his duty lay in the other.

He had almost completed his descent when, with a sound of rending metal, the vessel pitched nose down, and the lights went out. But he could still see quite well, for a shaft of sunlight streamed through the open hatch and the huge tear in the envelope. Many years ago he had stood in a great cathedral nave watching the light pouring through the stained-glass windows and forming pools of multicolored radiance on the ancient flagstones. The dazzling shaft of sunlight through the ruined fabric high above reminded him of that moment. He was in a cathedral of metal, falling down the sky.

When he reached the bridge, and was able for the first time to look outside, he was horrified to see how close the ship was to the ground. Only three thousand feet below were the beautiful and deadly pinnacles of rock and the red rivers of mud that were still carving their way down into the past. There was no level area anywhere in sight where a ship as large as the Queen could come to rest on an even keel.

A glance at the display board told him that all the ballast had gone. However, rate of descent had been reduced to a few yards a second; they still had a fighting chance.

Without a word, Falcon eased himself into the pilot's seat and took over such control as still remained. The instrument board showed him everything he wished to know; speech was superfluous. In the background, he could hear the Communications Officer giving a running report over the radio. By this time, all the news channels of Earth would have been preempted, and he could imagine the utter frustration of the program controllers. One of the most spectacular wrecks in history was occurring—without a single camera to record it. The last moments of the Queen would never fill millions with awe and terror, as had those of the Hindenburg, a century and a half before.

Now the ground was only about seventeen hundred feet away, still coming up slowly. Though he had full thrust, he had not dared to use it, lest the weakened structure collapse; but now he realized that he had no choice. The wind was taking them toward a fork in the canyon, where the river was split by a wedge of rock like the prow of some gigantic, fossilized ship of stone. If she continued on her present course, the Queen would straddle that triangular plateau and come to rest with at least a third of her length jutting out over nothingness; she would snap like a rotten stick.

Far away, above the sound of straining metal and escaping gas, came the familiar whistle of the jets as Falcon opened up the lateral thrusters. The ship staggered, and began to slew to port. The shriek of tearing metal was now almost continuous—and the rate of descent had started to increase ominously. A glance at the damage-control board showed that cell number five had just gone.

The ground was only yards away. Even now, he could not tell whether his maneuver would succeed or fail. He switched the thrust vectors over to vertical, giving maximum lift to reduce the force of impact.

The crash seemed to last forever. It was not violent—merely prolonged, and irresistible. It seemed that the whole universe was falling about them.

The sound of crunching metal came nearer, as if some great beast were eating its way through the dying ship.

Then floor and ceiling closed upon him like a vise.

2. "Because It's There"

"Why do you want to go to Jupiter?"

"As Springer said when he lifted for Pluto—'because it's there.' "

"Thanks. Now we've got *that* out of the way—the real reason."

Howard Falcon smiled, though only those who knew him well could have interpreted the slight, leathery grimace. Webster was one of them; for more than twenty years they had shared triumphs and disasters—including the greatest disaster of all.

"Well, Springer's cliché is still valid. We've landed on all the terrestrial planets, but none of the gas giants. They are the only real challenge left in the solar system."

"An expensive one. Have you worked out the cost?"

"As well as I can; here are the estimates. Remember, though—this isn't a one-shot mission, but a transportation system. Once it's proved out, it can be used over and over again. And it will open up not merely Jupiter, but all the giants."

Webster looked at the figures, and whistled.

"Why not start with an easier planet—Uranus, for example? Half the gravity, and less than half the escape velocity. Quieter weather, too—if that's the right word for it."

Webster had certainly done his homework. But that, of course, was why he was head of Long-Range Planning.

"There's very little saving—when you allow for the extra distance and the logistics problems. For Jupiter, we can use the facilities of Ganymede. Beyond Saturn, we'd have to establish a new supply base."

Logical, thought Webster; but he was sure that it was not the important reason. Jupiter was lord of the solar system; Falcon would be interested in no lesser challenge.

"Besides," Falcon continued, "Jupiter is a major scientific scandal. It's more than a hundred years since its radio storms were discovered, but we still don't know what causes them—and the Great Red Spot is as big a mystery as ever. That's why I can get matching funds from the Bureau of Astronautics. Do you know how many probes they have dropped into that atmosphere?"

"A couple of hundred, I believe."

"*Three* hundred and twenty-six, over the last fifty years—about a quarter of them total failures. Of course, they've learned a hell of a lot, but they've barely scratched the planet. Do you realize how *big it is?*"

"More than ten times the size of Earth."

"Yes, yes—but do you know what that really means?"

Falcon pointed to the large globe in the corner of Webster's office.

"Look at India—how small it seems. Well, if you skinned Earth and spread it out on the surface of Jupiter, it would look about as big as India does here."

There was a long silence while Webster contemplated the equation: Jupiter is to Earth as Earth is to India. Falcon had—deliberately, of course—chosen the best possible example. . . .

Was it already ten years ago? Yes, it must have been. The crash lay seven years in the past (*that* date was engraved on his heart), and those initial tests had taken place three years before the first and last flight of the *Queen Elizabeth.*

Ten years ago, then, Commander (no, Lieutenant) Falcon had invited him to a preview—a three-day drift across the northern plains of India, within sight of the Himalayas. "Perfectly safe," he had promised. "It will get you away from the office—and will teach you what this whole thing is about."

Webster had not been disappointed. Next to his first journey to the Moon, it had been the most memorable experience of his life. And yet, as Falcon had assured him, it had been perfectly safe, and quite uneventful.

They had taken off from Srinagar just before dawn, with the huge silver bubble of the balloon already catching the first light of the Sun. The ascent had been made in total silence; there were none of the roaring propane burners that had lifted the hot-air balloons of an earlier age. All the heat they needed came from the little pulsed-fusion reactor, weighing only about two hundred and twenty pounds, hanging in the open mouth of the envelope. While they were climbing, its laser was zapping ten times a second, igniting the merest whiff of deuterium fuel. Once they had reached altitude, it would fire only a few times a minute, making up for the heat lost through the great gasbag overhead.

And so, even while they were almost a mile above the ground, they could hear dogs barking, people shouting, bells ringing. Slowly the vast, Sun-smitten landscape expanded around them. Two hours later, they had leveled out at three miles and were taking frequent draughts of oxygen. They could relax and admire the scenery; the on-board instrumentation was doing all the work—gathering the information that would be required by the designers of the still-unnamed liner of the skies.

It was a perfect day. The southwest monsoon would not break for another month, and there was hardly a cloud in the sky. Time seemed to have come to a stop; they resented the hourly radio reports which interrupted their reverie. And all around, to the horizon and far beyond, was that infinite, ancient landscape, drenched with history—a patchwork of villages, fields, temples, lakes, irrigation canals . . .

With a real effort, Webster broke the hypnotic spell of that ten-year-old memory. It had converted him to lighter-than-air flight—and it had made him realize the enormous size of India, even in a world that could be circled within ninety minutes. And yet, he repeated to himself, Jupiter is to Earth as Earth is to India. . . .

"Granted your argument," he said, "and supposing the funds are available, there's another question you have to answer. Why should you do better than the—what is it—three hundred and twenty-six robot probes that have already made the trip?"

"I am better qualified than they were—as an observer, and as a pilot. *Especially* as a pilot. Don't forget—I've more experience of lighter-than-air flight than anyone in the world."

"You could still serve as controller, and sit safely on Ganymede."

"*But that's just the point!* They've already done that. Don't you remember what killed the *Queen?*"

Webster knew perfectly well; but he merely answered: "Go on."

"*Time lag—time lag!* That idiot of a platform controller thought he was using a local radio circuit. But he'd been accidentally switched through a satellite—oh, maybe it wasn't his fault, but he should have noticed. That's a half-second time lag for the round trip. Even then it wouldn't have mattered flying in calm air. It was the turbulence over the Grand Canyon that did it. When the platform tipped, and he corrected for that—it had already tipped the other way. Ever tried to drive a car over a bumpy road with a half-second delay in the steering?"

"No, and I don't intend to try. But I can imagine it."

"Well, Ganymede is a million kilometers from Jupiter. That means a round-trip delay of six seconds. No, you need a controller on the spot—to handle emergencies in real time. Let me show you something. Mind if I use this?"

"Go ahead."

Falcon picked up a postcard that was lying on Webster's desk; they were almost obsolete on Earth, but this one showed a 3-D view of a Martian landscape, and was decorated with exotic and expensive stamps. He held it so that it dangled vertically.

"This is an old trick, but helps to make my point. Place your thumb and finger on either side, not quite touching. That's right."

Webster put out his hand, almost but not quite gripping the card.

"Now catch it."

Falcon waited for a few seconds; then, without warning, he let go of the card. Webster's thumb and finger closed on empty air.

"I'll do it again, just to show there's no deception. You see?"

Once again, the falling card had slipped through Webster's fingers.

"Now you try it on me."

This time, Webster grasped the card and dropped it without warning. It had scarcely moved before Falcon had caught it. Webster almost imagined he could hear a click, so swift was the other's reaction.

"When they put me together again," Falcon remarked in an expressionless voice, "the surgeons made some improvements. This is one of them—and there are others. I want to make the most of them. Jupiter is the place where I can do it."

Webster stared for long seconds at the fallen card, absorbing the improbable colors of the Trivium Charontis Escarpment. Then he said quietly: "I understand. How long do you think it will take?"

"With your help, plus the Bureau, plus all the science foundation we can drag in—oh, three years. Then a year for trials—we'll have to send in at least two test models. So, with luck—five years."

"That's about what I thought. I hope you get your luck; you've earned it. But there's one thing I won't do."

"What's that?"

"Next time you go ballooning, don't expect *me* as passenger."

3. THE WORLD OF THE GODS

The fall from Jupiter V to Jupiter itself takes only three and a half hours. Few men could have slept on so awesome a journey. Sleep was a weakness that Howard Falcon hated, and the little he still required brought dreams that time had not yet been able to exorcise. But he could expect no rest in the three days that lay ahead, and must seize what he could during the long fall down into that ocean of clouds, some sixty thousand miles below.

As soon as *Kon-Tiki* had entered her transfer orbit and all the computer checks were satisfactory, he prepared for the last sleep he might ever know. It seemed appropriate that at almost the same moment Jupiter eclipsed the bright and tiny Sun as he swept into the monstrous shadow of the planet. For a few minutes a strange golden twilight enveloped the ship; then a quarter of the sky became an utterly black hole in space, while the rest was a blaze of stars. No matter how far one traveled across the solar system, they never changed; these same constellations now shone on Earth, millions of miles away. The only novelties here were the small, pale crescents of Callisto and Ganymede; doubtless there were a dozen other moons up there in the sky, but they were all much too tiny, and too distant, for the unaided eye to pick them out.

"Closing down for two hours," he reported to the mother ship, hanging almost a thousand miles above the desolate rocks of Jupiter V, in the radiation shadow of the tiny satellite. If it never served any other useful purpose, Jupiter V was a cosmic bulldozer perpetually sweeping up the charged particles that made it unhealthy to linger close to Jupiter. Its wake was almost free of radiation, and there a ship could park in perfect safety, while death sleeted invisibly all around.

Falcon switched on the sleep inducer, and consciousness faded swiftly out as the electric pulses surged gently through his brain. While *Kon-Tiki* fell toward Jupiter, gaining speed second by second in that enormous gravitational field, he slept without dreams. They always came when he awoke; and he had brought his nightmares with him from Earth.

Yet he never dreamed of the crash itself, though he often found himself again face to face with that terrified superchimp, as he descended the spiral stairway between the collapsing gasbags. None of the simps had survived; those that were not killed outright were so badly injured that they had been painlessly "euthed." He sometimes wondered why he dreamed only of this doomed creature—which he had never met before the last minutes of its life—and not of the friends and colleagues he had lost aboard the dying *Queen*.

The dreams he feared most always began with his first return to consciousness. There had been little physical pain; in fact, there had been no sensation of any kind. He was in darkness and silence, and did not even seem to be breathing. And—strangest of all—he could not locate his limbs. He could move neither his hands nor his feet, because he did not know where they were.

The silence had been the first to yield. After hours, or days, he had become aware of a faint throbbing, and eventually, after long thought, he deduced that this was the beating of his own heart. That was the first of his many mistakes.

Then there had been faint pinpricks, sparkles of light, ghosts of pressures upon still-unresponsive limbs. One by one his senses had returned, and pain had come with them. He had had to learn everything anew, recapitulating infancy and babyhood. Though his memory was unaffected, and he could understand words that were spoken to him, it was months before he was able to answer except by the flicker of an eyelid. He could remember the moments of triumph when he had spoken the first word, turned the page of a book—and, finally, learned to move under his own power. *That* was a victory indeed, and it had taken him almost two years to prepare for it. A hundred times he had envied that dead superchimp, but *he* had been given no choice. The doctors had made their decision—and now, twelve years later, he was where no human being had ever traveled before, and moving faster than any man in history.

Kon-Tiki was just emerging from shadow, and the Jovian dawn bridged the sky ahead in a titanic bow of light, when the persistent buzz of the alarm dragged Falcon up from sleep. The inevitable nightmares (he had been trying to summon a nurse, but did not even have the strength to push the button) swiftly faded from consciousness. The greatest—and perhaps last—adventure of his life was before him.

He called Mission Control, now almost sixty thousand miles away and falling swiftly below the curve of Jupiter, to report that everything was in order. His velocity had just passed thirty-one miles a second (*that* was one for the books) and in half an hour *Kon-Tiki* would hit the outer fringes of the atmosphere, as he started on the most difficult re-entry in the entire solar system. Although scores of probes had survived this flaming ordeal, they had been tough, solidly packed masses of instrumentation, able to withstand several hundred gravities of drag. *Kon-Tiki* would hit peaks of thirty g's, and would average more than ten, before she came to rest in the upper reaches of the Jovian atmosphere. Very carefully and thoroughly, Falcon began to attach the elaborate system of restraints that would anchor him to the walls of the cabin. When he had finished, he was virtually a part of the ship's structure.

The clock was counting backward; one hundred seconds to reentry. For better or worse, he was committed. In a minute and a half, he would graze the Jovian atmosphere, and would be caught irrevocably in the grip of the giant.

The countdown was three seconds late—not at all bad, considering the unknowns involved. From beyond the walls of the capsule came a ghostly sighing, which rose steadily to a high-pitched, screaming roar. The noise was quite different from that of a reentry on Earth or Mars; in this thin atmosphere of hydrogen and helium, all sounds were transformed a couple of octaves upward. On Jupiter, even thunder would have falsetto overtones.

With the rising scream came mounting weight; within seconds, he was completely immobilized. His field of vision contracted until it embraced only the clock and the accelerometer; fifteen g, and four hundred and eighty seconds to go. . . .

He never lost consciousness; but then, he had not expected to. *Kon-Tiki's* trail through the Jovian atmosphere must be really spectacular—by this time, thousands of miles long. Five hundred seconds after entry, the drag began to taper off: ten g, five g, two. . . . Then weight vanished almost completely. He was falling free, all his enormous orbital velocity destroyed.

There was a sudden jolt as the incandescent remnants of the heat shield were jettisoned. It had done its work and would not be needed again; Jupiter could have it now. He released all but two of the restraining buckles, and waited for the automatic sequencer to start the next, and most critical, series of events.

He did not see the first drogue parachute pop out, but he could feel the slight jerk, and the rate of fall diminished immediately. *Kon-Tiki* had lost all her horizontal speed and was going straight down at almost a thousand miles an hour. Everything depended on what happened in the next sixty seconds.

There went the second drogue. He looked up through the overhead window and saw, to his immense relief, that clouds of glittering foil were billowing out behind the falling ship. Like a great flower unfurling, the thousands of cubic yards of the balloon spread out across the sky, scooping up the thin gas until it was fully in-flated. *Kon-Tiki*'s rate of fall dropped to a few miles an hour and remained constant. Now there was plenty of time; it would take him days to fall all the way down to the surface of Jupiter.

But he would get there eventually, even if he did nothing about it. The balloon overhead was merely acting as an efficient para-chute. It was providing no lift; nor could it do so, while the gas inside and out was the same.

With its characteristic and rather disconcerting crack the fu-sion reactor started up, pouring torrents of heat into the envelope overhead. Within five minutes, the rate of fall had become zero; within six, the ship had started to rise. According to the radar altimeter, it had leveled out at about two hundred and sixty-seven miles above the surface—or whatever passed for a surface on Ju-piter.

Only one kind of balloon will work in an atmosphere of hy-drogen, which is the lightest of all gases—and that is a hot-hydrogen balloon. As long as the fuser kept ticking over, Falcon could remain aloft, drifting across a world that could hold a hundred Pacifics. After traveling over three hundred million miles, *Kon-Tiki* had at last begun to justify her name. She was an aerial raft, adrift upon the currents of the Jovian atmosphere.

Though a whole new world was lying around him, it was more than an hour before Falcon could examine the view. First he had to check all the capsule's systems and test its response to the controls. He had to learn how much extra heat was necessary to produce a desired rate of ascent, and how much gas he must vent in order to descend. Above all, there was the question of stability. He must adjust the length of the cables attaching his capsule to the huge, pear-shaped balloon, to damp out vibrations and get the smoothest possible ride. Thus far, he was lucky; at this level, the wind was steady, and the Doppler reading on the invisible surface gave him a ground speed of two hundred seventeen and a half miles an hour. For Jupiter, that was modest; winds of up to a thousand had been observed. But mere speed was, of course, unimportant; the real danger was turbulence. If he ran into that, only skill and experience and swift reaction could save him—and these were not matters that could yet be programed into a computer.

Not until he was satisfied that he had got the feel of his strange craft did Falcon pay any attention to Mission Control's pleadings. Then he deployed the booms carrying the instrumentation and the atmospheric samplers. The capsule now resembled a rather untidy Christmas tree, but still rode smoothly down the Jovian winds while it radioed its torrents of information to the recorders on the ship miles above. And now, at last, he could look around. . . .

His first impression was unexpected, and even a little disappointing. As far as the scale of things was concerned, he might have been ballooning over an ordinary cloudscape on Earth. The horizon seemed at a normal distance; there was no feeling at all that he was on a world eleven times the diameter of his own. Then he looked at the infrared radar, sounding the layers of atmosphere beneath him—and knew how badly his eyes had been deceived.

That layer of clouds apparently about three miles away was really more than thirty-seven miles below. And the horizon, whose distance he would have guessed at about one hundred and twenty-five, was actually eighteen hundred miles from the ship.

The crystalline clarity of the hydrohelium atmosphere and the enormous curvature of the planet had fooled him completely. It was even harder to judge distances here than on the Moon; everything he saw must be multiplied by at least ten.

It was a simple matter, and he should have been prepared for it. Yet somehow, it disturbed him profoundly. He did not feel that Jupiter was huge, but that *he* had shrunk—to a tenth of his normal size. Perhaps, with time, he would grow accustomed to the inhuman scale of this world; yet as he stared toward that unbelievably distant horizon, he felt as if a wind colder than the atmosphere around him was blowing through his soul. Despite all his arguments, this might never be a place for man. He could well be both the first and the last to descend through the clouds of Jupiter.

The sky above was almost black, except for a few wisps of ammonia cirrus perhaps twelve miles overhead. It was cold up there, on the fringes of space, but both pressure and temperature increased rapidly with depth. At the level where *Kon-Tiki* was drifting now, it was fifty below zero, and the pressure was five atmospheres. Sixty-five miles farther down, it would be as warm as equatorial Earth, and the pressure about the same as at the bottom of one of the shallower seas. Ideal conditions for life. . . .

A quarter of the brief Jovian day had already gone; the sun was halfway up the sky, but the light on the unbroken cloudscape below had a curious mellow quality. That extra three hundred million miles had robbed the Sun of all its power. Though the sky was clear, Falcon found himself continually thinking that it was a heavily overcast day. When night fell, the onset of darkness would be swift indeed; though it was still morning, there was a sense of autumnal twilight in the air. But autumn, of course, was something that never came to Jupiter. There were no seasons here.

Kon-Tiki had come down in the exact center of the equatorial zone—the least colorful part of the planet. The sea of clouds that stretched out to the horizon was tinted a pale salmon; there were none of the yellows and pinks and even reds that banded Jupiter at higher altitudes. The Great Red Spot itself—most spectacular of all of the planet's features—lay thousands of miles to the south. It had been a temptation to descend there, but the south tropical disturbance was unusually active, with currents reaching over nine hundred miles an hour. It would have been asking for trouble to head into that maelstrom of unknown forces. The Great Red Spot and its mysteries would have to wait for future expeditions.

The Sun, moving across the sky twice as swiftly as it did on Earth, was now nearing the zenith and had become eclipsed by the great silver canopy of the balloon. Kon-Tiki was still drifting swiftly and smoothly westward at a steady two hundred and seventeen and a half, but only the radar gave any indication of this. Was it always as calm here? Falcon asked himself. The scientists who had talked learnedly of the Jovian doldrums, and had predicted that the equator would be the quietest place, seemed to know what they were talking about, after all. He had been profoundly skeptical of all such forecasts, and had agreed with one unusually modest researcher who had told him bluntly: "There are no experts on Jupiter." Well, there would be at least one by the end of this day.

If he managed to survive until then.

4. THE VOICES OF THE DEEP

That first day, the Father of the Gods smiled upon him. It was as calm and peaceful here on Jupiter as it had been, years ago, when he was drifting with Webster across the plains of northern India. Falcon had time to master his new skills, until *Kon-Tiki* seemed an extension of his own body. Such luck was more than he had dared to hope for, and he began to wonder what price he might have to pay for it.

The five hours of daylight were almost over; the clouds below were full of shadows, which gave them a massive solidity they had not possessed when the Sun was higher. Color was swiftly draining from the sky, except in the west itself, where a band of deepening purple lay along the horizon. Above this band was the thin crescent of a closer moon, pale and bleached against the utter blackness beyond.

With a speed perceptible to the eye, the Sun went straight down over the edge of Jupiter, over eighteen hundred miles away. The stars came out in their legions—and there was the beautiful evening star of Earth, on the very frontier to twilight, reminding him how far he was from home. It followed the Sun down into the west. Man's first night on Jupiter had begun.

With the onset of darkness, *Kon-Tiki* started to sink. The balloon was no longer heated by the feeble sunlight and was losing a small part of its buoyancy. Falcon did nothing to increase lift; he had expected this and was planning to descend.

The invisible cloud deck was still over thirty miles below, and he would reach it about midnight. It showed up clearly on the infrared radar, which also reported that it contained a vast array of complex carbon compounds, as well as the usual hydrogen, helium, and ammonia. The chemists were dying for samples of that fluffy, pinkish stuff; though some atmospheric probes had already gathered a few grams, they had only whetted their appetites. Half the basic molecules of life were here, floating high above the surface of Jupiter. And where there was food, could life be far away? That was the question that, after more than a hundred years, no one had been able to answer.

The infrared was blocked by the clouds, but the microwave

radar sliced right through and showed layer after layer, all the way down to the hidden surface almost two hundred and fifty miles below. That was barred to him by enormous pressures and temperatures; not even robot probes had ever reached it intact. It lay in tantalizing inaccessibility at the bottom of the radar screen, slightly fuzzy, and showing a curious granular structure that his equipment could not resolve.

An hour after sunset, he dropped his first probe. It fell swiftly for about sixty miles, then began to float in the denser atmosphere, sending back torrents of radio signals, which he relayed to Mission Control. Then there was nothing else to do until sunrise, except to keep an eye on the rate of descent, monitor the instruments, and answer occasional queries. While she was drifting in this steady current, Kon-Tiki could look after herself.

Just before midnight, a woman controller came on watch and introduced herself with the usual pleasantries. Ten minutes later she called again, her voice at once serious and excited.

"Howard! Listen in on channel forty-six—high gain."

Channel forty-six? There were so many telemetering circuits that he knew the numbers of only those that were critical; but as soon as he threw the switch, he recognized this one. He was plugged in to the microphone on the probe, floating more than eighty miles below him in an atmosphere now almost as dense as water.

At first, there was only a soft hiss of whatever strange winds stirred down in the darkness of that unimaginable world. And then, out of the background noise, there slowly emerged a booming vibration that grew louder and louder, like the beating of a gigantic drum. It was so low that it was felt as much as heard, and the beats steadily increased their tempo, though the pitch never changed. Now it was a swift, almost infrasonic throbbing. Then, suddenly, in mid-vibration, it stopped—so abruptly that the mind could not accept the silence, but memory continued to manufacture a ghostly echo in the deepest caverns of the brain.

It was the most extraordinary sound that Falcon had ever heard, even among the multitudinous noises of Earth. He could think of no natural phenomenon that could have caused it; nor was it like the cry of any animal, not even one of the great whales. . . .

It came again, following exactly the same pattern. Now that

he was prepared for it, he estimated the length of the sequence; from first faint throb to final crescendo, it lasted just over ten seconds.

And this time there was a real echo, very faint and far away. Perhaps it came from one of the many reflecting layers, deeper in this stratified atmosphere; perhaps it was another, more distant source. Falcon waited for a second echo, but it never came.

Mission Control reacted quickly and asked him to drop another probe at once. With two microphones operating, it would be possible to find the approximate location of the sources. Oddly enough, none of *Kon-Tiki's* own external mikes could detect anything except wind noises. The boomings, whatever they were, must have been trapped and channeled beneath an atmospheric reflecting layer far below.

They were coming, it was soon discovered, from a cluster of sources about twelve hundred miles away. The distance gave no indication of their power; in Earth's oceans, quite feeble sounds could travel equally far. And as for the obvious assumption that living creatures were responsible, the Chief Exobiologist quickly ruled that out.

"I'll be very disappointed," said Dr. Brenner, "if there are no microorganisms or plants here. But nothing like animals, because there's no free oxygen. All biochemical reactions on Jupiter must be low-energy ones—there's just no way an active creature could generate enough power to function."

Falcon wondered if this was true; he had heard the argument before, and reserved judgment.

"In any case," continued Brenner, "some of those sound waves are a hundred yards long! Even an animal as big as a whale couldn't produce them. They *must* have a natural origin."

Yes, that seemed plausible, and probably the physicists would be able to come up with an explanation. What would a blind alien make, Falcon wondered, of the sounds he might hear when standing beside a stormy sea, or a geyser, or a volcano, or a waterfall? He might well attribute them to some huge beast.

About an hour before sunrise the voices of the deep died away, and Falcon began to busy himself with preparation for the dawn of his second day. *Kon-Tiki* was now only three miles above the nearest cloud layer; the external pressure had risen to ten atmospheres, and the temperature was a tropical thirty degrees. A man could be comfortable here with no more equipment than a breathing mask and the right grade of heliox mixture.

"We've some good news for you," Mission Control reported, soon after dawn. "The cloud layer's breaking up. You'll have partial clearing in an hour—but watch out for turbulence."

"I've already noticed some," Falcon answered. "How far down will I be able to see?"

"At least twelve miles, down to the second thermocline. *That* cloud deck is solid—it never breaks."

And it's out of my reach, Falcon told himself; the temperature down there must be over a hundred degrees. This was the first time that any balloonist had ever had to worry, not about his ceiling, but about his basement!

Ten minutes later he could see what Mission Control had already observed from its superior vantage point. There was a change in color near the horizon, and the cloud layer had become ragged and humpy, as if something had torn it open. He turned up his little nuclear furnace and gave Kon-Tiki another three miles of altitude, so that he could get a better view.

The sky below was clearing rapidly, completely, as if something was dissolving the solid overcast. An abyss was opening before his eyes. A moment later he sailed out over the edge of a cloud canyon about twelve miles deep and six hundred miles wide.

A new world lay spread beneath him; Jupiter had stripped away one of its many veils. The second layer of clouds, unattainably far below, was much darker in color than the first. It was almost salmon pink, and curiously mottled with little islands of brick red. They were all oval-shaped, with their long axes pointing east-west, in the direction of the prevailing wind. There were hundreds of them, all about the same size, and they reminded Falcon of puffy little cumulus clouds in the terrestrial sky.

He reduced buoyancy, and Kon-Tiki began to drop down the face of the dissolving cliff. It was then that he noticed the snow.

White flakes were forming in the air and drifting slowly downward. Yet it was much too warm for snow—and, in any event, there was scarcely a trace of water at this altitude. Moreover, there was no glitter or sparkle about these flakes as they went cascading down into the depths. When, presently, a few landed on an instrument boom outside the main viewing port, he saw that they were a dull, opaque white—not crystalline at all—and quite large—several inches across. They looked like wax, and Falcon guessed that this was precisely what they were. Some chemical reaction was taking place in the atmosphere around him, condensing out the hydrocarbons floating in the Jovian air.

About sixty miles ahead, a disturbance was taking place in the cloud layer. The little red ovals were being jostled around, and were beginning to form a spiral—the familiar cyclonic pattern so common in the meteorology of Earth. The vortex was emerging with astonishing speed; if that was a storm ahead, Falcon told himself, he was in big trouble.

And then his concern changed to wonder—and to fear. What was developing in his line of flight was not a storm at all. Something enormous—something scores of miles across—was rising through the clouds.

The reassuring thought that it, too, might be a cloud—a thunderhead boiling up from the lower levels of the atmosphere—lasted only a few seconds. No; this was *solid*. It shouldered its way through the pink-and-salmon overcast like an iceberg rising from the deeps.

An *iceberg* floating on hydrogen? That was impossible, of course; but perhaps it was not too remote an analogy. As soon as he focused the telescope upon the enigma, Falcon saw that it was a whitish, crystalline mass, threaded with streaks of red and brown. It must be, he decided, the same stuff as the "snowflakes" falling around him—a mountain range of wax. And it was not, he soon realized, as solid as he had thought; around the edges it was continually crumbling and reforming. . . .

"I know what it is," he radioed Mission Control, which for the last few minutes had been asking anxious questions. "It's a mass of bubbles—some kind of foam. Hydrocarbon froth. Get the chemists working on . . . *Just a minute!*"

"What is it?" called Mission Control. "What is it?"

He ignored the frantic pleas from space and concentrated all his mind upon the image in the telescope field. He had to be sure;

if he made a mistake, he would be the laughingstock of the solar system.

Then he relaxed, glanced at the clock, and switched off the nagging voice from Jupiter V.

"Hello, Mission Control," he said, very formally. "This is Howard Falcon aboard *Kon-Tiki*. Ephemeris Time nineteen hours twenty-one minutes fifteen seconds. Latitude zero degrees five minutes North. Longitude one hundred five degrees forty-two minutes, System One.

"Tell Dr. Brenner that there is life on Jupiter. And it's *big*. . . ."

5. THE WHEELS OF POSEIDON

"I'm very happy to be proved wrong," Dr. Brenner radioed back cheerfully. "Nature always has something up her sleeve. Keep the long-focus camera on target and give us the steadiest pictures you can."

The things moving up and down those waxen slopes were still too far away for Falcon to make out many details, and they must have been very large to be visible at all at such a distance. Almost black, and shaped like arrowheads, they maneuvered by slow undulations of their entire bodies, so that they looked rather like giant manta rays, swimming above some tropical reef.

Perhaps they were sky-borne cattle, browsing on the cloud pastures of Jupiter, for they seemed to be feeding along the dark, red-brown streaks that ran like dried-up river beds down the flanks of the floating cliffs. Occasionally, one of them would dive headlong into the mountain of foam and disappear completely from sight.

Kon-Tiki was moving only slowly with respect to the cloud layer below; it would be at least three hours before she was above those ephemeral hills. She was in a race with the Sun. Falcon hoped that darkness would not fall before he could get a good view of the mantas, as he had christened them, as well as the fragile landscape over which they flapped their way.

It was a long three hours. During the whole time, he kept the external microphones on full gain, wondering if here was the source of that booming in the night. The mantas were certainly large enough to have produced it; when he could get an accurate measurement, he discovered that they were almost a hundred yards across the wings. That was three times the length of the largest whale—though he doubted if they could weigh more than a few tons.

Half an hour before sunset, Kon-Tiki was almost above the "mountains."

"No," said Falcon, answering Mission Control's repeated questions about the mantas, "they're still showing no reaction to me. I don't think they're intelligent—they look like harmless vegetarians. And even if they try to chase me, I'm sure they can't reach my altitude."

Yet he was a little disappointed when the mantas showed not the slightest interest in him as he sailed high above their feeding ground. Perhaps they had no way of detecting his presence. When he examined and photographed them through the telescope, he could see no signs of any sense organs. The creatures were simply huge black deltas, rippling over hills and valleys that, in reality, were little more substantial than the clouds of Earth. Though they looked solid, Falcon knew that anyone who stepped on those white mountains would go crashing through them as if they were made of tissue paper.

At close quarters he could see the myriads of cellules or bubbles from which they were formed. Some of these were quite large—a yard or so in diameter—and Falcon wondered in what witches' cauldron of hydrocarbons they had been brewed. There must be enough petrochemicals deep down in the atmosphere of Jupiter to supply all Earth's needs for a million years.

The short day had almost gone when he passed over the crest of the waxen hills, and the light was fading rapidly along their lower slopes. There were no mantas on this western side, and for some reason the topography was very different. The foam was sculptured into long, level terraces, like the interior of a lunar crater. He could almost imagine that they were gigantic steps leading down to the hidden surface of the planet.

And on the lowest of those steps, just clear of the swirling clouds that the mountain had displaced when it came surging skyward, was a roughly oval mass, one or two miles across. It was difficult to see, since it was only a little darker than the gray-white foam on which it rested. Falcon's first thought was that he was looking at a forest of pallid trees, like giant mushrooms that had never seen the Sun.

Yes, it must be a forest—he could see hundreds of thin trunks, springing from the white waxy froth in which they were rooted. But the trees were packed astonishingly close together; there was scarcely any space between them. Perhaps it was not a forest, after all, but a single enormous tree—like one of the giant multi-trunked banyans of the East. Once he had seen a banyan tree in Java that was over six hundred and fifty yards across; this monster was at least ten times that size.

The light had almost gone. The cloudscape had turned purple with refracted sunlight, and in a few seconds that, too, would have vanished. In the last light of his second day on Jupiter, Howard Falcon saw—or thought he saw—something that cast the gravest doubts on his interpretation of the white oval.

Unless the dim light had totally deceived him, those hundreds of thin trunks were beating back and forth, in perfect synchronism, like fronds of kelp rocking in the surge.

And the tree was no longer in the place where he had first seen it.

"Sorry about this," said Mission Control, soon after sunset, "but we think Source Beta is going to blow within the next hour. Probability seventy percent."

Falcon glanced quickly at the chart. Beta—Jupiter latitude one hundred and forty degrees—was over eighteen thousand six hundred miles away and well below his horizon. Even though major eruptions ran as high as ten megatons, he was much too far away for the shock wave to be a serious danger. The radio storm that it would trigger was, however, quite a different matter.

The decameter outbursts that sometimes made Jupiter the most powerful radio source in the whole sky had been discovered back in the 1950s, to the utter astonishment of the astronomers. Now, more than a century later, their real cause was still a mystery. Only the symptoms were understood; the explanation was completely un-known.

The "volcano" theory had best stood the test of time, although no one imagined that this word had the same meaning on Jupiter as on Earth. At frequent intervals—often several times a day—titanic eruptions occurred in the lower depths of the atmosphere, probably on the hidden surface of the planet itself. A great column of gas, more than six hundred miles high, would start boiling up-ward as if determined to escape into space.

Against the most powerful gravitational field of all the planets, it had no chance. Yet some traces—a mere few million tons—usually managed to reach the Jovian ionosphere; and when they did, all hell broke loose.

The radiation belts surrounding Jupiter completely dwarf the feeble Van Allen belts of Earth. When they are short-circuited by an ascending column of gas, the result is an electrical discharge millions of times more powerful than any terrestrial flash of light-ning; it sends a colossal thunderclap of radio noise flooding across the entire solar system and on out to the stars.

It had been discovered that these radio outbursts came from four main areas of the planet. Perhaps there were weaknesses there that allowed the fires of the interior to break out from time to time. The scientists on Ganymede, largest of Jupiter's many moons, now thought that they could predict the onset of a decameter storm; their accuracy was about as good as a weather forecaster's of the early 1900s.

Falcon did not know whether to welcome or to fear a radio storm; it would certainly add to the value of the mission—if he survived it. His course had been planned to keep as far as possible from the main centers of disturbance, especially the most active one, Source Alpha. As luck would have it, the threatening Beta was the closest to him. He hoped that the distance, almost three-fourths the circumference of Earth, was safe enough.

"Probability ninety percent," said Mission Control with a dis-tinct note of urgency. "And forget that hour. Ganymede says it may be any moment."

The radio had scarcely fallen silent when the reading on the magnetic field-strength meter started to shoot upward. Before it could go off scale, it reversed and began to drop as rapidly as it had risen. Far away and thousands of miles below, something had given the planet's molten core a titanic jolt.

"There she blows!" called Mission Control.

"Thanks, I already know. When will the storm hit me?"

"You can expect onset in five minutes. Peak in ten."

Far around the curve of Jupiter, a funnel of gas as wide as the Pacific Ocean was climbing spaceward at thousands of miles an hour. Already the thunderstorms of the lower atmosphere would be raging around it—but they were nothing compared with the fury that would explode when the radiation belt was reached and began dumping its surplus electrons onto the planet. Falcon began to re-tract all the instrument booms that were extended out from the capsule. There were no other precautions he could take. It would be four hours before the atmospheric shock wave reached him—but the radio blast, traveling at the speed of light, would be here in a tenth of a second, once the discharge had been triggered.

The radio monitor, scanning back and forth across the spec-trum, still showed nothing unusual, just the normal mush of back-ground static. Then Falcon noticed that the noise level was slowly creeping upward. The explosion was gathering its strength.

At such a distance he had never expected to *see* anything. But suddenly a flicker as of far-off heat lightning danced along the east-ern horizon. Simultaneously, half the circuit breakers jumped out of the main switchboard, the lights failed, and all communications channels went dead.

He tried to move, but was completely unable to do so. The paralysis that gripped him was not merely psychological; he seemed to have lost all control of his limbs and could feel a painful tingling sensation over his entire body. It was impossible that the electric field could have penetrated this shielded cabin. Yet there was a flickering glow over the instrument board, and he could hear the unmistakable crackle of a brush discharge.

With a series of sharp bangs, the emergency systems went into operation, and the overloads reset themselves. The lights flickered on again. And Falcon's paralysis disappeared as swiftly as it had come.

After glancing at the board to make sure that all circuits were back to normal, he moved quickly to the viewing ports.

There was no need to switch on the inspection lamps—the cables supporting the capsule seemed to be on fire. Lines of light glowing an electric blue against the darkness stretched upward from the main lift ring to the equator of the giant balloon; and rolling slowly along several of them were dazzling balls of fire.

The sight was so strange and so beautiful that it was hard to read any menace in it. Few people, Falcon knew, had ever seen ball lightning from such close quarters—and certainly none had survived if they were riding a hydrogen-filled balloon back in the atmosphere of Earth. He remembered the flaming death of the *Hindenburg*, destroyed by a stray spark when she docked at Lakehurst in 1937; as it had done so often in the past, the horrifying old newsreel film flashed through his mind. But at least that could not happen here, though there was more hydrogen above his head than had ever filled the last of the Zeppelins. It would be a few billion years yet, before anyone could light a fire in the atmosphere of Jupiter.

With a sound like briskly frying bacon, the speech circuit came back to life.

"Hello, *Kon-Tiki*—are you receiving? Are you receiving?"

The words were chopped and badly distorted, but intelligible. Falcon's spirits lifted; he had resumed contact with the world of men.

"I receive you," he said. "Quite an electrical display, but no damage—so far."

"Thanks—thought we'd lost you. Please check telemetry channels three, seven, twenty-six. Also gain on camera two. And we don't quite believe the readings on the external ionization probes. . . ."

Reluctantly Falcon tore his gaze away from the fascinating pyrotechnic display around *Kon-Tiki*, though from time to time he kept glancing out of the windows. The ball lightning disappeared first, the fiery globes slowly expanding until they reached a critical size, at which they vanished in a gentle explosion. But even an hour later, there were still faint glows around all the exposed metal on the outside of the capsule; and the radio circuits remained noisy until well after midnight.

The remaining hours of darkness were completely uneventful—until just before dawn. Because it came from the east, Falcon assumed that he was seeing the first faint hint of sunrise. Then he realized that it was twenty minutes too early for this—and the glow that had appeared along the horizon was moving toward him even as he watched. It swiftly detached itself from the arch of stars that marked the invisible edge of the planet, and he saw that it was a relatively narrow band, quite sharply defined. The beam of an enormous searchlight appeared to be swinging beneath the clouds.

Perhaps sixty miles behind the first racing bar of light came another, parallel to it and moving at the same speed. And beyond that another, and another—until all the sky flickered with alternating sheets of light and darkness.

By this time, Falcon thought, he had been inured to wonders, and it seemed impossible that this display of pure, soundless luminosity could present the slightest danger. But it was so astonishing, and so inexplicable, that he felt cold, naked fear gnawing at his self-control. No man could look upon such a sight without feeling like a helpless pygmy in the presence of forces beyond his comprehension. Was it possible that, after all, Jupiter carried not only life but also intelligence? And, perhaps, an intelligence that only now was beginning to react to his alien presence?

"Yes, we see it," said Mission Control, in a voice that echoed his own awe. "We've no idea what it is. Stand by, we're calling Ganymede."

The display was slowly fading; the bands racing in from the far horizon were much fainter, as if the energies that powered them were becoming exhausted. In five minutes it was all over; the last faint pulse of light flickered along the western sky and then was gone. Its passing left Falcon with an overwhelming sense of relief. The sight was so hypnotic, and so disturbing, that it was not good for any man's peace of mind to contemplate it too long.

He was more shaken than he cared to admit. The electrical storm was something that he could understand; but *this* was totally incomprehensible.

Mission Control was still silent. He knew that the information banks up on Ganymede were now being searched as men and computers turned their minds to the problem. If no answer could be found there, it would be necessary to call Earth; that would mean a delay of almost an hour. The possibility that even Earth might be unable to help was one that Falcon did not care to contemplate.

He had never before been so glad to hear the voice of Mission Control as when Dr. Brenner finally came on the circuit. The biologist sounded relieved, yet subdued—like a man who has just come through some great intellectual crisis.

"Hello, Kon-Tiki. We've solved your problem, but we can still hardly believe it.

"What you've been seeing is bioluminescence, very similar to that produced by microorganisms in the tropical seas of Earth. Here they're in the atmosphere, not the ocean, but the principle is the same."

"But the pattern," protested Falcon, "was so regular—so *artificial*. And it was hundreds of miles across!"

"It was even larger than you imagine; you observed only a small part of it. The whole pattern was over three thousand miles wide and looked like a revolving wheel. You merely saw the spokes, sweeping past you at about six-tenths of a mile a second. . . ."

"A *second!*" Falcon could not help interjecting. "No animals could move that fast!"

"Of course not. Let me explain. What you saw was triggered by the shock wave from Source Beta, moving at the speed of sound."

"But what about the pattern?" Falcon insisted.

"That's the surprising part. It's a very rare phenomenon, but identical wheels of light—except that they're a thousand times smaller—have been observed in the Persian Gulf and the Indian Ocean. Listen to this: British India Company's *Patna*, Persian Gulf, May 1880, 11:30 P.M.—'an enormous luminous wheel, whirling round, the spokes of which appeared to brush the ship along. The spokes were 200 or 300 yards long . . . each wheel contained about sixteen spokes. . . .' And here's one from the Gulf of Omar, dated May 23, 1906: 'The intensely bright luminescence approached us rapidly, shooting sharply defined light rays to the west in rapid succession, like the beam from the searchlight of a warship. . . . To the left of us, a gigantic fiery wheel formed itself, with spokes that reached as far as one could see. The whole wheel whirled around for two or three minutes. . . .' The archive computer on Ganymede dug up about five hundred cases. It would have printed out the lot if we hadn't stopped it in time."

"I'm convinced—but still baffled."

"I don't blame you. The full explanation wasn't worked out until late in the twentieth century. It seems that these luminous wheels are the results of submarine earthquakes, and always occur in shallow waters where the shock waves can be reflected and cause standing wave patterns. Sometimes bars, sometimes rotating wheels—the 'Wheels of Poseidon,' they've been called. The theory was finally proved by making underwater explosions and photographing the results from a satellite. No wonder sailors used to be superstitious. Who would have believed a thing like *this?*"

So that was it, Falcon told himself. When Source Beta blew its top, it must have sent shock waves in all directions—through the compressed gas of the lower atmosphere, through the solid body of Jupiter itself. Meeting and crisscrossing, those waves must have canceled here, reinforced there; the whole planet must have rung like a bell.

Yet the explanation did not destroy the sense of wonder and awe; he would never be able to forget those flickering bands of light, racing through the unattainable depths of the Jovian atmosphere. He felt that he was not merely on a strange planet, but in some magical realm between myth and reality.

This was a world where absolutely *anything* could happen, and no man could possibly guess what the future would bring.

And he still had a whole day to go.

6. MEDUSA

When the true dawn finally arrived, it brought a sudden change of weather. *Kon-Tiki* was moving through a blizzard; waxen snowflakes were falling so thickly that visibility was reduced to zero. Falcon began to worry about the weight that might be accumulating on the envelope. Then he noticed that any flakes settling outside the windows quickly disappeared; *Kon-Tiki's* continual outpouring of heat was evaporating them as swiftly as they arrived.

If he had been ballooning on Earth, he would also have worried about the possibility of collision. At least that was no danger here; any Jovian mountains were several hundred miles below him. And as for the floating islands of foam, hitting them would probably be like plowing into slightly hardened soap bubbles.

Nevertheless, he switched on the horizontal radar, which until now had been completely useless; only the vertical beam, giving his distance from the invisible surface, had thus far been of any value. Then he had another surprise.

Scattered across a huge sector of the sky ahead were dozens of large and brilliant echoes. They were completely isolated from one another and apparently hung unsupported in space. Falcon remembered a phrase the earliest aviators had used to describe one of the hazards of their profession: "clouds stuffed with rocks." That was a perfect description of what seemed to lie in the track of *Kon-Tiki*.

It was a disconcerting sight; then Falcon again reminded himself that nothing *really* solid could possibly hover in this atmosphere. Perhaps it was some strange meteorological phenomenon. In any case, the nearest echo was about a hundred and twenty-five miles.

He reported to Mission Control, which could provide no explanation. But it gave the welcome news that he would be clear of the blizzard in another thirty minutes.

It did not warn him, however, of the violent cross wind that abruptly grabbed *Kon-Tiki* and swept it almost at right angles to its previous track. Falcon needed all his skill and the maximum use of what little control he had over his ungainly vehicle to prevent it from being capsized. Within minutes he was racing northward at over three hundred miles an hour. Then, as suddenly as it had started, the turbulence ceased; he was still moving at high speed, but in smooth air. He wondered if he had been caught in the Jovian equivalent of a jet stream.

The snow storm dissolved; and he saw what Jupiter had been preparing for him.

Kon-Tiki had entered the funnel of a gigantic whirlpool, some six hundred miles across. The balloon was being swept along a curving wall of cloud. Overhead, the sun was shining in a clear sky; but far beneath, this great hole in the atmosphere drilled down to

unknown depths until it reached a misty floor where lightning flickered almost continuously.

Though the vessel was being dragged downward so slowly that
it was in no immediate danger, Falcon increased the flow of heat
into the envelope until Kon-Tiki hovered at a constant altitude.
Not until then did he abandon the fantastic spectacle outside and
consider again the problem of the radar.

The nearest echo was now only about twenty-five miles away.
All of them, he quickly realized, were distributed along the wall of
the vortex, and were moving with it, apparently caught in the
whirlpool like Kon-Tiki itself. He aimed the telescope along the
radar bearing and found himself looking at a curious mottled cloud
that almost filled the field of view.

It was not easy to see, being only a little darker than the whirling wall of mist that formed its background. Not until he had been
staring for several minutes did Falcon realize that he had met it
once before.

The first time it had been crawling across the drifting mountains of foam, and he had mistaken it for a giant, many-trunked
tree. Now at last he could appreciate its real size and complexity
and could give it a better name to fix its image in his mind. It did
not resemble a tree at all, but a jellyfish—a medusa, such as might
be met trailing its tentacles as it drifted along the warm eddies of
the Gulf Stream.

This medusa was more than a mile across and its scores of dangling tentacles were hundreds of feet long. They swayed slowly back
and forth in perfect unison, taking more than a minute for each
complete undulation—almost as if the creature was clumsily rowing
itself through the sky.

The other echoes were more distant medusae. Falcon focused
the telescope on half a dozen and could see no variations in shape
or size. They all seemed to be of the same species, and he wondered
just why they were drifting lazily around in this six-hundred-mile
orbit. Perhaps they were feeding upon the aerial plankton sucked
in by the whirlpool, as Kon-Tiki itself had been.

"Do you realize, Howard," said Dr. Brenner, when he had recovered from his initial astonishment, "that this thing is about a
hundred thousand times as large as the biggest whale? And even if

it's only a gasbag, it must still weigh a million tons! I can't even guess at its metabolism. It must generate megawatts of heat to maintain its buoyancy."

"But if it's just a gasbag, why is it such a damn good radar reflector?"

"I haven't the faintest idea. Can you get any closer?"

Brenner's question was not an idle one. If he changed altitude to take advantage of the differing wind velocities, Falcon could approach the medusa as closely as he wished. At the moment, however, he preferred his present twenty-five miles and said so, firmly.

"I see what you mean," Brenner answered, a little reluctantly. "Let's stay where we are for the present." That "we" gave Falcon a certain wry amusement; an extra sixty thousand miles made a considerable difference in one's point of view.

For the next two hours Kon-Tiki drifted uneventfully in the gyre of the great whirlpool, while Falcon experimented with filters and camera contrast, trying to get a clear view of the medusa. He began to wonder if its elusive coloration was some kind of camouflage; perhaps, like many animals of Earth, it was trying to lose itself against its background. That was a trick used by both hunters and hunted.

In which category was the medusa? That was a question he could hardly expect to have answered in the short time that was left to him. Yet just before noon, without the slightest warning, the answer came. . . .

Like a squadron of antique jet fighters, five mantas came sweeping through the wall of mist that formed the funnel of the vortex. They were flying in a V formation directly toward the pallid gray cloud of the medusa; and there was no doubt, in Falcon's mind, that they were on the attack. He had been quite wrong to assume that they were harmless vegetarians.

Yet everything happened at such a leisurely pace that it was like watching a slow-motion film. The mantas undulated along at perhaps thirty miles an hour; it seemed ages before they reached the medusa, which continued to paddle imperturbably along at an even slower speed. Huge though they were, the mantas looked tiny beside the monster they were approaching. When they flapped down on its back, they appeared about as large as birds landing on a whale.

Could the medusa defend itself? Falcon wondered. He did not see how the attacking mantas could be in danger as long as they avoided those huge clumsy tentacles. And perhaps their host was not even aware of them; they could be insignificant parasites, tolerated as are fleas upon a dog.

But now it was obvious that the medusa was in distress. With agonizing slowness, it began to tip over like a capsizing ship. After ten minutes it had tilted forty-five degrees; it was also rapidly losing altitude. It was impossible not to feel a sense of pity for the beleaguered monster, and to Falcon the sight brought bitter memories. In a grotesque way, the fall of the medusa was almost a parody of the dying *Queen's* last moments.

Yet he knew that his sympathies were on the wrong side. High intelligence could develop only among predators—not among the drifting browsers of either sea or air. The mantas were far closer to him than was this monstrous bag of gas. And anyway, who could *really* sympathize with a creature a hundred thousand times larger than a whale?

Then he noticed that the medusa's tactics seemed to be having some effect. The mantas had been disturbed by its slow roll and were flapping heavily away from its back—like gorging vultures interrupted at mealtime. But they did not move very far, continuing to hover a few yards from the still-capsizing monster.

There was a sudden, blinding flash of light synchronized with a crash of static over the radio. One of the mantas, slowly twisting end over end, was plummeting straight downward. As it fell, a plume of black smoke trailed behind it. The resemblance to an aircraft going down in flames was quite uncanny.

In unison, the remaining mantas dived steeply away from the medusa, gaining speed by losing altitude. They had, within minutes, vanished back into the wall of cloud from which they had emerged. And the medusa, no longer falling, began to roll back toward the horizontal. Soon it was sailing along once more on an even keel, as if nothing had happened.

"Beautiful!" said Dr. Brenner, after a moment of stunned silence. "It's developed electric defenses, like some of our eels and rays. But that must have been about a million volts! Can you see any organs that might produce the discharge? Anything looking like electrodes?"

"No," Falcon answered, after switching to the highest power of the telescope. "But here's something odd. Do you see this pattern? Check back on the earlier images. I'm sure it wasn't there before."

A broad, mottled band had appeared along the side of the medusa. It formed a startlingly regular checkerboard, each square of which was itself speckled in a complex subpattern of short horizontal lines. They were spaced at equal distances in a geometrically perfect array of rows and columns.

"You're right," said Dr. Brenner, with something very much like awe in his voice. "That's just appeared. And I'm afraid to tell you what I think it is."

"Well, I have no reputation to lose—at least as a biologist. Shall I give my guess?"

"Go ahead."

"That's a large meter-band radio array. The sort of thing they used back at the beginning of the twentieth century."

"I was afraid you'd say that. Now we know why it gave such a massive echo."

"But why has it just appeared?"

"Probably an aftereffect of the discharge."

"I've just had another thought," said Falcon, rather slowly. "Do you suppose it's *listening* to us?"

"On this frequency? I doubt it. Those are meter—no, *decameter* antennas—judging by their size. Hmm . . . that's an idea!"

Dr. Brenner fell silent, obviously contemplating some new line of thought. Presently he continued: "I bet they're tuned to the radio outbursts! That's something nature never got around to do on Earth. . . . We have animals with sonar and even electric senses, but nothing ever developed a radio sense. Why bother where there was so much light?

"But it's different here. Jupiter is *drenched* with radio energy. It's worth while using it—maybe even tapping it. That thing could be a floating power plant!"

A new voice cut into the conversation.

"Mission Commander here. This is all very interesting, but there's a much more important matter to settle. *Is it intelligent?* If so, we've got to consider the First Contact directives."

"Until I came here," said Dr. Brenner, somewhat ruefully, "I would have sworn that anything that could make a shortwave antenna system *must* be intelligent. Now, I'm not sure. This could have evolved naturally. I suppose it's no more fantastic than the human eye."

"Then we have to play safe and assume intelligence. For the present, therefore, this expedition comes under all the clauses of the Prime directive."

There was a long silence while everyone on the radio circuit absorbed the implications of this. For the first time in the history of space flight, the rules that had been established through more than a century of argument might have to be applied. Man had—it was hoped—profited from his mistakes on Earth. Not only moral considerations, but also his own self-interest demanded that he should not repeat them among the planets. It could be disastrous to treat a superior intelligence as the American settlers had treated the Indians, or as almost everyone had treated the Africans. . . .

The first rule was: keep your distance. Make no attempt to approach, or even to communicate, until "they" have had plenty of time to study you. Exactly what was meant by "plenty of time," no one had ever been able to decide. It was left to the discretion of the man on the spot.

A responsibility of which he had never dreamed had descended upon Howard Falcon. In the few hours that remained to him on Jupiter, he might become the first ambassador of the human race.

And *that* was an irony so delicious that he almost wished the surgeons had restored to him the power of laughter.

7. Prime Directive

It was growing darker, but Falcon scarcely noticed as he strained his eyes toward that living cloud in the field of the telescope. The wind that was steadily sweeping *Kon-Tiki* around the funnel of the great whirlpool had now brought him within twelve miles of the creature.

If he got much closer than six, he would take evasive action. Though he felt certain that the medusa's electric weapons were short-ranged, he did not wish to put the matter to the test. That would be a problem for future explorers, and he wished them luck.

Now it was quite dark in the capsule. That was strange, because sunset was still hours away. Automatically, he glanced at the horizontally scanning radar, as he had done every few minutes. Apart from the medusa he was studying, there was no other object within about sixty miles of him.

Suddenly, with startling power, he heard the sound that had come booming out of the Jovian night—the throbbing beat that grew more and more rapid, then stopped in mid-crescendo. The whole capsule vibrated with it like a pea in a kettledrum.

Falcon realized two things almost simultaneously during the sudden, aching silence. *This* time the sound was not coming from thousands of miles away, over a radio circuit. It was in the very atmosphere around him.

The second thought was even more disturbing. He had quite forgotten—it was inexcusable, but there had been other apparently more important things on his mind—that most of the sky above him was completely blanked out by *Kon-Tiki*'s gas-bag. Being lightly silvered to conserve its heat, the great balloon was an effective shield both to radar and to vision.

He had known this, of course; it had been a minor defect of the design, tolerated because it did not appear important. It seemed very important to Howard Falcon now—as he saw that fence of gigantic tentacles, thicker than the trunks of any tree, descending all around the capsule.

He heard Brenner yelling: "Remember the Prime directive! Don't alarm it!" Before he could make an appropriate answer that overwhelming drum beat started again and drowned all other sounds.

The sign of a really skilled test pilot is how he reacts not to foreseeable emergencies, but to ones that nobody could have anticipated. Falcon did not hesitate for more than a second to analyze the situation. In a lightning-swift movement, he pulled the rip cord.

That word was an archaic survival from the days of the first hydrogen balloons; on *Kon-Tiki*, the rip cord did not tear open the gasbag, but merely operated a set of louvers around the upper curve of the envelope. At once the hot gas started to rush out; Kon-Tiki, deprived of her lift, began to fall swiftly in this gravity field two and a half times as strong as Earth's.

Falcon had a momentary glimpse of great tentacles whipping upward and away. He had just time to note that they were studded with large bladders or sacs, presumably to give them buoyancy, and that they ended in multitudes of thin feelers like the roots of a plant. He half expected a bolt of lightning—but nothing happened.

His precipitous rate of descent was slackening as the atmosphere thickened and the deflated envelope acted as a parachute. When Kon-Tiki had dropped about two miles, he felt that it was safe to close the louvers again. By the time he had restored buoyancy and was in equilibrium once more, he had lost another mile of altitude and was getting dangerously near his safety limit.

He peered anxiously through the overhead windows, though he did not expect to see anything except the obscuring bulk of the balloon. But he had sideslipped during his descent, and part of the medusa was just visible a couple of miles above him. It was much closer than he expected—and it was still coming down, faster than he would have believed possible.

Mission Control was calling anxiously. He shouted: "I'm O.K.— but it's still coming after me. I can't go any deeper."

That was not quite true. He could go a lot deeper—about one hundred and eighty miles. But it would be a one-way trip, and most of the journey would be of little interest to him.

Then, to his great relief, he saw that the medusa was leveling off, not quite a mile above him. Perhaps it had decided to approach this strange intruder with caution; or perhaps it, too, found this deeper layer uncomfortably hot. The temperature was over fifty degrees centigrade, and Falcon wondered how much longer his life-support system could handle matters.

Dr. Brenner was back on the circuit, still worrying about the Prime directive.

"Remember—it may only be inquisitive!" he cried, without much conviction. "Try not to frighten it!"

Falcon was getting rather tired of this advice and recalled a TV discussion he had once seen between a space lawyer and an astronaut. After the full implications of the Prime directive had been carefully spelled out, the incredulous spacer had exclaimed: "Then if there was no alternative, I must sit still and let myself be eaten?" The lawyer had not even cracked a smile when he answered: "That's an *excellent* summing up."

It had seemed funny at the time; it was not at all amusing now.

And then Falcon saw something that made him even more unhappy. The medusa was still hovering about a mile above him—but one of its tentacles was becoming incredibly elongated, and was stretching down toward *Kon-Tiki*, thinning out at the same time. As a boy he had once seen the funnel of a tornado descending from a storm cloud over the Kansas plains. The thing coming toward him now evoked vivid memories of that black, twisting snake in the sky.

"I'm rapidly running out of options," he reported to Mission Control. "I now have only a choice between frightening it—and giving it a bad stomach-ache. I don't think it will find *Kon-Tiki* very digestible, if that's what it has in mind."

He waited for comments from Brenner, but the biologist remained silent.

"Very well. It's twenty-seven minutes ahead of time, but I'm starting the ignition sequencer. I hope I'll have enough reserve to correct my orbit later."

He could no longer see the medusa; once more it was directly overhead. But he knew that the descending tentacle must now be very close to the balloon. It would take almost five minutes to bring the reactor up to full thrust. . . .

The fuser was primed. The orbit computer had not rejected the situation as wholly impossible. The air scoops were open, ready to gulp in tons of the surrounding hydrohelium on demand. Even under optimum conditions, this would have been the moment of truth—for there had been no way of testing how a nuclear ramjet would *really* work in the strange atmosphere of Jupiter.

Very gently something rocked *Kon-Tiki*. Falcon tried to ignore it.

Ignition had been planned at six miles higher, in an atmosphere of less than a quarter of the density and thirty degrees cooler. Too bad.

What was the shallowest dive he could get away with, for the air scoops to work? When the ram ignited, he'd be heading toward Jupiter with two and a half g's to help him get there. Could he possibly pull out in time?

A large, heavy hand patted the balloon. The whole vessel bobbed up and down, like one of the yo-yo's that had just become the craze on Earth.

Of course, Brenner *might* be perfectly right. Perhaps it was just trying to be friendly. Maybe he should try to talk to it over the radio. Which should it be: "Pretty pussy"? "Down, Fido"? Or "Take me to your leader"?

The tritium-deuterium ratio was correct. He was ready to light the candle, with a hundred-million-degree match.

The thin tip of the tentacle came slithering around the edge of the balloon some sixty yards away. It was about the size of an elephant's trunk, and by the delicate way it was moving appeared to be almost as sensitive. There were little palps at its end, like questing mouths. He was sure that Dr. Brenner would be fascinated.

This seemed about as good a time as any. He gave a swift scan of the entire control board, started the final four-second ignition count, broke the safety seal, and pressed the JETTISON switch.

There was a sharp explosion and an instant loss of weight. *Kon-Tiki* was falling freely, nose down. Overhead, the discarded balloon was racing upward, dragging the inquisitive tentacle with it. Falcon had no time to see if the gasbag actually hit the medusa, because at that moment the ramjet fired and he had other matters to think about.

A roaring column of hot hydrohelium was pouring out of the reactor nozzles, swiftly building up thrust—but *toward* Jupiter, not away from it. He could not pull out yet, for vector control was too sluggish. Unless he could gain complete control and achieve horizontal flight within the next five seconds, the vehicle would dive too deeply into the atmosphere and would be destroyed.

With agonizing slowness—those five seconds seemed like fifty— he managed to flatten out, then pull the nose upward. He glanced back only once and caught a final glimpse of the medusa, many miles away. *Kon-Tiki*'s discarded gasbag had apparently escaped from its grasp, for he could see no sign of it.

Now he was master once more—no longer drifting helplessly

on the winds of Jupiter, but riding his own column of atomic fire back to the stars. He was confident that the ramjet would steadily give him velocity and altitude until he had reached near-orbital speed at the fringes of the atmosphere. Then, with a brief burst of pure rocket power, he would regain the freedom of space.

Halfway to orbit, he looked south and saw the tremendous enigma of the Great Red Spot—that floating island twice the size of Earth—coming up over the horizon. He stared into its mysterious beauty until the computer warned him that conversion to rocket thrust was only sixty seconds ahead. He tore his gaze reluctantly away.

"Some other time," he murmured.

"What's that?" said Mission Control. "What did you say?"

"It doesn't matter," he replied.

8. Between Two Worlds

"You're a hero now, Howard," said Webster, "not just a celebrity. You've given them something to think about—injected some excitement into their lives. Not one in a million will actually travel to the Outer Giants, but the whole human race will go in imagination. And that's what counts."

"I'm glad to have made your job a little easier."

Webster was too old a friend to take offense at the note of irony. Yet it surprised him. And this was not the first change in Howard that he had noticed since the return from Jupiter.

The Administrator pointed to the famous sign on his desk, borrowed from an impresario of an earlier age: ASTONISH ME!

"I'm not ashamed of my job. New knowledge, new resources— they're all very well. But men also need novelty and excitement. Space travel has become routine; you've made it a great adventure once more. It will be a long, long time before we get Jupiter pigeonholed. And maybe longer still before we understand those medusae. I still think that one *knew* where your blind spot was. Anyway, have you decided on your next move? Saturn, Uranus, Neptune—you name it."

"I don't know. I've thought about Saturn, but I'm not really needed there. It's only one gravity, not two and a half like Jupiter. So men can handle it."

Men, thought Webster. He said "men." He's never done that before. And when did I last hear him use the word "we"? He's changing, slipping away from us. . . .

"Well," he said aloud, rising from his chair to conceal his slight uneasiness, "let's get the conference started. The cameras are all set up and everyone's waiting. You'll meet a lot of old friends."

He stressed the last word, but Howard showed no response. The leather mask of his face was becoming more and more difficult to read. Instead, he rolled back from the Administrator's desk, unlocked his undercarriage so that it no longer formed a chair, and rose on his hydraulics to his full seven feet of height. It had been good psychology on the part of the surgeons to give him that extra twelve inches, to compensate somewhat for all that he had lost when the *Queen* had crashed.

Falcon waited until Webster had opened the door, then pivoted neatly on his balloon tires and headed for it at a smooth and silent twenty miles an hour. The display of speed and precision was not flaunted arrogantly; rather, it had become quite unconscious.

Howard Falcon, who had once been a man and could still pass for one over a voice circuit, felt a calm sense of achievement—and, for the first time in years, something like peace of mind. Since his return from Jupiter, the nightmares had ceased. He had found his role at last.

He now knew why he had dreamed about that superchimp aboard the doomed *Queen Elizabeth*. Neither man nor beast, it was between two worlds; and so was he.

He alone could travel unprotected on the lunar surface. The life-support system inside the metal cylinder that had replaced his fragile body functioned equally well in space or under water. Gravity fields ten times that of Earth were an inconvenience, but nothing more. And no gravity was best of all. . . .

The human race was becoming more remote, the ties of kinship more tenuous. Perhaps these air-breathing, radiation-sensitive bundles of unstable carbon compounds had no right beyond the atmosphere; they should stick to their natural homes—Earth, Moon, Mars.

Some day the real masters of space would be machines, not men—and he was neither. Already conscious of his destiny, he took a somber pride in his unique loneliness—the first immortal midway between two orders of creation.

He would, after all, be an ambassador; between the old and the new—between the creatures of carbon and the creatures of metal who must one day supersede them.

Both would have need of him in the troubled centuries that lay ahead.

ISAAC ASIMOV

1920–1992

Isaac Asimov was born in Russia, in a small town near the city of Smolensk, but he didn't stay there. When he was three years old, his father sought a better life in America. The family emigrated to Brooklyn, New York, a borough from which Isaac hardly strayed for the next fifteen years of his life.

Although young Isaac was not geographically adventurous in the flesh, his mind wandered far from the little candy store his parents owned. Isaac was a reader. He read everything that came to his hand. (He was the only person I knew who had read the current edition of the *Encyclopedia Britannica* all the way through.) By his early teens his vicarious voyaging was spreading over galaxies, for he had found the reading he enjoyed most in the science fiction magazines.

From reading science fiction it was only a step to trying to write those stories for himself, and when he was seventeen he made the effort.

John Campbell's *Astounding* was the class magazine in the field, and Isaac aimed at the top. He was not an immediate success with Campbell. Campbell bounced his first couple of stories, "Marooned off Vesta" and "The Weapon Too Dreadful to Use," but they were not a total loss; Isaac promptly resubmitted them to the competing *Amazing Stories*, which snapped them up. But Isaac's diligence and talent won Campbell over, and before long he was a regular in *Astounding*. (Those two early rejections may have been a lucky break for Isaac. Bearing in mind Campbell's predilection for WASPish bylines, Isaac Asimov may narrowly have escaped being persuaded to become something like "Anson MacIsaacs"—saved by the fact that by the time Campbell got around to buying something from him, Isaac already had an established presence under his own name.)

Isaac's family finally settled down at 174 Windsor Place in Brooklyn, where the candy store they operated was just a block or two from Brooklyn's wonderful Prospect Park. It happened that at the time I lived diagonally across the park, on St. John's Place. We had met as fellow sf fans and wannabee writers—members of that nest of wannabees, the fan club called the "Futurians." (A good many of us Futurian wannabees did in fact make it, including C. M. Kornbluth, Damon Knight, James Blish, Donald A. Wollheim, Robert A. W. Lowndes, and Judith Merril, among others.) It was no trouble for a teenager to stroll a mile or so across the park for a visit on a nice day—especially in my own case, since I had the extra incentive of getting a free malted milk at the candy store from Isaac's mother—and Isaac and I became good friends, staying that way for nearly sixty years.

The late 1930s were a busy time for Isaac. Candy stores are open for long hours. When Isaac's parents weren't in the store, Isaac or one of his siblings (sister Marcia, brother Stanley) had to take over. That chore was not always a dead loss for Isaac, because when business was slow he spent the time reading. Not all the reading was overtly recreational (although reading of all kinds was always recreational for Isaac), since by then he had entered Columbia University and had to study to prepare for his planned entry into medical school.

Medical school didn't happen for Isaac. Those were the days of a pervasive genteel anti-Semitism in American society. Some important people somewhere were of the opinion that there were more Jewish doctors than was appropriate, and so "Jewish quotas" were established in medical schools. Isaac didn't make the cut, and had ultimately to settle for a Ph.D in biochemistry instead of the M.D. he had wanted. Too bad for his possible future patients, because he would have made a fine doctor; not so bad for the rest of us, because if Isaac had taken on the responsibilities of a physician, when would he have had time to write?

He did write. Found time somehow, kept it up. In those early years with Campbell at *Astounding* he began the continued works that are most closely associated with his name. First there were the "positronic robot" stories, later collected as *I, Robot* and half a dozen other volumes. Then some of that recreational reading produced a large dividend. Isaac had just finished *The Decline and Fall of the Roman Empire*, thought it suggested an interesting theme for science fiction stories, and wrote the novelette called *Foundation*.

Although I read nearly everything Isaac wrote until the 1950s, after which his massive production got hopelessly ahead of me, it is an odd fact that I never actually read the first few of the *Foundation* stories. I didn't have to. By then I had become a magazine editor on my own and had moved to Knickerbocker Village, down near the Manhattan Bridge in New York. On Sundays Isaac was likely to take the subway over for a visit. We'd go for a long walk— sometimes through nearby Chinatown, sometimes across the bridge to the Brooklyn side—and he would tell me the stories he had been writing. So when they came out in the magazines they were already old news to me.

When Isaac wrote his first robot story, he had no plans for a long-lasting series. It had simply occurred to him that a robot might make a good nursemaid for a small child, and so he wrote the story called "Robbie." Naturally he gave it first to Campbell, who bounced it at once. The trouble was, Campbell explained to Isaac, he hadn't really thought about what robots were actually going to be like. They couldn't just be clanking machines that did whatever their mechanical minds dictated. They had to be invested (the word *programmed* had not yet become fashionable) with certain basic constraints, else there was no telling what kind of trouble they might get into. Isaac took the point at once. The result was the famous "Three Laws of Robotics," which became gospel for all the robot stories which followed.

(Of course, that particular problem of self-willed robots has never arisen. No machine intelligence has yet shown any signs of enough self-awareness to need constraining. Actually, when the great computer guru, Marvin Minsky, became a graduate student at MIT he remembered those stories, and so one of his first projects was to try to program the three laws into an actual computer. That turned out to be impossible, but in the process Minsky learned something about the nature of hierarchical programming.)

After Campbell bounced "Robbie," Isaac did what came naturally, he gave it to me for one of my new magazines, and I published it, changing the title to "Strange Playfellow." (Isaac hated the title change. Over the years I changed a lot of his titles, and he always hated it, and always had the last word. Every one of his stories got republished time and again, and he changed the titles back.)

Although from the beginning Isaac was part of that astonishing efflorescence of new writers that made up the golden age of *Astounding*, the place in the pantheon earned by his earliest stories was relatively inconspicuous. The thing that decisively marked him as a unique voice in that wonderful chorus wasn't a story at all; it was an "article" about a fascinating, but entirely imaginary, chemical compound called thiotimoline, which had the unique property of time-traveling by going into solution even before the solvent was added. The article was a splendid joke, taken as gospel by a few of the more credulous readers, denounced as irresponsible fraud by others, but enjoyed by just about all. From then on it was clear that this writer was something special.

During World War II Isaac remained a civilian, but became a part of that interesting research team at the Philadelphia Navy Yard that included our other Grand Masters, Heinlein and de Camp (see volume one). It wasn't until the war was over that the draft caught Isaac. He spent a few uncomfortable months in the Pacific (very nearly getting to be one of the soldiers ordered to witness some A-bomb tests), and got out to finish his pursuit of a doctorate and get back to writing.

One of the things he wrote was a short novel, on order for the magazine *Startling Stories*. It was called *Grow Old with Me* (from Robert Browning's poem, "Rabbi ben Ezra"), and the editor of *Startling* didn't like the title or, for that matter, the story itself. Although he had asked Isaac to write it, he rejected it outright.

It was then no longer possible for Isaac to turn his rejects over to me to publish in one of my magazines, because I hadn't returned to editing at that time. What I had done, though, was to become a literary agent.

Something new had been added to the field of science fiction publishing after World War II. Until then almost no American science fiction appeared in book form; if you didn't read the magazines, you didn't read American science fiction. But in the late 1940s a few fans began to set up their own little semiprofessional publishing companies, reprinting in volume form some of the great magazine serials of the past. As the salesmen for the big trade houses visited bookstores, they took note of this new publishing category that seemed to have an active market. When they got back from their sales trips, they told their home offices about it; and so a couple of the big New York publishers decided to experiment with a science fiction line. As an agent, I began doing business with some of them, and persuaded Isaac to take *Grow Old with Me* out of the file drawer and let me show it to Doubleday, who bought it, changing the title to *Pebble in the Sky*. (That title Isaac never changed back. Clearly, he was more afraid of Walter I. Bradbury, Doubleday's editor, than he had ever been of me.)

Thus began the long history of Isaac's career as Doubleday's—and maybe the world's—premier sf author. Isaac had contributed a section to a text on biochemistry a little earlier, but *Pebble in the Sky* was the first book of his own to see print. More than four hundred followed.

As writers go, Isaac Asimov was obsessed. I do not think the man ever saw a piece of paper he didn't want to write on. He wrote incessantly, wherever he was, all the time.

He and I cruised together once, on the Holland-American ship *Rotterdam*. It was a most memorable voyage, stopping at exotic ports in the Caribbean and pausing just off the coast of Cape Canaveral to observe the glorious night-time launch of *Apollo 17* to the Moon. Isaac showed up for meals and to watch with the rest of us as that wonderful plume of rocket fire leaped up from the launch pad and crossed the sky overhead, but that was about it. Every other time, as I happened to pass his stateroom, I could hear the steady clickety-clack of his portable typewriter going inside.

It wasn't just science fiction that he wrote. Isaac had the wonderful trait of being able to read and absorb a score or a hundred books and journal articles, and then to pour the essence of them into one of his volumes explaining science—indeed, explaining *everything*—to his world of readers. He was a marvel. For a while he carried a jokey calling card, made for him by a friend, which described him simply as:

ISAAC ASIMOV
NATIONAL RESOURCE

And indeed he was.

Recommended Reading
by Isaac Asimov

Foundation
I, Robot
The Gods Themselves
Pebble in the Sky
I. Asimov

THE LAST QUESTION

The last question was asked for the first time, half in jest, on May 21, 2061, at a time when humanity first stepped into the light. The question came about as a result of a five-dollar bet over highballs, and it happened this way:

Alexander Adell and Bertram Lupov were two of the faithful attendants of Multivac. As well as any human beings could, they knew what lay behind the cold, clicking, flashing face—miles and miles of face—of that giant computer. They had at least a vague notion of the general plan of relays and circuits that had long since grown past the point where any single human could possibly have a firm grasp of the whole.

Multivac was self-adjusting and self-correcting. It had to be, for nothing human could adjust and correct it quickly enough or even adequately enough. So Adell and Lupov attended the monstrous giant only lightly and superficially, yet as well as any men could. They fed it data, adjusted questions to its needs and translated the answers that were issued. Certainly they, and all others like them, were fully entitled to share in the glory that was Multivac's.

For decades, Multivac had helped design the ships and plot the trajectories that enabled man to reach the Moon, Mars, and Venus, but past that, Earth's poor resources could not support the ships. Too much energy was needed for the long trips. Earth exploited its coal and uranium with increasing efficiency, but there was only so much of both.

But slowly Multivac learned enough to answer deeper questions more fundamentally, and on May 14, 2061, what had been theory, became fact.

The energy of the sun was stored, converted, and utilized directly on a planet-wide scale. All Earth turned off its burning coal, its fissioning uranium, and flipped the switch that connected all of it to a small station, one mile in diameter, circling the Earth at half the distance of the Moon. All Earth ran by invisible beams of sunpower.

Seven days had not sufficed to dim the glory of it and Adell and Lupov finally managed to escape from the public functions, and to meet in quiet where no one would think of looking for them, in the deserted underground chambers, where portions of the mighty buried body of Multivac showed. Unattended, idling, sorting data with contented lazy clickings, Multivac, too, had earned its vacation and the boys appreciated that. They had no intention, originally, of disturbing it.

They had brought a bottle with them, and their only concern at the moment was to relax in the company of each other and the bottle.

"It's amazing when you think of it," said Adell. His broad face had lines of weariness in it, and he stirred his drink slowly with a glass rod, watching the cubes of ice slur clumsily about. "All the energy we can possibly ever use for free. Enough energy, if we wanted to draw on it, to melt all Earth into a big drop of impure liquid iron, and still never miss the energy so used. All the energy we could ever use, forever and forever and forever."

Lupov cocked his head sideways. He had a trick of doing that when he wanted to be contrary, and he wanted to be contrary now, partly because he had had to carry the ice and glassware. "Not forever," he said.

"Oh, hell, just about forever. Till the sun runs down, Bert."

"That's not forever."

"All right, then. Billions and billions of years. Ten billion, maybe. Are you satisfied?"

Lupov put his fingers through his thinning hair as though to reassure himself that some was still left and sipped gently at his own drink. "Ten billion years isn't forever."

"Well, it will last our time, won't it?"

"So would the coal and uranium."

"All right, but now we can hook up each individual spaceship to the Solar Station, and it can go to Pluto and back a million times without ever worrying about fuel. You can't do *that* on coal and uranium. Ask Multivac, if you don't believe me."

"I don't have to ask Multivac. I know that."

"Then stop running down what Multivac's done for us," said Adell, blazing up, "It did all right."

"Who says it didn't? What I say is that a sun won't last forever. That's all I'm saying. We're safe for ten billion years, but then what?" Lupov pointed a slightly shaky finger at the other. "And don't say we'll switch to another sun."

There was a silence for a while. Adell put his glass to his lips only occasionally, and Lupov's eyes slowly closed. They rested.

Then Lupov's eyes snapped open. "You're thinking we'll switch to another sun when ours is done, aren't you?"

"I'm not thinking."

"Sure you are. You're weak on logic, that's the trouble with you. You're like the guy in the story who was caught in a sudden shower and who ran to a grove of trees and got under one. He wasn't worried, you see, because he figured when one tree got wet through, he would just get under another one."

"I get it," said Adell. "Don't shout. When the sun is done, the other stars will be gone, too."

"Darn right they will," muttered Lupov. "It all had a beginning in the original cosmic explosion, whatever that was, and it'll all have an end when all the stars run down. Some run down faster than others. Hell, the giants won't last a hundred million years. The sun will last ten billion years and maybe the dwarfs will last two hundred billion for all the good they are. But just give us a trillion years and everything will be dark. Entropy has to increase to maximum, that's all."

"I know all about entropy," said Adell, standing on his dignity.

"The hell you do."

"I know as much as you do."

"Then you know everything's got to run down someday."

"All right. Who says they won't?"

"You did, you poor sap. You said we had all the energy we needed, forever. You said 'forever.' "

It was Adell's turn to be contrary. "Maybe we can build things up again someday," he said.

"Never."

"Why not? Someday."

"Never."

"Ask Multivac."

"*You* ask Multivac. I dare you. Five dollars says it can't be done."

Adell was just drunk enough to try, just sober enough to be able to phrase the necessary symbols and operations into a question which, in words, might have corresponded to this: Will mankind one day without the net expenditure of energy be able to restore the sun to its full youthfulness even after it had died of old age?

Or maybe it could be put more simply like this: How can the net amount of entropy of the universe be massively decreased?

Multivac fell dead and silent. The slow flashing of lights ceased, the distant sounds of clicking relays ended.

Then, just as the frightened technicians felt they could hold their breath no longer, there was a sudden springing to life of the teletype attached to that portion of Multivac. Five words were printed: INSUFFICIENT DATA FOR MEANINGFUL ANSWER.

"No bet," whispered Lupov. They left hurriedly.

By next morning, the two, plagued with throbbing head and cottony mouth, had forgotten the incident.

Jerrodd, Jerrodine, and Jerrodette I and II watched the starry picture in the visiplate change as the passage through hyperspace was completed in its non-time lapse. At once, the even powdering of stars gave way to the predominance of a single bright shining disk, the size of a marble, centered on the viewing-screen.

"That's X-23," said Jerrodd confidently. His thin hands clamped tightly behind his back and the knuckles whitened.

The little Jerrodettes, both girls, had experienced the hyperspace passage for the first time in their lives and were self-conscious over the momentary sensation of inside-outness. They buried their giggles and chased one another wildly about their mother, screaming, "We've reached X-23—we've reached X-23—we've—"

"Quiet, children," said Jerrodine sharply. "Are you sure, Jerrodd?"

"What is there to be but sure?" asked Jerrodd, glancing up at the bulge of featureless metal just under the ceiling. It ran the length of the room, disappearing through the wall at either end. It was as long as the ship.

Jerrodd scarcely knew a thing about the thick rod of metal except that it was called a Microvac, that one asked it questions if one wished; that if one did not it still had its task of guiding the ship to a preordered destination; of feeding on energies from the various Subgalactic Power Stations; of computing the equations for the hyperspatial jumps.

Jerrodd and his family had only to wait and live in the comfortable residence quarters of the ship.

Someone had once told Jerrodd that the "ac" at the end of "Microvac" stood for "automatic computer" in ancient English, but he was on the edge of forgetting even that.

Jerrodine's eyes were moist as she watched the visiplate. "I can't help it. I feel funny about leaving Earth."

"Why, for Pete's sake?" demanded Jerrodd. "We had nothing there. We'll have everything on X-23. You won't be alone. You won't be a pioneer. There are over a million people on the planet already. Good Lord, our great-grandchildren will be looking for new worlds because X-23 will be overcrowded." Then, after a reflective pause, "I tell you, it's a lucky thing the computers worked out interstellar travel the way the race is growing."

"I know, I know," said Jerrodine miserably.

Jerrodette I said promptly, "Our Microvac is the best Microvac in the world."

"I think so, too," said Jerrodd, tousling her hair.

It was a nice feeling to have a Microvac of your own and Jerrodd was glad he was part of his generation and no other. In his father's youth, the only computers had been tremendous machines taking up a hundred square miles of land. There was only one to a planet. Planetary ACs they were called. They had been growing in size steadily for a thousand years and then, all at once, came refinement. In place of transistors, had come molecular valves so that even the largest Planetary AC could be put into a space only half the volume of a spaceship.

Jerrodd felt uplifted, as he always did when he thought that his own personal Microvac was many times more complicated than the ancient and primitive Microvac that had first tamed the Sun, and almost as complicated as Earth's Planetary AC (the largest) that had first solved the problem of hyperspatial travel and had made trips to the stars possible.

"So many stars, so many planets," sighed Jerrodine, busy with her own thoughts. "I suppose families will be going to new planets forever, the way we are now."

"Not forever," said Jerrodd, with a smile. "It will all stop someday, but not for billions of years. Many billions. Even the stars run down, you know. Entropy must increase."

"What's entropy, Daddy?" shrilled Jerrodette II.

"Entropy, little sweet, is just a word which means the amount of running-down of the universe. Everything runs down, you know, like your little walkie-talkie robot, remember?"

"Can't you just put in a new power-unit, like with my robot?"

"The stars *are* the power-units, dear. Once they're gone, there are no more power-units."

Jerrodette I at once set up a howl. "Don't let them, Daddy. Don't let the stars run down."

"Now look what you've done," whispered Jerrodine, exasperated.

"How was I to know it would frighten them?" Jerrodd whispered back.

"Ask the Microvac," wailed Jerrodette I. "Ask him how to turn the stars on again."

"Go ahead," said Jerrodine. "It will quiet them down." (Jerrodette II was beginning to cry, also.)

Jerrodd shrugged. "Now, now, honeys. I'll ask Microvac. Don't worry, he'll tell us."

He asked the Microvac, adding quickly, "Print the answer."

Jerrodd cupped the strip of thin cellufilm and said cheerfully,

"See now, the Microvac says it will take care of everything when the time comes so don't worry."

Jerrodine said, "And now, children, it's time for bed. We'll be in our new home soon."

Jerrodd read the words on the cellufilm again before destroying it: INSUFFICIENT DATA FOR MEANINGFUL ANSWER.

He shrugged and looked at the visiplate, X-23 was just ahead.

VJ-23X of Lameth stared into the black depths of the three-dimensional, small-scale map of the Galaxy and said, "Are we ridiculous, I wonder, in being so concerned about the matter?"

MQ-17J of Nicron shook his head. "I think not. You know the Galaxy will be filled in five years at the present rate of expansion."

Both seemed in their early twenties, both were tall and perfectly formed.

"Still," said VJ-23X, "I hesitate to submit a pessimistic report to the Galactic Council."

"I wouldn't consider any other kind of report. Stir them up a bit. We've got to stir them up."

VJ-23X sighed. "Space is infinite. A hundred billion Galaxies are there for the taking. More."

"A hundred billion is not infinite and it's getting less infinite all the time. Consider! Twenty thousand years ago, mankind first solved the problem of utilizing stellar energy, and a few centuries later, interstellar travel became possible. It took mankind a million years to fill one small world and then only fifteen thousand years to fill the rest of the Galaxy. Now the population doubles every ten years—"

VJ-23X interrupted. "We can thank immortality for that."

"Very well. Immortality exists and we have to take it into account. I admit it has its seamy side, this immortality. The Galactic AC has solved many problems for us, but in solving the problem of preventing old age and death, it has undone all its other solutions."

"Yet you wouldn't want to abandon life, I suppose."

"Not at all," snapped MQ-17J, softening it at once to, "Not yet. I'm by no means old enough. How old are you?"

"Two hundred twenty-three. And you?"

"I'm still under two hundred. —But to get back to my point. Population doubles every ten years. Once this Galaxy is filled, we'll have filled another in ten years. Another ten years and we'll have filled two more. Another decade, four more. In a hundred years, we'll have filled a thousand Galaxies. In a thousand years, a million Galaxies. In ten thousand years, the entire known Universe. Then what?"

VJ-23X said, "As a side issue, there's a problem of transportation. I wonder how many sunpower units it will take to move Galaxies of individuals from one Galaxy to the next."

"A very good point. Already, mankind consumes two sunpower units per year."

"Most of it's wasted. After all, our own Galaxy alone pours out a thousand sunpower units a year and we only use two of those."

"Granted, but even with a hundred per cent efficiency, we only stave off the end. Our energy requirements are going up in a geometric progression even faster than our population. We'll run out of energy even sooner than we run out of Galaxies. A good point. A very good point."

"We'll just have to build new stars out of interstellar gas."

"Or out of dissipated heat?" asked MQ-17J, sarcastically.

"There may be some way to reverse entropy. We ought to ask the Galactic AC."

VJ-23X was not really serious, but MQ-17J pulled out his AC-contact from his pocket and placed it on the table before him.

"I've half a mind to," he said. "It's something the human race will have to face someday."

He stared somberly at his small AC-contact. It was only two inches cubed and nothing in itself, but it was connected through hyperspace with the great Galactic AC that served all mankind. Hyperspace considered, it was an integral part of the Galactic AC.

MQ-17J paused to wonder if someday in his immortal life he would get to see the Galactic AC. It was on a little world of its own, a spider webbing of force beams holding the matter within which surges of submesons took the place of the old clumsy molecular valves. Yet despite its sub-etheric workings, the Galactic AC was known to be a full thousand feet across.

MQ-17J asked suddenly of his AC-contact, "Can entropy ever be reversed?"

VJ-23X looked startled and said at once, "Oh, say, I didn't really mean to have you ask that."

"Why not?"

"We both know entropy can't be reversed. You can't turn smoke and ash back into a tree."

"Do you have trees on your world?" asked MQ-17J.

The sound of the Galactic AC startled them into silence. Its voice came thin and beautiful out of the small AC-contact on the desk. It said: THERE IS INSUFFICIENT DATA FOR A MEAN-INGFUL ANSWER.

VJ-23X said, "See!"

The two men thereupon returned to the question of the report they were to make to the Galactic Council.

Zee Prime's mind spanned the new Galaxy with a faint interest in the countless twists of stars that powdered it. He had never seen this one before. Would he ever see them all? So many of them, each with its load of humanity. —But a load that was almost a dead weight. More and more, the real essence of men was to be found out here, in space.

Minds, not bodies! The immortal bodies remained back on the planets, in suspension over the eons. Sometimes they roused for material activity but that was growing rarer. Few new individuals were coming into existence to join the incredibly mighty throng, but what matter? There was little room in the Universe for new individuals.

Zee Prime was roused out of his reverie upon coming across the wispy tendrils of another mind.

"I am Zee Prime," said Zee Prime. "And you?"

"I am Dee Sub Wun. Your Galaxy?"

"We call it only the Galaxy. And you?"

"We call ours the same. All men call their Galaxy their Galaxy and nothing more. Why not?"

"True. Since all Galaxies are the same."

"Not all Galaxies. On one particular Galaxy the race of man must have originated. That makes it different."

Zee Prime said, "On which one?"

"I cannot say. The Universal AC would know."

"Shall we ask him? I am suddenly curious."

Zee Prime's perceptions broadened until the Galaxies themselves shrank and became a new, more diffuse powdering on a much larger background. So many hundreds of billions of them, all with their immortal beings, all carrying their load of intelligences with minds that drifted freely through space. And yet one of them was unique among them all in being the original Galaxy. One of them had, in its vague and distant past, a period when it was the only Galaxy populated by man.

Zee Prime was consumed with curiosity to see this Galaxy and he called out: "Universal AC! On which Galaxy did mankind originate?"

The Universal AC heard, for on every world and throughout space, it had its receptors ready, and each receptor lead through hyperspace to some unknown point where the Universal AC kept itself aloof.

Zee Prime knew of only one man whose thoughts had penetrated within sensing distance of Universal AC, and he reported only a shining globe, two feet across, difficult to see.

"But how can that be all of Universal AC?" Zee Prime had asked.

"Most of it," had been the answer, "is in hyperspace. In what form it is there I cannot imagine."

Nor could anyone, for the day had long since passed, Zee Prime knew, when any man had any part of the making of a Universal AC. Each Universal AC designed and constructed its successor. Each, during its existence of a million years or more accumulated the necessary data to build a better and more intricate, more capable successor in which its own store of data and individuality would be submerged.

The Universal AC interrupted Zee Prime's wandering thoughts, not with words, but with guidance. Zee Prime's mentality was guided into the dim sea of Galaxies and one in particular enlarged into stars.

A thought came, infinitely distant, but infinitely clear. "THIS IS THE ORIGINAL GALAXY OF MAN."

But it was the same after all, the same as any other, and Zee Prime stifled his disappointment.

Dee Sub Wun, whose mind had accompanied the other, said suddenly, "And is one of these stars the original star of Man?"

The Universal AC said, "MAN'S ORIGINAL STAR HAS GONE NOVA. IT IS A WHITE DWARF."

"Did the men upon it die?" asked Zee Prime, startled and without thinking.

The Universal AC said, "A NEW WORLD, AS IN SUCH CASES WAS CONSTRUCTED FOR THEIR PHYSICAL BODIES IN TIME."

"Yes, of course," said Zee Prime, but a sense of loss overwhelmed him even so. His mind released its hold on the original Galaxy of Man, let it spring back and lose itself among the blurred pinpoints. He never wanted to see it again.

Dee Sub Wun said, "What is wrong?"

"The stars are dying. The original star is dead."

"They must all die. Why not?"

"But when all energy is gone, our bodies will finally die, and you and I with them."

"It will take billions of years."

"I do not wish it to happen even after billions of years. Universal AC! How may stars be kept from dying?"

Dee Sub Wun said in amusement, "You're asking how entropy might be reversed in direction."

And the Universal AC answered: "THERE IS AS YET INSUFFICIENT DATA FOR A MEANINGFUL ANSWER."

Zee Prime's thoughts fled back to his own Galaxy. He gave no further thought to Dee Sub Wun, whose body might be waiting on a Galaxy a trillion light-years away, or on the star next to Zee Prime's own. It didn't matter.

Unhappily, Zee Prime began collecting interstellar hydrogen out of which to build a small star of his own. If the stars must someday die, at least some could yet be built.

•   •   •

Man considered with himself, for in a way, Man, mentally, was one. He consisted of a trillion, trillion, trillion ageless bodies, each in its place, each resting quiet and incorruptible, each cared for by perfect automatons, equally incorruptible, while the minds of all the bodies freely melted one into the other, indistinguishable.

Man said, "The Universe is dying."

Man looked about at the dimming Galaxies. The giant stars, spendthrifts, were gone long ago, back in the dimmest of the dim far past. Almost all stars were white dwarfs, fading to the end.

New stars had been built of the dust between the stars, some by natural processes, some by Man himself, and those were going, too. White dwarfs might yet be crashed together and of the mighty forces so released, new stars built, but only one star for every thousand white dwarfs destroyed, and those would come to an end, too.

Man said, "Carefully husbanded, as directed by the Cosmic AC, the energy that is even yet left in all the Universe will last for billions of years."

"But even so," said Man, "eventually it will all come to an end. However it may be husbanded, however stretched out, the energy once expended is gone and cannot be restored. Entropy must increase forever to the maximum."

Man said, "Can entropy not be reversed? Let us ask the Cosmic AC."

The Cosmic AC surrounded them but not in space. Not a fragment of it was in space. It was in hyperspace and made of something that was neither matter nor energy. The question of its size and nature no longer had meaning in any terms that Man could comprehend.

"Cosmic AC," said Man, "how may entropy be reversed?"

The Cosmic AC said, "THERE IS AS YET INSUFFICIENT DATA FOR A MEANINGFUL ANSWER."

Man said, "Collect additional data."

The Cosmic AC said, "I WILL DO SO. I HAVE BEEN DOING SO FOR A HUNDRED BILLION YEARS. MY PREDECESSORS AND I HAVE BEEN ASKED THIS QUESTION MANY TIMES. ALL THE DATA I HAVE REMAINS INSUFFICIENT."

"Will there come a time," said Man, "when data will be sufficient or is the problem insoluble in all conceivable circumstances?"

The Cosmic AC said, "NO PROBLEM IS INSOLUBLE IN ALL CONCEIVABLE CIRCUMSTANCES."

Man said, "When will you have enough data to answer the question?"

The Cosmic AC said, "THERE IS AS YET INSUFFICIENT DATA FOR A MEANINGFUL ANSWER."

"Will you keep working on it?" asked Man.

The Cosmic AC said, "I WILL."

Man said, "We shall wait."

The stars and Galaxies died and snuffed out, and space grew black after ten trillion years of running down.

One by one Man fused with AC, each physical body losing its mental identity in a manner that was somehow not a loss but a gain.

Man's last mind paused before fusion, looking over a space that included nothing but the dregs of one last dark star and nothing besides but incredibly thin matter, agitated randomly by the tag ends of heat wearing out, asymptotically, to the absolute zero.

Man said, "AC, is this the end? Can this chaos not be reversed into the Universe once more? Can that not be done?"

AC said, "THERE IS AS YET INSUFFICIENT DATA FOR A MEANINGFUL ANSWER."

Man's last mind fused and only AC existed—and that in hyperspace.

Matter and energy had ended and with it space and time. Even AC existed only for the sake of the one last question that it had never answered from the time a half-drunken computer ten trillion years before had asked the question of a computer that was to AC far less than was a man to Man.

All other questions had been answered, and until this last question was answered also, AC might not release his consciousness.

All collected data had come to a final end. Nothing was left to be collected.

But all collected data had yet to be completely correlated and put together in all possible relationships.

A timeless interval was spent in doing that.

And it came to pass that AC learned how to reverse the direction of entropy.

But there was now no man to whom AC might give the answer of the last question. No matter. The answer—by demonstration—would take care of that, too.

For another timeless interval, AC thought how best to do this. Carefully, AC organized the program.

The consciousness of AC encompassed all of what had once been a Universe and brooded over what was now Chaos. Step by step, it must be done.

And AC said, "LET THERE BE LIGHT!"

And there was light—

IT'S SUCH A BEAUTIFUL DAY

On April 12, 2117, the field-modulator brake-valve in the Door belonging to Mrs. Richard Hanshaw depolarized for reasons unknown. As a result, Mrs. Hanshaw's day was completely upset and her son, Richard, Jr., first developed his strange neurosis.

It was not the type of thing you would find listed as a neurosis in the usual textbooks and certainly young Richard behaved, in most respects, just as a well-brought-up twelve-year-old in prosperous circumstances ought to behave.

And yet from April 12 on, Richard Hanshaw, Jr., could only with regret ever persuade himself to go through a Door.

Of all this, on April 12, Mrs. Hanshaw had no premonition. She woke in the morning (an ordinary morning) as her mekkano slithered gently into her room, with a cup of coffee on a small tray. Mrs. Hanshaw was planning a visit to New York in the afternoon and she had several things to do first that could not quite be trusted to a mekkano, so after one or two sips, she stepped out of bed.

The mekkano backed away, moving silently along the diamagnetic field that kept its oblong body half an inch above the floor, and moved back to the kitchen, where its simple computer was quite adequate to set the proper controls on the various kitchen appliances in order that an appropriate breakfast might be prepared.

Mrs. Hanshaw, having bestowed the usual sentimental glance

upon the cubograph of her dead husband, passed through the stages of her morning ritual with a certain contentment. She could hear her son across the hall clattering through his, but she knew she need not interfere with him. The mekkano was well adjusted to see to it, as a matter of course, that he was showered, that he had on a change of clothing, and that he would eat a nourishing breakfast.

The tergoshower she had had installed the year before made the morning wash and dry so quick and pleasant that, really, she felt certain Dickie would wash even without supervision.

On a morning like this, when she was busy, it would certainly not be necessary for her to do more than deposit a casual peck on the boy's cheek before he left. She heard the soft chime the mekkano sounded to indicate approaching school time and she floated down the force-lift to the lower floor (her hair-style for the day only sketchily designed, as yet) in order to perform that motherly duty.

She found Richard standing at the door, with his text-reels and pocket projector dangling by their strap and a frown on his face.

"Say, Mom," he said, looking up, "I dialed the school's co-ords but nothing happens."

She said, almost automatically, "Nonsense, Dickie. I never heard of such a thing."

"Well, you try."

Mrs. Hanshaw tried a number of times. Strange, the school door was always set for general reception. She tried other co-ordinates. Her friends' Doors might not be set for reception, but there would be a signal at least, and then she could explain.

But nothing happened at all. The Door remained an inactive gray barrier despite all her manipulations. It was obvious that the Door was out of order—and only five months after its annual fall inspection by the company.

She was quite angry about it.

It *would* happen on a day when she had so much planned. She thought petulantly of the fact that a month earlier she had decided against installing a subsidiary Door on the ground that it was an unnecessary expense. How was she to know that Doors were getting to be so *shoddy?*

She stepped to the visiphone while the anger still burned in her and said to Richard, "You just go down the road, Dickie, and use the Williamsons' Door."

Ironically, in view of later developments, Richard balked. "Aw, gee, Mom, I'll get dirty. Can't I stay home till the Door is fixed?"

And, as ironically, Mrs. Hanshaw insisted. With her finger on the combination board of the phone, she said, "You won't get dirty if you put flexies on your shoes, and don't forget to brush yourself well before you go into their house."

"But, golly—"

"No back-talk, Dickie. You've got to be in school. Just let me see you walk out of here. And quickly, or you'll be late."

The mekkano, an advanced model and very responsive, was already standing before Richard with flexies in one appendage.

Richard pulled the transparent plastic shields over his shoes and moved down the hall with visible reluctance. "I don't even know how to work this thing, Mom."

"You just push that button," Mrs. Hanshaw called. "The red button. Where it says 'For Emergency Use.' And don't dawdle. Do you want the mekkano to go along with you?"

"Gosh, no," he called back, morosely, "what do you think I am? A baby? Gosh!" His muttering was cut off by a slam.

With flying fingers, Mrs. Hanshaw punched the appropriate combination on the phone board and thought of the things she intended saying to the company about this.

Joe Bloom, a reasonable young man, who had gone through technology school with added training in force-field mechanics, was at the Hanshaw residence in less than half an hour. He was really quite competent, though Mrs. Hanshaw regarded his youth with deep suspicion.

She opened the movable house-panel when he first signaled and her sight of him was as he stood there, brushing at himself vigorously to remove the dust of the open air. He took off his flexies and dropped them where he stood. Mrs. Hanshaw closed the house-panel against the flash of raw sunlight that had entered. She found herself irrationally hoping that the step-by-step trip from the public Door had been an unpleasant one. Or perhaps that the public Door itself had been out of order and the youth had had to lug his tools even farther than the necessary two hundred yards. She wanted the

Company, or its representative at least, to suffer a bit. It would teach them what broken Doors meant.

But he seemed cheerful and unperturbed as he said, "Good morning, ma'am. I came to see about your Door."

"I'm glad someone did," said Mrs. Hanshaw, ungraciously. "My day is quite ruined."

"Sorry, ma'am. What seems to be the trouble?"

"It just won't work. Nothing at all happens when you adjust co-ords," said Mrs. Hanshaw. "There was no warning at all. I had to send my son out to the neighbors through that—that thing."

She pointed to the entrance through which the repair man had come.

He smiled and spoke out of the conscious wisdom of his own specialized training in Doors. "That's a door, too, ma'am. You don't give that kind a capital letter when you write it. It's a hand-door, sort of. It used to be the only kind once."

"Well, at least it works. My boy's had to go out in the dirt and germs."

"It's not bad outside today, ma'am," he said, with the connoisseur like air of one whose profession forced him into the open nearly every day. "Sometimes it *is* real unpleasant. But I guess you want I should fix this here Door, ma'am, so I'll get on with it."

He sat down on the floor, opened the large tool case he had brought in with him and in half a minute, by use of a point-demagnetizer, he had the control panel removed and a set of intricate vitals exposed.

He whistled to himself as he placed the fine electrodes of the field-analyzer on numerous points, studying the shifting needles on the dials. Mrs. Hanshaw watched him, arms folded.

Finally, he said, "Well, here's something," and with a deft twist, he disengaged the brake-valve.

He tapped it with a fingernail and said, "This here brake-valve is depolarized, ma'am. There's your whole trouble." He ran his finger along the little pigeonholes in his tool case and lifted out a duplicate of the object he had taken from the door mechanism. "These things just go all of a sudden. Can't predict it."

He put the control panel back and stood up. "It'll work now, ma'am."

He punched a reference combination, blanked it, then punched another. Each time, the dull gray of the Door gave way to a deep, velvety blackness. He said, "Will you sign here, ma'am? and put down your charge number, too, please? Thank you, ma'am."

He punched a new combination, that of his home factory, and with a polite touch of finger to forehead, he stepped through the Door. As his body entered the blackness, it cut off sharply. Less and less of him was visible and the tip of his tool case was the last thing that showed. A second after he had passed through completely, the Door turned back to dull gray.

Half an hour later, when Mrs. Hanshaw had finally completed her interrupted preparations and was fuming over the misfortune of the morning, the phone buzzed annoyingly and her real troubles began.

Miss Elizabeth Robbins was distressed. Little Dick Hanshaw had always been a good pupil. She hated to report him like this. And yet, she told herself, his actions were certainly queer. And she would talk to his mother, not to the principal.

She slipped out to the phone during the morning study period, leaving a student in charge. She made her connection and found herself staring at Mrs. Hanshaw's handsome and somewhat formidable head.

Miss Robbins quailed, but it was too late to turn back. She said, diffidently, "Mrs. Hanshaw, I'm Miss Robbins." She ended on a rising note.

Mrs. Hanshaw looked blank, then said, "Richard's teacher?" That, too, ended on a rising note.

"That's right. I called you, Mrs. Hanshaw," Miss Robbins plunged right into it, "to tell you that Dick was quite late to school this morning."

"He *was*? But that couldn't be. I saw him leave."

Miss Robbins looked astonished. She said, "You mean you saw him use the Door?"

Mrs. Hanshaw said quickly, "Well, no. Our Door was temporarily out of order. I sent him to a neighbor and he used that Door."

"Are you sure?"

"Of course I'm sure. I wouldn't lie to you."

"No, no, Mrs. Hanshaw. I wasn't implying that at all. I meant are you sure he found the way to the neighbor? He might have got lost."

"Ridiculous. We have the proper maps, and I'm sure Richard knows the location of every house in District A-3." Then, with the quiet pride of one who knows what is her due, she added, "Not that he ever needs to know, of course. The co-ords are all that are necessary at any time."

Miss Robbins, who came from a family that had always had to economize rigidly on the use of its Doors (the price of the power being what it was) and who had therefore run errands on foot until quite an advanced age, resented the pride. She said, quite clearly, "Well, I'm afraid, Mrs. Hanshaw, that Dick did not use the neighbor's Door. He was over an hour late to school and the condition of his flexies made it quite obvious that he tramped cross-country. They were *muddy*."

"*Muddy?*" Mrs. Hanshaw repeated the emphasis on the word. "What did he say? What was his excuse?"

Miss Robbins couldn't help but feel a little glad at the discomfiture of the other woman. She said, "He wouldn't talk about it. Frankly, Mrs. Hanshaw, he seems ill. That's why I called you. Perhaps you might want to have a doctor look at him."

"Is he running a temperature?" The mother's voice went shrill.

"Oh, no. I don't mean physically ill. It's just his attitude and the look in his eyes." She hesitated, then said with every attempt at delicacy, "I thought perhaps a routine checkup with a psychic probe—"

She didn't finish. Mrs. Hanshaw, in a chilled voice and with what was as close to a snort as her breeding would permit, said, "Are you implying that Richard is *neurotic?*"

"Oh, no, Mrs. Hanshaw, but—"

"It certainly sounded so. The idea! He has always been perfectly healthy. I'll take this up with him when he gets home. I'm sure there's a perfectly normal explanation which he'll give to *me*."

The connection broke abruptly, and Miss Robbins felt hurt and uncommonly foolish. After all she had only tried to help, to fulfill what she considered an obligation to her students.

She hurried back to the classroom with a glance at the metal face of the wall clock. The study period was drawing to an end. English Composition next.

But her mind wasn't completely on English Composition. Automatically, she called the students to have them read selections from their literary creations. And occasionally she punched one of those selections on tape and ran it through the small vocalizer to show the students how English *should* be read.

The vocalizer's mechanical voice, as always, dripped perfection, but, again as always, lacked character. Sometimes, she wondered if it was wise to try to train the students into a speech that was divorced from individuality and geared only to a mass-average accent and intonation.

Today, however, she had no thought for that. It was Richard Hanshaw she watched. He sat quietly in his seat, quite obviously indifferent to his surroundings. He was lost deep in himself and just not the same boy he had been. It was obvious to her that he had had some unusual experience that morning and, really, she was right to call his mother, although perhaps she ought not to have made the remark about the probe. Still it was quite the thing these days. All sorts of people get probed. There wasn't any disgrace attached to it. Or there shouldn't be, anyway.

She called on Richard, finally. She had to call twice, before he responded and rose to his feet.

The general subject assigned had been: "If you had your choice of traveling on some ancient vehicle, which would you choose, and why?" Miss Robbins tried to use the topic every semester. It was a good one because it carried a sense of history with it. It forced the youngster to think about the manner of living of people in past ages.

She listened while Richard Hanshaw read in a low voice.

"If I had my choice of ancient vehicles," he said, pronouncing the "h" in vehicles, "I would choose the stratoliner. It travels slow like all vehicles but it is clean. Because it travels in the stratosphere, it must be all enclosed so that you are not likely to catch disease. You can see the stars if it is night time almost as good as in a planetarium. If you look down you can see the Earth like a map or maybe see clouds—" He went on for several hundred more words.

She said brightly when he had finished reading, "It's pronounced vee-ick-ulls, Richard. No 'h.' Accent on the first syllable. And you don't say 'travels slow' or 'see good.' What do you say, class?"

There was a small chorus of responses and she went on, "That's right. Now what is the difference between an adjective and an adverb? Who can tell me?"

And so it went. Lunch passed. Some pupils stayed to eat; some went home. Richard stayed. Miss Robbins noted that, as usually he didn't.

The afternoon passed, too, and then there was the final bell and the usual upsurging hum as twenty-five boys and girls rattled their belongings together and took their leisurely place in line.

Miss Robbins clapped her hands together. "Quickly, children. Come, Zelda, take your place."

"I dropped my tape-punch, Miss Robbins," shrilled the girl, defensively.

"Well, pick it up, pick it up. Now children, be brisk, be brisk."

She pushed the button that slid a section of the wall into a recess and revealed the gray blankness of a large Door. It was not the usual Door that the occasional student used in going home for lunch, but an advanced model that was one of the prides of this well-to-do private school.

In addition to its double width, it possessed a large and impressively gear-filled "automatic serial finder" which was capable of adjusting the Door for a number of different co-ordinates at automatic intervals.

At the beginning of the semester, Miss Robbins always had to spend an afternoon with the mechanic, adjusting the device for the coordinates of the homes of the new class. But then, thank goodness, it rarely needed attention for the remainder of the term.

The class lined up alphabetically, first girls, then boys. The Door went velvety black and Hester Adams waved her hand and stepped through. "By-y-y—"

The "bye" was cut off in the middle, as it almost always was.

The Door went gray, then black again, and Theresa Cantrocchi went through. Gray, black, Zelda Charlowicz. Gray, black, Patricia Coombs. Gray, black, Sara May Evans.

The line grew smaller as the Door swallowed them one by one, depositing each in her home. Of course, an occasional mother forgot to leave the house Door on special reception at the appropriate time and then the school Door remained gray. Automatically, after a minute-long wait, the Door went on to the next combination in line and the pupil in question had to wait till it was all over, after which a phone call to the forgetful parent would set things right. This was always bad for the pupils involved, especially the sensitive ones who took seriously the implication that they were little thought of at home. Miss Robbins always tried to impress this on visiting parents, but it happened at least once every semester just the same.

The girls were all through now. John Abramowitz stepped through and then Edwin Byrne—

Of course, another trouble, and a more frequent one was the boy or girl who got into line out of place. They *would* do it despite the teacher's sharpest watch, particularly at the beginning of the term when the proper order was less familiar to them.

When that happened, children would be popping into the wrong houses by the half-dozen and would have to be sent back. It always meant a mixup that took minutes to straighten out and parents were invariably irate.

Miss Robbins was suddenly aware that the line had stopped. She spoke sharply to the boy at the head of the line.

"Step through, Samuel. What are you waiting for?"

Samuel Jones raised a complacent countenance and said, "It's not my combination, Miss Robbins."

"Well, whose is it?" She looked impatiently down the line of five remaining boys. Who was out of place?

"It's Dick Hanshaw's, Miss Robbins."

"Where is he?"

Another boy answered, with the rather repulsive tone of self-righteousness all children automatically assume in reporting the deviations of their friends to elders in authority, "He went through the fire door, Miss Robbins."

"What?"

The schoolroom Door had passed on to another combination and Samuel Jones passed through. One by one, the rest followed.

Miss Robbins was alone in the classroom. She stepped to the fire door. It was a small affair, manually operated, and hidden behind a bend in the wall so that it would not break up the uniform structure of the room. She opened it a crack. It was there as a means of escape from the building in case of fire, a device which was enforced by an anachronistic law that did not take into account the modern methods of automatic fire-fighting that all public buildings used. There was nothing outside, but the—outside. The sunlight was harsh and a dusty wind was blowing.

Miss Robbins closed the door. She was glad she had called Mrs. Hanshaw. She had done her duty. More than ever, it was obvious that something was wrong with Richard. She suppressed the impulse to phone again.

Mrs. Hanshaw did not go to New York that day. She remained home in a mixture of anxiety and an irrational anger, the latter directed against the impudent Miss Robbins.

Some fifteen minutes before school's end, her anxiety drove her to the Door. Last year she had had it equipped with an automatic device which activated it to the school's co-ordinates at five of three and kept it so, barring manual adjustment, until Richard arrived.

Her eyes were fixed on the Door's dismal gray (why couldn't an inactive force-field be any other color, something more lively and cheerful?) and waited. Her hands felt cold as she squeezed them together.

The Door turned black at the precise second but nothing happened. The minutes passed and Richard was late. Then quite late. Then very late.

It was a quarter of four and she was distracted. Normally, she would have phoned the school, but she couldn't, she couldn't. Not after that teacher had deliberately cast doubts on Richard's mental well-being. How could she?

Mrs. Hanshaw moved about restlessly, lighting a cigarette with fumbling fingers, then smudging it out. Could it be something quite normal? Could Richard be staying after school for some reason?

Surely he would have told her in advance. A gleam of light struck her; he knew she was planning to go to New York and might not be back till late in the evening—

No, he would surely have told her. Why fool herself?

Her pride was breaking. She would have to call the school, or even (she closed her eyes and teardrops squeezed through between the lashes) the police.

And when she opened her eyes, Richard stood before her, eyes on the ground and his whole bearing that of someone waiting for a blow to fall.

"Hello, Mom."

Mrs. Hanshaw's anxiety transmuted itself instantly (in a manner known only to mothers) into anger. "Where have you been, Richard?"

And then, before she could go further into the refrain concerning careless, unthinking sons and broken-hearted mothers, she took note of his appearance in greater detail, and gasped in utter horror.

She said, "You've been in the open."

Her son looked down at his dusty shoes (minus flexies), at the dirt marks that streaked his lower arms and at the small, but definite tear in his shirt. He said, "Gosh, Mom, I just thought I'd—" and he faded out.

She said, "Was there anything wrong with the school Door?"

"No, Mom."

"Do you realize I've been worried sick about you?" She waited vainly for an answer. "Well, I'll talk to you afterward, young man. First, you're taking a bath, and every stitch of your clothing is being thrown out. Mekkano!"

But the mekkano had already reacted properly to the phrase "taking a bath" and was off to the bathroom in its silent glide.

"You take your shoes off right here," said Mrs. Hanshaw, "then march after mekkano."

Richard did as he was told with a resignation that placed him beyond futile protest.

Mrs. Hanshaw picked up the soiled shoes between thumb and forefinger and dropped them down the disposal chute which hummed in faint dismay at the unexpected load. She dusted her hands carefully on a tissue which she allowed to float down the chute after the shoes.

She did not join Richard at dinner but let him eat in the worse-than-lack-of-company of the mekkano. This, she thought, would be an active sign of her displeasure and would do more than any amount of scolding or punishment to make him realize that he had done wrong. Richard, she frequently told herself, was a sensitive boy.

But she went up to see him at bedtime.

She smiled at him and spoke softly. She thought that would be the best way. After all, he had been punished already.

She said, "What happened today, Dickie-boy?" She had called him that when he was a baby and just the sound of the name softened her nearly to tears.

But he only looked away and his voice was stubborn and cold. "I just don't like to go through those darn Doors, Mom."

"But why ever not?"

He shuffled his hands over the filmy sheet (fresh, clean, antiseptic and, of course, disposable after each use) and said, "I just don't like them."

"But then how do you expect to go to school, Dickie?"

"I'll get up early," he mumbled.

"But there's nothing wrong with Doors."

"Don't like 'em." He never once looked up at her.

She said, despairingly, "Oh, well, you have a good sleep and tomorrow morning you'll feel much better."

She kissed him and left the room, automatically passing her hand through the photo-cell beam and in that manner dimming the room lights.

But she had trouble sleeping herself that night. Why should Dickie dislike Doors so suddenly? They had never bothered him before. To be sure, the Door had broken down in the morning but that should make him appreciate them all the more.

Dickie was behaving so unreasonably.

Unreasonably? That reminded her of Miss Robbins and her diagnosis and Mrs. Hanshaw's soft jaw set in the darkness and privacy of her bedroom. Nonsense! The boy was upset and a night's sleep was all the therapy he needed.

But the next morning when she arose, her son was not in the house. The mekkano could not speak but it could answer questions with gestures of its appendages equivalent to a yes or no, and it did not take Mrs. Hanshaw more than half a minute to ascertain that the boy had arisen thirty minutes earlier than usual, skimped his shower, and darted out of the house.

But not by way of the Door.

Out the other way—through the door. Small "d."

Mrs. Hanshaw's visiphone signaled genteelly at 3:10 P.M. that day. Mrs. Hanshaw guessed the caller and having activated the receiver, saw that she had guessed correctly. A quick glance in the mirror to see that she was properly calm after a day of abstracted concern and worry and then she keyed in her own transmission.

"Yes, Miss Robbins," she said coldly.

Richard's teacher was a bit breathless. She said, "Mrs. Hanshaw, Richard has deliberately left through the fire door although I told him to use the regular Door. I do not know where he went."

Mrs. Hanshaw said, carefully, "He left to come home."

Miss Robbins looked dismayed, "Do you approve of this?"

Pale-faced, Mrs. Hanshaw set about putting the teacher in her place. "I don't think it is up to you to criticize. If my son does not choose to use the Door, it is his affair and mine. I don't think there is any school ruling that would force him to use the Door, is there?" Her bearing quite plainly intimated that if there were she would see to it that it was changed.

Miss Robbins flushed and had time for one quick remark before contact was broken. She said, "I'd have him probed. I really would."

Mrs. Hanshaw remained standing before the quartzinium plate, staring blindly at its blank face. Her sense of family placed her for a few moments quite firmly on Richard's side. Why *did* he have to use the Door if he chose not to? And then she settled down to wait and pride battled the gnawing anxiety that something after all was wrong with Richard.

He came home with a look of defiance on his face, but his mother, with a strenuous effort at self-control, met him as though nothing were out of the ordinary.

For weeks, she followed that policy. It's nothing, she told herself. It's a vagary. He'll grow out of it.

It grew into an almost normal state of affairs. Then, too, every once in a while, perhaps three days in a row, she would come down to breakfast to find Richard waiting sullenly at the Door, then using it when school time came. She always refrained from commenting on the matter.

Always, when he did that, and especially when he followed it up by arriving home via the Door, her heart grew warm and she thought, "Well, it's over." But always with the passing of one day, two or three, he would return like an addict to his drug and drift silently out by the door—small "d"—before she woke.

And each time she thought despairingly of psychiatrists and probes, and each time the vision of Miss Robbins' low-bred satisfaction at (possibly) learning of it, stopped her, although she was scarcely aware that that was the true motive.

Meanwhile, she lived with it and made the best of it. The mekkano was instructed to wait at the door—small "d"—with a Tergo kit and a change of clothing. Richard washed and changed without resistance. His underthings, socks and flexies were disposable in any case, and Mrs. Hanshaw bore uncomplainingly the expense of daily disposal of shirts. Trousers she finally allowed to go a week before disposal on condition of rigorous nightly cleansing.

One day she suggested that Richard accompany her on a trip to New York. It was more a vague desire to keep him in sight than part of any purposeful plan. He did not object. He was even happy. He stepped right through the Door, unconcerned. He didn't hesitate. He even lacked the look of resentment he wore on those mornings he used the Door to go to school.

Mrs. Hanshaw rejoiced. This could be a way of weaning him back into Door usage, and she racked her ingenuity for excuses to make trips with Richard. She even raised her power bill to quite unheard-of heights by suggesting, and going through with, a trip to Canton for the day in order to witness a Chinese festival.

That was on a Sunday, and the next morning Richard marched directly to the hole in the wall he always used. Mrs. Hanshaw, having wakened particularly early, witnessed that. For once, badgered past endurance, she called after him plaintively, "Why not the Door, Dickie?"

He said, briefly, "It's all right for Canton," and stepped out of the house.

So that plan ended in failure. And then, one day, Richard came home soaking wet. The mekkano hovered about him uncertainly and Mrs. Hanshaw, just returned from a four-hour visit with her sister in Iowa, cried, "Richard Hanshaw!"

He said, hang-dog fashion, "It started raining. All of a sudden, it started raining."

For a moment, the word didn't register with her. Her own school days and her studies of geography were twenty years in the past. And then she remembered and caught the vision of water pouring recklessly and endlessly down from the sky—a mad cascade of water with no tap to turn off, no button to push, no contact to break.

She said, "And you stayed out in it?"

He said, "Well, gee, Mom, I came home fast as I could. I didn't know it was going to rain."

Mrs. Hanshaw had nothing to say. She was appalled and the sensation filled her too full for words to find a place.

Two days later, Richard found himself with a running nose, and a dry, scratchy throat. Mrs. Hanshaw had to admit that the virus of disease had found a lodging in her house, as though it were a miserable hovel of the Iron Age.

It was over that that her stubbornness and pride broke and she admitted to herself that, after all, Richard had to have psychiatric help.

Mrs. Hanshaw chose a psychiatrist with care. Her first impulse was to find one at a distance. For a while, she considered stepping directly into the San Francisco Medical Center and choosing one at random.

And then it occurred to her that by doing that she would become merely an anonymous consultant. She would have no way of obtaining any greater consideration for herself than would be forthcoming to any public-Door user of the city slums. Now if she remained in her own community, her word would carry weight—

She consulted the district map. It was one of that excellent series prepared by Doors, Inc., and distributed free of charge to their clients. Mrs. Hanshaw couldn't quite suppress that little thrill of civic pride as she unfolded the map. It wasn't a fine-print directory of Door co-ordinates only. It was an actual map, with each house carefully located.

And why not? District A-3 was a name of moment in the world, a badge of aristocracy. It was the first community on the planet to have been established on a completely Doored basis. The first, the largest, the wealthiest, the best-known. It needed no factories, no stores. It didn't even need roads. Each house was a little secluded castle, the Door of which had entry anywhere the world over where other Doors existed.

Carefully, she followed down the keyed listing of the five thousand families of District A-3. She knew it included several psychiatrists. The learned professions were well represented in A-3.

Doctor Hamilton Sloane was the second name she arrived at and her finger lingered upon the map. His office was scarcely two miles from the Hanshaw residence. She liked his name. The fact that he lived in A-3 was evidence of worth. And he was a neighbor, practically a neighbor. He would understand that it was a matter of urgency—and confidential.

Firmly, she put in a call to his office to make an appointment.

Doctor Hamilton Sloane was a comparatively young man, not quite forty. He was of good family and he had indeed heard of Mrs. Hanshaw.

He listened to her quietly and then said, "And this all began with the Door breakdown."

"That's right, Doctor."

"Does he show any fear of the Doors?"

"Of course not. What an idea!" She was plainly startled.

"It's possible, Mrs. Hanshaw, it's possible. After all, when you stop to think of how a Door works it is rather a frightening thing, really. You step into a Door, and for an instant your atoms are converted into field-energies, transmitted to another part of space and reconverted into matter. For that instant you're not alive."

"I'm sure no one thinks of such things."

"But your son may. He witnessed the breakdown of the Door. He may be saying to himself, 'What if the Door breaks down just as I'm half-way through?' "

"But that's nonsense. He still uses the Door. He's even been to Canton with me; Canton, China. And as I told you, he uses it for school about once or twice a week."

"Freely? Cheerfully?"

"Well," said Mrs. Hanshaw, reluctantly, "he does seem a bit put out by it. But really, Doctor, there isn't much use talking about it, is there? If you would do a quick probe, see where the trouble was," and she finished on a bright note, "why, that would be all. I'm sure it's quite a minor thing."

Dr. Sloane sighed. He detested the word "probe" and there was scarcely any word he heard oftener.

"Mrs. Hanshaw," he said patiently, "there is no such thing as a quick probe. Now I know the mag-strips are full of it and it's a rage in some circles, but it's much overrated."

"Are you serious?"

"Quite. The probe is very complicated and the theory is that it traces mental circuits. You see, the cells of the brains are inter-connected in a large variety of ways. Some of those interconnected paths are more used than others. They represent habits of thought, both conscious and unconscious. Theory has it that these paths in any given brain can be used to diagnose mental ills early and with certainty."

"Well, then?"

"But subjection to the probe is quite a fearful thing, especially to a child. It's a traumatic experience. It takes over an hour. And even then, the results must be sent to the Central Psychoanalytical Bureau for analysis, and that could take weeks. And on top of all that, Mrs. Hanshaw, there are many psychiatrists who think the theory of probe-analyses to be most uncertain."

Mrs. Hanshaw compressed her lips. "You mean nothing can be done."

Dr. Sloane smiled. "Not at all. There were psychiatrists for centuries before there were probes. I suggest that you let me talk to the boy."

"Talk to him? Is that all?"

"I'll come to you for background information when necessary, but the essential thing, I think, is to talk to the boy."

"Really, Dr. Sloane, I doubt if he'll discuss the matter with you. He won't talk to me about it and I'm his mother."

"That often happens," the psychiatrist assured her. "A child will sometimes talk more readily to a stranger. In any case, I cannot take the case otherwise."

Mrs. Hanshaw rose, not at all pleased. "When can you come, Doctor?"

"What about this coming Saturday? The boy won't be in school. Will you be busy?"

"We will be ready."

She made a dignified exit. Dr. Sloane accompanied her through the small reception room to his office Door and waited while she punched the co-ordinates of her house. He watched her pass through. She became a half-woman, a quarter-woman, an isolated elbow and foot, a nothing.

It *was* frightening.

Did a Door ever break down during passage, leaving half a body here and half there? He had never heard of such a case, but he imagined it could happen.

He returned to his desk and looked up the time of his next appointment. It was obvious to him that Mrs. Hanshaw was annoyed and disappointed at not having arranged for a psychic probe treatment.

Why, for God's sake? Why should a thing like the probe, an obvious piece of quackery in his own opinion, get such a hold on the general public? It must be part of this general trend toward machines. Anything man can do, machines can do better. Machines! More machines! Machines for anything and everything! O tempora! O mores!

Oh, hell!

His resentment of the probe was beginning to bother him. Was it a fear of technological unemployment, a basic insecurity on his part, a mechanophobia, if that was the word—

He made a mental note to discuss this with his own analyst.

Dr. Sloane had to feel his way. The boy wasn't a patient who had come to him, more or less anxious to talk, more or less anxious to be helped.

Under the circumstances it would have been best to keep his first meeting with Richard short and noncommittal. It would have been sufficient merely to establish himself as something less than a total stranger. The next time he would be someone Richard had seen before. The time after he would be an acquaintance, and after that a friend of the family.

Unfortunately, Mrs. Hanshaw was not likely to accept a long-drawn-out process. She would go searching for a probe and, of course, she would find it.

And harm the boy. He was certain of that.

It was for that reason he felt he must sacrifice a little of the proper caution and risk a small crisis.

An uncomfortable ten minutes had passed when he decided he must try. Mrs. Hanshaw was smiling in a rather rigid way, eyeing him narrowly, as though she expected verbal magic from him. Richard wriggled in his seat, unresponsive to Dr. Sloane's tentative comments, overcome with boredom and unable not to show it.

Dr. Sloane said, with casual suddenness, "Would you like to take a walk with me, Richard?"

The boy's eyes widened and he stopped wriggling. He looked directly at Dr. Sloane. "A walk, sir?"

"I mean, outside."

"Do you go—outside?"

"Sometimes. When I feel like it."

Richard was on his feet, holding down a squirming eagerness. "I didn't think anyone did."

"I do. And I like company."

The boy sat down, uncertainly. "Mom?"

Mrs. Hanshaw had stiffened in her seat, her compressed lips radiating horror, but she managed to say, "Why certainly, Dickie. But watch yourself."

And she managed a quick and baleful glare at Dr. Sloane.

•   •   •

In one respect, Dr. Sloane had lied. He did not go outside "sometimes." He hadn't been in the open since early college days. True, he had been athletically inclined (still was to some extent) but in his time the indoor ultraviolet chambers, swimming pools, and tennis courts had flourished. For those with the price, they were much more satisfactory than the outdoor equivalents, open to the elements as they were, could possibly be. There was no occasion to go outside.

So there was a crawling sensation about his skin when he felt wind touch it, and he put down his flexied shoes on bare grass with a gingerly movement.

"Hey, look at that." Richard was quite different now, laughing, his reserve broken down.

Dr. Sloane had time only to catch a flash of blue that ended in a tree. Leaves rustled and he lost it.

"What was it?"

"A bird," said Richard. "A blue kind of bird."

Dr. Sloane looked about him in amazement. The Hanshaw residence was on a rise of ground, and he could see for miles. The area was only lightly wooded and between clumps of trees, grass gleamed brightly in the sunlight.

Colors set in deeper green made red and yellow patterns. They were flowers. From the books he had viewed in the course of his lifetime and from the old video shows, he had learned enough so that all this had an eerie sort of familiarity.

And yet the grass was so trim, the flowers so patterned. Dimly, he realized he had been expecting something wilder. He said, "Who takes care of all this?"

Richard shrugged. "I dunno. Maybe the mekkanos do it."

"Mekkanos?"

"There's loads of them around. Sometimes they got a sort of atomic knife they hold near the ground. It cuts the grass. And they're always fooling around with the flowers and things. There's one of them over there."

It was a small object, half a mile away. Its metal skin cast back highlights as it moved slowly over the gleaming meadow, engaged in some sort of activity that Dr. Sloane could not identify.

Dr. Sloane was astonished. Here it was a perverse sort of es-theticism, a kind of conspicuous consumption—

"What's that?" he asked suddenly.

Richard looked. He said, "That's a house. Belongs to the Froeh-lichs. Co-ordinates, A-3, 23, 461. That little pointy building over there is the public Door."

Dr. Sloane was staring at the house. Was that what it looked like from the outside? Somehow he had imagined something much more cubic, and taller.

"Come along," shouted Richard, running ahead.

Dr. Sloane followed more sedately. "Do you know all the houses about here?"

"Just about."

"Where is A-23, 26, 475?" It was his own house, of course.

Richard looked about. "Let's see. Oh, sure, I know where it is—you see that water there?"

"Water?" Dr. Sloane made out a line of silver curving across the green.

"Sure. Real water. Just sort of running over rocks and things. It keeps running all the time. You can get across it if you step on the rocks. It's called a river."

More like a creek, thought Dr. Sloane. He had studied geog-raphy, of course, but what passed for the subject these days was really economic and cultural geography. Physical geography was al-most an extinct science except among specialists. Still, he knew what rivers and creeks were, in a theoretical sort of way.

Richard was still talking. "Well, just past the river, over that hill with the big clump of trees and down the other side a way is A-23, 26, 475. It's a light green house with a white roof."

"It is?" Dr. Sloane was genuinely astonished. He hadn't known it was green.

Some small animal disturbed the grass in its anxiety to avoid the oncoming feet. Richard looked after it and shrugged. "You can't catch them. I tried."

A butterfly flitted past, a wavering bit of yellow. Dr. Sloane's eyes followed it.

There was a low hum that lay over the fields, interspersed with an occasional harsh, calling sound, a rattle, a twittering, a chatter that rose, then fell. As his ear accustomed itself to listening, Dr. Sloane heard a thousand sounds, and none were man-made.

A shadow fell upon the scene, advancing toward him, covering him. It was suddenly cooler and he looked upward, startled.

Richard said, "It's just a cloud. It'll go away in a minute—looka these flowers. They're the kind that smell."

They were several hundred yards from the Hanshaw residence. The cloud passed and the sun shone once more. Dr. Sloane looked back and was appalled at the distance they had covered. If they moved out of sight of the house and if Richard ran off, would he be able to find his way back?

He pushed the thought away impatiently and looked out toward the line of water (nearer now) and past it to where his own house must be. He thought wonderingly: Light green?

He said, "You must be quite an explorer."

Richard said, with a shy pride, "When I go to school and come back, I always try to use a different route and see new things."

"But you don't go outside every morning, do you? Sometimes you use the Doors, I imagine."

"Oh, sure."

"Why is that, Richard?" Somehow, Dr. Sloane felt there might be significance in that point.

But Richard quashed him. With his eyebrows up and a look of astonishment on his face, he said, "Well, gosh, some mornings it rains and I *have* to use the Door. I hate that, but what can you do? About two weeks ago, I got caught in the rain and I—" he looked about him automatically, and his voice sank to a whisper "—caught a cold, and wasn't Mom upset, though."

Dr. Sloane sighed. "Shall we go back now?"

There was a quick disappointment on Richard's face. "Aw, what for?"

"You remind me that your mother must be waiting for us."

"I guess so." The boy turned reluctantly.

They walked slowly back. Richard was saying, chattily, "I wrote a composition at school once about how if I could go on some ancient vehicle" (he pronounced it with exaggerated care) "I'd go in a stratoliner and look at stars and clouds and things. Oh, boy, I was sure nuts."

"You'd pick something else now?"

"You bet. I'd go in an aut'm'bile, real slow. Then I'd see every-thing there was."

Mrs. Hanshaw seemed troubled, uncertain. "You don't think it's abnormal, then, Doctor?"

"Unusual, perhaps, but not abnormal. He likes the outside."

"But how can he? It's so dirty, so unpleasant."

"That's a matter of individual taste. A hundred years ago our ancestors were all outside most of the time. Even today, I dare say there are a million Africans who have never seen a Door."

"But Richard's always been taught to behave himself the way a decent person in District A-3 is supposed to behave," said Mrs. Hanshaw, fiercely. "Not like an African or—or an ancestor."

"That may be part of the trouble, Mrs. Hanshaw. He feels this urge to go outside and yet he feels it to be wrong. He's ashamed to talk about it to you or to his teacher. It forces him into sullen retreat and it could eventually be dangerous."

"Then how can we persuade him to stop?"

Dr. Sloane said, "Don't try. Channel the activity instead. The day your Door broke down, he was forced outside, found he liked it, and that set a pattern. He used the trip to school and back as an excuse to repeat that first exciting experience. Now suppose you agree to let him out of the house for two hours on Saturdays and Sundays. Suppose he gets it through his head that after all he can go outside without necessarily having to go anywhere in the pro-cess. Don't you think he'll be willing to use the Door to go to school and back thereafter? And don't you think that will stop the trouble he's now having with his teacher and probably with his fellow-pupils?"

"But then will matters remain so? Must they? Won't he ever be normal again?"

Dr. Sloane rose to his feet. "Mrs. Hanshaw, he's as normal as need be right now. Right now, he's tasting the joys of the forbidden. If you cooperate with him, show that you don't disapprove, it will lose some of its attraction right there. Then, as he grows older, he will become more aware of the expectations and demands of society. He will learn to conform. After all, there is a little of the rebel in all of us, but it generally dies down as we grow old and tired. Unless, that is, it is unreasonably suppressed and allowed to build up pressure. Don't do that. Richard will be all right."

He walked to the Door.

Mrs. Hanshaw said, "And you don't think a probe will be necessary, Doctor?"

He turned and said vehemently, "No, definitely not! There is nothing about the boy that requires it. Understand? Nothing."

His fingers hesitated an inch from the combination board and the expression on his face grew lowering.

"What's the matter, Dr. Sloane?" asked Mrs. Hanshaw.

But he didn't hear her because he was thinking of the Door and the psychic probe and all the rising, choking tide of machinery. There is a little of the rebel in all of us, he thought.

So he said in a soft voice, as his hand fell away from the board and his feet turned away from the Door, "You know, it's such a beautiful day that I think I'll walk."

STRIKEBREAKER

E lvis Blei rubbed his plump hands and said, "Self-containment is the word." He smiled uneasily as he helped Steven Lamorak of Earth to a light. There was uneasiness all over his smooth face with its small wide-set eyes.

Lamorak puffed smoke appreciatively and crossed his lanky legs. His hair was powered with gray and he had a large and powerful jawbone. "Home grown?" he asked, staring critically at the cigarette. He tried to hide his own disturbance at the other's tension.

"Quite," said Blei.

"I wonder," said Lamorak, "that you have room on your small world for such luxuries."

(Lamorak thought of his first view of Elsevere from the spaceship visiplate. It was a jagged, airless planetoid, some hundred miles in diameter—just a dust-gray rough-hewn rock, glimmering dully in the light of its sun, 200,000,000 miles distant. It was the only object more than a mile in diameter that circled that sun, and now men had burrowed into that miniature world and constructed a society in it. And he himself, as a sociologist, had come to study the world and see how humanity had made itself fit into that queerly specialized niche.)

Blei's polite fixed smile expanded a hair. He said, "We are not a small world, Dr. Lamorak; you judge us by two-dimensional standards. The surface area of Elsevere is only three quarters that of the State of New York, but that's irrelevant. Remember, we can occupy, if we wish, the entire interior of Elsevere. A sphere of fifty miles radius has a volume of well over half a million cubic miles. If all of Elsevere were occupied by levels fifty feet apart, the total surface area within the planetoid would be 56,000,000 square miles, and that is equal to the total land area of Earth. And none of these square miles, Doctor, would be unproductive."

Lamorak said, "Good Lord," and stared blankly for a moment. "Yes, of course you're right. Strange I never thought of it that way. But then, Elsevere is the only thoroughly exploited asteroid world in the Galaxy; the rest of us simply can't get away from thinking of two-dimensional surfaces, as you pointed out. Well, I'm more than ever glad that your Council has been so cooperative as to give me a free hand in this investigation of mine."

Blei nodded convulsively at that.

Lamorak frowned slightly and thought: He acts for all the world as though he wished I had not come. Something's wrong.

Blei said, "Of course, you understand that we are actually much smaller than we could be; only minor portions of Elsevere have as yet been hollowed out and occupied. Nor are we particularly anxious to expand, except very slowly. To a certain extent we are limited by the capacity of our pseudo-gravity engines and Solar energy converters."

"I understand. But tell me, Councillor Blei—as a matter of personal curiosity, and not because it is of prime importance to my project—could I view some of your farming and herding levels first? I am fascinated by the thought of fields of wheat and herds of cattle inside a planetoid."

"You'll find the cattle small by your standards, Doctor, and we don't have much wheat. We grow yeast to a much greater extent. But there will be some wheat to show you. Some cotton and rice, too. Even fruit trees."

"Wonderful. As you say, self-containment. You recirculate everything, I imagine."

Lamorak's sharp eyes did not miss the fact that this last remark twinged Blei. The Elseverian's eyes narrowed to slits that hid his expression.

He said, "We must recirculate, yes. Air, water, food, minerals—everything that is used up—must be restored to its original state; waste products are reconverted to raw materials. All that is needed is energy and we have enough of that. We don't manage with one hundred percent efficiency, of course; there is a certain seepage. We import a small amount of water each year; and if our needs grow, we may have to import some coal and oxygen."

Lamorak said, "When can we start our tour, Councillor Blei?"

Blei's smile lost some of its negligible warmth. "As soon as we can, Doctor. There are some routine matters that must be arranged."

Lamorak nodded, and having finished his cigarette, stubbed it out.

Routine matters? There was none of this hesitancy during the preliminary correspondence. Elsevere had seemed proud that its unique asteroid existence had attracted the attention of the Galaxy.

He said, "I realize I would be a disturbing influence in a tightly knit society," and watched grimly as Blei leaped at the explanation and made it his own.

"Yes," said Blei, "we feel marked off from the rest of the Galaxy. We have our own customs. Each individual Elseverian fits into a comfortable niche. The appearance of a stranger without fixed caste is unsettling."

"The caste system does involve a certain inflexibility."

"Granted," said Blei quickly, "but there is also a certain self-assurance. We have firm rules of intermarriage and rigid inheritance of occupation. Each man, woman, and child knows his place, accepts it, and is accepted in it; we have virtually no neurosis or mental illness."

"And are there no misfits?" asked Lamorak.

Blei shaped his mouth as though to say no, then clamped it suddenly shut, biting the word into silence; a frown deepened on his forehead. He said, at length, "I will arrange for the tour, Doctor. Meanwhile, I imagine you would welcome a chance to freshen up and to sleep."

They rose together and left the room, Blei politely motioning the Earthman to precede him out the door.

•   •   •

Lamorak felt oppressed by the vague feeling of crisis that had pervaded his discussion with Blei.

The newspaper reinforced that feeling. He read it carefully before getting into bed, with what was at first merely a clinical interest. It was an eight-page tabloid of synthetic paper. One quarter of its items consisted of "personals": births, marriages, deaths, record quotas, expanding habitable volume (not area! three dimensions!). The remainder included scholarly essays, educational material, and fiction. Of news, in the sense to which Lamorak was accustomed, there was virtually nothing.

One item only could be so considered and that was chilling in its incompleteness.

It said, under a small headline: DEMANDS UNCHANGED: *There has been no change in his attitude of yesterday. The Chief Councillor, after a second interview, announced that his demands remain completely unreasonable and cannot be met under any circumstances.*

Then, in parenthesis, and in different type, there was the statement: *The editors of this paper agree that Elsevere cannot and will not jump to his whistle, come what may.*

Lamorak read it over three times. *His* attitude. *His* demands. *His* whistle.

Whose?

He slept uneasily, that night.

He had no time for newspapers in the days that followed; but spasmodically, the matter returned to his thoughts.

Blei, who remained his guide and companion for most of the tour, grew ever more withdrawn.

On the third day (quite artificially clock-set in an Earthlike twenty-four-hour pattern), Blei stopped at one point, and said, "Now this level is devoted entirely to chemical industries. That section is not important—"

But he turned away a shade too rapidly, and Lamorak seized his arm. "What are the products of that section?"

"Fertilizers. Certain organics," said Blei stiffly.

Lamorak held him back, looking for what sight Blei might be evading. His gaze swept over the close-by horizons of lined rock and the buildings squeezed and layered between the levels.

Lamorak said, "Isn't that a private residence there?"

Blei did not look in the indicated direction.

Lamorak said, "I think that's the largest one I've seen yet. Why is it here on a factory level?" That alone made it noteworthy. He had already seen that the levels on Elsevere were divided rigidly among the residential, the agricultural, and the industrial.

He looked back and called, "Councillor Blei!"

The councillor was walking away and Lamorak pursued him with hasty steps. "Is there something wrong, sir?"

Blei muttered, "I am rude, I know. I am sorry. There are matters that prey on my mind—" He kept up his rapid pace.

"Concerning *his* demands."

Blei came to a full halt. "What do *you* know about that?"

"No more than I've said. I read that much in the newspaper."

Blei muttered something to himself.

Lamorak said, "Ragusnik? What's that?"

Blei sighed heavily. "I suppose you ought to be told. It's humiliating, deeply embarrassing. The Council thought that matters would certainly be arranged shortly and that your visit need not be interfered with, that you need not know or be concerned. But it is almost a week now. I don't know what will happen and, appearances notwithstanding, it might be best for you to leave. No reason for an Outworlder to risk death."

The Earthman smiled incredulously. "Risk death? In this little world, so peaceful and busy. I can't believe it."

The Elseverian councillor said, "I can explain. I think it best I should." He turned his head away. "As I told you, everything on Elsevere must recirculate. You understand that."

"Yes."

"That includes—uh, human wastes."

"I assumed so," said Lamorak.

"Water is reclaimed from it by distillation and absorption. What remains is converted into fertilizer for yeast use; some of it is used as a source of fine organics and other by-products. These factories you see are devoted to this."

"Well?" Lamorak had experienced a certain difficulty in the drinking of water when he first landed on Elsevere, because he had been realistic enough to know what it must be reclaimed from; but he had conquered the feeling easily enough. Even on Earth, water was reclaimed by natural processes from all sorts of unpalatable substances.

Blei, with increasing difficulty, said, "Igor Ragusnik is the man who is in charge of the industrial processes immediately involving the wastes. The position has been in his family since Elsevere was first colonized. One of the original settlers was Mikhail Ragusnik and he—he—"

"Was in charge of waste reclamation."

"Yes. Now that residence you singled out is the Ragusnik residence; it is the best and most elaborate on the asteroid. Ragusnik gets many privileges the rest of us do not have; but, after all—" Passion entered the Councillor's voice with great suddenness. "We cannot *speak* to him."

"What?"

"He demands full social equality. He wants his children to mingle with ours, and our wives to visit—Oh!" It was a groan of utter disgust.

Lamorak thought of the newspaper item that could not even bring itself to mention Ragusnik's name in print, or to say anything specific about his demands. He said, "I take it he's an outcast because of his job."

"Naturally. Human wastes and—" Words failed Blei. After a pause, he said more quietly, "As an Earthman, I suppose you don't understand."

"As a sociologist, I think I do." Lamorak thought of the Untouchables in ancient India, the ones who handled corpses. He thought of the position of swineherds in ancient Judea.

He went on, "I gather Elsevere will not give in to those demands."

"Never," said Blei, energetically. "Never."

"And so?"

"Ragusnik has threatened to cease operations."

"Go on strike, in other words."

"Yes."

"Would that be serious?"

"We have enough food and water to last quite a while; reclamation is not essential in that sense. But the wastes would accumulate; they would infect the asteroid. After generations of careful disease control, we have low natural resistance to germ diseases. Once an epidemic started—and one would—we would drop by the hundred."

"Is Ragusnik aware of this?"

"Yes, of course."

"Do you think he is likely to go through with his threat, then?"

"He is mad. He has already stopped working; there has been no waste reclamation since the day before you landed." Blei's bulbous nose sniffed at the air as though it already caught the whiff of excrement.

Lamorak sniffed mechanically at that, but smelled nothing.

Blei said, "So you see why it might be wise for you to leave. We are humiliated, of course, to have to suggest it."

But Lamorak said, "Wait; not just yet. Good Lord, this is a matter of great interest to me professionally. May I speak to the Ragusnik?"

"On no account," said Blei, alarmed.

"But I would like to understand the situation. The sociological conditions here are unique and not to be duplicated elsewhere. In the name of science—"

"How do you mean, speak? Would image-reception do?"

"Yes."

"I will ask the Council," muttered Blei.

They sat about Lamorak uneasily, their austere and dignified expressions badly marred with anxiety. Blei, seated in the midst of them, studiously avoided the Earthman's eyes.

The Chief Councillor, gray-haired, his face harshly wrinkled, his neck scrawny, said in a soft voice, "If in any way you can persuade him, sir, out of your own convictions, we will welcome that. In no case, however, are you to imply that we will, in any way, yield."

A gauzy curtain fell between the Council and Lamorak. He could make out the individual councillors still, but now he turned sharply toward the receiver before him. It glowed to life.

A head appeared in it, in natural color and with great realism. A strong dark head, with massive chin faintly stubbled, and thick, red lips set into a firm horizontal line.

The image said, suspiciously, "Who are you?"

Lamorak said, "My name is Steven Lamorak; I am an Earthman."

"An Outworlder?"

"That's right. I am visiting Elsevere. You are Ragusnik?"

"Igor Ragusnik, at your service," said the image, mockingly. "Except that there is no service and will be none until my family and I are treated like human beings."

Lamorak said, "Do you realize the danger that Elsevere is in? The possibility of epidemic disease?"

"In twenty-four hours, the situation can be made normal, if they allow me humanity. The situation is theirs to correct."

"You sound like an educated man, Ragusnik."

"So?"

"I am told you're denied no material comforts. You are housed and clothed and fed better than anyone on Elsevere. Your children are the best educated."

"Granted. But all by servo-mechanism. And motherless girl-babies are sent us to care for until they grow to be our wives. And they die young for loneliness. Why?" There was sudden passion in his voice. "Why must we live in isolation as if we were all monsters, unfit for human beings to be near? Aren't we human beings like others, with the same needs and desires and feelings. Don't we perform an honorable and useful function?"

There was a rustling of sighs from behind Lamorak. Ragusnik heard it, and raised his voice. "I see you of the Council behind there. Answer me: Isn't it an honorable and useful function? It is *your* waste made into food for *you*. Is the man who purifies corruption worse than the man who produces it?—Listen, Councillors, I will *not* give in. Let all of Elsevere die of disease—including myself and my son, if necessary—but I will not give in. My family will be better dead of disease, than living as now."

Lamorak interrupted. "You've led this life since birth, haven't you?"

"And if I have?"

"Surely you're used to it."

"Never. Resigned, perhaps. My father was resigned, and I was resigned for a while; but I have watched my son, my only son, with no other little boy to play with. My brother and I had each other, but my son will never have anyone, and I am no longer resigned. I am through with Elsevere and through with talking."

The receiver went dead.

The Chief Councillor's face had paled to an aged yellow. He and Blei were the only ones of the group left with Lamorak. The Chief Councillor said, "The man is deranged; I do not know how to force him."

He had a glass of wine at his side; as he lifted it to his lips, he spilled a few drops that stained his white trousers with purple splotches.

Lamorak said, "Are his demands so unreasonable? Why can't he be accepted into society?"

There was momentary rage in Blei's eyes. "A dealer in excrement." Then he shrugged. "You are from Earth."

Incongruously, Lamorak thought of another unacceptable, one of the numerous classic creations of the medieval cartoonist, Al Capp. The variously named "inside man at the skonk works."

He said, "Does Ragusnik really deal with excrement? I mean, is there physical contact? Surely, it is all handled by automatic machinery."

"Of course," said the Chief Councillor.

"Then exactly what is Ragusnik's function?"

"He manually adjusts the various controls that assure the proper functioning of the machinery. He shifts units to allow repairs to be made; he alters functional rates with the time of day; he varies end production with demand." He added sadly, "If we had the space to make the machinery ten times as complex, all this could be done automatically; but that would be such needless waste."

"But even so," insisted Lamorak, "all Ragusnik does he does simply by pressing buttons or closing contacts or things like that."

"Yes."

"Then his work is no different from any Elseverian's."

Blei said, stiffly, "You don't understand."

"And for that you will risk the death of your children?"

"We have no other choice," said Blei. There was enough agony in his voice to assure Lamorak that the situation was torture for him, but that he had no other choice indeed.

Lamorak shrugged in disgust. "Then break the strike. Force him."

"How?" said the Chief Councillor. "Who would touch him or go near him? And if we kill him by blasting from a distance, how will that help us?"

Lamorak said, thoughtfully, "Would you know how to run his machinery?"

The Chief Councillor came to his feet. "I?" he howled.

"I don't mean *you*," cried Lamorak at once. "I used the pronoun in its indefinite sense. Could *someone* learn how to handle Ragusnik's machinery?"

Slowly, the passion drained out of the Chief Councillor. "It is in the handbooks, I am certain—though I assure you I have never concerned myself with it."

"Then couldn't someone learn the procedure and substitute for Ragusnik until the man gives in?"

Blei said, "Who would agree to do such a thing? Not I, under any circumstances."

Lamorak thought fleetingly of Earthly taboos that might be almost as strong. He thought of cannibalism, incest, a pious man cursing God. He said, "But you must have made provision for vacancy in the Ragusnik job. Suppose he died."

"Then his son would automatically succeed to his job, or his nearest other relative," said Blei.

"What if he had no adult relatives? What if all his family died at once?"

"That has never happened; it will never happen."

The Chief Councillor added, "If there were danger of it, we might, perhaps, place a baby or two with the Ragusniks and have it raised to the profession."

"Ah. And how would you choose that baby?"

"From among children of mothers who died in childbirth, as we choose the future Ragusnik bride."

"Then choose a substitute Ragusnik now, by lot," said Lamorak.

The Chief Councillor said. "No! Impossible! How can you suggest that? If we select a baby, that baby is brought up to the life; it knows no other. At this point, it would be necessary to choose an adult and subject him to Ragusnik-hood. No, Dr. Lamorak, we are neither monsters nor abandoned brutes."

No use, thought Lamorak helplessly. No use, unless—

He couldn't bring himself to face that unless just yet.

That night, Lamorak slept scarcely at all. Ragusnik asked for only the basic elements of humanity. But opposing that were thirty thousand Elseverians who faced death.

The welfare of thirty thousand on one side; the just demands of one family on the other. Could one say that thirty thousand who would support such injustice deserved to die? Injustice by what standards? Earth's? Elsevere's? And who was Lamorak that he should judge?

And Ragusnik? He was willing to let thirty thousand die, including men and women who merely accepted a situation they had been taught to accept and could not change if they wished to. And children who had nothing at all to do with it.

Thirty thousand on one side; a single family on the other.

Lamorak made his decision in something that was almost despair; in the morning he called the Chief Councillor.

He said, "Sir, if you can find a substitute, Ragusnik will see that he has lost all chance to force a decision in his favor and will return to work."

"There can be no substitute," sighed the Chief Councillor; "I have explained that."

"No substitute among the Elseverians, but I am not an Elseverian; it doesn't matter to me. I will substitute."

They were excited, much more excited than Lamorak himself. A dozen times they asked him if he was serious.

Lamorak had not shaved, and he felt sick. "Certainly, I'm serious. And any time Ragusnik acts like this, you can always import a substitute. No other world has the taboo and there will always be plenty of temporary substitutes available if you pay enough."

(He was betraying a brutally exploited man, and he knew it. But he told himself desperately: *Except for ostracism, he's very well treated. Very well.*)

They gave him the handbooks and he spent six hours, reading and rereading. There was no use asking questions. None of the Elseverians knew anything about the job, except for what was in the handbook; and all seemed uncomfortable if the details were as much as mentioned.

"Maintain zero reading of galvanometer A-2 at all times during red signal of the Lunge-howler," read Lamorak. "Now what's a Lunge-howler?"

"There will be a sign," muttered Blei, and the Elseverians looked at each other hang-dog and bent their heads to stare at their fingerends.

They left him long before he reached the small rooms that were the central headquarters of generations of working Ragusniks, serving their world. He had specific instructions concerning which turnings to take and what level to reach, but they hung back and let him proceed alone.

He went through the rooms painstakingly, identifying the instruments and controls, following the schematic diagrams in the handbook.

There's a Lunge-howler, he thought, with gloomy satisfaction.

The sign did indeed say so. It had a semicircular face bitten into holes that were obviously designed to glow in separate colors. Why a "howler" then?

He didn't know.

Somewhere, thought Lamorak, *somewhere wastes are accumulating pushing against gears and exits, pipelines and stills, waiting to be handled in half a hundred ways. Now they just accumulate.*

Not without a tremor, he pulled the first switch as indicated by the handbook in its directions for "Initiation." A gentle murmur of life made itself felt through the floors and walls. He turned a knob and lights went on.

At each step, he consulted the handbook, though he knew it by heart; and with each step, the rooms brightened and the dial-indicators sprang into motion and a humming grew louder.

Somewhere deep in the factories, the accumulated wastes were being drawn into the proper channels.

A high-pitched signal sounded and startled Lamorak out of his painful concentration. It was the communications signal and Lamorak fumbled his receiver into action.

Ragusnik's head showed, startled; then slowly, the incredulity and outright shock faded from his eyes. *"That's* how it is, then."

"I'm not an Elseverian, Ragusnik; I don't mind doing this."

"But what business is it of yours? Why do you interfere?"

"I'm on your side, Ragusnik, but I must do this."

"Why, if you're on my side? Do they treat people on your world as they treat me here?"

"Not any longer. But even if you are right, there are thirty thousand people on Elsevere to be considered."

"They would have given in; you've ruined my only chance."

"They would *not* have given in. And in a way, you've won; they know now that you're dissatisfied. Until now, they never dreamed a Ragusnik could be unhappy, that he could make trouble."

"What if they know? Now all they need do is hire an Outworlder anytime."

Lamorak shook his head violently. He had thought this through in these last bitter hours. "The fact that they know means that the Elseverians will begin to think about you; some will begin to wonder if it's right to treat a human so. And if Outworlders are hired, they'll spread the word that this goes on upon Elsevere and Galactic public opinion will be in your favor."

"And?"

"Things will improve. In your son's time, things will be much better."

"In my son's time," said Ragusnik, his cheeks sagging. "I might have had it now. Well, I lose. I'll go back to the job."

Lamorak felt an overwhelming relief. "If you'll come here now, sir, you may have your job and I'll consider it an honor to shake your hand."

Ragusnik's head snapped up and filled with a gloomy pride. "You call me 'sir' and offer to shake my hand. Go about your business, Earthman, and leave me to my work, for I would not shake yours."

Lamorak returned the way he had come, relieved that the crisis was over, and profoundly depressed, too.

He stopped in surprise when he found a section of corridor cordoned off, so he could not pass. He looked about for alternate routes, then startled at a magnified voice above his head. "Dr. Lamorak, do you hear me? This is Councillor Blei."

Lamorak looked up. The voice came over some sort of public address system, but he saw no sign of an outlet.

He called out, "Is anything wrong? Can you hear me?"

"I hear you."

Instinctively, Lamorak was shouting. "Is anything wrong? There seems to be a block here. Are there complications with Ragusnik?"

"Ragusnik has gone to work," came Blei's voice. "The crisis is over, and you must make ready to leave."

"Leave?"

"Leave Elsevere; a ship is being made ready for you now."

"But wait a bit." Lamorak was confused by this sudden leap of events. "I haven't completed my gathering of data."

Blei's voice said, "This cannot be helped. You will be directed to the ship and your belongings will be sent after you by servo-mechanisms. We trust—we trust—"

Something was becoming clear to Lamorak. "You trust *what?*"

"We trust you will make no attempt to see or speak directly to any Elseverian. And of course we hope you will avoid embarrassment by not attempting to return to Elsevere at any time in the future. A colleague of yours would be welcome if further data concerning us is needed."

"I understand," said Lamorak, tonelessly. Obviously, he had himself become a Ragusnik. He had handled the controls that in turn had handled the wastes; he was ostracized. He was a corpse-handler, a swineherd, an inside man at the skonk works.

He said, "Good-bye."

Blei's voice said, "Before we direct you, Dr. Lamorak—on behalf of the Council of Elsevere, I thank you for your help in this crisis."

"You're welcome," said Lamorak, bitterly.

THE MARTIAN WAY

1

From the doorway of the short corridor between the only two rooms in the travel-head of the spaceship, Mario Esteban Rioz watched sourly as Ted Long adjusted the video dials painstakingly. Long tried a touch clockwise, then a touch counter. The picture was lousy.

Rioz knew it would stay lousy. They were too far from Earth and at a bad position facing the Sun. But then Long would not be expected to know that. Rioz remained standing in the doorway for an additional moment, head bent to clear the upper lintel, body turned half sidewise to fit the narrow opening. Then he jerked into the galley like a cork popping out of a bottle.

"What are you after?" he asked.

"I thought I'd get Hilder," said Long.

Rioz propped his rump on the corner of a table shelf. He lifted a conical can of milk from the companion shelf just above his head. Its point popped under pressure. He swirled it gently as he waited for it to warm.

"What for?" he said. He upended the cone and sucked noisily.

"Thought I'd listen."

"I think it's a waste of power."

Long looked up, frowning. "It's customary to allow free use of personal video sets."

"Within reason," retorted Rioz.

Their eyes met challengingly. Rioz had the rangy body, the gaunt, cheek-sunken face that was almost the hallmark of the Martian Scavenger, those Spacers who patiently haunted the space routes between Earth and Mars. Pale blue eyes were set keenly in the brown, lined face which, in turn, stood darkly out against the white surrounding syntho-fur that lined the upturned collar of his leathtic space jacket.

Long was altogether paler and softer. He bore some of the marks of the Grounder, although no second-generation Martian could be a Grounder in the sense that Earthmen were. His own collar was thrown back and his dark brown hair freely exposed.

"What do you call within reason?" demanded Long.

Rioz's thin lips grew thinner. He said, "Considering that we're not even going to make expenses this trip, the way it looks, any power drain at all is outside reason."

Long said, "If we're losing money, hadn't you better get back to your post? It's your watch."

Rioz grunted and ran a thumb and forefinger over the stubble on his chin. He got up and trudged to the door, his soft, heavy boots muting the sound of his steps. He paused to look at the thermostat, then turned with a flare of fury.

"I *thought* it was hot. Where do you think you are?"

Long said, "Forty degrees isn't excessive."

"For you it isn't, maybe. But this is space, not a heated office at the iron mines." Rioz swung the thermostat control down to minimum with a quick thumb movement. "Sun's warm enough."

"The galley isn't on Sunside."

"It'll percolate through, damn it."

Rioz stepped through the door and Long stared after him for a long moment, then turned back to the video. He did not turn up the thermostat.

The picture was still flickering badly, but it would have to do. Long folded a chair down out of the wall. He leaned forward, waiting through the formal announcement, the momentary pause before the slow dissolution of the curtain, the spotlight picking out the well-known bearded figure which grew as it was brought forward until it filled the screen. The voice, impressive even through the flutings and croakings induced by the electron storms of twenty millions of miles, began, "Friends! My fellow citizens of Earth . . ."

2

Rioz's eye caught the flash of the radio signal as he stepped into the pilot room. For one moment, the palms of his hands grew clammy when it seemed to him that it was a radar pip; but that was only his guilt speaking. He should not have left the pilot room while on duty theoretically, though all Scavengers did it. Still, it was the standard nightmare, this business of a strike turning up during just those five minutes when one knocked off for a quick coffee because it seemed certain that space was clear. And the nightmare had been known to happen, too.

Rioz threw in the multiscanner. It was a waste of power, but while he was thinking about it, he might as well make sure.

Space was clear except for the far-distant echoes from the neighboring ships on the scavenging line.

He hooked up the radio circuit, and the blond, long-nosed head of Richard Swenson, copilot of the next ship on the Mars-ward side, filled it.

"Hey, Mario," said Swenson.

"Hi. What's new?"

There was a second and a fraction of pause between that and Swenson's next comment, since the speed of electromagnetic radiation is not infinite.

"What a day I've *had*."

"Something happened?" Rioz asked.

"I had a strike."

"Well, good."

"Sure, if I'd roped it in," said Swenson morosely.

"What happened?"

"Damn it, I headed in the wrong direction."

Rioz knew better than to laugh. He said, "How did you do that?"

"It wasn't my fault. The trouble was the shell was moving way out of the ecliptic. Can you imagine the stupidity of a pilot who can't work the release maneuver decently? How was I to know? I got the distance of the shell and let it go at that. I just assumed its orbit was in the usual trajectory family. Wouldn't you? I started along what I thought was a good line of intersection and it was five minutes before I noticed the distance was still going up. The pips were taking their sweet time returning. So then I took the angular projections of the thing, and it was too late to catch up with it."

"Any of the other boys getting it?"

"No. It's 'way out of the ecliptic and'll keep on going forever. That's not what bothers me so much. It was only an inner shell. But I hate to tell you how many tons of propulsion I wasted getting up speed and then getting back to station. You should have heard Canute."

Canute was Richard Swenson's brother and partner.

"Mad, huh?" said Rioz.

"Mad? Like to have killed me! But then we've been out five months now and it's getting kind of sticky. You know."

"I know."

"How are you doing, Mario?"

Rioz made a spitting gesture. "About that much this trip. Two shells in the last two weeks and I had to chase each one for six hours."

"Big ones?"

"Are you kidding? I could have scaled them down to Phobos by hand. This is the worst trip I've ever had."

"How much longer are you staying?"

"For my part, we can quit tomorrow. We've only been out two months and it's got so I'm chewing Long out all the time."

There was a pause over and above the electromagnetic lag.

Swenson said, "What's he like, anyway? Long, I mean."

Rioz looked over his shoulder. He could hear the soft, crackly mutter of the video in the galley. "I can't make him out. He says to me about a week after the start of the trip, 'Mario, why are you a Scavenger?' I just look at him and say, 'To make a living. Why do you suppose?' I mean, what the hell kind of a question is that? Why is anyone a Scavenger?

"Anyway, he says, 'That's not it, Mario.' *He's* telling *me*, you see. He says, 'You're a Scavenger because this is part of the Martian way.'"

Swenson said, "And what did he mean by that?"

Rioz shrugged. "I never asked him. Right now he's sitting in there listening to the ultramicrowave from Earth. He's listening to some Grounder called Hilder."

"Hilder? A Grounder politician, an Assemblyman or something, isn't he?"

"That's right. At least, I think that's right. Long is always doing things like that. He brought about fifteen pounds of books with him, all about Earth. Just plain dead weight, you know."

"Well, he's your partner. And talking about partners, I think I'll get back on the job. If I miss another strike, there'll be murder around here."

He was gone and Rioz leaned back. He watched the even green line that was the pulse scanner. He tried the multiscanner a moment. Space was still clear.

He felt a little better. A bad spell is always worse if the Scavengers all about you are pulling in shell after shell, if the shells go spiraling down the Phobos scrap forges with everyone's brand welded on except your own. Then, too, he had managed to work off some of his resentment toward Long.

It was a mistake teaming up with Long. It was always a mistake to team up with a tenderfoot. They thought what you wanted was conversation, especially Long, with his eternal theories about Mars and its great new role in human progress. That was the way he said it—Human Progress: the Martian Way; the New Creative Minority. And all the time what Rioz wanted wasn't talk, but a strike, a few shells to call their own.

At that, he hadn't any choice, really. Long was pretty well known down on Mars and made good pay as a mining engineer. He was a friend of Commissioner Sankov and he'd been out on one or two short scavenging missions before. You can't turn a fellow down flat before a tryout, even though it did look funny. Why should a mining engineer with a comfortable job and good money want to muck around in space?

Rioz never asked Long that question. Scavenger partners are forced too close together to make curiosity desirable, or sometimes even safe. But Long talked so much that he answered the question.

"I had to come out here, Mario," he said. "The future of Mars isn't in the mines; it's in space."

Rioz wondered how it would be to try a trip alone. Everyone said it was impossible. Even discounting lost opportunities when one man had to go off watch to sleep or attend to other things, it was well known that one man alone in space would become intolerably depressed in a relatively short while.

Taking a partner along made a six-month trip possible. A regular crew would be better, but no Scavenger could make money on a ship large enough to carry one. The capital it would take in propulsion alone!

Even two didn't find it exactly fun in space. Usually you had to change partners each trip and you could stay out longer with some than with others. Look at Richard and Canute Swenson. They teamed up every five or six trips because they were brothers. And yet whenever they did, it was a case of constantly mounting tension and antagonism after the first week.

Oh, well. Space was clear. Rioz would feel a little better if he went back in the galley and smoothed down some of the bickering with Long. He might as well show he was an old spacehand who took the irritations of space as they came.

He stood up, walked the three steps necessary to reach the short, narrow corridor that tied together the two rooms of the spaceship.

3

Once again Rioz stood in the doorway for a moment, watching. Long was intent on the flickering screen.

Rioz said gruffly, "I'm shoving up the thermostat. It's all right— we can spare the power."

Long nodded. "If you like."

Rioz took a hesitant step forward. Space was clear, so to hell with sitting and looking at a blank, green, pipless line. He said, "What's the Grounder been talking about?"

"History of space travel mostly. Old stuff, but he's doing it well. He's giving the whole works—color cartoons, trick photography, stills from old films, everything."

As if to illustrate Long's remarks, the bearded figure faded out of view, and a cross-sectional view of a spaceship flitted onto the screen. Hilder's voice continued, pointing out features of interest that appeared in schematic color. The communications system of the ship outlined itself in red as he talked about it, the storerooms, the proton micropile drive, the cybernetic circuits . . .

Then Hilder was back on the screen. "But this is only the travel-head of the ship. What moves it? What gets it off the Earth?"

Everyone knew what moved a spaceship, but Hilder's voice was like a drug. He made spaceship propulsion sound like the secret of the ages, like an ultimate revelation. Even Rioz felt a slight tingling of suspense, though he had spent the greater part of his life aboard ship.

Hilder went on. "Scientists call it different names. They call it the Law of Action and Reaction. Sometimes they call it Newton's Third Law. Sometimes they call it Conservation of Momentum. But we don't have to call it any name. We can just use our common sense. When we swim, we push water backward and move forward ourselves. When we walk, we push back against the ground and move forward. When we fly a gyro-flivver, we push air backward and move forward.

"Nothing can move forward unless something else moves backward. It's the old principle of "You can't get something for nothing."

"Now imagine a spaceship that weighs a hundred thousand tons lifting off Earth. To do that, something else must be moved downward. Since a spaceship is extremely heavy, a great deal of material must be moved downward. So much material, in fact, that there is no place to keep it all aboard ship. A special compartment must be built behind the ship to hold it."

Again Hilder faded out and the ship returned. It shrank and a truncated cone appeared behind it. In bright yellow, words appeared within it: MATERIAL TO BE THROWN AWAY.

"But now," said Hilder, "the total weight of the ship is much greater. You need still more propulsion and still more."

The ship shrank enormously to add on another larger shell and still another immense one. The ship proper, the travel-head, was a little dot on the screen, a glowing red dot.

Rioz said, "Hell, this is kindergarten stuff."

"Not to the people he's speaking to, Mario," replied Long. "Earth isn't Mars. There must be billions of Earth people who've never even seen a spaceship; don't know the first thing about it."

Hilder was saying, "When the material inside the biggest shell is used up, the shell is detached. It's thrown away, too."

The outermost shell came loose, wobbled about the screen.

"Then the second one goes," said Hilder, "and then, if the trip is a long one, the last is ejected."

The ship was just a red dot now, with three shells shifting and moving, lost in space.

Hilder said, "These shells represent a hundred thousand tons of tungsten, magnesium, aluminum, and steel. They are gone forever from Earth. Mars is ringed by Scavengers, waiting along the routes of space travel, waiting for the cast-off shells, netting and branding them, saving them for Mars. Not one cent of payment reaches Earth for them. They are salvage. They belong to the ship that finds them."

Rioz said, "We risk our investment and our lives. If we don't pick them up, no one gets them. What loss is that to Earth?"

"Look," said Long, "he's been talking about nothing but the drain that Mars, Venus, and the Moon put on Earth. This is just another item of loss."

"They'll get their return. We're mining more iron every year."

"And most of it goes right back into Mars. If you can believe his figures, Earth has invested two hundred billion dollars in Mars and received back about five billion dollars' worth of iron. It's put five hundred billion dollars into the Moon and gotten back a little over twenty-five billion dollars of magnesium, titanium, and assorted light metals. It's put fifty billion dollars into Venus and gotten back nothing. And that's what the taxpayers of Earth are really interested in—tax money out; nothing in."

The screen was filled, as he spoke, with diagrams of the Scavengers on the route to Mars; little, grinning caricatures of ships, reaching out wiry, tenuous arms that groped for the tumbling, empty shells, seizing and snaking them in, branding them MARS PROPERTY in glowing letters, then scaling them down to Phobos. Then it was Hilder again. "They tell us eventually they will return it all to us. Eventually! Once they are a going concern! We don't know when that will be. A century from now? A thousand years? A million? 'Eventually.' Let's take them at their word. Someday they will give us back all our metals. Someday they will grow their own food, use their own power, live their own lives.

"But one thing they can never return. Not in a hundred million years. Water!

"Mars has only a trickle of water because it is too small. Venus has no water at all because it is too hot. The Moon has none because it is too hot and too small. So Earth must supply not only drinking water and washing water for the Spacers, water to run their industries, water for the hydroponic factories they claim to be setting up—but even water to throw away by the millions of tons.

"What is the propulsive force that spaceships use? What is it they throw out behind so that they can accelerate forward? Once it was the gases generated from explosives. That was very expensive. Then the proton micropile was invented—a cheap power source that could heat up any liquid until it was a gas under tremendous pressure. What is the cheapest and most plentiful liquid available? Why, water, of course.

"Each spaceship leaves Earth carrying nearly a million tons— not pounds, tons—of water, for the sole purpose of driving it into space so that it may speed up or slow down.

"Our ancestors burned the oil of Earth madly and willfully. They destroyed its coal recklessly. We despise and condemn them for that, but at least they had this excuse—they thought that when the need arose, substitutes would be found. And they were right. We have our plankton farms and our proton micropiles.

"But there is no substitute for water. None! There never can be. And when our descendants view the desert we will have made of Earth, what excuse will they find for us? When the droughts come and grow—"

Long leaned forward and turned off the set. He said, "That bothers me. The damn fool is deliberately—What's the matter?"

Rioz had risen uneasily to his feet. "I ought to be watching the pips."

"The hell with the pips." Long got up likewise, followed Rioz through the narrow corridor, and stood just inside the pilot room. "If Hilder carries this through, if he's got the guts to make a real issue out of it—*Wow!*"

He had seen it too. The pip was a Class A, racing after the outgoing signal like a greyhound after a mechanical rabbit.

Rioz was babbling, "Space was clear, I tell you, *clear*. For Mars' sake, Ted, don't just freeze on me. See if you can spot it visually."

Rioz was working speedily and with an efficiency that was the result of nearly twenty years of scavenging. He had the distance in two minutes. Then, remembering Swenson's experience, he measured the angle of declination and the radial velocity as well.

He yelled at Long, "One point seven six radians. You can't miss it, man."

Long held his breath as he adjusted the vernier. "It's only half a radian off the Sun. It'll only be crescent-lit."

He increased magnification as rapidly as he dared, watching for the one "star" that changed position and grew to have a form, revealing itself to be no star.

"I'm starting, anyway," said Rioz. "We can't wait."

"I've got it. I've got it." Magnification was still too small to give it a definite shape, but the dot Long watched was brightening and dimming rhythmically as the shell rotated and caught sunlight on cross sections of different sizes.

"Hold on."

The first of many fine spurts of steam squirted out of the proper vents, leaving long trails of microcrystals of ice gleaming mistily in the pale beams of the distant Sun. They thinned out for a hundred miles or more. One spurt, then another, then another, as the Scavenger ship moved out of its stable trajectory and took up a course tangential to that of the shell.

"It's moving like a comet at perihelion!" yelled Rioz. "Those damned Grounder pilots knock the shells off that way on purpose. I'd like to—"

He swore his anger in a frustrated frenzy as he kicked steam backward and backward recklessly, till the hydraulic cushioning of his chair had soughed back a full foot and Long had found himself all but unable to maintain his grip on the guardrail.

"Have a heart," he begged.

But Rioz had his eye on the pips. "If you can't take it, man, stay on Mars!" The steam spurts continued to boom distantly.

The radio came to life. Long managed to lean forward through what seemed like molasses and closed contact. It was Swenson, eyes glaring.

Swenson yelled, "Where the hell are you guys going? You'll be in my sector in ten seconds."

Rioz said, "I'm chasing a shell."

"In *my* sector?"

"It started in mine and you're not in position to get it. Shut off that radio, Ted."

The ship thundered through space, a thunder that could be heard only within the hull. And then Rioz cut the engines in stages large enough to make Long flail forward. The sudden silence was more ear-shattering than the noise that had preceded it.

Rioz said, "All right. Let me have the 'scope."

They both watched. The shell was a definite truncated cone now, tumbling with slow solemnity as it passed along among the stars.

"It's a Class A shell, all right," said Rioz with satisfaction. A giant among shells, he thought. It would put them into the black.

Long said, "We've got another pip on the scanner. I think it's Swenson taking after us."

Rioz scarcely gave it a glance. "He won't catch us."

The shell grew larger still, filling the visiplate.

Rioz's hands were on the harpoon lever. He waited, adjusted the angle microscopically twice, played out the length allotment. Then he yanked, tripping the release.

For a moment, nothing happened. Then a metal mesh cable snaked out onto the visiplate, moving toward the shell like a striking cobra. It made contact, but it did not hold. If it had, it would have snapped instantly like a cobweb strand. The shell was turning with a rotational momentum amounting to thousands of tons. What the cable did do was to set up a powerful magnetic field that acted as a brake on the shell.

Another cable and another lashed out. Rioz sent them out in an almost heedless expenditure of energy.

"I'll get this one! By Mars, I'll get this one!"

With some two dozen cables stretching between ship and shell, he desisted. The shell's rotational energy, converted by braking into heat, had raised its temperature to a point where its radiation could be picked up by the ship's meters.

Long said, "Do you want me to put our brand on?"

"Suits me. But you don't have to if you don't want to. It's my watch."

"I don't mind."

Long clambered into his suit and went out the lock. It was the surest sign of his newness to the game that he could count the number of times he had been out in space in a suit. This was the fifth time.

He went out along the nearest cable, hand over hand, feeling the vibration of the mesh against the metal of his mitten.

He burned their serial number in the smooth metal of the shell. There was nothing to oxidize the steel in the emptiness of space. It simply melted and vaporized, condensing some feet away from the energy beam, turning the surface it touched into a gray, powdery dullness.

Long swung back toward the ship.

Inside again, he took off his helmet, white and thick with frost that collected as soon as he had entered.

The first thing he heard was Swenson's voice coming over the radio, almost unrecognizable in his rage: ". . . straight to the Commissioner. Damn it, there are rules to this game!"

Rioz sat back, unbothered. "Look, it hit my sector. I was late spotting it and I chased it into yours. You couldn't have gotten it with Mars for a backstop. That's all there is to it—You back, Long?"

He cut contact.

The signal button raged at him, but he paid no attention.

"He's going to the Commissioner?" Long asked.

"Not a chance. He just goes on like that because it breaks the monotony. He doesn't mean anything by it. He knows it's our shell. And how do you like that hunk of stuff, Ted?"

"Pretty good."

"Pretty good? It's terrific! Hold on. I'm setting it swinging."

The side jets spat steam and the ship started a slow rotation about the shell. The shell followed it. In thirty minutes, they were a gigantic bola spinning in emptiness. Long checked the *Ephemeris* for the position of Deimos.

At a precisely calculated moment, the cables released their magnetic field and the shell went streaking off tangentially in a trajectory that would, in a day or so, bring it within pronging distance of the shell stores on the Martian satellite.

Rioz watched it go. He felt good. He turned to Long. "This is one fine day for us."

"What about Hilder's speech?" asked Long.

"What? Who? Oh, that. Listen, if I had to worry about every thing some damned Grounder said, I'd never get any sleep. Forget it."

"I don't think we should forget it."

"You're nuts. Don't bother me about it, will you? Get some sleep instead."

4

Ted Long found the breadth and height of the city's main thoroughfare exhilarating. It had been two months since the Commissioner had declared a moratorium on scavenging and had pulled all ships out of space, but this feeling of a stretched-out vista had not stopped thrilling Long. Even the thought that the moratorium was called pending a decision on the part of Earth to enforce its new insistence on water economy, by deciding upon a ration limit for scavenging, did not cast him entirely down.

The roof of the avenue was painted a luminous light blue, perhaps as an old-fashioned imitation of Earth's sky, Ted wasn't sure. The walls were lit with the store windows that pierced them.

Off in the distance, over the hum of traffic and the sloughing noise of people's feet passing him, he could hear the intermittent blasting as new channels were being bored into Mars' crust. All his life he remembered such blastings. The ground he walked on had been part of solid, unbroken rock when he was born. The city was growing and would keep on growing—if Earth would only let it.

He turned off at a cross street, narrower, not quite as brilliantly lit, shop windows giving way to apartment houses, each with its row of lights along the front façade. Shoppers and traffic gave way to slower-paced individuals and to squawling youngsters who had as yet evaded the maternal summons to the evening meal.

At the last minute, Long remembered the social amenities and stopped off at a corner water store.

He passed over his canteen. "Fill 'er up."

The plump storekeeper unscrewed the cap, cocked an eye into the opening. He shook it a little and let it gurgle. "Not much left," he said cheerfully.

"No," agreed Long.

The storekeeper trickled water in, holding the neck of the canteen close to the hose tip to avoid spillage. The volume gauge whirred. He screwed the cap back on.

Long passed over the coins and took his canteen. It clanked against his hip now with a pleasing heaviness. It would never do to visit a family without a full canteen. Among the boys, it didn't matter. Not as much, anyway.

He entered the hallway of No. 27, climbed a short flight of stairs, and paused with his thumb on the signal.

The sound of voices could be heard plainly.

One was a woman's voice, somewhat shrill. "It's all right for you to have your Scavenger friends here, isn't it? I'm supposed to be thankful you manage to get home two months a year. Oh, it's quite enough that you spend a day or two with me. After that, it's the Scavengers again."

"I've been home for a long time now," said a male voice, "and this is business. For Mars' sake, let up, Dora. They'll be here soon."

Long decided to wait a moment before signaling. It might give them a chance to hit a more neutral topic.

"What do I care if they come?" retorted Dora. "Let them hear me. And I'd just as soon the Commissioner kept the moratorium on permanently. You hear me?"

"And what would we live on?" came the male voice hotly. "You tell me that."

"I'll tell you. You can make a decent, honorable living right here on Mars, just like everybody else. I'm the only one in this apartment house that's a Scavenger widow. That's what I am—a widow. I'm worse than a widow, because if I were a widow, I'd at least have a chance to marry someone else—What did you say?"

"Nothing. Nothing at all."

"Oh, I know what you said. Now listen here, Dick Swenson—"

"I only said," cried Swenson, "that now I know why Scavengers usually don't marry."

"You shouldn't have either. I'm tired of having every person in the neighborhood pity me and smirk and ask when you're coming home. Other people can be mining engineers and administrators and even tunnel borers. At least tunnel borers' wives have a decent homelife and their children don't grow up like vagabonds. Peter might as well not have a father—"

A thin boy-soprano voice made its way through the door. It was somewhat more distant, as though it were in another room. "Hey, Mom, what's a vagabond?"

Dora's voice rose a notch. "Peter! You keep your mind on your homework."

Swenson said in a low voice, "It's not right to talk this way in front of the kid. What kind of notions will he get about me?"

"Stay home then and teach him better notions."

Peter's voice called out again. "Hey, Mom, I'm going to be a Scavenger when I grow up."

Footsteps sounded rapidly. There was a momentary hiatus in the sounds, then a piercing, "Mom! Hey, Mom! Leggo my ear! What did I do?" and a snuffling silence.

Long seized the chance. He worked the signal vigorously.

Swenson opened the door, brushing down his hair with both hands.

"Hello, Ted," he said in a subdued voice. Then loudly, "Ted's here, Dora. Where's Mario, Ted?"

Long said, "He'll be here in a while."

Dora came bustling out of the next room, a small, dark woman with a pinched nose, and hair, just beginning to show touches of gray, combed off the forehead.

"Hello, Ted. Have you eaten?"

"Quite well, thanks. I haven't interrupted you, have I?"

"Not at all. We finished ages ago. Would you like some coffee?"

"I think so." Ted unslung his canteen and offered it.

"Oh, goodness, that's all right. We've plenty of water."

"I insist."

"Well, then—"

Back into the kitchen she went. Through the swinging door, Long caught a glimpse of dishes sitting in Secoterg, the "waterless cleaner that soaks up and absorbs grease and dirt in a twinkling. One ounce of water will rinse eight square feet of dish surface clean as clean. Buy Secoterg. Secoterg just cleans it right, makes your dishes shiny bright, does away with water waste—"

The tune started whining through his mind and Long crushed it with speech. He said, "How's Pete?"

"Fine, fine. The kid's in the fourth grade now. You know I don't get to see him much. Well, sir, when I came back last time, he looked at me and said . . ."

It went on for a while and wasn't too bad as bright sayings of bright children as told by dull parents go.

The door signal burped and Mario Rioz came in, frowning and red.

Swenson stepped to him quickly. "Listen, don't say anything about shell-snaring. Dora still remembers the time you fingered a Class A shell out of my territory and she's in one of her moods now."

"Who the hell wants to talk about shells?" Rioz slung off a fur-lined jacket, threw it over the back of the chair, and sat down.

Dora came through the swinging door, viewed the newcomer with a synthetic smile, and said, "Hello, Mario. Coffee for you, too?"

"Yeah," he said, reaching automatically for his canteen.

"Just use some more of my water, Dora," said Long quickly. "He'll owe it to me."

"Yeah," said Rioz.

"What's wrong, Mario?" asked Long.

Rioz said heavily, "Go on. Say you told me so. A year ago when Hilder made that speech, you told me so. Say it."

Long shrugged.

Rioz said, "They've set up the quota. Fifteen minutes ago the news came out."

"Well?"

"Fifty thousand tons of water per trip."

"What?" yelled Swenson, burning. "You can't get off Mars with fifty thousand!"

"That's the figure. It's a deliberate piece of gutting. No more scavenging."

Dora came out with the coffee and set it down all around.

"What's all this about no more scavenging?" She sat down very firmly and Swenson looked helpless.

"It seems," said Long, "that they're rationing us at fifty thousand tons and that means we can't make any more trips."

"Well, what of it?" Dora sipped her coffee and smiled gaily. "If you want my opinion, it's a good thing. It's time all you Scavengers found yourselves nice, steady jobs here on Mars. I mean it. It's no life to be running all over space—"

"Please, Dora," said Swenson.

Rioz came close to a snort.

Dora raised her eyebrows. "I'm just giving my opinions."

Long said, "Please feel free to do so. But I would like to say something. Fifty thousand is just a detail. We know that Earth—or at least Hilder's party—wants to make political capital out of a campaign for water economy, so we're in a bad hole. We've got to get water somehow or they'll shut us down altogether, right?"

"Well, sure," said Swenson.

"But the question is how, right?"

"If it's only getting water," said Rioz in a sudden gush of words, "there's only one thing to do and you know it. If the Grounders won't give us water, we'll take it. The water doesn't belong to them just because their fathers and grandfathers were too damned sick-yellow ever to leave their fat planet. Water belongs to people wherever they are. We're people and the water's ours, too. We have a right to it."

"How do you propose taking it?" asked Long.

"Easy! They've got oceans of water on Earth. They can't post a guard over every square mile. We can sink down on the night side of the planet any time we want, fill our shells, then get away. How can they stop us?"

"In half a dozen ways, Mario. How do you spot shells in space up to distances of a hundred thousand miles? One thin metal shell in all that space. How? By radar. Do you think there's no radar on Earth? Do you think that if Earth ever gets the notion we're engaged in waterlegging, it won't be simple for them to set up a radar network to spot ships coming in from space?"

Dora broke in indignantly. "I'll tell you one thing, Mario Rioz. My husband isn't going to be part of any raid to get water to keep up his scavenging with."

"It isn't just scavenging," said Mario. "Next they'll be cutting down on everything else. We've got to stop them now."

"But we don't need their water, anyway," said Dora. "We're not the Moon or Venus. We pipe enough water down from the polar caps for all we need. We have a water tap right in this apartment. There's one in every apartment on this block."

Long said, "Home use is the smallest part of it. The mines use water. And what do we do about the hydroponic tanks?"

"That's right," said Swenson. "What about the hydroponic tanks, Dora? They've got to have water and it's about time we arranged to grow our own fresh food instead of having to live on the condensed crud they ship us from Earth."

"Listen to him," said Dora scornfully. "What do you know about fresh food? You've never eaten any."

"I've eaten more than you think. Do you remember those carrots I picked up once?"

"Well, what was so wonderful about them? If you ask me, good baked protomeal is much better. And healthier, too. It just seems to be the fashion now to be talking fresh vegetables because they're increasing taxes for these hydroponics. Besides, all this will blow over."

Long said, "I don't think so. Not by itself, anyway. Hilder will probably be the next Coordinator, and then things may really get bad. If they cut down on food shipments, too—"

"Well, then," shouted Rioz, "what do we do? I still say take it! Take the water!"

"And I say we can't do that, Mario. Don't you see that what you're suggesting is the Earth way, the Grounder way? You're trying to hold on to the umbilical cord that ties Mars to Earth. Can't you get away from that? Can't you see the Martian way?"

"No, I can't. Suppose you tell me."

"I will, if you'll listen. When we think about the Solar System, what do we think about? Mercury, Venus, Earth, Moon, Mars, Phobos, and Deimos. There you are—seven bodies, that's all. But that doesn't represent one per cent of the Solar System. We Martians are right at the edge of the other ninety-nine per cent. Out there, farther from the Sun, there's unbelievable amounts of water!"

The others stared.

Swenson said uncertainly, "You mean the layers of ice on Jupiter and Saturn?"

"Not that specifically, but it is water, you'll admit. A thousand-mile-thick layer of water is a lot of water."

"But it's all covered up with layers of ammonia or—or something, isn't it?" asked Swenson. "Besides, we can't land on the major planets."

"I know that," said Long, "but I haven't said that was the answer. The major planets aren't the only objects out there. What about the asteroids and the satellites? Vesta is a two-hundred-mile-diameter asteroid that's hardly more than a chunk of ice. One of the moons of Saturn is mostly ice. How about that?"

Rioz said, "Haven't you ever been in space, Ted?"

"You know I have. Why do you ask?"

"Sure, I know you have, but you still talk like a Grounder. Have you thought of the distances involved? The average asteroid is a hundred twenty million miles from Mars at the closest. That's twice the Venus-Mars hop and you know that hardly any liners do even that in one jump. They usually stop off at Earth or the Moon. After all, how long do you expect anyone to stay in space, man?"

"I don't know. What's your limit?"

"You know the limit. You don't have to ask me. It's six months. That's handbook data. After six months, if you're still in space you're psychotherapy meat. Right, Dick?"

Swenson nodded.

"And that's just the asteroids," Rioz went on. "From Mars to Jupiter is three hundred thirty million miles, and to Saturn it's seven hundred million. How can anyone handle that kind of distance? Suppose you hit standard velocity or, to make it even, say you get up to a good two hundred kilomiles an hour. It would take you—let's see, allowing time for acceleration and deceleration—about six or seven months to get to Jupiter and nearly a year to get to Saturn. Of course, you could hike the speed to a million miles an hour, theoretically, but where would you get the water to do that?"

"Gee," said a small voice attached to a smutty nose and round eyes. "Saturn!"

Dora whirled in her chair. "Peter, march right back into your room."

"Aw, Ma."

"Don't 'Aw, Ma' me." She began to get out of the chair, and Peter scuttled away.

Swenson said, "Say, Dora, why don't you keep him company for a while? It's hard to keep his mind on homework if we're all out here talking."

Dora sniffed obstinately and stayed put. "I'll sit right here until I find out what Ted Long is thinking of. I tell you right now I don't like the sound of it."

Swenson said nervously, "Well, never mind Jupiter and Saturn. I'm sure Ted isn't figuring on that. But what about Vesta? We could make it in ten or twelve weeks there and the same back. And two hundred miles in diameter. That's four million cubic miles of ice!"

"So what?" said Rioz. "What do we do on Vesta? Quarry the ice? Set up mining machinery? Say, do you know how long that would take?"

Long said, "I'm talking about Saturn, not Vesta."

Rioz addressed an unseen audience. "I tell him seven hundred million miles and he keeps on talking."

"All right," said Long, "suppose you tell me how you know we can only stay in space six months, Mario?"

"It's common knowledge, damn it."

"Because it's in the *Handbook of Space Flight*. It's data compiled by Earth scientists from experience with Earth pilots and spacemen. You're still thinking Grounder style. You won't think the Martian way."

"A Martian may be a Martian, but he's still a man."

"But how can you be so blind? How many times have you fellows been out for over six months without a break?"

Rioz said, "That's different."

"Because you're Martians? Because you're professional Scavengers?"

"No. Because we're not on a flight. We can put back for Mars any time we want to."

"But you *don't* want to. That's my point. Earthmen have tremendous ships with libraries of films, with a crew of fifteen plus passengers. Still, they can only stay out six months maximum. Martian Scavengers have a two-room ship with only one partner. But we can stick it out more than six months."

Dora said, "I suppose you want to stay in a ship for a year and go to Saturn."

"Why not, Dora?" said Long. "We can do it. Don't you see we can? Earthmen can't. They've got a real world. They've got open sky and fresh food, all the air and water they want. Getting into a ship is a terrible change for them. More than six months is too much for them for that very reason. Martians are different. We've been living on a ship our entire lives.

"That's all Mars is—a ship. It's just a big ship forty-five hundred miles across with one tiny room in it occupied by fifty thousand people. It's closed in like a ship. We breathe packaged air and drink packaged water, which we repurify over and over. We eat the same food rations we eat aboard ship. When we get into a ship; it's the same thing we've known all our lives. We can stand it for a lot more than a year if we have to."

Dora said, "Dick, too?"

"We all can."

"Well, Dick can't. It's all very well for you, Ted Long, and this shell stealer here, this Mario, to talk about jaunting off for a year. You're not married. Dick is. He has a wife and he has a child and that's enough for him. He can just get a regular job right here on Mars. Why, my goodness, suppose you go to Saturn and find there's no water there. How'll you get back? Even if you had water left, you'd be out of food. It's the most ridiculous thing I ever heard of."

"No. Now listen," said Long tightly. "I've thought this thing out. I've talked to Commissioner Sankov and he'll help. But we've got to have ships and men. I can't get them. The men won't listen to me. I'm green. You two are known and respected. You're veterans. If you back me, even if you don't go yourselves, if you'll just help me sell this thing to the rest, get volunteers—"

"First," said Rioz grumpily, "you'll have to do a lot more explaining. Once we get to Saturn, where's the water?"

"That's the beauty of it," said Long. "That's why it's got to be Saturn. The water there is just floating around in space for the taking."

5

When Hamish Sankov had come to Mars, there was no such thing as a native Martian. Now there were two-hundred-odd babies whose grandfathers had been born on Mars—native in the third generation.

When he had come as a boy in his teens, Mars had been scarcely more than a huddle of grounded space ships connected by sealed underground tunnels. Through the years, he had seen buildings grow and burrow widely, thrusting blunt snouts up into the thin, unbreathable atmosphere. He had seen huge storage depots spring up into which spaceships and their loads could be swallowed whole. He had seen the mines grow from nothing to a huge gouge in the Martian crust, while the population of Mars grew from fifty to fifty thousand.

It made him feel old, these long memories—they and the even dimmer memories induced by the presence of this Earthman before him. His visitor brought up those long-forgotten scraps of thought about a soft-warm world that was as kind and gentle to mankind as the mother's womb.

The Earthman seemed fresh from that womb. Not very tall, not very lean; in fact, distinctly plump. Dark hair with a neat little wave in it, a neat little mustache, and neatly scrubbed skin. His clothing was right in style and as fresh and neatly turned as plastek could be.

Sankov's own clothes were of Martian manufacture, serviceable and clean, but many years behind the times. His face was craggy and lined, his hair was pure white, and his Adam's apple wobbled when he talked.

The Earthman was Myron Digby, member of Earth's General Assembly. Sankov was Martian Commissioner.

Sankov said, "This all hits us hard, Assemblyman."

"It's hit most of us hard, too, Commissioner."

"Uh-huh. Can't honestly say then that I can make it out. Of course, you understand, I don't make out that I can understand Earth ways, for all that I was born there. Mars is a hard place to live, Assemblyman, and you have to understand that. It takes a lot of shipping space just to bring us food, water, and raw materials so we can live. There's not much room left for books and news films. Even video programs can't reach Mars, except for about a month when Earth is in conjunction, and even then nobody has much time to listen.

"My office gets a weekly summary film from Planetary Press. Generally, I don't have time to pay attention to it. Maybe you'd call us provincial, and you'd be right. When something like this happens, all we can do is kind of helplessly look at each other."

Digby said slowly, "You can't mean that your people on Mars haven't heard of Hilder's anti-Waster campaign."

"No, can't exactly say that. There's a young Scavenger, son of a good friend of mine who died in space—" Sankov scratched the side of his neck doubtfully—"who makes a hobby out of reading up on Earth history and things like that. He catches video broadcasts when he's out in space and he listened to this man Hilder. Near as I can make out, that was the first talk Hilder made about Wasters.

"The young fellow come to me with that. Naturally, I didn't take him very serious. I kept an eye on the Planetary Press films for a while after that, but there wasn't much mention of Hilder and what there was made him out to look pretty funny."

"Yes, Commissioner," said Digby, "it all seemed quite a joke when it started."

Sankov stretched out a pair of long legs to one side of his desk and crossed them at the ankles. "Seems to me it's still pretty much of a joke. What's his argument? We're using up water. Has he tried looking at some figures? I got them all here. Had them brought to me when this committee arrived.

"Seems that Earth has four hundred million cubic miles of water in its oceans and each cubic mile weighs four and a half billion tons. That's a lot of water. Now we use some of that heap in space flight. Most of the thrust is inside Earth's gravitational field, and that means the water thrown out finds its way back to the oceans. Hilder doesn't figure that in. When he says a million tons of water is used up per flight, he's a liar. It's less than a hundred thousand tons.

"Suppose, now, we have fifty thousand flights a year. We don't, of course; not even fifteen hundred. But let's say there are fifty thousand. I figure there's going to be considerable expansion as time goes on. With fifty thousand flights, one cubic mile of water would be lost to space each year. That means that in a million years, Earth would *lose one quarter of one per cent* of its total water supply!"

Digby spread his hands, palms upward, and let them drop. "Commissioner, Interplanetary Alloys has used figures like that in their campaign against Hilder, but you can't fight a tremendous, emotion-filled drive with cold mathematics. This man Hilder has invented a name, 'Wasters.' Slowly he has built this name up into a gigantic conspiracy; a gang of brutal, profit-seeking wretches raping Earth for their own immediate benefit.

"He has accused the government of being riddled with them, the Assembly of being dominated by them, the press of being owned by them. None of this, unfortunately, seems ridiculous to the average man. He knows all too well what selfish men can do to Earth's resources. He knows what happened to Earth's oil during the Time of Troubles, for instance, and the way topsoil was ruined.

"When a farmer experiences a drought, he doesn't care that the amount of water lost in space flight isn't a droplet in a fog as far as Earth's overall water supply is concerned. Hilder has given him something to blame and that's the strongest possible consolation for disaster. He isn't going to give that up for a diet of figures."

Sankov said, "That's where I get puzzled. Maybe it's because I don't know how things work on Earth, but it seems to me that there aren't just droughty farmers there. As near as I could make out from the news summaries, these Hilder people are a minority. Why is it Earth goes along with a few farmers and some crackpots that egg them on?"

"Because, Commissioner, there are such things as worried human beings. The steel industry sees that an era of space flight will stress increasingly the light, nonferrous alloys. The various miners' unions worry about extraterrestrial competition. Any Earthman who can't get aluminum to build a prefab is certain that it is because the aluminum is going to Mars. I know a professor of archaeology who's an anti-Waster because he can't get a government grant to cover his excavations. He's convinced that all government money is going into rocketry research and space medicine, and he resents it."

Sankov said, "That doesn't sound like Earth people are much different from us here on Mars. But what about the General Assembly? Why do they have to go along with Hilder?"

Digby smiled sourly. "Politics isn't pleasant to explain. Hilder introduced this bill to set up a committee to investigate waste in space flight. Maybe three-fourths or more of the General Assembly was against such an investigation as an intolerable and useless extension of bureaucracy—which it is. But then how could any legislator be against a mere investigation of waste? It would sound as though he had something to fear or to conceal. It would sound as though he were himself profiting from waste. Hilder is not in the least afraid of making such accusations, and whether true or not, they would be a powerful factor with the voters in the next election. The bill passed.

"And then there came the question of appointing the members of the committee. Those who were against Hilder shied away from membership, which would have meant decisions that would be continually embarrassing. Remaining on the sidelines would make one that much less a target for Hilder. The result is that I am the only member of the committee who is outspokenly anti-Hilder and it may cost me reelection."

Sankov said, "I'd be sorry to hear that, Assemblyman. It looks as though Mars didn't have as many friends as we thought we had.

We wouldn't like to lose one. But if Hilder wins out—what's he after, anyway?"

"I should think," said Digby, "that that is obvious. He wants to be the next Global Coordinator."

"Think he'll make it?"

"If nothing happens to stop him, he will."

"And then what? Will he drop this Waster campaign then?"

"I can't say. I don't know if he's laid his plans past the Coordinacy. Still, if you want my guess, he couldn't abandon the campaign and maintain his popularity. It's gotten out of hand."

Sankov scratched the side of his neck. "All right. In that case, I'll ask you for some advice. What can we folks on Mars do? You know Earth. You know the situation. We don't. Tell us what to do."

Digby rose and stepped to the window. He looked out upon the low domes of other buildings; red, rocky, completely desolate plain in between; a purple sky and a shrunken sun.

He said without turning, "Do you people really like it on Mars?"

Sankov smiled. "Most of us don't exactly know any other world, Assemblyman. Seems to me Earth would be something queer and uncomfortable to them."

"But wouldn't Martians get used to it? Earth isn't hard to take after this. Wouldn't your people learn to enjoy the privilege of breathing air under an open sky? You once lived on Earth. You remember what it was like."

"I sort of remember. Still, it doesn't seem to be easy to explain. Earth is just there. It fits people and people fit it. People take Earth the way they find it. Mars is different. It's sort of raw and doesn't fit people. People got to make something out of it. They got to build a world, and not take what they find. Mars isn't much yet, but we're building, and when we're finished, we're going to have just what we like. It's sort of a great feeling to know you're building a world. Earth would be kind of unexciting after that."

The Assemblyman said, "Surely the ordinary Martian isn't such a philosopher that he's content to live this terribly hard life for the sake of a future that must be hundreds of generations away."

"No-o, not just like that." Sankov put his right ankle on his left knee and cradled it as he spoke. "Like I said, Martians are a lot like Earthmen, which means they're sort of human beings, and human beings don't go in for philosophy much. Just the same, there's something to living in a growing world, whether you think about it much or not.

"My father used to send me letters when I first came to Mars. He was an accountant and he just sort of stayed an accountant. Earth wasn't much different when he died from what it was when he was born. He didn't see anything happen. Everyday was like every other day, and living was just a way of passing time until he died.

"On Mars, it's different. Every day there's something new—the city's bigger, the ventilation system gets another kick, the water lines from the poles get slicked up. Right now, we're planning to set up a news-film association of our own. We're going to call it Mars Press. If you haven't lived when things are growing all about you, you'll never understand how wonderful it feels.

"No, Assemblyman, Mars is hard and tough and Earth is a lot more comfortable, but seems to me if you take our boys to Earth, they'll be unhappy. They probably wouldn't be able to figure out why, most of them, but they'd feel lost; lost and useless. Seems to me lots of them would never make the adjustment."

Digby turned away from the window and the smooth, pink skin of his forehead was creased into a frown. "In that case, Commissioner, I am sorry for you. For all of you."

"Why?"

"Because I don't think there's anything your people on Mars can do. Or the people on the Moon or Venus. It won't happen now; maybe it won't happen for a year or two, or even five years. But pretty soon you'll all have to come back to Earth, unless—"

Sankov's white eyebrows bent low over his eyes. "Well?"

"Unless you can find another source of water besides the planet Earth."

Sankov shook his head. "Don't seem likely, does it?"

"Not very."

"And except for that, seems to you there's no chance?"

"None at all."

Digby said that and left, and Sankov stared for a long time at nothing before he punched a combination of the local communi-line.

After a while, Ted Long looked out at him.

Sankov said, "You were right, son. There's nothing they can do. Even the ones that mean well see no way out. How did you know?"

"Commissioner," said Long, "when you've read all you can about the Time of Troubles, particularly about the twentieth century, nothing political can come as a real surprise."

"Well, maybe. Anyway, son, Assemblyman Digby is sorry for us, quite a piece sorry, you might say, but that's all. He says we'll have to leave Mars—or else get water somewhere else. Only he thinks that we can't get water somewhere else."

"You know we can, don't you, Commissioner?"

"I know we *might*, son. It's a terrible risk."

"If I find enough volunteers, the risk is our business."

"How is it going?"

"Not bad. Some of the boys are on my side right now. I talked Mario Rioz into it, for instance, and you know he's one of the best."

"That's just it—the volunteers will be the best men we have. I hate to allow it."

"If we get back, it will be worth it."

"If! It's a big word, son."

"And a big thing we're trying to do."

"Well, I gave my word that if there was no help on Earth, I'll see that the Phobos water hole lets you have all the water you'll need. Good luck."

6

Half a million miles above Saturn, Mario Rioz was cradled on nothing and sleep was delicious. He came out of it slowly and for a while, alone in his suit, he counted the stars and traced lines from one to another.

At first, as the weeks flew past, it was scavenging all over again, except for the gnawing feeling that every minute meant an additional number of thousands of miles away from all humanity. That made it worse.

They had aimed high to pass out of the ecliptic while moving through the Asteroid Belt. That had used up water and had probably been unnecessary. Although tens of thousands of worldlets look as thick as vermin in two-dimensional projection upon a photographic plate, they are nevertheless scattered so thinly through the quadrillions of cubic miles that make up their conglomerate orbit that only the most ridiculous of coincidences would have brought about a collision.

Still, they passed over the Belt and someone calculated the chances of collision with a fragment of matter large enough to do damage. The value was so low, so impossibly low, that it was perhaps inevitable that the notion of the "space-float" should occur to someone.

The days were long and many, space was empty, only one man was needed at the controls at any one time. The thought was a natural.

First, it was a particularly daring one who ventured out for fifteen minutes or so. Then another who tried half an hour. Eventually, before the asteroids were entirely behind, each ship regularly had its off-watch member suspended in space at the end of a cable.

It was easy enough. The cable, one of those intended for operations at the conclusion of their journey, was magnetically attached at both ends, one to the space suit to start with. Then you clambered out the lock onto the ship's hull and attached the other end there. You paused awhile, clinging to the metal skin by the electromagnets in your boots. Then you neutralized those and made the slightest muscular effort.

Slowly, ever so slowly, you lifted from the ship and even more slowly the ship's larger mass moved an equivalently shorter distance downward. You floated incredibly, weightlessly, in solid, speckled black. When the ship had moved far enough away from you, your gauntleted hand, which kept touch upon the cable, tightened its grip slightly. Too tightly, and you would begin moving back toward the ship and it toward you. Just tightly enough, and friction would halt you. Because your motion was equivalent to that of the ship, it seemed as motionless below you as though it had been painted against an impossible background while the cable between you hung in coils that had no reason to straighten out.

It was a half ship to your eye. One half was lit by the light of the feeble Sun, which was still too bright to look at directly without the heavy protection of the polarized space-suit visor. The other half was black on black, invisible.

Space closed in and it was like sleep. Your suit was warm, it renewed its air automatically, it had food and drink in special containers from which it could be sucked with a minimal motion of the head, it took care of wastes appropriately. Most of all, more than anything else, there was the delightful euphoria of weightlessness.

You never felt so well in your life. The days stopped being too long, they weren't long enough, and there weren't enough of them.

They had passed Jupiter's orbit at a spot some thirty degrees from its then position. For months, it was the brightest object in the sky, always excepting the glowing white pea that was the Sun. At its brightest, some of the Scavengers insisted they could make out Jupiter as a tiny sphere, one side squashed out of true by the night shadow.

Then over a period of additional months it faded, while another dot of light grew until it was brighter than Jupiter. It was Saturn, first as a dot of brilliance, then as an oval, glowing splotch. ("Why oval?" someone asked, and after a while, someone else said, "The rings, of course," and it was obvious.)

Everyone space-floated at all possible times toward the end, watching Saturn incessantly.

("Hey, you jerk, come on back in, damn it. You're on duty." "Who's on duty? I've got fifteen minutes more by my watch." "You set your watch back. Besides, I gave you twenty minutes yesterday." "You wouldn't give two minutes to your grandmother." "Come on in, damn it, or I'm coming out anyway." "All right, I'm coming. Holy howlers, what a racket over a lousy minute." But no quarrel could possibly be serious, not in space. It felt too good.)

Saturn grew until at last it rivaled and then surpassed the Sun. The rings, set at a broad angle to their trajectory of approach, swept grandly about the planet, only a small portion being eclipsed. Then, as they approached, the span of the rings grew still wider, yet narrower as the angle of approach constantly decreased.

The larger moons showed up in the surrounding sky like serene fireflies.

Mario Rioz was glad he was awake so that he could watch again. Saturn filled half the sky, streaked with orange, the night shadow cutting it fuzzily nearly one quarter of the way in from the right. Two round little dots in the brightness were shadows of two of the moons. To the left and behind him (he could look over his left shoulder to see, and as he did so, the rest of his body inched slightly to the right to conserve angular momentum) was the white diamond of the Sun.

Most of all he liked to watch the rings. At the left, they emerged from behind Saturn, a tight, bright triple band of orange light. At the right, their beginnings were hidden in the night shadow, but showed up closer and broader. They widened as they came, like the flare of a horn, growing hazier as they approached, until, while the eye followed them, they seemed to fill the sky and lose themselves.

From the position of the Scavenger fleet just inside the outer rim of the outermost ring, the rings broke up and assumed their true identity as a phenomenal cluster of solid fragments rather than the tight, solid band of light they seemed.

Below him, or rather in the direction his feet pointed, some twenty miles away, was one of the ring fragments. It looked like a large, irregular splotch, marring the symmetry of space, three quarters in brightness and the night shadow cutting it like a knife. Other fragments were farther off, sparkling like star dust, dimmer and thicker, until, as you followed them down, they became rings once more.

The fragments were motionless, but that was only because the ships had taken up an orbit about Saturn equivalent to that of the outer edge of the rings.

The day before, Rioz reflected, he had been on that nearest fragment, working along with more than a score of others to mold it into the desired shape. Tomorrow he would be at it again.

Today—today he was space-floating.

"Mario?" The voice that broke upon his earphones was questioning.

Momentarily Rioz was flooded with annoyance. Damn it, he wasn't in the mood for company.

"Speaking," he said.

"I thought I had your ship spotted. How are you?"

"Fine. That you, Ted?"

"That's right," said Long.

"Anything wrong on the fragment?"

"Nothing. I'm out here floating."

"You?"

"It gets me, too, occasionally. Beautiful, isn't it?"

"Nice," agreed Rioz.

"You know, I've read Earth books—"

"Grounder books, you mean." Rioz yawned and found it diffi-cult under the circumstances to use the expression with the proper amount of resentment.

"—and sometimes I read descriptions of people lying on grass," continued Long. "You know that green stuff like thin, long pieces of paper they have all over the ground down there, and they look up at the blue sky with clouds in it. Did you ever see any films of that?"

"Sure. It didn't attract me. It looked cold."

"I suppose it isn't, though. After all, Earth is quite close to the Sun, and they say their atmosphere is thick enough to hold the heat. I must admit that personally I would hate to be caught under open sky with nothing on but clothes. Still, I imagine they like it."

"Grounders are nuts!"

"They talk about the trees, big brown stalks, and the winds, air movements, you know."

"You mean drafts. They can keep that, too."

"It doesn't matter. The point is they describe it beautifully, almost passionately. Many times I've wondered, 'What's it really like? Will I ever feel it or is this something only Earthmen can possibly feel?' I've felt so often that I was missing something vital. Now I know what it must be like. It's this. Complete peace in the middle of a beauty-drenched universe."

Rioz said, "They wouldn't like it. The Grounders, I mean. They're so used to their own lousy little world they wouldn't ap-preciate what it's like to float and look down on Saturn." He flipped his body slightly and began swaying back and forth about his center of mass, slowly, soothingly.

Long said, "Yes, I think so too. They're slaves to their planet. Even if they come to Mars, it will only be their children that are free. There'll be starships someday; great, huge things that can carry thousands of people and maintain their self-contained equilibrium for decades, maybe centuries. Mankind will spread through the whole Galaxy. But people will have to live their lives out on shipboard until new methods of interstellar travel are developed, so it will be Martians, not planet-bound Earthmen, who will colonize the Universe. That's inevitable. It's got to be. It's the Martian way."

But Rioz made no answer. He had dropped off to sleep again, rocking and swaying gently, half a million miles above Saturn.

7

The work shift of the ring fragment was the tail of the coin. The weightlessness, peace, and privacy of the space-float gave place to something that had neither peace nor privacy. Even the weightlessness, which continued, became more a purgatory than a paradise under the new conditions.

Try to manipulate an ordinarily nonportable heat projector. It could be lifted despite the fact that it was six feet high and wide and almost solid metal, since it weighed only a fraction of an ounce. But its inertia was exactly what it had always been, which meant that if it wasn't moved into position very slowly, it would just keep on going, taking you with it. Then you would have to hike the pseudo-grav field of your suit and come down with a jar.

Keralski had hiked the field a little too high and he came down a little too roughly, with the projector coming down with him at a dangerous angle. His crushed ankle had been the first casualty of the expedition.

Rioz was swearing fluently and nearly continuously. He continued to have the impulse to drag the back of his hand across his forehead in order to wipe away the accumulating sweat. The few times that he had succumbed to the impulse, metal had met silicone with a clash that rang loudly inside his suit, but served no useful purpose. The desiccators within the suit were sucking at maximum and, of course, recovering the water and restoring ion-exchanged liquid, containing a careful proportion of salt, into the appropriate receptacle.

Rioz yelled, "Damn it, Dick, wait till I give the word, will you?"

And Swenson's voice rang in his ears, "Well, how long am I supposed to sit here?"

"Till I say," replied Rioz.

He strengthened pseudo-grav and lifted the projector a bit. He released pseudo-grav, ensuring that the projector would stay in place for minutes even if he withdrew support altogether. He kicked the cable out of the way (it stretched beyond the close "horizon" to a power source that was out of sight) and touched the release.

The material of which the fragment was composed bubbled and vanished under its touch. A section of the lip of the tremendous cavity he had already carved into its substance melted away and a roughness in its contour had disappeared.

"Try it now," called Rioz.

Swenson was in the ship that was hovering nearly over Rioz's head.

Swenson called, "All clear?"

"I told you to go ahead."

It was a feeble flicker of steam that issued from one of the ship's forward vents. The ship drifted down toward the ring fragment. Another flicker adjusted a tendency to drift sidewise. It came down straight.

A third flicker to the rear slowed it to a feather rate.

Rioz watched tensely. "Keep her coming. You'll make it. You'll make it."

The rear of the ship entered the hole, nearly filling it. The bellying walls came closer and closer to its rim. There was a grinding vibration as the ship's motion halted.

It was Swenson's turn to curse. "It doesn't fit," he said.

Rioz threw the projector groundward in a passion and went flailing up into space. The projector kicked up a white crystalline dust all about it, and when Rioz came down under pseudo-grav, he did the same.

He said, "You went in on the bias, you dumb Grounder."

"I hit it level, you dirt-eating farmer."

Backward-pointing side jets of the ship were blasting more

strongly than before, and Rioz hopped to get out of the way.

The ship scraped up from the pit, then shot into space half a mile before forward jets could bring it to a halt.

Swenson said tensely, "We'll spring half a dozen plates if we do this once again. Get it right, will you?"

"I'll get it right. Don't worry about it. Just you come in right."

Rioz jumped upward and allowed himself to climb three hundred yards to get an overall look at the cavity. The gouge marks of the ship were plain enough. They were concentrated at one point halfway down the pit. He would get that.

It began to melt outward under the blaze of the projector.

Half an hour later the ship snuggled neatly into its cavity, and Swenson, wearing his space suit, emerged to join Rioz.

Swenson said, "If you want to step in and climb out of the suit I'll take care of the icing."

"It's all right," said Rioz. "I'd just as soon sit here and watch Saturn."

He sat down at the lip of the pit. There was a six-foot gap between it and the ship. In some places about the circle, it was two feet; in a few places, even merely a matter of inches. You couldn't expect a better fit out of handwork. The final adjustment would be made by steaming ice gently and letting it freeze into the cavity between the lip and the ship.

Saturn moved visibly across the sky, its vast bulk inching below the horizon.

Rioz said, "How many ships are left to put in place?"

Swenson said, "Last I heard, it was eleven. We're in now, so that means only ten. Seven of the ones that are placed are iced in. Two or three are dismantled."

"We're coming along fine."

"There's plenty to do yet. Don't forget the main jets at the other end. And the cables and the power lines. Sometimes I wonder if we'll make it. On the way out, it didn't bother me so much, but just now I was sitting at the controls and I was saying, 'We won't make it. We'll sit out here and starve and die with nothing but Saturn over us.' It makes me feel—"

He didn't explain how it made him feel. He just sat there.

Rioz said, "You think too damn much."

"It's different with you," said Swenson. "I keep thinking of Pete—and Dora."

"What for? She said you could go, didn't she? The Commissioner gave her that talk on patriotism and how you'd be a hero and set for life once you got back, and she said you could go. You didn't sneak out the way Adams did."

"Adams is different. That wife of his should have been shot when she was born. Some women can make hell for a guy, can't they? She didn't want him to go—but she'd probably rather he didn't come back if she can get his settlement pay."

"What's your kick, then? Dora wants you back, doesn't she?"

Swenson sighed. "I never treated her right."

"You turned over your pay, it seems to me. I wouldn't do that for any woman. Money for value received, not a cent more."

"Money isn't it. I get to thinking out here. A woman likes company. A kid needs his father. What am I doing 'way out here?"

"Getting set to go home."

"Ah-h, you don't understand."

8

Ted Long wandered over the ridged surface of the ring fragment with his spirits as icy as the ground he walked on. It had all seemed perfectly logical back on Mars, but that was Mars. He had worked it out carefully in his mind in perfectly reasonable steps. He could still remember exactly how it went.

It didn't take a ton of water to move a ton of ship. It was not mass equals mass, but mass times velocity equals mass times velocity. It didn't matter, in other words, whether you shot out a ton of water at a mile a second or a hundred pounds of water at twenty miles a second. You got the same final velocity out of the ship.

That meant the jet nozzles had to be made narrower and the steam hotter. But then drawbacks appeared. The narrower the nozzle, the more energy was lost in friction and turbulence. The hotter the steam, the more refractory the nozzle had to be and the shorter its life. The limit in that direction was quickly reached.

Then, since a given weight of water could move considerably

more than its own weight under the narrow-nozzle conditions, it paid to be big. The bigger the water-storage space, the larger the size of the actual travel-head, even in proportion. So they started to make liners heavier and bigger. But then the larger the shell, the heavier the bracings, the more difficult the weldings, the more exacting the engineering requirements. At the moment, the limit in that direction had been reached also.

And then he had put his finger on what had seemed to him to be the basic flaw—the original unswervable conception that the fuel had to be placed *inside* the ship; the metal had to be built to encircle a million tons of water.

Why? Water did not have to be water. It could be ice, and ice could be shaped. Holes could be melted into it. Travel-heads and jets could be fitted into it. Cables could hold travel-heads and jets stiffly together under the influence of magnetic field-force grips.

Long felt the trembling of the ground he walked on. He was at the head of the fragment. A dozen ships were blasting in and out of sheaths carved in its substance, and the fragment shuddered under the continuing impact.

The ice didn't have to be quarried. It existed in proper chunks in the rings of Saturn. That's all the rings were—pieces of nearly pure ice, circling Saturn. So spectroscopy stated and so it had turned out to be. He was standing on one such piece now, over two miles long, nearly one mile thick. It was almost half a billion tons of water, all in one piece, and he was standing on it.

But now he was face to face with the realities of life. He had never told the men just how quickly he had expected to set up the fragment as a ship, but in his heart, he had imagined it would be two days. It was a week now and he didn't dare to estimate the remaining time. He no longer even had any confidence that the task was a possible one. Would they be able to control jets with enough delicacy through leads slung across two miles of ice to manipulate out of Saturn's dragging gravity?

Drinking water was low, though they could always distill more out of the ice. Still, the food stores were not in a good way either.

He paused, looked up into the sky, eyes straining. *Was the* object growing larger? He ought to measure its distance. Actually, he lacked the spirit to add that trouble to the others. His mind slid back to greater immediacies.

Morale, at least, was high. The men seemed to enjoy being out Saturn-way. They were the first humans to penetrate this far, the first to pass the asteroids, the first to see Jupiter like a glowing pebble to the naked eye, the first to see Saturn—like that.

He didn't think fifty practical, case-hardened, shell-snatching Scavengers would take time to feel that sort of emotion. But they did. And they were proud.

Two men and a half-buried ship slid up the moving horizon as he walked.

He called crisply, "Hello, there!"

Rioz answered, "That you, Ted?"

"You bet. Is that Dick with you?"

"Sure. Come on, sit down. We were just getting ready to ice in and we were looking for an excuse to delay."

"I'm not," said Swenson promptly. "When will we be leaving, Ted?"

"As soon as we get through. That's no answer, is it?"

Swenson said dispiritedly, "I suppose there isn't any other answer."

Long looked up, staring at the irregular bright splotch in the sky. Rioz followed his glance. "What's the matter?"

For a moment, Long did not reply. The sky was black otherwise and the ring fragments were an orange dust against it. Saturn was more than three fourths below the horizon and the rings were going with it. Half a mile away a ship bounded past the icy rim of the planetoid into the sky, was orange-lit by Saturnlight, and sank down again.

The ground trembled gently.

Rioz said, "Something bothering you about the Shadow?"

They called it that. It was the nearest fragment of the rings, quite close considering that they were at the outer rim of the rings, where the pieces spread themselves relatively thin. It was perhaps twenty miles off, a jagged mountain, its shape clearly visible.

"How does it look to you?" asked Long.

Rioz shrugged. "Okay, I guess. I don't see anything wrong."

"Doesn't it seem to be getting larger?"

"Why should it?"

"Well, doesn't it?" Long insisted.

Rioz and Swenson stared at it thoughtfully.

"It does look bigger," said Swenson.

"You're just putting the notion into our minds," Rioz argued. "If it were getting bigger, it would be coming closer."

"What's impossible about that?"

"These things are on stable orbits."

"They were when we came here," said Long. "There, did you feel that?"

The ground had trembled again.

Long said, "We've been blasting this thing for a week now. First, twenty-five ships landed on it, which changed its momentum right there. Not much, of course. Then we've been melting parts of it away and our ships have been blasting in and out of it—all at one end, too. In a week, we may have changed its orbit just a bit. The two fragments, this one and the Shadow, might be converging."

"It's got plenty of room to miss us in." Rioz watched it thoughtfully. "Besides, if we can't even tell for sure that it's getting bigger, how quickly can it be moving? Relative to us, I mean."

"It doesn't have to be moving quickly. Its momentum is as large as ours, so that, however gently it hits, we'll be nudged completely out of our orbit, maybe in toward Saturn, where we don't want to go. As a matter of fact, ice has a very low tensile strength, so that both planetoids might break up into gravel."

Swenson rose to his feet. "Damn it, if I can tell how a shell is moving a thousand miles away, I can tell what a mountain is doing twenty miles away." He turned toward the ship.

Long didn't stop him.

Rioz said, "There's a nervous guy."

The neighboring planetoid rose to zenith, passed overhead, began sinking. Twenty minutes later, the horizon opposite that portion behind which Saturn had disappeared burst into orange flame as its bulk began lifting again.

Rioz called into his radio, "Hey, Dick, are you dead in there?"

"I'm checking," came the muffled response.

"Is it moving?" asked Long.

"Yes."

"Toward us?"

There was a pause. Swenson's voice was a sick one. "On the nose, Ted. Intersection of orbits will take place in three days."

"You're crazy!" yelled Rioz.

"I checked four times," said Swenson.

Long thought blankly, What do we do now?

9

Some of the men were having trouble with the cables. They had to be laid precisely; their geometry had to be very nearly perfect for the magnetic field to attain maximum strength. In space, or even in air, it wouldn't have mattered. The cables would have lined up automatically once the juice went on.

Here it was different. A gouge had to be plowed along the planetoid's surface and into it the cable had to be laid. If it were not lined up within a few minutes of arc of the calculated direction, a torque would be applied to the entire planetoid, with consequent loss of energy, none of which could be spared. The gouges then had to be redriven, the cables shifted and iced into the new positions.

The men plodded wearily through the routine.

And then the word reached them:

"All hands to the jets!"

Scavengers could not be said to be the type that took kindly to discipline. It was a grumbling, growling, muttering group that set about disassembling the jets of the ships that yet remained intact, carrying them to the tail end of the planetoid, grubbing them into position, and stringing the leads along the surface.

It was almost twenty-four hours before one of them looked into the sky and said, "Holy jeepers!" followed by something less printable.

His neighbor looked and said, "I'll be damned!"

Once they noticed, all did. It became the most astonishing fact in the Universe.

"Look at the Shadow!"

It was spreading across the sky like an infected wound. Men looked at it, found it had doubled its size, wondered why they hadn't noticed that sooner.

Work came to a virtual halt. They besieged Ted Long.

He said, "We can't leave. We don't have the fuel to see us back to Mars and we don't have the equipment to capture another planetoid. So we've got to stay. Now the Shadow is creeping in on us because our blasting has thrown us out of orbit. We've got to change that by continuing the blasting. Since we can't blast the front end any more without endangering the ship we're building, let's try another way."

They went back to work on the jets with a furious energy that received impetus every half hour when the Shadow rose again over the horizon, bigger and more menacing than before.

Long had no assurance that it would work. Even if the jets would respond to the distant controls, even if the supply of water, which depended upon a storage chamber opening directly into the icy body of the planetoid, with built-in heat projectors steaming the propulsive fluid directly into the driving cells, were adequate, there was still no certainty that the body of the planetoid without a magnetic cable sheathing would hold together under the enormously disruptive stresses.

"Ready!" came the signal in Long's receiver.

Long called, "Ready!" and depressed the contact.

The vibration grew about him. The star field in the visiplate trembled.

In the rearview, there was a distant gleaming spume of swiftly moving ice crystals.

"It's blowing!" was the cry.

It kept on blowing. Long dared not stop. For six hours, it blew, hissing, bubbling, steaming into space; the body of the planetoid converted to vapor and hurled away.

The Shadow came closer until men did nothing but stare at the mountain in the sky, surpassing Saturn itself in spectacularity.

It's every groove and valley was a plain scar upon its face. But when it passed through the planetoid's orbit, it crossed more than half a mile behind its then position.

The steam jet ceased.

Long bent in his seat and covered his eyes. He hadn't eaten in two days. He could eat now, though. Not another planetoid was close enough to interrupt them, even if it began an approach that very moment.

Back on the planetoid's surface, Swenson said, "All the time I watched that damned rock coming down, I kept saying to myself, 'This can't happen. We can't let it happen.' "

"Hell," said Rioz, "we were all nervous. Did you see Jim Davis? He was green. I was a little jumpy myself."

"That's not it. It wasn't just—dying, you know. I was thinking—I know it's funny, but can't help it—I was thinking that Dora warned me I'd get myself killed, she'll never let me hear the last of it. Isn't that a crummy sort of attitude at a time like that?"

"Listen," said Rioz, "you wanted to get married, so you got married. Why come to me with your troubles?"

10

The flotilla, welded into a single unit, was returning over its mighty course from Saturn to Mars. Each day it flashed over a length of space that had taken nine days outward.

Ted Long had put the entire crew on emergency. With twenty-five ships embedded in the planetoid taken out of Saturn's rings and unable to move or maneuver independently, the coordination of their power sources into unified blasts was a ticklish problem. The jarring that took place on the first day of travel nearly shook them out from under their hair.

That, at least, smoothed itself out as the velocity raced upward under the steady thrust from behind. They passed the one-hundred-thousand-mile-an-hour mark late on the second day, and climbed steadily toward the million-mile mark and beyond.

Long's ship, which formed the needle point of the frozen fleet, was the only one which possessed a five-way view of space. It was an uncomfortable position under the circumstances. Long found himself watching tensely, imagining somehow that the stars would slowly begin to slip backward, to whizz past them, under the influence of the multiship's tremendous rate of travel.

They didn't, of course. They remained nailed to the black backdrop, their distance scorning with patient immobility any speed mere man could achieve.

The men complained bitterly after the first few days. It was not only that they were deprived of the space-float. They were burdened by much more than the ordinary pseudo-gravity field of the ships, by the effects of the fierce acceleration under which they were living. Long himself was weary to death of the relentless pressure against hydraulic cushions.

They took to shutting off the jet thrusts one hour out of every four and Long fretted.

It had been just over a year that he had last seen Mars shrinking in an observation window from this ship, which had then been an independent entity. What had happened since then? Was the colony still there?

In something like a growing panic, Long sent out radio pulses toward Mars daily, with the combined power of twenty-five ships behind it. There was no answer. He expected none. Mars and Saturn were on opposite sides of the Sun now, and until he mounted high enough above the ecliptic to get the Sun well beyond the line connecting himself and Mars, solar interference would prevent any signal from getting through.

High above the outer rim of the Asteroid Belt, they reached maximum velocity. With short spurts of power from first one side jet, then another, the huge vessel reversed itself. The composite jet in the rear began its mighty roaring once again, but now the result was deceleration.

They passed a hundred million miles over the Sun, curving down to intersect the orbit of Mars.

A week out of Mars, answering signals were heard for the first time, fragmentary, ether-torn, and incomprehensible, but they were coming from Mars. Earth and Venus were at angles sufficiently different to leave no doubt of that.

Long relaxed. There were still humans on Mars, at any rate.

Two days out of Mars, the signal was strong and clear and Sankov was at the other end.

Sankov said, "Hello, son. It's three in the morning here. Seems like people have no consideration for an old man. Dragged me right out of bed."

"I'm sorry, sir."

"Don't be. They were following orders. I'm afraid to ask, son. Anyone hurt? Maybe dead?"

"No deaths, sir. Not one."

"And—and the water? Any left?"

Long said, with an effort at nonchalance, "Enough."

"In that case, get home as fast as you can. Don't take any chances, of course."

"There's trouble, then."

"Fair to middling. When will you come down?"

"Two days. Can you hold out that long?"

"I'll hold out."

Forty hours later Mars had grown to a ruddy-orange ball that filled the ports and they were in the final planet-landing spiral.

"Slowly," Long said to himself, "slowly." Under these conditions, even the thin atmosphere of Mars could do dreadful damage if they moved through it too quickly.

Since they came in from well above the ecliptic, their spiral passed from north to south. A polar cap shot whitely below them, then the much smaller one of the summer hemisphere, the large one again, the small one, at longer and longer intervals. The planet approached closer, and the landscape began to show features.

"Prepare for landing!" called Long.

11

Sankov did his best to look placid, which was difficult considering how closely the boys had shaved their return. But it had worked out well enough.

Until a few days ago, he had no sure knowledge that they had survived. It seemed more likely—inevitable, almost—that they were nothing but frozen corpses somewhere in the trackless stretches from Mars to Saturn, new planetoids that had once been alive.

The Committee had been dickering with him for weeks before the news had come. They had insisted on his signature to the paper for the sake of appearances. It would look like an agreement, voluntarily and mutually arrived at. But Sankov knew well that, given complete obstinacy on his part, they would act unilaterally and be damned with appearances. It seemed fairly certain that Hilder's election was secure now and they would take the chance of arousing a reaction of sympathy for Mars.

So he dragged out the negotiations, dangling before them always the possibility of surrender.

And then he heard from Long and concluded the deal quickly.

The papers had lain before him and he had made a last statement for the benefit of the reporters who were present.

He said, "Total imports of water from Earth are twenty million tons a year. This is declining as we develop our own piping system. If I sign this paper agreeing to an embargo, our industry will be paralyzed, any possibilities of expansion will halt. It looks to me as if that can't be what's in Earth's mind, can it?"

Their eyes met his and held only a hard glitter. Assemblyman Digby had already been replaced and they were unanimous against him.

The Committee Chairman impatiently pointed out, "You have said all this before."

"I know, but right now I'm kind of getting ready to sign and I want it clear in my head. Is Earth set and determined to bring us to an end here?"

"Of course not. Earth is interested in conserving its irreplaceable water supply, nothing else."

"You have one and a half quintillion tons of water on Earth."

The Committee Chairman said, "We cannot spare water."

And Sankov had signed.

That had been the final note he wanted. Earth had one and a half quintillion tons of water and could spare none of it.

Now, a day and a half later, the Committee and the reporters waited in the spaceport dome. Through thick, curving windows, they could see the bare and empty grounds of Mars Spaceport.

The Committee Chairman asked with annoyance, "How much longer do we have to wait? And, if you don't mind, what are we waiting for?"

Sankov said, "Some of our boys have been out in space, out past the asteroids."

The Committee Chairman removed a pair of spectacles and cleaned them with a snowy-white handkerchief. "And they're returning?"

"They are."

The Chairman shrugged, lifted his eyebrows in the direction of the reporters.

In the smaller room adjoining, a knot of women and children clustered about another window. Sankov stepped back a bit to cast a glance toward them. He would much rather have been with them, been part of their excitement and tension. He, like them, had waited over a year now. He, like them, had thought, over and over again, that the men must be dead.

"You see that?" said Sankov, pointing.

"Hey!" cried a reporter. "It's a ship!"

A confused shouting came from the adjoining room.

It wasn't a ship so much as a bright dot obscured by a drifting white cloud. The cloud grew larger and began to have form. It was a double streak against the sky, the lower ends billowing out and upward again. As it dropped still closer, the bright dot at the upper end took on a crudely cylindrical form.

It was rough and craggy, but where the sunlight hit, brilliant high lights bounced back.

The cylinder dropped toward the ground with the ponderous slowness characteristic of space vessels. It hung suspended on those blasting jets and settled down upon the recoil of tons of matter hurling downward like a tired man dropping into his easy chair.

And as it did so, a silence fell upon all within the dome. The women and children in one room, the politicians and reporters in the other remained frozen, heads craned incredulously upward.

The cylinder's landing flanges, extending far below the two rear jets, touched ground and sank into the pebbly morass. And then the ship was motionless and the jet action ceased.

But the silence continued in the dome. It continued for a long time.

Men came clambering down the sides of the immense vessel, inching down, down the two-mile trek to the ground, with spikes on their shoes and ice axes in their hands. They were gnats against the blinding surface.

One of the reporters croaked, "What is it?"

"That," said Sankov calmly, "happens to be a chunk of matter that spent its time scooting around Saturn as part of its rings. Our boys fitted it out with travel-head and jets and ferried it home. It just turns out the fragments in Saturn's rings are made up out of ice."

He spoke into a continuing deathlike silence. "That thing that looks like a spaceship is just a mountain of hard water. If it were standing like that on Earth, it would be melting into a puddle and maybe it would break under its own weight. Mars is colder and has less gravity, so there's no such danger.

"Of course, once we get this thing really organized, we can have water stations on the moons of Saturn and Jupiter and on the asteroids. We can scale in chunks of Saturn's rings and pick them up and send them on at the various stations. Our Scavengers are good at that sort of thing.

"We'll have all the water we need. That one chunk you see is just under a cubic mile—or about what Earth would send us in two hundred years. The boys used quite a bit of it coming back from Saturn. They made it in five weeks, they tell me, and used up about a hundred million tons. But, Lord, that didn't make any dent at all in that mountain. Are you getting all this, boys?"

He turned to the reporters. There was no doubt they were getting it.

He said, "Then get this, too. Earth is worried about its water supply. It only has one and a half quintillion tons. It can't spare us a single ton out of it. Write down that we folks on Mars are worried about Earth and don't want anything to happen to Earth people. Write down that we'll sell water to Earth. Write down that we'll let them have million-ton lots for a reasonable fee. Write down that in ten years, we figure we can sell it in cubic-mile lots. Write down that Earth can quit worrying because Mars can sell it all the water it needs and wants."

The Committee Chairman was past hearing. He was feeling the future rushing in. Dimly he could see the reporters grinning as they wrote furiously.

Grinning.

He could hear the grin become laughter on Earth as Mars turned the tables so neatly on the anti-Wasters. He could hear the laughter thunder from every continent when word of the fiasco spread. And he could see the abyss, deep and black as space, into which would drop forever the political hopes of John Hilder and of every opponent of space flight left on Earth—his own included, of course.

In the adjoining room, Dora Swenson screamed with joy, and Peter, grown two inches, jumped up and down, calling, "Daddy! Daddy!"

Richard Swenson had just stepped off the extremity of the flange and, face showing clearly through the clear silicone of the headpiece, marched toward the dome.

"Did you ever see a guy look so happy?" asked Ted Long. "Maybe there's something in this marriage business."

"Ah, you've just been out in space too long," Rioz said.

ALFRED BESTER

1913–1987

In 1939 the magazine *Thrilling Wonder Stories* was running a contest for new writers. Alfred Bester, then in his early twenties, had just written his first short science fiction story, "The Broken Arrow." He entered it in the contest, won handily, and saw it published in the April 1939 issue of the magazine. (Interestingly, this was the same contest that another Grand Master, Robert A. Heinlein, decided at the last minute *not* to enter with his own first story, "Lifeline." It's worth a little musing to speculate on which would have won if the two stories had been in competition . . . and what would have been the effect on both writers' later careers.)

Over the next three years Bester published a dozen or so additional stories, competent journeyman science fiction for the time but of no marked distinction. They weren't particularly profitable, either. At the prevailing rates (seldom much more than a penny a word, often less), Bester's total income from three years of writing science fiction was somewhere over, but not much over, one thousand dollars. It was not a figure that impressed Bester, so around 1942 he moved his efforts to the better-paying field of writing comics, then to writing radio plays, finally to a post as a contributing editor on the travel magazine, *Holiday*.

Bester's then wife, Rollie, was a radio actress, and a good one. While I was working on Madison Avenue, not long after World War II, I used to run into them from time to time in the restaurant in the old CBS building. Alfie was always interested in the latest shoptalk about science fiction, but had, he said, no intention of ever coming back to it as a writer—well, maybe an occasional short story now and then, just for the fun of it, but nothing *serious*.

It was Horace Gold who changed Bester's mind for him. When Gold became editor of the new science fiction magazine, *Galaxy*, in 1950, Alfie Bester was one of the first writers Horace got after to write for him. Horace Gold was a powerfully persuasive man. Alfie didn't have a chance. It took a couple of years, but it was for Horace Gold's magazine that Alfred J. Bester made his reappearance as a major science fiction writer with such powerful serials as *The Demolished Man* (notable for its semicomic view of telepathic reality as well as some fascinatingly innovative typographical tricks) and *The Stars My Destination* (*The Count of Monte Cristo* retold and set in the twenty-fifth century, as Bester himself described it, but even better than the original), as well as a flood of fine shorter pieces.

Although *Galaxy* had a lock on Bester's major works, his short stories were appearing all over the field. Many came out in *The Magazine of Fantasy and Science Fiction*, and the one called "Disappearing Act" wound up in an anthology of original stories I was editing at the time, *Star Science Fiction*. Let me give you an idea of how those stories were received by Bester's writing peers. My frequent collaborator, Cyril M. Kornbluth, was staying with me, grimly slugging his way through a commissioned story he didn't much like, when I accepted "Disappearing Act." I was so taken with Bester's story that I gave Cyril the manuscript to read. When he had finished it, he flung it down angrily, saying, "What's the matter with you, Fred? You show me this story *now*? How am I supposed to go back to writing space opera?"

The last time I saw Alfie was in Dublin, Ireland. We were both in town for an international meeting of science fiction writers. With a little free time before the meeting began, I had gone for a walk along the Liffey River; I saw Alfie walking down the street and called to him. He cut me dead. Later that night, at the con, I asked him what I had done to offend him. "Not a damn thing," he said sadly. "Fact is, I'm pretty near blind. People don't have faces for me until they're within two feet; I just didn't see you."

Blind or not, Alfie was in good form at the con, and good form still when he and I, with our spouses, then flew to Newcastle-on-

Tyne to give readings at a literary festival. Our plan was for all of us to rent a car and explore northern England together as soon as the festivities were over, but that didn't happen. The morning after our readings Alfie was too ill to get out of bed, much less to go for long touristy drives. So, regretfully, my wife and I took off for Hadrian's Wall and the Scottish border without him.

We never met again. A few years later, when Alfie was up for his Grand Master Award, his health had become so bad that it seemed unlikely that he would live long enough to accept it, as was the custom, at that year's SFWA awards banquet. For the only time in history, it was arranged to present his award to him several months early, at the annual science fiction world convention.

That didn't work out, either. Alfie's health deteriorated rapidly. He died even before the worldcon, which is why he is the only writer ever to have received the Grand Master Award posthumously.

Recommended Reading
by Alfred Bester

The Demolished Man
The Stars My Destination
Golem$_{100}$
Starburst
Starlight: The Great Short Fiction of Alfred Bester

DISAPPEARING ACT

This one wasn't the last war or a war to end war. They called it the War for the American Dream. General Carpenter struck that note and sounded it constantly.

There are fighting generals (vital to an army), political generals (vital to an administration), and public relations generals (vital to a war). General Carpenter was a master of public relations. Forthright and Four-Square, he had ideals as high and as understandable as the mottoes on money. In the mind of America he *was* the army, the administration, the nation's shield and sword and stout right arm. His ideal was the American dream.

"We are not fighting for money, for power, or for world domination," General Carpenter announced at the Press Association dinner.

"We are fighting solely for the American dream," he said to the 162nd Congress.

"Our aim is not aggression or the reduction of nations to slavery," he said at the West Point Annual Officer's Dinner.

"We are fighting for the Meaning of Civilization," he told the San Francisco Pioneers' Club.

"We are struggling for the Ideal of Civilization; for Culture, for Poetry, for the Only Things Worth Preserving," he said at the Chicago Wheat Pit Festival.

"This is a war for survival," he said. "We are not fighting for ourselves, but for our Dreams; for the Better Things in Life which must not disappear from the face of the earth."

America fought. General Carpenter asked for one hundred million men. The army was given one hundred million men. General Carpenter asked for ten thousand U-Bombs. Ten thousand U-Bombs were delivered and dropped. The enemy also dropped ten thousand U-Bombs and destroyed most of America's cities.

"We must dig in against the hordes of barbarism," General Carpenter said. "Give me a thousand engineers."

One thousand engineers were forthcoming and a hundred cities were dug and hollowed out beneath the rubble.

"Give me five hundred sanitation experts, eight hundred traffic managers, two hundred air-conditioning experts, one hundred city managers, one thousand communication chiefs, seven hundred personnel experts. . . ."

The list of General Carpenter's demand for technical experts was endless. America did not know how to supply them.

"We must become a nation of experts," General Carpenter informed the National Association of American Universities. "Every man and woman must be a specific tool for a specific job, hardened and sharpened by your training and education to win the fight for the American Dream."

"Our Dream," General Carpenter said at the Wall Street Bond Drive Breakfast, "is at one with the gentle Greeks of Athens, with the noble Romans of . . . er . . . Rome. It is a dream of the Better Things in Life. Of Music and Art and Poetry and Culture. Money is only a weapon to be used in the fight for this dream. Ambition is only a ladder to climb to this dream. Ability is only a tool to shape this dream."

Wall Street applauded. General Carpenter asked for one hundred and fifty billion dollars, fifteen hundred dedicated dollar-a-year men, three thousand experts in mineralogy, petrology, mass production, chemical warfare, and air-traffic time study. They were delivered. The country was in high gear. General Carpenter had only to press a button and an expert would be delivered.

In March of A.D. 2112 the war came to a climax and the American Dream was resolved, not on any one of the seven fronts where millions of men were locked in bitter combat, not in any of the staff headquarters or any of the capitals of the warring nations, not in any of the production centers spewing forth arms and supplies, but in Ward T of the United States Army Hospital buried three hundred feet below what had once been St. Albans, New York.

Ward T was something of a mystery at St. Albans. Like all army hospitals, St. Albans was organized with specific wards reserved for specific injuries. Right-arm amputees were gathered in one ward; left-arm amputees in another. Radiation burns, head injuries, eviscerations, secondary gamma poisonings, and so on were each assigned their specific location in the hospital organization. The Army Medical Corps had established nineteen classes of combat injury which included every possible kind of damage to brain and tissue. These used up letters A to S. What, then, was in Ward T?

No one knew. The doors were double-locked. No visitors were permitted to enter. No patients were permitted to leave. Physicians were seen to arrive and depart. Their perplexed expressions stimulated the wildest speculations but revealed nothing. The nurses who ministered to Ward T were questioned eagerly but they were closed mouthed.

There were dribs and drabs of information, unsatisfying and self-contradictory. A charwoman asserted that she had been in to clean up and there had been no one in the ward. Absolutely no one. Just two dozen beds and nothing else. Had the beds been slept in? Yes. They were rumpled, some of them. Were there signs of the ward being in use? Oh yes. Personal things on the tables and so on. But dusty, kind of. Like they hadn't been used in a long time.

Public opinion decided it was a ghost ward. For spooks only.

But a night orderly reported passing the locked ward and hearing singing from within. What kind of singing? Foreign language, like. What language? The orderly couldn't say. Some of the words sounded like . . . well, like: Cow dee on us eager tour . . .

Public opinion started to run a fever and decided it was an alien ward. For spies only.

St. Albans enlisted the help of the kitchen staff and checked the food trays. Twenty-four trays went into Ward T three times a day. Twenty-four came out. Sometimes the returning trays were emptied. Most times they were untouched.

Public opinion started to run a fever and decided it was a racket. It was an informal club for goldbricks and staff grafters who caroused within. Cow dee on us eager tour indeed!

For gossip, a hospital can put a small town sewing circle to shame with ease, but sick people are easily goaded into passion by trivia. It took just three months for idle speculation to turn into downright fury. In January, 2112, St. Albans was a sound, well-run hospital. By March, 2112, St. Albans was in a ferment, and the psychological unrest found its way into the official records. The percentage of recoveries fell off. Malingering set in. Petty infractions increased. Mutinies flared. There was a staff shake-up. It did no good. Ward T was inciting the patients to riot. There was another shake-up, and another, and still the unrest fumed.

The news finally reached General Carpenter's desk through official channels.

"In our fight for the American Dream," he said, "we must not ignore those who have already given of themselves. Send me a Hospital Administration expert."

The expert was delivered. He could do nothing to heal St. Albans. General Carpenter read the reports and fired him.

"Pity," said General Carpenter, "is the first ingredient of civilization. Send me a Surgeon General."

A Surgeon General was delivered. He could not break the fury of St. Albans, and General Carpenter broke him. But by this time Ward T was being mentioned in the dispatches.

"Send me," General Carpenter said, "the expert in charge of Ward T."

St. Albans sent a doctor, Captain Edsel Dimmock. He was a stout young man, already bald, only three years out of medical school, but with a fine record as an expert in psychotherapy. General Carpenter liked experts. He liked Dimmock. Dimmock adored the general as the spokesman for a culture which he had been too specially trained to seek up to now, but which he hoped to enjoy after the war was won.

"Now look here, Dimmock," General Carpenter began. "We're

all of us tools, today—hardened and sharpened to do a specific job. You know our motto: a job for everyone and everyone on the job. Somebody's not on the job at Ward T and we've got to kick him out. Now, in the first place what the hell is Ward T?"

Dimmock stuttered and fumbled. Finally he explained that it was a special ward set up for special combat cases. Shock cases.

"Then you do have patients in the ward?"

"Yes, sir. Ten women and fourteen men."

Carpenter brandished a sheaf of reports. "Says here the St. Albans patients claim nobody's in Ward T."

Dimmock was shocked. That was untrue, he assured the general.

"All right, Dimmock. So you've got your twenty-four crocks in there. Their job's to get well. Your job's to cure them. What the hell's upsetting the hospital about that?"

"W-well, sir. Perhaps it's because we keep them locked up."

"You keep Ward T locked?"

"Yes, sir."

"Why?"

"To keep the patients in, General Carpenter."

"Keep 'em in? What d'you mean? Are they trying to get out? They violent, or something?"

"No, sir. Not violent."

"Dimmock, I don't like your attitude. You're acting damned sneaky and evasive. And I'll tell you something else I don't like. That T classification. I checked with a Filing Expert from the Medical Corps and there is no T classification. What the hell are you up to at St. Albans?"

"W-well, sir . . . We invented the T classification. It . . . They . . . They're rather special cases, sir. We don't know what to do about them or how to handle them. W-we've been trying to keep it quiet until we've worked out a modus operandi, but it's brand new, General Carpenter. Brand new!" Here the expert in Dimmock triumphed over discipline. "It's sensational. It'll make medical history, by God! It's the biggest damned thing ever."

"What is it, Dimmock? Be specific."

"Well, sir, they're shock cases. Blanked out. Almost catatonic. Very little respiration. Slow pulse. No response."

"I've seen thousands of shock cases like that," Carpenter grunted. "What's so unusual?"

"Yes, sir, so far it sounds like the standard Q or R classification. But here's something unusual. They don't eat and they don't sleep."

"Never?"

"Some of them never."

"Then why don't they die?"

"We don't know. The metabolism cycle's broken, but only on the anabolism side. Catabolism continues. In other words, sir, they're eliminating waste products, but they're not taking anything in. They're eliminating fatigue poisons and rebuilding worn tissue, but without food and sleep. God knows how. It's fantastic."

"That why you've got them locked up? Mean to say . . . D'you suspect them of stealing food and catnaps somewhere else?"

"N-No, sir." Dimmock looked shamefaced. "I don't know how to tell you this, General Carpenter. . . . We lock them up because of the real mystery. They . . . Well, they disappear."

"They what?"

"They disappear, sir. Vanish. Right before your eyes."

"The hell you say."

"I do say, sir. They'll be sitting on a bed or standing around. One minute you see them, the next minute you don't. Sometimes there's two dozen in Ward T. Other times none. They disappear and reappear without rhyme or reason. That's why we've got the ward locked, General Carpenter. In the entire history of combat and combat injury, there's never been a case like this before. We don't know how to handle it."

"Bring me three of those cases," General Carpenter said.

Nathan Riley ate French toast, eggs benedict; consumed two pints of brown ale, smoked a John Drew, belched delicately and arose from the breakfast table. He nodded quietly to Gentleman Jim Corbett, who broke off his conversation with Diamond Jim Brady to intercept him on the way to the cashier's desk.

"Who do you like for the pennant this year, Nat?" Gentleman Jim inquired.

"The Dodgers," Nathan Riley answered.

"They've got no pitching."

"They've got Snider and Furillo and Campanella. They'll take the pennant this year, Jim. I'll bet they take it earlier than any team ever did. By September 13. Make a note. See if I'm right."

"You're always right, Nat," Corbett said.

Riley smiled, paid his check, sauntered out into the street and caught a horsecar bound for Madison Square Garden.

He got off at the corner of Fiftieth Street and Eighth Avenue and walked upstairs to a handbook office over a radio repair shop. The bookie glanced at him, produced an envelope, and counted out $15,000.

"Rocky Marciano by a TKO over Roland La Starza in the eleventh," he said. "How the hell do you call them so accurate, Nat?"

"That's the way I make a living." Riley smiled. "Are you making book on the elections?"

"Eisenhower twelve to five. Stevenson—"

"Never mind Adlai." Riley placed $20,000 on the counter. "I'm backing Ike. Get this down for me."

He left the handbook office and went to his suite in the Waldorf where a tall, thin young man was waiting for him anxiously.

"Oh yes," Nathan Riley said. "You're Ford, aren't you? Harold Ford?"

"Henry Ford, Mr. Riley."

"And you need financing for that machine in your bicycle shop. What's it called?"

"I call it an Ipsimobile, Mr. Riley."

"Hmmm. Can't say I like that name. Why not call it an automobile?"

"That's a wonderful suggestion, Mr. Riley. I'll certainly take it."

"I like you, Henry. You're young, eager, adaptable. I believe in your future and I believe in your automobile. I'll invest two hundred thousand dollars in your company."

Riley wrote a check and ushered Henry Ford out. He glanced at his watch and suddenly felt impelled to go back and look around for a moment. He entered his bedroom, undressed, put on a gray shirt and gray slacks. Across the pocket of the shirt were large blue letters: U.S.A.H.

He locked the bedroom door and disappeared.

He reappeared in Ward T of the United States Army Hospital in St. Albans, standing alongside his bed which was one of twenty-four lining the walls of a long, light steel barracks. Before he could draw another breath, he was seized by three pairs of hands. Before he could struggle, he was shot by a pneumatic syringe and poleaxed by 1½ cc of sodium thiomorphate.

"We've got one," someone said.

"Hang around," someone else answered. "General Carpenter said he wanted three."

After Marcus Junius Brutus left her bed, Lela Machan clapped her hands. Her slave women entered the chamber and prepared her bath. She bathed, dressed, scented herself, and breakfasted on Smyrna figs, rose oranges, and a flagon of Lacrima Christi. Then she smoked a cigarette and ordered her litter.

The gates of her house were crowded as usual by adoring hordes from the Twentieth Legion. Two centurions removed her chair-bearers from the poles of the litter and bore her on their stout shoulders. Lela Machan smiled. A young man in a sapphire-blue cloak thrust through the mob and ran toward her. A knife flashed in his hand. Lela braced herself to meet death bravely.

"Lady!" he cried. "Lady Lela!"

He slashed his left arm with the knife and let the crimson blood stain her robe.

"This blood of mine is the least I have to give you," he cried.

Lela touched his forehead gently.

"Silly boy," she murmured. "Why?"

"For love of you, my lady."

"You will be admitted tonight at nine," Lela whispered. He stared at her until she laughed. "I promise you. What is your name, pretty boy?"

"Ben Hur."

"Tonight at nine, Ben Hur."

The litter moved on. Outside the forum, Julius Caesar passed in hot argument with Savonarola. When he saw the litter he motioned sharply to the centurions, who stopped at once. Caesar swept back the curtains and stared at Lela, who regarded him languidly. Caesar's face twitched.

"Why?" he asked hoarsely. "I have begged, pleaded, bribed, wept, and all without forgiveness. Why, Lela? Why?"

"Do you remember Boadicea?" Lela murmured.

"Boadicea? Queen of the Britons? Good God, Lela, what can she mean to our love? I did not love Boadicea. I merely defeated her in battle."

"And killed her, Caesar."

"She poisoned herself, Lela."

"She was my mother, Caesar!" Suddenly Lela pointed her finger at Caesar. "Murderer. You will be punished. Beware the Ides of March, Caesar!"

Caesar recoiled in horror. The mob of admirers that had gathered around Lela uttered a shout of approval. Amidst a shower of rose petals and violets, she continued on her way across the Forum to the Temple of the Vestal Virgins where she abandoned her adoring suitors and entered the sacred temple.

Before the altar she genuflected, intoned a prayer, dropped a pinch of incense on the altar flame and disrobed. She examined her beautiful body reflected in a silver mirror, then experienced a momentary twinge of homesickness. She put on a gray blouse and a gray pair of slacks. Across the pocket of the blouse was lettered U.S.A.H.

She smiled once at the altar and disappeared.

She reappeared in Ward T of the United States Army Hospital where she was instantly felled by 1½ cc of sodium thiomorphate injected subcutaneously by a pneumatic syringe.

"That's two," somebody said.

"One more to go."

George Hanmer paused dramatically and stared around . . . at the opposition benches, at the Speaker on the woolsack, at the silver mace on a crimson cushion before the Speaker's chair. The entire House of Parliament, hypnotized by Hanmer's fiery oratory, waited breathlessly for him to continue.

"I can say no more," Hanmer said at last. His voice was choked with emotion. His face was blanched and grim. "I will fight for this bill at the beachheads. I will fight in the cities, the towns, the fields and the hamlets. I will fight for this bill to the death and, God willing, I will fight for it after death. Whether this be a challenge or a prayer, let the consciences of the right honorable gentlemen determine; but of one thing I am sure and determined: England must own the Suez Canal."

Hanmer sat down. The house exploded. Through the cheering and applause he made his way out into the division lobby where Gladstone, Churchill, and Pitt stopped him to shake his hand. Lord Palmerston eyed him coldly, but Pam was shouldered aside by Disraeli who limped up, all enthusiasm, all admiration.

"We'll have a bite at Tattersall's," Dizzy said. "My car's waiting."

Lady Beaconsfield was in the Rolls Royce outside the Houses of Parliament. She pinned a primrose on Dizzy's lapel and patted Hanmer's cheek affectionately.

"You've come a long way from the schoolboy who used to bully Dizzy, Georgie," she said.

Hanmer laughed. Dizzy sang: *"Gaudeamus igitur . . ."* and Hanmer chanted the ancient scholastic song until they reached Tattersall's. There Dizzy ordered Guinness and grilled bones while Hanmer went upstairs in the club to change.

For no reason at all he had the impulse to go back for a last look. Perhaps he hated to break with his past completely. He divested himself of his surtout, nankeen waistcoat, pepper and salt trousers, polished Hessians and undergarments. He put on a gray shirt and gray trousers and disappeared.

He reappeared in Ward T of the St. Albans hospital where he was rendered unconscious by 1 ½ cc of sodium thiomorphate.

"That's three," somebody said.

"Take 'em to Carpenter."

So there they sat in General Carpenter's office, PFC Nathan Riley, M/Sgt Lela Machan, and Corp/2 George Hanmer. They were in their hospital grays. They were torpid with sodium thiomorphate.

The office had been cleared and it blazed with light. Present were experts from Espionage, Counter-Espionage, Security, and Central Intelligence. When Captain Edsel Dimmock saw the steel-faced ruthless squad awaiting the patients and himself, he started. General Carpenter smiled grimly.

"Didn't occur to you that we mightn't buy your disappearance story, eh Dimmock?"

"S-Sir?"

"I'm an expert too, Dimmock. I'll spell it out for you. The war's going badly. Very badly. There've been intelligence leaks. The St. Albans mess might point to you."

"B-But they do disappear, sir. I—"

"My experts want to talk to you and your patients about this disappearing act, Dimmock. They'll start with you."

The experts worked over Dimmock with preconscious softeners, id releases, and superego blocks. They tried every truth serum in the books and every form of physical and mental pressure. They brought Dimmock, squealing, to the breaking point three times, but there was nothing to break.

"Let him stew for now," Carpenter said. "Get on to the patients."

The experts appeared reluctant to apply pressure to the sick men and the woman.

"For God's sake, don't be squeamish," Carpenter raged. "We're fighting a war for civilization. We've got to protect our ideals no matter what the price. Get to it!"

The experts from Espionage, Counter-Espionage, Security, and Central Intelligence got to it. Like three candles, PFC Nathan Riley, M/Sgt Lela Machan and Corp/2 George Hanmer snuffed out and disappeared. One moment they were seated in chairs surrounded by violence. The next moment they were not.

The experts gasped. General Carpenter did the handsome thing. He stalked to Dimmock. "Captain Dimmock, I apologize. Colonel Dimmock, you've been promoted for making an important discovery . . . only what the hell does it mean? We've got to check ourselves first."

Carpenter snapped up the intercom. "Get me a combat-shock expert and an alienist."

The two experts entered and were briefed. They examined the witnesses. They considered.

"You're all suffering from a mild case of shock," the combat-shock expert said. "War jitters."

"You mean we didn't see them disappear?"

The shock expert shook his head and glanced at the alienist who also shook his head.

"Mass illusion," the alienist said.

At that moment PFC Riley, M/Sgt Machan, and Corp/2 Hanmer reappeared. One moment they were a mass illusion; the next, they were back sitting in their chairs surrounded by confusion.

"Dope 'em again, Dimmock," Carpenter cried. "Give 'em a gallon." He snapped up the intercom. "I want every expert we've got. Emergency meeting in my office at once."

Thirty-seven experts, hardened and sharpened tools all, inspected the unconscious shock cases and discussed them for three hours. Certain facts were obvious: This must be a new fantastic syndrome brought on by the new and fantastic horrors of the war. As combat technique develops, the response of victims of this technique must also take new roads. For every action there is an equal and opposite reaction. Agreed.

This new syndrome must involve some aspects of teleportation . . . the power of mind over space. Evidently combat shock, while destroying certain known powers of the mind must develop other latent powers hitherto unknown. Agreed.

Obviously, the patients must only be able to return to the point of departure, otherwise they would not continue to return to Ward T nor would they have returned to General Carpenter's office. Agreed.

Obviously, the patients must be able to procure food and sleep wherever they go, since neither was required in Ward T. Agreed.

"One small point," Colonel Dimmock said. "They seem to be returning to Ward T less frequently. In the beginning they would come and go every day or so. Now most of them stay away for weeks and hardly ever return."

"Never mind that," Carpenter said. "Where do they go?"

"Do they teleport behind the enemy lines?" someone asked. "There's those intelligence leaks."

"I want Intelligence to check," Carpenter snapped. "Is the enemy having similar difficulties with, say, prisoners of war who appear and disappear from their POW camps? They might be some of ours from Ward T."

"They might simply be going home," Colonel Dimmock suggested.

"I want Security to check," Carpenter ordered. "Cover the home life and associations of every one of those twenty-four disappearers. Now . . . about our operations in Ward T. Colonel Dimmock has a plan."

"We'll set up six extra beds in Ward T," Edsel Dimmock explained. "We'll send in six experts to live there and observe. Information must be picked up indirectly from the patients. They're catatonic and nonresponsive when conscious, and incapable of answering questions when drugged."

"Gentlemen," Carpenter summed it up. "This is the greatest potential weapon in the history of warfare. I don't have to tell you what it can mean to us to be able to teleport an entire army behind enemy lines. We can win the war for the American Dream in one day if we can win this secret hidden in those shattered minds. We must win!"

The experts hustled, Security checked, Intelligence probed. Six hardened and sharpened tools moved into Ward T in St. Albans Hospital and slowly got acquainted with the disappearing patients who reappeared less and less frequently. The tension increased.

Security was able to report that not one case of strange appearance had taken place in America in the past year. Intelligence reported that the enemy did not seem to be having similar difficulties with their own shock cases or with POWs.

Carpenter fretted. "This is all brand new. We've got no specialists to handle it. We've got to develop new tools." He snapped up his intercom. "Get me a college," he said.

They got him Yale.

"I want some experts in mind over matter. Develop them," Carpenter ordered. Yale at once introduced three graduate courses in Thaumaturgy, Extrasensory Perception, and Telekinesis.

The first break came when one of the Ward T experts requested the assistance of another expert. He needed a Lapidary.

"What the hell for?" Carpenter wanted to know.

"He picked up a reference to a gemstone," Colonel Dimmock explained. "He's a personnel specialist and he can't relate it to anything in his experience."

"And he's not supposed to," Carpenter said approvingly. "A job for every man and every man on the job." He flipped up the intercom. "Get me a Lapidary."

An expert Lapidary was given leave of absence from the army arsenal and asked to identify a type of diamond called Jim Brady. He could not.

"We'll try it from another angle," Carpenter said. He snapped up his intercom. "Get me a Semanticist."

The Semanticist left his desk in the War Propaganda Department but could make nothing of the words "Jim Brady." They were names to him. No more. He suggested a Genealogist.

A Genealogist was given one day's leave from his post with the Un-American Ancestors Committee, but could make nothing of the name Brady beyond the fact that it had been a common name in America for five hundred years. He suggested an Archaeologist.

An Archaeologist was released from the Cartography Division of Invasion Command and instantly identified the name Diamond Jim Brady. It was a historic personage who had been famous in the city of Little Old New York sometime between Governor Peter Stuyvesant and Governor Fiorello La Guardia.

"Christ!" Carpenter marveled. "That's ages ago. Where the hell did Nathan Riley get that? You'd better join the experts in Ward T and follow this up."

The Archaeologist followed it up, checked his references and sent in his report. Carpenter read it and was stunned. He called an emergency meeting of his staff of experts.

"Gentlemen," he announced "Ward T is something bigger than teleportation. Those shock patients are doing something far more incredible . . . far more meaningful. Gentlemen, they're traveling through time."

The staff rustled uncertainly. Carpenter nodded emphatically.

"Yes, gentlemen. Time travel is here. It has not arrived the way we expected it . . . as a result of expert research by qualified specialists; it has come as a plague . . . an infection . . . a disease of the war . . . a result of combat injury to ordinary men. Before I continue, look through these reports for documentation."

The staff read the stenciled sheets. PFC Nathan Riley . . . disappearing into the early twentieth century in New York; M/Sgt Lela Machan . . . visiting the first century in Rome; Corp/2 George Hanmer . . . journeying into the nineteenth century in England. And all the rest of the twenty-four patients, escaping the turmoil and horrors of modern war in the twenty-second century by fleeing to Venice and the Doges, to Jamaica and the buccaneers, to China and the Han Dynasty, to Norway and Eric the Red, to any place and any time in the world.

"I needn't point out the colossal significance of this discovery," General Carpenter pointed out. "Think what it would mean to the war if we could send an army back in time a week or a month or a year. We could win the war before it started. We could protect our Dream . . . Poetry and Beauty and the Culture of America . . . from barbarism without ever endangering it."

The staff tried to grapple with the problem of winning battles before they started.

"The situation is complicated by the fact that these men and women of Ward T are *non compos*. They may or may not know how they do what they do, but in any case they're incapable of communicating with the experts who could reduce this miracle to method. It's for us to find the key. They can't help us."

The hardened and sharpened specialists looked around uncertainly.

"We'll need experts," General Carpenter said.

The staff relaxed. They were on familiar ground again.

"We'll need a Cerebral Mechanist, a Cyberneticist, a Psychiatrist, an Anatomist, an Archaeologist, and a first-rate Historian. They'll go into that ward and they won't come out until their job is done. They must learn the technique of time travel."

The first five experts were easy to draft from other war departments. All America was a tool chest of hardened and sharpened specialists. But there was trouble locating a first-class Historian until the Federal Penitentiary cooperated with the army and released Dr.

Bradley Scrim from his twenty years at hard labor. Dr. Scrim was acid and jagged. He had held the chair of Philosophic History at a Western university until he spoke his mind about the war for the American Dream. That got him the twenty years hard.

Scrim was still intransigent, but induced to play ball by the intriguing problem of Ward T.

"But I'm not an expert," he snapped. "In this benighted nation of experts, I'm the last singing grasshopper in the ant heap."

Carpenter snapped up the intercom. "Get me an Entomologist," he said.

"Don't bother," Scrim said. "I'll translate. You're a nest of ants . . . all working and toiling and specializing. For what?"

"To preserve the American Dream," Carpenter answered hotly. "We're fighting for Poetry and Culture and Education and the Finer Things in Life."

"Which means you're fighting to preserve me," Scrim said. "That's what I've devoted my life to. And what do you do with me? Put me in jail."

"You were convicted of enemy sympathizing and fellow-travelling," Carpenter said.

"I was convicted of believing in my American Dream," Scrim said. "Which is another way of saying I was jailed for having a mind of my own."

Scrim was also intransigent in Ward T. He stayed one night, enjoyed three good meals, read the reports, threw them down, and began hollering to be let out.

"There's a job for everyone and everyone must be on the job," Colonel Dimmock told him. "You don't come out until you've got the secret of time travel."

"There's no secret I can get," Scrim said.

"Do they travel in time?"

"Yes and no."

"The answer has to be one or the other. Not both. You're evading the—"

"Look," Scrim interrupted wearily. "What are you an expert in?"

"Psychotherapy."

"Then how the hell can you understand what I'm talking about? This is a philosophic concept. I tell you there's no secret here that the army can use. There's no secret any group can use. It's a secret for individuals only."

"I don't understand you."

"I didn't think you would. Take me to Carpenter."

They took Scrim to Carpenter's office where he grinned at the general malignantly, looking for all the world like a red-headed, underfed devil.

"I'll need ten minutes," Scrim said. "Can you spare them out of your toolbox?"

Carpenter nodded.

"Now listen carefully. I'm going to give you the clues to something so vast and so strange that it will need all your fine edge to cut into it."

Carpenter looked expectant.

"Nathan Riley goes back in time to the early twentieth century. There he lives the life of his fondest dreams. He's a big-time gambler, the friend of Diamond Jim Brady and others. He wins money betting on events because he always knows the outcome in advance. He won money betting on Eisenhower to win an election. He won money betting on a prizefighter named Marciano to beat another prizefighter named La Starza. He made money investing in an automobile company owned by Henry Ford. There are the clues. They mean anything to you?"

"Not without a Sociological Analyst," Carpenter answered. He reached for the intercom.

"Don't order one, I'll explain later. Let's try some more clues. Lela Machan, for example. She escapes into the Roman Empire where she lives the life of her dreams as a *femme fatale*. Every man loves her. Julius Caesar, Savonarola, the entire Twentieth Legion, a man named Ben Hur. Do you see the fallacy?"

"No."

"She also smokes cigarettes."

"Well?" Carpenter asked after a pause.

"I continue," Scrim said, "George Hanmer escapes into England of the nineteenth century where he's a member of Parliament and the friend of Gladstone, Winston Churchill, and Disraeli, who takes him riding in his Rolls Royce. Do you know what a Rolls Royce is?"

"No."

"It was the name of an automobile."

"So?"

"You don't understand yet?"

"No."

Scrim paced the floor in exaltation. "Carpenter, this is a bigger discovery than teleportation or time travel. This can be the salvation of man. I don't think I'm exaggerating. Those two dozen shock victims in Ward T have been U-Bombed into something so gigantic that it's no wonder your specialists and experts can't understand it."

"What the hell's bigger than time travel, Scrim?"

"Listen to this, Carpenter. Eisenhower did not run for office until the middle of the twentieth century. Nathan Riley could not have been a friend of Diamond Jim Brady's and bet on Eisenhower to win an election . . . not simultaneously. Brady was dead a quarter of a century before Ike was President. Marciano defeated La Starza fifty years after Henry Ford started his automobile company. Nathan Riley's time traveling is full of similar anachronisms."

Carpenter looked puzzled.

"Lela Machan could not have had Ben Hur for a lover. Ben Hur never existed in Rome. He never existed at all. He was a character in a novel. She couldn't have smoked. They didn't have tobacco then. You see? More anachronisms. Disraeli could never have taken George Hanmer for a ride in a Rolls Royce because automobiles weren't invented until long after Disraeli's death."

"The hell you say," Carpenter exclaimed. "You mean they're all lying?"

"No. Don't forget, they don't need sleep. They don't need food. They're not lying. They're going back in time, all right. They're eating and sleeping back there."

"But you just said their stories don't stand up. They're full of anachronisms."

"Because they travel back into a time of their own imagination. Nathan Riley has his own picture of what America was like in the early twentieth century. It's faulty and anachronistic because he's no scholar, but it's real for him. He can live there. The same is true for the others."

Carpenter goggled.

"The concept is almost beyond understanding. These people have discovered how to turn dreams into reality. They know how to enter their dream realities. They can stay there, live there, perhaps forever. My God, Carpenter, *this* is your American dream. It's miracle-working, immortality, Godlike creation, mind over matter. . . . It must be explored. It must be studied. It must be given to the world."

"Can you do it, Scrim?"

"No, I cannot. I'm an historian. I'm noncreative, so it's beyond me. You need a poet . . . an artist who understands the creation of dreams. From creating dreams on paper it oughtn't be too difficult to take the step to creating dreams in actuality."

"A poet? Are you serious?"

"Certainly I'm serious. Don't you know what a poet is? You've been telling us for five years that this war is being fought to save the poets."

"Don't be facetious, Scrim, I—"

"Send a poet into Ward T. He'll learn how they do it. He's the only man who can. A poet is half doing it anyway. Once he learns, he can teach your psychologists and anatomists. Then they can teach us; but the poet is the only man who can interpret between those shock cases and your experts."

"I believe you're right, Scrim."

"Then don't delay, Carpenter. Those patients are returning to this world less and less frequently. We've got to get at that secret before they disappear forever. Send a poet to Ward T."

Carpenter snapped up his intercom. "Send me a poet," he said.

He waited, and waited . . . and waited . . . while America sorted feverishly through its two hundred and ninety millions of hardened and sharpened experts, its specialized tools to defend the American Dream of Beauty and Poetry and the Better Things in Life. He waited for them to find a poet, not understanding the endless delay, the fruitless search; not understanding why Bradley Scrim laughed and laughed and laughed at this final, fatal disappearance.

FONDLY FAHRENHEIT

He doesn't know which of us I am these days, but they know one truth. You must own nothing but yourself. You must make your own life, live your own life and die your own death . . . or else you will die another's.

The rice fields on Paragon III stretch for hundreds of miles like checkerboard tundras, a blue and brown mosaic under a burning sky of orange. In the evening, clouds whip like smoke, and the paddies rustle and murmur.

A long line of men marched across the paddies the evening we escaped from Paragon III. They were silent, armed, intent; a long rank of silhouetted statues looming against the smoking sky. Each man carried a gun. Each man wore a walkie-talkie belt pack, the speaker button in his ear, the microphone bug clipped to his throat, the glowing view-screen strapped to his wrist like a green-eyed watch. The multitude of screens showed nothing but a multitude of individual paths through the paddies. The annunciators uttered no sound but the rustle and splash of steps. The men spoke infrequently, in heavy grunts, all speaking to all.

"Nothing here."

"Where's here?"

"Jenson's fields."

"You're drifting too far west."

"Close in the line there."

"Anybody covered the Grimson paddy?"

"Yeah. Nothing."

"She couldn't have walked this far."

"Could have been carried."

"Think she's alive?"

"Why should she be dead?"

The slow refrain swept up and down the long line of beaters advancing toward the smoky sunset. The line of beaters wavered like a writhing snake, but never ceased its remorseless advance. One hundred men spaced fifty feet apart. Five thousand feet of ominous search. One mile of angry determination stretching from east to west across a compass of heat. Evening fell. Each man lit his search lamp. The writhing snake was transformed into a necklace of wavering diamonds.

"Clear here. Nothing."

"Nothing here."

"Nothing."

"What about the Allen paddies?"

"Covering them now."

"Think we missed her?"

"Maybe."

"We'll beat back and check."

"This'll be an all-night job."

"Allen paddies clear."

"God damn! We've got to find her!"

"We'll find her."

"Here she is. Sector seven. Tune in."

The line stopped. The diamonds froze in the heat. There was silence. Each man gazed into the glowing green screen on his wrist, tuning to sector seven. All tuned to one. All showed a small nude figure awash in the muddy water of a paddy. Alongside the figure an owner's stake of bronze read: VANDALEUR. The ends of the line converged toward the Vandaleur field. The necklace turned into a cluster of stars. One hundred men gathered around a small nude body, a child dead in a rice paddy. There was no water in her mouth. There were no fingermarks on her throat. Her innocent face was battered. Her body was torn. Clotted blood on her skin was crusted and hard.

"Dead three-four hours at least."

"Her mouth is dry."

"She wasn't drowned. Beaten to death."

In the dark evening heat the men swore softly. They picked up the body. One stopped the others and pointed to the child's fingernails. She had fought her murderer. Under the nails were particles of flesh and bright drops of scarlet blood, still liquid, still uncoagulated.

"That blood ought to be clotted, too."

"Funny."

"Not so funny. What kind of blood don't clot?"

"Android."

"Looks like she was killed by one."

"Vandaleur owns an android."

"She couldn't be killed by an android."

"That's android blood under her nails."

"The police better check."

"The police'll prove I'm right."

"But andys can't kill."

"That's android blood, ain't it?"

"Androids can't kill. They're made that way."

"Looks like one android was made wrong."

"Jesus!"

And the thermometer that day registered 92.9° gloriously Fahrenheit.

So there we were aboard the *Paragon Queen* en route for Megaster V, James Vandaleur and his android. James Vandaleur counted his money and wept. In the second-class cabin with him was his android, a magnificent synthetic creature with classic features and wide blue eyes. Raised on its forehead in a cameo of flesh were the letters MA, indicating that this was one of the rare multiple-aptitude androids, worth $57,000 on the current exchange. There we were, weeping and counting and calmly watching.

"Twelve, fourteen, sixteen. Sixteen hundred dollars," Vandaleur wept. "That's all. Sixteen hundred dollars. My house was worth ten thousand. The land was worth five. There was furniture, cars, my paintings, etchings, my plane, my—And nothing to show for everything but sixteen hundred dollars. Christ!"

I leaped up from the table and turned on the android. I pulled a strap from one of the leather bags and beat the android. It didn't move.

"I must remind you," the android said, "that I am worth fifty-seven thousand dollars on the current exchange. I must warn you that you are endangering valuable property."

"You damned crazy machine," Vandaleur shouted.

"I am not a machine," the android answered. "The robot is a machine. The android is a chemical creation of synthetic tissue."

"What got into you?" Vandaleur cried. "Why did you do it? Damn you!" He beat the android savagely.

"I must remind you that I cannot be punished," I said. "The pleasure-pain syndrome is not incorporated in the android synthesis."

"Then why did you kill her?" Vandaleur shouted. "If it wasn't for kicks, why did you—"

"I must remind you," the android said, "that the second-class cabins in these ships are not soundproofed."

Vandaleur dropped the strap and stood panting, staring at the creature he owned.

"Why did you do it? Why did you kill her?" I asked.

"I don't know," I answered.

"First it was malicious mischief. Small things. Petty destruction. I should have known there was something wrong with you then. Androids can't destroy. They can't harm. They—"

"There is no pleasure-pain syndrome incorporated in the android synthesis."

"Then it got to arson. Then serious destruction. Then assault . . . that engineer on Rigel. Each time worse. Each time we had to get out faster. Now it's murder. Christ! What's the matter with you? What's happened?"

"There are no self-check relays incorporated in the android brain."

"Each time we had to get out it was a step downhill. Look at me. In a second-class cabin. Me. James Paleologue Vandaleur. There was a time when my father was the wealthiest—Now, sixteen hundred dollars in the world. That's all I've got. And you. Christ damn you!"

Vandaleur raised the strap to beat the android again, then dropped it and collapsed on a berth, sobbing. At last he pulled himself together.

"Instructions," he said.

The multiple android responded at once. It arose and awaited orders.

"My name is now Valentine. James Valentine. I stopped off on Paragon III for only one day to transfer to this ship for Megaster V. My occupation: Agent for one privately owned MA android which is for hire. Purpose of visit: To settle on Megaster V. Fix the papers."

The android removed Vandaleur's passport and papers from a bag, got pen and ink and sat down at the table. With an accurate, flawless hand—an accomplished hand that could draw, write, paint, carve, engrave, etch, photograph, design, create, and build—it meticulously forged new credentials for Vandaleur. Its owner watched me miserably.

"Create and build," I muttered, "And now destroy. Oh God! What am I going to do? Christ! If I could only get rid of you. If I didn't have to live off you. God! If only I'd inherited some guts instead of you."

Dallas Brady was Megaster's leading jewelry designer. She was short, stocky, amoral, and a nymphomaniac. She hired Vandaleur's multiple-aptitude android and put me to work in her shop. She seduced Vandaleur. In her bed one night, she asked abruptly, "Your name's Vandaleur, isn't it?"

"Yes," I murmured. Then: "No! It's Valentine. James Valentine."

"What happened on Paragon?" Dallas Brady asked. "I thought androids couldn't kill or destroy property. Prime Directives and Inhibitions set up for them when they're synthesized. Every company guarantees they can't."

"Valentine!" Vandaleur insisted.

"Oh come off it," Dallas Brady said. "I've known for a week. I haven't hollered copper, have I?"

"The name is Valentine."

"You want to prove it? You want I should call the cops?" Dallas reached out and picked up the phone.

"For God's sake, Dallas!" Vandaleur leaped up and struggled to take the phone from her. She fended him off, laughing at him, until he collapsed and wept in shame and helplessness.

"How did you find out?" he asked at last.

"The papers are full of it. And Valentine was a little too close to Vandaleur. That wasn't smart, was it?"

"I guess not. I'm not very smart."

"Your android's got quite a record, hasn't it? Assault. Arson. Destruction. What happened on Paragon?"

"It kidnapped a child. Took her out into the rice fields and murdered her."

"Raped her?"

"I don't know."

"They're going to catch up with you."

"Don't I know it? Christ! We've been running for two years now. Seven planets in two years. I must have abandoned fifty thousand dollars' worth of property in two years."

"You better find out what's wrong with it."

"How can I? Can I walk into a repair clinic and ask for an overhaul? What am I going to say? 'My android's just turned killer. Fix it.' They'd call the police right off." I began to shake. "They'd have that android dismantled inside one day. I'd probably be booked as accessory to murder."

"Why didn't you have it repaired before it got to murder?"

"If they started fooling around with lobotomies and body chemistry and endocrine surgery, they might have destroyed its aptitudes. What would I have left to hire out? How would I live?"

"You could work yourself. People do."

"Work at what? You know I'm good for nothing. How could I

compete with specialist androids and robots? Who can, unless he's got a terrific talent for a particular job?"

"Yeah. That's true."

"I lived off my old man all my life. Damn him! He had to go bust just before he died. Left me the android and that's all. The only way I can get along is living off what it earns."

"You better sell it before the cops catch up with you. You can live off fifty grand. Invest it."

"At three percent? Fifteen hundred a year? When the android returns fifteen percent on its value? Eight thousand a year. That's what it earns. No, Dallas. I've got to go along with it."

"What are you going to do about its violence kick?"

"I can't do anything . . . except watch it and pray. What are you going to do about it?"

"Nothing. It's none of my business. Only one thing . . . I ought to get something for keeping my mouth shut."

"What?"

"The android works for me for free. Let somebody else pay you, but I get it for free."

The multiple-aptitude android worked. Vandaleur collected its fees. His expenses were taken care of. His savings began to mount. As the warm spring of Megaster V turned to hot summer, I began investigating farms and properties. It would be possible, within a year or two, for us to settle down permanently, provided Dallas Brady's demands did not become rapacious.

On the first hot day of summer, the android began singing in Dallas Brady's workshop. It hovered over the electric furnace which, along with the weather, was broiling the shop, and sang an ancient tune that had been popular half a century before.

> Oh, it's no feat to beat the heat.
> All reet! All reet!
> So jeet your seat
> Be fleet be fleet
> Cool and discreet
> Honey . . .

It sang in a strange, halting voice, and its accomplished fingers were clasped behind its back, writhing in a strange rumba all their own. Dallas Brady was surprised.

"You happy or something?" she asked.

"I must remind you that the pleasure-pain syndrome is not incorporated in the android synthesis," I answered. "All reet! All reet! Be fleet be fleet, cool and discreet, honey . . ."

Its fingers stopped their writhing and picked up a heavy pair of iron tongs. The android poked them into the glowing heart of the furnace, leaning far forward to peer into the lovely heat.

"Be careful, you damned fool!" Dallas Brady exclaimed. "You want to fall in?"

"I must remind you that I am worth fifty-seven thousand dollars on the current exchange," I said. "It is forbidden to endanger valuable property. All reet! All reet! Honey . . ."

It withdrew a crucible of glowing gold from the electric furnace, turned, capered hideously, sang crazily, and splashed a sluggish gobbet of molten gold over Dallas Brady's head. She screamed and collapsed, her hair and clothes flaming, her skin crackling. The android poured again while it capered and sang.

"Be fleet be fleet, cool and discreet, honey . . ." It sang and slowly poured and poured the molten gold. Then I left the workshop and rejoined James Vandaleur in his hotel suite. The android's charred clothes and squirming fingers warned its owner that something was very much wrong.

Vandaleur rushed to Dallas Brady's workshop, stared once, vomited, and fled. I had enough time to pack one bag and raise nine hundred dollars on portable assets. He took a third-class cabin on the *Megaster Queen*, which left that morning for Lyra Alpha. He took me with him. He wept and counted his money and I beat the android again.

And the thermometer in Dallas Brady's workshop registered 98.1° beautifully Fahrenheit.

On Lyra Alpha we holed up in a small hotel near the university. There, Vandaleur carefully bruised my forehead until the letters MA were obliterated by the swelling and the discoloration. The letters would reappear again, but not for several months, and in the meantime Vandaleur hoped the hue and cry for an MA android would be forgotten. The android was hired out as a common laborer in the university power plant. Vandaleur, as James Venice, eked out life on the android's small earnings.

I wasn't too unhappy. Most of the other residents in the hotel were university students, equally hard up, but delightfully young and enthusiastic. There was one charming girl with sharp eyes and a quick mind. Her name was Wanda, and she and her beau, Jed Stark, took a tremendous interest in the killing android which was being mentioned in every paper in the galaxy.

"We've been studying the case," she and Jed said at one of the casual student parties which happened to be held this night in Vandaleur's room. "We think we know what's causing it. We're going to do a paper." They were in a high state of excitement.

"Causing what?" somebody wanted to know.

"The android rampage."

"Obviously out of adjustment, isn't it? Body chemistry gone haywire. Maybe a kind of synthetic cancer, yes?"

"No." Wanda gave Jed a look of suppressed triumph.

"Well, what is it?"

"Something specific."

"What?"

"That would be telling."

"Oh come on."

"Nothing doing."

"Won't you tell us?" I asked intently. "I . . . We're very much interested in what could go wrong with an android."

"No, Mr. Venice," Wanda said. "It's a unique idea and we've got to protect it. One thesis like this and we'll be set up for life. We can't take the chance of somebody stealing it."

"Can't you give us a hint?"

"No. Not a hint. Don't say a word, Jed. But I'll tell you this much, Mr. Venice. I'd hate to be the man who owns that android."

"You mean the police?" I asked.

"I mean projection, Mr. Venice. Projection! That's the danger . . . and I won't say any more. I've said too much as is."

I heard steps outside, and a hoarse voice singing softly: "Be fleet be fleet cool and discreet, honey . . ." My android entered the room, home from its tour of duty at the university power plant. It was not introduced. I motioned to it and I immediately responded to the command and went to the beer keg and took over Vandaleur's job of serving the guests. Its accomplished fingers writhed in a private rumba of their own. Gradually they stopped their squirming, and the strange humming ended.

Androids were not unusual at the university. The wealthier students owned them along with cars and planes. Vandaleur's android provoked no comment, but young Wanda was sharp-eyed and quick-witted. She noted my bruised forehead and she was intent on the history-making thesis she and Jed Stark were going to write. After the party broke up, she consulted with Jed walking upstairs to her room.

"Jed, why'd that android have a bruised forehead?"

"Probably hurt itself, Wanda. It's working in the power plant. They fling a lot of heavy stuff around."

"That all?"

"What else?"

"It could be a convenient bruise."

"Convenient for what?"

"Hiding what's stamped on its forehead."

"No point to that, Wanda. You don't have to see marks on a forehead to recognize an android. You don't have to see a trademark on a car to know it's a car."

"I don't mean it's trying to pass as a human. I mean it's trying to pass as a lower-grade android."

"Why?"

"Suppose it had 'MA' on its forehead."

"Multiple aptitude? Then why in hell would Venice waste it stoking furnaces if it could earn more—Oh. Oh! You mean it's—?"

Wanda nodded.

"Jesus!" Stark pursed his lips. "What do we do? Call the police?"

"No. We don't know if it's an MA for a fact. If it turns out to be an MA and the killing android, our paper comes first anyway. This is our big chance, Jed. It it's *that* android we can run a series of controlled tests and—"

"How do we find out for sure?"

"Easy. Infrared film. That'll show what's under the bruise. Borrow a camera. Buy some film. We'll sneak down to the power plant tomorrow afternoon and take some pictures. Then we'll know."

They stole down into the university power plant the following afternoon. It was a vast cellar, deep under the earth. It was dark, shadowy, luminous with burning light from the furnace doors. Above the roar of the fires they could hear a strange voice shouting and chanting in the echoing vault: "All reet! All reet! So jeet your seat. Be fleet be fleet, cool and discreet, honey . . ." And they could see a capering figure dancing a lunatic rumba in time to the music it shouted. The legs twisted. The arms waved. The fingers writhed.

Jed Stark raised the camera and began shooting his spool of infrared film, aiming the camera sights at that bobbing head. Then Wanda shrieked, for I saw them and came charging down on them, brandishing a polished steel shovel. It smashed the camera. It felled the girl and then the boy. Jed fought me for a desperate hissing moment before he was bludgeoned into helplessness. Then the android dragged them to the furnace and fed them to the flames, slowly, hideously. It capered and sang. Then it returned to my hotel.

The thermometer in the power plant registered 100.9° murderously Fahrenheit. All reet! All reet!

We bought steerage on the *Lyra Queen*, and Vandaleur and the android did odd jobs for their meals. During the night watches, Vandaleur would sit alone in the steerage head with a cardboard portfolio on his lap, puzzling over its contents. That portfolio was all he had managed to bring with him from Lyra Alpha. He had stolen it from Wanda's room. It was labeled ANDROID. It contained the secret of my sickness.

And it contained nothing but newspapers. Scores of newspapers from all over the galaxy, printed, microfilmed, engraved, etched, offset, photostated . . . Rigel *Star-Banner* . . . Paragon *Picayune* . . . Megaster *Times-Leader* . . . La lande *Herald* . . . Lacaille *Journal* . . . Indi *Intelligencer* . . . Eridani *Telegram-News*. All reet! All reet!

Nothing but newspapers. Each paper contained an account of one crime in the android's ghastly career. Each paper also contained news, domestic and foreign, sports, society, weather, shipping news, stock exchange quotations, human interest stories, features, contests, puzzles. Somewhere in that mass of uncollated facts was the secret Wanda and Jed Stark had discovered. Vandaleur pored over the papers helplessly. It was beyond him. So jeet your seat!

"I'll sell you," I told the android. "Damn you. When we land on Terra, I'll sell you. I'll settle for three percent on whatever you're worth."

"I am worth fifty-seven thousand dollars on the current exchange," I told him.

"If I can't sell you, I'll turn you in to the police," I said.

"I am valuable property," I answered. "It is forbidden to endanger valuable property. You won't have me destroyed."

"Christ damn you!" Vandaleur cried. "What? Are you arrogant? Do you know you can trust me to protect you? Is that the secret?"

The multiple-aptitude android regarded him with calm accomplished eyes. "Sometimes," it said, "it is a good thing to be property."

It was three below zero when the *Lyra Queen* dropped at Croydon Field. A mixture of ice and snow swept across the field, fizzing and exploding into steam under the *Queen*'s tail jets. The passengers trotted numbly across the blackened concrete to customs inspection, and thence to the airport bus that was to take them to London. Vandaleur and the android were broke. They walked.

By midnight they reached Piccadilly Circus. The December ice storm had not slackened, and the statue of Eros was encrusted with ice. They turned right, walked down to Trafalgar Square and then along the Strand shaking with cold and wet. Just above Fleet Street, Vandaleur saw a solitary figure coming from the direction of St. Paul's. He drew the android into an alley.

"We've got to have money," he whispered. He pointed at the approaching figure. "He has money. Take it from him."

"The order cannot be obeyed," the android said.

"Take it from him," Vandaleur repeated. "By force. Do you understand? We're desperate."

"It is contrary to my prime directive," I said. "I cannot endanger life or property. The order cannot be obeyed."

"For God's sake!" Vandaleur burst out. "You've attacked, destroyed, murdered. Don't gibber about prime directives. You haven't any left. Get his money. Kill him if you have to. I tell you, we're desperate!"

"It is contrary to my prime directive," I said. "I cannot endanger life or property. The order cannot be obeyed."

I thrust the android back and leaped out at the stranger. He was tall, austere, competent. He had an air of hope curdled by cynicism. He carried a cane. I saw he was blind.

"Yes?" he said. "I hear you near me. What is it?"

"Sir . . ." Vandaleur hesitated. "I'm desperate."

"We are all desperate," the stranger replied. "Quietly desperate."

"Sir . . . I've got to have some money."

"Are you begging or stealing?" The sightless eyes passed over Vandaleur and the android.

"I'm prepared for either."

"Ah. So are we all. It is the history of our race." The stranger motioned over his shoulder. "I have been begging at St. Paul's, my friend. What I desire cannot be stolen. What is it you desire that you are lucky enough to be able to steal?"

"Money," Vandaleur said.

"Money for what? Come, my friend, let us exchange confidences. I will tell you why I beg, if you will tell me why you steal. My name is Blenheim."

"My name is . . . Vole."

"I was not begging for sight at St. Paul's, Mr. Vole. I was begging for a number."

"A number?"

"Ah yes. Numbers rational, numbers irrational, numbers imaginary. Positive integers. Negative integers. Fractions, positive and negative. Eh? You have never heard of Blenheim's immortal treatise on Twenty Zeros, or The Differences in Absence of Quantity?" Blenheim smiled bitterly. "I am the wizard of the Theory of Number, Mr. Vole, and I have exhausted the charm of number for myself. After fifty years of wizardry, senility approaches and the appetite vanishes. I have been praying in St. Paul's for inspiration. Dear God, I prayed, if You exist, send me a number."

Vandaleur slowly lifted the cardboard portfolio and touched Blenheim's hand with it. "In here," he said, "is a number. A hidden number. A secret number. The number of a crime. Shall we exchange, Mr. Blenheim? Shelter for a number?"

"Neither begging nor stealing, eh?" Blenheim said. "But a bargain. So all life reduces itself to the banal." The sightless eyes again passed over Vandaleur and the android. "Perhaps the All-Mighty is not God but a merchant. Come home with me."

On the top floor of Blenheim's house we shared a room—two beds, two closets, two washstands, one bathroom. Vandaleur bruised my forehead again and sent me out to find work, and while the android worked, I consulted with Blenheim and read him the papers from the portfolio, one by one. All reet! All reet!

Vandaleur told him so much and no more. He was a student, I said, attempting a thesis on the murdering android. In these papers which he had collected were the facts that would explain the crimes of which Blenheim had heard nothing. There must be a correlation, a number, a statistic, something which would account for my derangement, I explained, and Blenheim was piqued by the mystery, the detective story, the human interest of number.

We examined the papers. As I read them aloud, he listed them and their contents in his blind, meticulous writing. And then I read his notes to him. He listed the papers by type, by typeface, by fact, by fancy, by article, spelling, words, theme, advertising, pictures, subject, politics, prejudices. He analyzed. He studied. He meditated. And we lived together in that top floor, always a little cold, always a little terrified, always a little closer . . . brought together by our fear of it, our hatred between us. Like a wedge driven into a living tree and splitting the trunk, only to be forever incorporated into the scar tissue, we grew together. Vandaleur and the android. Be fleet be fleet!

And one afternoon Blenheim called Vandaleur into his study and displayed his notes. "I think I've found it," he said, "but I can't understand it."

Vandaleur's heart leaped.

"Here are the correlations," Blenheim continued. "In fifty papers there are accounts of the criminal android. What is there, outside the depredations, that is also in fifty papers?"

"I don't know, Mr. Blenheim."

"It was a rhetorical question. Here is the answer. The weather."

"What?"

"The weather." Blenheim nodded. "Each crime was committed on a day when the temperature was above ninety degrees Fahrenheit."

"But that's impossible," Vandaleur exclaimed. "It was cool on Lyra Alpha."

"We have no record of any crime committed on Lyra Alpha. There is no paper."

"No. That's right, I—" Vandaleur was confused. Suddenly he exclaimed. "No. You're right. The furnace room. It was hot there. Hot! Of course. My God, yes! That's the answer. Dallas Brady's electric furnace . . . the rice deltas on Paragon. So jeet your seat. Yes. But why? Why? My God, why?"

I came into the house at that moment, and passing the study, saw Vandaleur and Blenheim. I entered, awaiting commands, my multiple aptitudes devoted to service.

"That's the android, eh?" Blenheim said after a long moment.

"Yes," Vandaleur answered, still confused by the discovery. "And that explains why it refused to attack you that night on the Strand. It wasn't hot enough to break the prime directive. Only in the heat . . . The heat, all reet!" He looked at the android. A silent lunatic command passed from man to android. I refused. It is forbidden to endanger life. Vandaleur gestured furiously, then seized Blenheim's shoulders and yanked him back out of his desk chair to the floor. Blenheim shouted once. Vandaleur leaped on him like a tiger, pinning him to the floor and sealing his mouth with one hand.

"Find a weapon," he called to the android.

"It is forbidden to endanger life."

"This is a fight for self-preservation. Bring me a weapon!" He held the squirming mathematician with all his weight. I went at once to a cupboard where I knew a revolver was kept. I checked it. It was loaded with five cartridges. I handed it to Vandaleur. I took it, rammed the barrel against Blenheim's head and pulled the trigger. He shuddered once. We had three hours before the cook returned from her day off. We looted the house. We took Blenheim's money and jewels. We packed a bag with clothes. We took Blenheim's notes, destroyed the newspapers; and we left, carefully locking the door behind us. In Blenheim's study we left a pile of crumpled papers under a half inch of burning candle. And we soaked the rug around it with kerosene. No, I did all that. The android refused. I am forbidden to endanger life or property.

All reet!

They took the tubes to Leicester Square, changed trains, and rode to the British Museum. There they got off and went to a small Georgian house just off Russell Square. A shingle in the window read: NAN WEBB, PSYCHOMETRIC CONSULTANT. Vandaleur had made a note of the address some weeks earlier. They went into the house. The android waited in the foyer with the bag. Vandaleur entered Nan Webb's office.

She was a tall woman with gray shingled hair, very fine English complexion, and very bad English legs. Her features were blunt, her expression acute. She nodded to Vandaleur, finished a letter, sealed it and looked up.

"My name," I said, "is Vanderbilt. James Vanderbilt."

"Quite."

"I'm an exchange student at London University."

"Quite."

"I've been researching on the killing android, and I think I've discovered something very interesting. I'd like your advice on it. What is your fee?"

"What is your college at the University?"

"Why?"

"There is a discount for students."

"Merton College."

"That will be two pounds, please."

Vandaleur placed two pounds on the desk and added to the fee

Blenheim's notes. "There is a correlation," he said, "between the crimes of the android and the weather. You will note that each crime was committed when the temperature rose above ninety degrees Fahrenheit. Is there a psychometric answer for this?"

Nan Webb nodded, studied the notes for a moment, put down the sheets of paper, and said: "Synesthesia, obviously."

"What?"

"Synesthesia," she repeated. "When a sensation, Mr. Vanderbilt, is interpreted immediately in terms of a sensation from a different sense organ from the one stimulated, it is called synesthesia. For example: A sound stimulus gives rise to a simultaneous sensation of definite color. Or color gives rise to a sensation of taste. Or a light stimulus gives rise to a sensation of sound. There can be confusion or short circuiting of any sensation of taste, smell, pain, pressure, temperature, and so on. D'you understand?"

"I think so."

"Your research has uncovered the fact that the android most probably reacts to temperature stimulus above the ninety-degree level synthetically. Most probably there is an endocrine response. Probably a temperature linkage with the android adrenal surrogate. High temperature brings about a response of fear, anger, excitement, and violent physical activity . . . all within the province of the adrenal gland."

"Yes. I see. Then if the android were to be kept in cold climates . . ."

"There would be neither stimulus nor response. There would be no crimes. Quite."

"I see. What is projection?"

"How do you mean?"

"Is there any danger of projection with regard to the owner of the android?"

"Very interesting. Projection is a throwing forward. It is the process of throwing out upon another the ideas or impulses that belong to oneself. The paranoid, for example, projects upon others his conflicts and disturbances in order to externalize them. He accuses, directly or by implication, other men of having the very sicknesses with which he is struggling himself."

"And the danger of projection?"

"It is the danger of believing what is implied. If you live with a psychotic who projects his sickness upon you, there is a danger of falling into his psychotic pattern and becoming virtually psychotic yourself. As, no doubt, is happening to you, Mr. Vandaleur."

Vandaleur leaped to his feet.

"You are an ass," Nan Webb went on crisply. She waved the sheets of notes. "This is no exchange student's writing. It's the unique cursive of the famous Blenheim. Every scholar in England knows this blind writing. There is no Merton College at London University. That was a miserable guess. Merton is one of the Oxford colleges. And you, Mr. Vandaleur, are so obviously infected by association with your deranged android ... by projection, if you will ... that I hesitate between calling the Metropolitan Police and the Hospital for the Criminally Insane."

I took out the gun and shot her.

Reet!

"Antares II, Alpha Aurigae, Acrux IV, Pollux IX, Rigel Centaurus," Vandaleur said. "They're all cold. Cold as a witch's kiss. Mean temperatures of forty degrees Fahrenheit. Never gets hotter than seventy. We're in business again. Watch that curve."

The multiple-aptitude android swung the wheel with its accomplished hands. The car took the curve sweetly and sped on through the northern marshes, the reeds stretching for miles, brown and dry, under the cold English sky. The sun was sinking swiftly. Overhead, a lone flight of bustards flapped clumsily eastward. High above the flight, a lone helicopter drifted toward home and warmth.

"No more warmth for us," I said. "No more heat. We're safe when we're cold. We'll hole up in Scotland, make a little money, get across to Norway, build a bankroll, and then ship out. We'll settle on Pollux. We're safe. We've licked it. We can live again."

There was a startling *bleep* from overhead, and then a ragged roar: "ATTENTION, JAMES VANDALEUR AND ANDROID. ATTENTION, JAMES VANDALEUR AND ANDROID!"

Vandaleur started and looked up. The lone helicopter was floating above them. From its belly came amplified commands: "YOU ARE SURROUNDED. THE ROAD IS BLOCKED. YOU ARE

TO STOP YOUR CAR AT ONCE AND SUBMIT TO ARREST.
STOP AT ONCE!"

I looked at Vandaleur for orders.

"Keep driving," Vandaleur snapped.

The helicopter dropped lower: "ATTENTION, ANDROID.
YOU ARE IN CONTROL OF THE VEHICLE. YOU ARE TO
STOP AT ONCE. THIS IS A STATE DIRECTIVE SUPERSED-
ING ALL PRIVATE COMMANDS."

"What the hell are you doing?" I shouted.

"A state directive supersedes all private commands," the android answered. "I must point out to you that—"

"Get the hell away from the wheel," Vandaleur ordered. I
clubbed the android, yanked him sideways, and squirmed over him
to the wheel. The car veered off the road in that moment and went
churning through the frozen mud and dry reeds. Vandaleur regained
control and continued westward through the marshes toward a parallel highway five miles distant.

"We'll beat their goddamned block," he grunted.

The car pounded and surged. The helicopter dropped even
lower. A searchlight blazed from the belly of the plane.

"ATTENTION, JAMES VANDALEUR AND ANDROID.
SUBMIT TO ARREST. THIS IS A STATE DIRECTIVE SUPER-
SEDING ALL PRIVATE COMMANDS."

"He can't submit," Vandaleur shouted wildly. "There's no one
to submit to. He can't and I won't."

"Christ!" I muttered. "We'll beat them yet. We'll beat the
block. We'll beat the heat. We'll—"

"I must point out to you," I said, "that I am required by my
prime directive to obey state directives which supersede all private
commands. I must submit to arrest."

"Who says it's a state directive?" Vandaleur said. "Them? Up
in that plane? They've got to show credentials. They've got to prove
it's state authority before you submit. How d'you know they're not
crooks trying to trick us?"

Holding the wheel with one arm, he reached into his side
pocket to make sure the gun was still in place. The car skidded.
The tires squealed on frost and reeds. The wheel was wrenched
from his grasp and the car yawed up a small hillock and overturned.

The motor roared and the wheels screamed. Vandaleur crawled out and dragged the android with him. For the moment we were outside the circle of light boring down from the helicopter. We blundered off into the marsh, into the blackness, into concealment. . . . Vandaleur running with a pounding heart, hauling the android along. The helicopter circled and soared over the wrecked car, searchlight peering, loudspeaker braying. On the highway we had left, lights appeared as the pursuing and blocking parties gathered and followed radio directions from the plane. Vandaleur and the android continued deeper and deeper into the marsh, working their way toward the parallel road and safety. It was night by now. The sky was a black matte. Not a star showed. The temperature was dropping. A southeast night wind knifed us to the bone.

Far behind there was a dull concussion. Vandaleur turned, gasping. The car's fuel had exploded. A geyser of flame shot up like a lurid fountain. It subsided into a low crater of burning reeds. Whipped by the wind, the distant hem of flame fanned up into a wall, ten feet high. The wall began marching down on us, cracking fiercely. Above it, a pall of oil smoke surged forward. Behind it, Vandaleur could make out the figures of men . . . a mass of beaters searching the marsh.

"Christ!" I cried and searched desperately for safety. He ran, dragging me with him, until their feet crunched through the surface ice of a pool. He trampled the ice furiously, then flung himself down in the numbing water, pulling the android with us.

The wall of flame approached. I could hear the crackle and feel the heat. He could see the searchers clearly. Vandaleur reached into his side pocket for the gun. The pocket was torn. The gun was gone. He groaned and shook with cold and terror. The light from the marsh fire was blinding. Overhead, the helicopter floated helplessly to one side, unable to fly through the smoke and flames and aid the searchers who were beating far to the right of us.

"They'll miss us," Vandaleur whispered. "Keep quiet. That's an order. They'll miss us. We'll beat them. We'll beat the fire. We'll—"

Three distinct shots sounded less than a hundred feet from the fugitives. *Blam! Blam! Blam!* They came from the last three cartridges in my gun as the marsh fire reached it where it had dropped, and exploded the shells. The searchers turned toward the sound and began working directly toward us. Vandaleur cursed hysterically and tried to submerge even deeper to escape the intolerable heat of the fire. The android began to twitch.

The wall of flame surged up to them. Vandaleur took a deep breath and prepared to submerge until the flame passed over them. The android shuddered and burst into an earsplitting scream.

"All reet! All reet!" it shouted. "Be fleet be fleet!"

"Damn you!" I shouted. I tried to drown it.

"Damn you!" I cursed him. I smashed his face.

The android battered Vandaleur, who fought it off until it exploded out of the mud and staggered upright. Before I could return to the attack, the live flames captured it hypnotically. It danced and capered in a lunatic rumba before the wall of fire. Its legs twisted. Its arms waved. The fingers writhed in a private rumba of their own. It shrieked and sang and ran in a crooked waltz before the embrace of the heat, a muddy monster silhouetted against the brilliant sparkling flare.

The searchers shouted. There were shots. The android spun around twice and then continued its horrid dance before the face of the flames. There was a rising gust of wind. The fire swept around the capering figure and enveloped it for a roaring moment. Then the fire swept on, leaving behind it a sobbing mass of synthetic flesh oozing scarlet blood that would never coagulate.

The thermometer would have registered 1200° wondrously Fahrenheit.

Vandaleur didn't die. I got away. They missed him while they watched the android caper and die. But I don't know which of us he is these days. Projection, Wanda warned me. Projection, Nan Webb told him. If you live with a crazy man or a crazy machine long enough, I become crazy too. Reet!

But we know one truth. We know they were wrong. The new robot and Vandaleur know that because the new robot's started twitching too. Reet! Here on cold Pollux, the robot is twitching and singing. No heat, but my fingers writhe. No heat, but it's taken the little Talley girl off for a solitary walk. A cheap labor robot. A servo-mechanism . . . all I could afford . . . but it's twitching and humming and walking alone with the child somewhere and I can't find them. Christ! Vandaleur can't find me before it's too late. Cool and discreet, honey, in the dancing frost while the thermometer registers 10° fondly Fahrenheit.

COMMENT ON
"FONDLY FAHRENHEIT"

I've always been fascinated by the way craftsmen work in their profession, and I'll spend hours with pawnbrokers, computer engineers, exterminators, anyone, in an effort to discover the backstage problems of their work. Perhaps this is a habit created by years of interviewing for the magazine for which I write and edit; perhaps it is the built-in curiosity of the writer. I don't know. But it occurred to me that readers might be interested in the backstage problems of writing "Fondly Fahrenheit."

I must describe my working methods first, otherwise this journal of the writing of the story will seem cold-blooded and mechanistic. I write out of fever. I cannot write anything until I'm so saturated with it, involved with it, bursting with it, that it must come out or I will have no rest.

Over the years I've evolved a technique for igniting this fever. It starts with outlining, first general, then increasingly detailed as the story develops. When I have what I believe to be the final outline (it never is), I begin running the story through my head over and over again; not in words, I don't tell it to myself, but in a sort of sensory cinema. I listen to the sound, visualize the scenes, feel the tempo of the characters and their conflicts.

It's at this point that the pacing begins. At home I have a good seventy-five-foot straightaway, and I walk the length of the apartment, back and forth, endlessly. In the office I have a wide corridor, the length *of a football field. The staff and the secretaries are used to my peculiarity by now and kindly clear the way for me. The pacing and the repetitions continue, the heat mounts, and, if I'm lucky, the ignition point is reached. Then I run like hell for the typewriter.*

The idea for "Fondly Fahrenheit" first came to me out of a reminiscence of Mark Twain, I think in Life on the Mississippi, *but I'm not sure, it was so long ago. He wrote that the first Negro slave was hanged for murder near Hannibal, Missouri. The slave had criminally assualted and killed a young girl. Twain said that the slave had been guilty of a similar crime in another state, but that his owner had smuggled him out because he was too valuable to be given up to justice and destroyed.*

It seemed to me that there might be an interesting story in this conflict between master and slave; the slave aware of his value and the hold it gives him over his owner, the master constrained by greed to condone criminal acts which he abhors. It was impossible for me to set the story in antebellum days; I didn't know enough about the period or the scene. Contemporary treatment was clearly out of the question; we do have economic forms of slavery, but no chattel slavery. I decided to set the story in the future, postulating an android-slave society. The note went into my Commonplace Book, which has been the storehouse for ideas, fragments, bits of dialogue, odd situations, and gimmicks since I began my writing career. It remained there for several years.

I would think about it, off and on, but I was also thinking about dozens of other ideas which seemed to have priority. I sometimes regard story ideas as an eager crowd, jostling and elbowing each other, trying to attract your attention. The master-slave idea managed to attract my serious attention one evening, and I outlined the first three or four scenes. I could get no further, and rather than waste time struggling with it, I put it away. One of the luxuries of reaching a certain financial plateau is that the writer can take his time and give inchoate ideas a chance to sort themselves out in the unconscious. Many writers, working under the gun, are so beset by the pressure of meeting bills that they haven't the time to do their best work. I've been through it myself, and I'm deeply sympathetic.

When I looked through my outlines and notes a few months later, the unconscious had done its work. It dawned on me that what was holding me up was the fact that I hadn't thought through the android slave's criminal behavior; I'd more or less written him off as a murderer, period. Now I asked myself why. Why does a carefully conditioned android go berserk? I remembered a note I'd made long before on the statistics of crime, relating crime rate to temperature. (This was a decade before the long, hot summer riots had become a commonplace.) "Good," I said. "The android breaks his conditioning only when the temperature rises above a certain level."

At this point it was possible to add a mystery to the chase structure. Will the owner discover what's wrong with his android? I went back, reoutlined in these terms, changing the settings to accommodate the temperature gimmick, and continued blocking forward. Then I came up against another wall. So he does discover the secret. So what? It felt like a letdown. I needed more of a climax. Once again I put the notes away to give the real writer, who lives somewhere deep down inside me, a chance to do some work.

Much later I was going through my Commonplace Book, looking for something else, when I came across a note I'd made on psychiatric projection, transcribed from one of Karen Horney's books. These are cases where disturbed people attribute their own strange behavior to others.

"That's it!" the real writer, an alert opportunist, said.

"That's what?" I asked. "I'm looking for notes on Western frontier customs."

"That's the final twist for the android story," he said. "Temperature may break the android's conditioning, but the master is really the criminal. We'll extrapolate the projection theme. The master unconsciously but actually imposes his own insanity on the slave."

We dropped everything else, worked out a detailed scene-by-scene outline, and began to pace. Suddenly an idea came, one we'd been toying with for years, that of telling a story from a multiple point of view. Here it would be the omniscient, the master's and the slave's. That was the ignition point. The fever set in, and I ran like hell for the typewriter.

What you've just read is the result of all this; years of notes, months of dovetailing ideas, weeks of outlining. Someone once asked me how long it took to write "Fondly Fahrenheit." I hedged. "Well, it took me two days to type it," I said. What else could I say?

THE FOUR-HOUR FUGUE

Fear carries a scent with it
that most humans can't detect.
Most, but not all.

B y now, of course, the Northeast Corridor was the Northeast
slum, stretching from Canada to the Carolinas and as far west as
Pittsburgh. It was a fantastic jungle of rancid violence inhabited by
a steaming, restless population with no visible means of support and
no fixed residence, so vast that census takers, birth-control super-
visors, and the social services had given up all hope. It was a gigantic raree-show that everyone denounced and enjoyed. Even the
privileged few who could afford to live highly protected lives in
highly expensive Oases and could live anywhere else they pleased
never thought of leaving. The jungle grabbed you.

There were thousands of everyday survival problems but one of
the most exasperating was the shortage of fresh water. Most of the
available potable water had long since been impounded by pro-
gressive industries for the sake of a better tomorrow and there was
very little left to go around. Rainwater tanks on the roofs, of course.
A black market, naturally. That was about all. So the jungle stank.
It stank worse than the court of Queen Elizabeth, which could have

bathed but didn't believe in it. The Corridor just couldn't bathe, wash clothes, or clean house, and you could smell its noxious effluvium from ten miles out at sea. Welcome to the Fun Corridor.

Sufferers near the shore would have been happy to clean up in salt water, but the Corridor beaches had been polluted by so much crude oil seepage for so many generations that they were all owned by deserving oil reclamation companies. *Keep Out! No Trespassing!* And armed guards. The rivers and lakes were electrically fenced; no need for guards, just skull and crossbones signs and if you didn't know what they were telling you, tough.

Not to believe that everybody minded stinking as they skipped merrily over the rotting corpses in the streets, but a lot did and their only remedy was perfumery. There were dozens of competing companies producing perfumes but the leader, far and away, was the Continental Can Company, which hadn't manufactured cans in two centuries. They'd switched to plastics and had the good fortune about a hundred stockholders' meetings back to make the mistake of signing a sales contract with and delivering to some cockamamie perfume brewer an enormous quantity of glowing neon containers. The corporation went bust and CCC took it over in hopes of getting some of their money back. That takeover proved to be their salvation when the perfume explosion took place: it gave them entrée to the most profitable industry of the times.

But it was neck-and-neck with the rivals until Blaise Skiaki joined CCC: then it turned into a runaway. Blaise Skiaki. Origins: French, Japanese, Black African, and Irish. Education: BA, Princeton; ME, MIT; PhD. Dow Chemical. (It was Dow that had secretly tipped CCC that Skiaki was a winner and lawsuits brought by the competition were still pending before the ethics board.) Blaise Skiaki: Age, thirty-one; unmarried, straight, genius.

His sense of scent was his genius and he was privately referred to at CCC as "The Nose." He knew everything about perfumery: the animal products, ambergris, castor, civet, musk; the essential oils distilled from plants and flowers: the balsams extruded by tree and shrub wounds, benzoin, opopanax, Peru, Talu, storax, myrrh: the synthetics created from the combination of natural and chemical scents, the latter mostly the esters of fatty acids.

He had created for CCC their most successful sellers: "Vulva,"

"Assuage," "Oxter" (a much more attractive brand name than "Armpitto"), "Preparation F," "Tongue War," et cetera. He was treasured by CCC, paid a salary generous enough to enable him to live in an Oasis and, best of all, granted unlimited supplies of fresh water. No girl in the Corridor could resist the offer of taking a shower with him.

But he paid a high price for these advantages. He could never use scented soaps, shaving creams, pomades, or depilatories. He could never eat seasoned foods. He could drink nothing but pure water. All this, you understand, to keep The Nose pure and un-contaminated so that he could smell around in his sterile laboratory and devise new creations. He was presently composing a rather promising unguent provisionally named "Correctum," but he'd been on it for six months without any positive results and CCC was alarmed by the delay. His genius had never before taken so long.

There was a meeting of the top-level executives, names withheld on the grounds of corporate privilege.

"What's the matter with him anyway?"

"Has he lost his touch?"

"It hardly seems likely."

"Maybe he needs a rest."

"Why, he had a week's holiday last month."

"What did he do?"

"Ate up a storm, he told me."

"Could that be it?"

"No. He said he purged himself before he came back to work."

"Is he having trouble here at CCC? Difficulties with middle management?"

"Absolutely not, Mr. Chairman. They wouldn't dare touch him."

"Maybe he wants a raise."

"No. He can't spend the money he makes now."

"Has our competition got to him?"

"They get to him all the time, General, and he laughs them off."

"Then it must be something personal."

"Agreed."

"Woman trouble?"

"My God! We should have such trouble."

"Family trouble?"

"He's an orphan, Mr. Chairman."

"Ambition? Incentive? Should we make him an officer of CCC?"

"I offered that to him the first of the year, sir, and he turned me down. He just wants to play in his laboratory."

"Then why isn't he playing?"

"Apparently he's got some kind of creative block."

"What the hell is the matter with him anyway?"

"Which is how you started this meeting."

"I did not."

"You did."

"Not."

"Governor, will you play back the bug."

"Gentlemen, gentlemen, please! Obviously Dr. Skiaki has personal problems which are blocking his genius. We must solve that for him. Suggestions?"

"Psychiatry?"

"That won't work without voluntary cooperation. I doubt whether he'd cooperate. He's an obstinate gook."

"Senator, I beg you! Such expressions must not be used with reference to one of our most valuable assets."

"Mr. Chairman, the problem is to discover the source of Dr. Skiaki's block."

"Agreed. Suggestions?"

"Why, the first step should be to maintain twenty-four-hour surveillance. All of the gook's—excuse me—the good doctor's activities, associates, contacts."

"By CCC?"

"I would suggest not. There are bound to be leaks which would only antagonize the good gook—doctor!"

"Outside surveillance?"

"Yes, sir."

"Very good. Agreed. Meeting adjourned."

Skip-Tracer Associates were perfectly furious. After one month they threw the case back into CCC's lap, asking for nothing more than their expenses.

"Why in hell didn't you tell us that we were assigned to a pro, Mr. Chairman, sir? Our tracers aren't trained for that."

"Wait a minute, please. What d'you mean, 'pro'?"

"A professional Rip."

"A what?"

"Rip. Gorill. Gimpster. Crook."

"Dr. Skiaki a crook? Preposterous."

"Look, Mr. Chairman. I'll frame it for you and you draw your own conclusions. Yes?"

"Go ahead."

"It's all detailed in this report anyway. We put double tails on Skiaki every day to and from your shop. When he left they followed him home. He always went home. They staked in double shifts. He had dinner sent in from the Organic Nursery every night. They checked the messengers bringing the dinners. Legit. They checked the dinners; sometimes for one, sometimes for two. They traced some of the girls who left his penthouse. All clean. So far, all clean, yes?"

"And?"

"The crunch. Couple of nights a week he leaves the house and goes into the city. He leaves around midnight and doesn't come back until four, more or less."

"Where does he go?"

"We don't know because he shakes his tails like the pro that he is. He weaves through the Corridor like a whore or a fag cruising for trade—excuse me—and he always loses our men. I'm not taking anything away from him. He's smart, shifty, quick, and a real pro. He has to be; and he's too much for Skip-Tracers to handle."

"Then you have no idea of what he does or who he meets between midnight and four?"

"No, sir. We've got nothing and you've got a problem. Not ours any more."

"Thank you. Contrary to the popular impression, corporations are not altogether idiotic. CCC understands that negatives are also results. You'll receive your expenses and the agreed-upon fee."

"Mr. Chairman, I—"

"No, no, please. You've narrowed it down to those missing four hours. Now, as you say, they're our problem."

•   •   •

CCC summoned Salem Burne. Mr. Burne always insisted that he was neither a physician nor a psychiatrist: he did not care to be associated with what he considered to be the drek of the professions. Salem Burne was a witch doctor; more precisely, a warlock. He made the most remarkable and penetrating analyses of disturbed people, not so much through his coven rituals of pentagons, incantations, incense, and the like as through his remarkable sensitivity to Body English and his acute interpretation of it. And this might be witchcraft after all.

Mr. Burne entered Blaise Skiaki's immaculate laboratory with a winning smile and Dr. Skiaki let out a rending howl of anguish.

"I told you to sterilize before you came."

"But I did, Doctor. Faithfully."

"You did not. You reek of anise, ilang-ilang, and methyl anthranilate. You've polluted my day. Why?"

"Dr. Skiaki, I assure you that I—" Suddenly Salem Burne stopped. "Oh my God!" he groaned. "I used my wife's towel this morning."

Skiaki laughed and turned up the ventilators to full force. "I understand. No hard feelings. Now let's get your wife out of here. I have an office about half a mile down the hall. We can talk there."

They sat down in the vacant office and looked at each other. Mr. Burne saw a pleasant, youngish man with cropped black hair, small expressive ears, high telltale cheekbones, slitty eyes that would need careful watching and graceful hands that would be a dead giveaway.

"Now, Mr. Burne, how can I help you?" Skiaki said while his hands asked. "Why the hell have you come pestering me?"

"Dr. Skiaki, I'm a colleague in a sense: I'm a professional witch doctor. One crucial part of my ceremonies is the burning of various forms of incense, but they're all rather conventional. I was hoping that your expertise might suggest something different with which I could experiment."

"I see. Interesting. You've been burning stacte, onycha, galbanum, frankincense . . . that sort of thing?"

"Yes. All quite conventional."

"Most interesting. I could, of course, make many suggestions for new experiments and yet—" Here Skiaki stopped and stared into space.

After a long pause the warlock asked, "Is anything wrong, Doctor?"

"Look here," Skiaki burst out. "You're on the wrong track. It's the burning of incense that's conventional and old-fashioned, and trying different scents won't solve your problem. Why not experiment with an altogether different approach?"

"And what would that be?"

"The Odophone principle."

"Odophone?"

"Yes. There's a scale that exists among scents as among sounds. Sharp smells correspond to high notes and heavy smells with low notes. For example, ambergris is in the treble clef while violet is in the bass. I could draw up a scent scale for you, running perhaps two octaves. Then it would be up to you to compose the music."

"This is positively brilliant, Dr. Skiaki."

"Isn't it?" Skiaki beamed. "But in all honesty I should point out that we're collaborators in brilliance. I could never have come up with the idea if you hadn't presented me with a most original challenge."

They made contact on this friendly note and talked shop enthusiastically, lunched together, told each other about themselves, and made plans for the witchcraft experiments in which Skiaki volunteered to participate despite the fact that he was no believer in diabolism.

"And yet the irony lies in the fact that he is indeed devil-ridden," Salem Burne reported.

The Chairman could make nothing of this.

"Psychiatry and diabolism use different terms for the same phenomenon," Burne explained. "So perhaps I'd better translate. Those missing four hours are fugues."

The Chairman was not enlightened. "Do you mean the musical expression, Mr. Burne?"

"No, sir. A fugue is also the psychiatric description of a more advanced form of somnambulism . . . sleepwalking."

"Blaise Skiaki walks in his sleep?"

"Yes, sir, but it's more complicated than that. The sleepwalker is a comparatively simple case. He is never in touch with his surroundings. You can speak to him, shout at him, address him by name, and he remains totally oblivious."

"And the fugue?"

"In the fugue the subject is in touch with his surroundings. He can converse with you. He has awareness and memory for the events that take place within the fugue, but while he is within his fugue he is a totally different person from the man he is in real life. And—and this is most important, sir—after the fugue he remembers nothing of it."

"Then in your opinion Dr. Skiaki has these fugues two or three times a week."

"That is my diagnosis, sir."

"And he can tell us nothing of what transpires during the fugue?"

"Nothing."

"Can you?"

"I'm afraid not, sir. There's a limit to my powers."

"Have you any idea what is causing these fugues?"

"Only that he is driven by something. I would say that he is possessed by the devil, but that is the cant of my profession. Others may use different terms—compulsion or obsession. The terminology is unimportant. The basic fact is that something possessing him is compelling him to go out nights to do—what? I don't know. All I do know is that this diabolical drive most probably is what is blocking his creative work for you."

One does not summon Gretchen Nunn, not even if you're CCC whose common stock has split twenty-five times. You work your way up through the echelons of her staff until you are finally admitted to the Presence. This involves a good deal of backing and forthing between your staff and hers, and ignites a good deal of exasperation, so the Chairman was understandably put out when at last he was ushered into Miss Nunn's workshop, which was cluttered with the books and apparatus she used for her various investigations.

Gretchen Nunn's business was working miracles; not in the sense of the extraordinary, anomalous or abnormal brought about by a superhuman agency, but rather in the sense of the extraordinary and/or abnormal perception and manipulation of reality. In any situation she could and did achieve the impossible begged by her desperate clients, and her fees were so enormous that she was thinking of going public.

Naturally the Chairman had anticipated Miss Nunn as looking like Merlin in drag. He was flabbergasted to discover that she was a Watusi princess with velvety black skin, aquiline features, great black eyes, tall, slender, twentyish, ravishing in red.

She dazzled him with a smile, indicated a chair, sat in one opposite and said, "My fee is one hundred thousand. Can you afford it?"

"I can. Agreed."

"And your difficulty—is it worth it?"

"It is."

"Then we understand each other so far. Yes, Alex?"

The young secretary who had bounced into the workshop said, "Excuse me. LeClerque insists on knowing how you made the positive identification of the mold as extraterrestrial."

Miss Nunn clicked her tongue impatiently. "He knows that I never give reasons. I only give results."

"Yes'N."

"Has he paid?"

"Yes'N."

"All right, I'll make an exception in his case. Tell him that it was based on the levo and dextro probability in amino acids and tell him to have a qualified exobiologist carry on from there. He won't regret the cost."

"Yes'N. Thank you."

She turned to the Chairman as the secretary left. "You heard that. I only give results."

"Agreed, Miss Nunn."

"Now your difficulty. I'm not committed yet. Understood?"

"Yes. Miss Nunn."

"Go ahead. Everything. Stream of consciousness, if necessary."

An hour later she dazzled him with another smile and said,

"Thank you. This one is really unique. A welcome change. It's a contract, if you're still willing."

"Agreed, Miss Nunn. Would you like a deposit or an advance?"

"Not from CCC."

"What about expenses? Should that be arranged?"

"No. My responsibility."

"But what if you have to—if you're required to—if—"

She laughed. "My responsibility. I never give reasons and I never reveal methods. How can I charge for them? Now don't forget; I want that Skip-Trace report."

A week later Gretchen Nunn took the unusual step of visiting the Chairman in his office at CCC. "I'm calling on you, sir, to give you the opportunity of withdrawing from our contract."

"Withdraw? But why?"

"Because I believe you're involved in something far more serious than you anticipated."

"But what?"

"You won't take my word for it?"

"I must know."

Miss Nunn compressed her lips. After a moment she sighed. "Since this is an unusual case I'll break my rules. Look at this, sir." She unrolled a large map of a segment of the Corridor and flattened it on the Chairman's desk. There was a star in the center of the map. "Skiaki's residence," Miss Nunn said. There was a large circle scribed around the star. "The limits to which a man can walk in two hours." Miss Nunn said. The circle was crisscrossed by twisting trails all emanating from the star. "I got this from the Skip-Trace report. This is how the tails traced Skiaki."

"Very ingenious, but I see nothing serious in this, Miss Nunn."

"Look closely at the trails. What do you see?"

"Why . . . each ends in a red cross."

"And what happens to each trail before it reaches the red cross?"

"Nothing. Nothing at all, except—except that the dots change to dashes."

"And that's what makes it serious."

"I don't understand, Miss Nunn."

"I'll explain. Each cross represents the scene of a murder. The dashes represent the backtracking of the actions and whereabouts of each murder victim just prior to death."

"Murder!"

"They could trace their actions just so far back and no further. Skip-Trace could tail Skiaki just so far forward and no further. Those are the dots. The dates join up. What's your conclusion?"

"It must be coincidence," the Chairman shouted. "This brilliant charming young man. Murder? Impossible!"

"Do you want the factual data I've drawn up?"

"No, I don't. I want the truth. Proof positive without any inferences from dots, dashes and dates."

"Very well, Mr. Chairman. You'll get it."

She rented the professional beggar's pitch alongside the entrance to Skiaki's Oasis for a week. No success. She hired a Revival Band and sang hymns with it before the Oasis. No success. She finally made the contact after she promoted a job with the Organic Nursery. The first three dinners she delivered to the penthouse she came and went unnoticed; Skiaki was entertaining a series of girls, all scrubbed and sparkling with gratitude. When she made the fourth delivery he was alone and noticed her for the first time.

"Hey," he grinned. "How long has this been going on?"

"Sir?"

"Since when has Organic been using girls for delivery boys?"

"I am a delivery person, sir," Miss Nunn answered with dignity. "I have been working for the Organic Nursery since the first of the month."

"Knock off the sir bit."

"Thank you, s—Dr. Skiaki."

"How the devil do you know that I've got a doctorate?"

She'd slipped. He was listed at the Oasis and the Nursery merely as B. Skiaki, and she should have remembered. As usual, she turned her mistake into an advantage. "I know all about you, sir. Dr. Blaise Skiaki, Princeton, MIT, Dow Chemical. Chief Scent Chemist at CCC."

"You sound like 'Who's Who.'"

"That's where I read it, Dr. Skiaki."

"You read me up in 'Who's Who'? Why on earth?"

"You're the first famous man I've ever met."

"Whatever gave you the idea that I'm famous, which I'm not."
She gestured around. "I knew you had to be famous to live like this."

"Very flattering. What's your name, love?"

"Gretchen, sir."

"What's your last name?"

"People from my class don't have last names, sir."

"Will you be the delivery b—person tomorrow, Gretchen?"

"Tomorrow is my day off, Doctor."

"Perfect. Bring dinner for two."

So the affair began and Gretchen discovered, much to her aston-ishment, that she was enjoying it very much. Blaise was indeed a brilliant, charming young man, always entertaining, always consid-erate, always generous. In gratitude he gave her (remember he be-lieved she came from the lowest Corridor class) one of his most prized possessions, a five-carat diamond he had synthesized at Dow. She responded with equal style; she wore it in her navel and prom-ised that it was for his eyes only.

Of course he always insisted on her scrubbing up each time she visited, which was a bit of a bore; in her income bracket she prob-ably had more fresh water than he did. However, one convenience was that she could quit her job at the Organic Nursery and attend to other contracts while she was attending to Skiaki.

She always left his penthouse around eleven-thirty but stayed outside until one. She finally picked him up one night just as he was leaving the Oasis. She'd memorized the Salem Burne report and knew what to expect. She overtook him quickly and spoke in an agitated voice, "Mistuh. Mistuh."

He stopped and looked at her kindly without recognition. "Yes, my dear?"

"If yuh gone this way kin I come too. I scared."

"Certainly, my dear."

"Thanks, mistuh. I gone home. You gone home?"

"Well, not exactly."

"Where you gone? Y'ain't up to nothin' bad, is you? I don't want no part."

"Nothing bad, my dear. Don't worry."

"Then what you up to?"

He smiled secretly. "I'm following something."

"Somebody?"

"No, something."

"What kine something?"

"My, you're curious, aren't you. What's your name?"

"Gretchen. How 'bout you?"

"Me?"

"What's your name?"

"Wish. Call me Mr. Wish." He hesitated for a moment and then said, "I have to turn left here."

"Thas OK, Mistuh Wish. I go left, too."

She could see that all his senses were prickling, and reduced her prattle to a background of unobtrusive sound. She stayed with him as he twisted, turned, sometimes doubling back, through streets, alleys, lanes and lots, always assuring him that this was her way home too. At a rather dangerous-looking refuse dump he gave her a fatherly pat and cautioned her to wait while he explored its safety. He explored, disappeared and never reappeared.

"I replicated this experience with Skiaki six times," Miss Nunn reported to CCC. "They were all significant. Each time he revealed a little more without realizing it and without recognizing me. Burne was right. It is fugue."

"And the cause, Miss Nunn?"

"Pheromone trails."

"What?"

"I thought you gentlemen would know the term, being in the chemistry business. I see I'll have to explain. It will take some time so I insist that you do not require me to describe the induction and deduction that led me to my conclusion. Understood?"

"Agreed, Miss Nunn."

"Thank you, Mr. Chairman. Surely you all know hormones, from the Greek *hormaein*, meaning 'to excite'. They're internal secretions which excite other parts of the body into action. Pheromones are external secretions which excite other creatures into action. It's a mute chemical language.

"The best example of the pheromone language is the ant. Put

a lump of sugar somewhere outside an ant hill. A forager will come across it, feed, and return to the nest. Within an hour the entire commune will be single-filing to and from the sugar, following the pheromone trail first laid down quite undeliberately by the first discoverer. It's an unconscious but compelling stimulant."

"Fascinating. And Dr. Skiaki?"

"He follows human pheromone trails. They compel him; he goes into fugue and follows them."

"Ah! An outré aspect of The Nose. It makes sense, Miss Nunn. It really does. But what trails is he compelled to follow?"

"The death-wish."

"Miss Nunn!"

"Surely you're aware of this aspect of the human psyche. Many people suffer from an unconscious but powerful death-wish, especially in these despairing times. Apparently this leaves a pheromone trail which Dr. Skiaki senses, and he is compelled to follow it."

"And then?"

"Apparently he grants the wish."

"Apparently! Apparently!" the Chairman shouted. "I ask you for proof positive of this monstrous accusation."

"You'll get it, sir. I'm not finished with Blaise Skiaki yet. There are one or two things I have to wrap up with him, and in the course of that I'm afraid he's in for a shock. You'll have your proof pos—"

That was a half-lie from a woman half in love. She knew she had to see Blaise again but her motives were confused. To find out whether she really loved him, despite what she knew? To find out whether he loved her? To tell him the truth about herself? To warn him or save him or run away with him? To fulfill her contract in a cool, professional style? She didn't know. Certainly she didn't know that she was in for a shock from Skiaki.

"Were you born blind?" he murmured that night.

She sat bolt upright in the bed. "What? Blind? What?"

"You heard me."

"I've had perfect sight all my life."

"Ah. Then you don't know, darling. I rather suspected that might be it."

"I certainly don't know what you're talking about, Blaise."

"Oh, you're blind all right," he said calmly. "But you've never known because you're blessed with a fantastic freak facility. You have extrasensory perception of other people's senses. You see through other people's eyes. For all I know you may be deaf and hear through their ears. You may feel with their skin. We must explore it some time."

"I never heard of anything more absurd in all my life," she said angrily.

"I can prove it to you, if you like, Gretchen."

"Go ahead, Blaise. Prove the impossible."

"Come into the lounge."

In the living room he pointed to a vase. "What color is that?"

"Brown, of course."

"What color is that?" A tapestry.

"Gray."

"And that lamp?"

"Black."

"QED," Skiaki said. "It has been demonstrated."

"What's been demonstrated?"

"That you're seeing through my eyes."

"How can you say that?"

"Because I'm color-blind. That's what gave me the clue in the first place."

"What?"

He took her in his arms to quiet her trembling. "Darling Gretchen, the vase is green. The tapestry is amber and gold. The lamp is crimson. I can't see the colors but the decorator told me and I remember. Now why the terror? You're blind, yes, but you're blessed with something far more miraculous than mere sight: you see through the eyes of the world. I'd change places with you any time."

"It can't be true," she cried.

"It's true, love."

"What about when I'm alone?"

"When are you alone? When is anybody in the Corridor ever alone?"

She snatched up a shift and ran out of the penthouse, sobbing hysterically. She ran back to her own Oasis nearly crazed with terror. And yet she kept looking around and there were all the colors:

red, orange, yellow, green, indigo, blue, violet. But there were also people swarming through the labyrinths of the Corridor as they always were, twenty-four hours a day.

Back in her apartment she was determined to put the disaster to the test. She dismissed her entire staff with stern orders to get the hell out and spend the night somewhere else. She stood at the door and counted them out, all amazed and unhappy. She slammed the door and looked around. She could still see.

"The lying son-of-a-bitch." she muttered and began to pace furiously. She raged through the apartment, swearing venomously. It proved one thing: never get into personal relationships. They'll betray you, they'll try to destroy you, and she'd made a fool of herself. But why, in God's name, did Blaise use this sort of dirty trick to destroy her? Then she smashed into something and was thrown back. She recovered her balance and looked to see what she had blundered into. It was a harpsichord.

"But . . . but I don't own a harpsichord," she whispered in bewilderment. She started forward to touch it and assure herself of its reality. She smashed into the something again, grabbed it, and felt it. It was the back of a couch. She looked around frantically. This was not one of her rooms. The harpsichord. Vivid Brueghels hanging on the walls. Jacobean furniture. Linenfold paneled doors. Crewel drapes.

"But . . . this is the . . . the Raxon apartment downstairs. I must be seeing through their eyes. I must . . . he was right. I . . . ." She closed her eyes and looked. She saw a mélange of apartments, streets, crowds, people, events. She had always seen this sort of montage on occasion but had always thought it was merely the total visual recall which was a major factor in her extraordinary abilities and success. Now she knew the truth.

She began to sob again. She felt her way around the couch and sat down, despairing. When at last the convulsion spent itself she wiped her eyes courageously, determined to face reality. She was no coward. But when she opened her eyes she was shocked by another bombshell. She saw her familiar room in tones of gray. She saw Blaise Skiaki standing in the open door smiling at her.

"Blaise?" she whispered.

"The name is Wish, my dear. Mr. Wish. What's yours?"

"Blaise, for God's sake, not me! Not me. I left no death-wish trail."

"What's your name my dear? We've met before?"

"Gretchen," she screamed. "I'm Gretchen Nunn and I have no death-wish."

"Nice meeting you again, Gretchen," he said in glassy tones, smiling the glassy smile of Mr. Wish. He took two steps toward her. She jumped up and ran behind the couch.

"Blaise, listen to me. You are not Mr. Wish. There is no Mr. Wish. You are Dr. Blaise Skiaki, a famous scientist. You are chief chemist at CCC and have created many wonderful perfumes."

He took another step toward her, unwinding the scarf he wore around his neck.

"Blaise, I'm Gretchen. We've been lovers for two months. You must remember. Try to remember. You told me about my eyes to-night . . . being blind. You must remember that."

He smiled and whirled the scarf into a cord.

"Blaise, you're suffering from fugue. A blackout. A change of psyche. This isn't the real you. It's another creature driven by a pheromone. But I left no pheromone trail. I couldn't. I've never wanted to die."

"Yes, you do, my dear. Only happy to grant your wish. That's why I'm called Mr. Wish."

She squealed like a trapped rat and began darting and dodging while he closed in on her. She feinted him to one side, twisted to the other with a clear chance of getting out the door ahead of him, only to crash into three grinning goons standing shoulder to shoulder. They grabbed and held her.

Mr. Wish did not know that he also left a pheromone trail. It was a pheromone trail of murder.

"Oh, it's you again." Mr. Wish sniffed.

"Hey, old buddy-boy, got a looker this time, huh?"

"And loaded. Dig this layout."

"Great. Makes up for the last three which was nothin'. Thanks buddy-boy. You can go home now."

"Why don't I ever get to kill one?" Mr. Wish exclaimed petulantly.

"Now, now. No sulks. We got to protect our bird dog. You lead. We follow and do the rest."

"And if anything goes wrong, you're the setup," one of the goons giggled.

"Go home, buddy-boy. The rest is ours. No arguments. We already explained the standoff to you. We know who you are but you don't know who we are."

"I know who I am," Mr. Wish said with dignity. "I am Mr. Wish and I still think I have the right to kill at least one."

"All right, all right. Next time. That's a promise. Now blow."

As Mr. Wish exited resentfully, they ripped Gretchen naked and let out a huge wow when they saw the five-carat diamond in her navel. Mr. Wish turned and saw its scintillation too.

"But that's mine," he said in a confused voice. "That's only for my eyes. I—Gretchen said she would never—" Abruptly Dr. Blaise Skiaki spoke in a tone accustomed to command: "Gretchen, what the hell are you doing here? What's this place? Who are these creatures? What's going on?"

When the police arrived they found three dead bodies and a composed Gretchen Nunn sitting with a laser pistol in her lap. She told a perfectly coherent story of forcible entry, an attempt at armed rape and robbery, and how she was constrained to meet force with force. There were a few loopholes in her account. The bodies were not armed, but if the men had said they were armed Miss Nunn, of course, would have believed them. The three were somewhat battered, but goons were always fighting. Miss Nunn was commended for her courage and cooperation.

After her final report to the Chairman (which was not the truth, the whole truth and nothing but the truth) Miss Nunn received her check and went directly to the perfume laboratory, which she entered without warning. Dr. Skiaki was doing strange mysterious things with pipettes, flasks, and reagent bottles. Without turning he ordered. "Out. Out. Out."

"Good morning, Dr. Skiaki."

He turned, displaying a mauled face and black eyes, and smiled. "Well, well, well. The famous Gretchen Nunn, I presume. Voted Person of the Year three times in succession."

"No, sir. People from my class don't have last names."

"Knock off the sir bit."

"Yes s—Mr. Wish."

"Oi!" He winced. "Don't remind me of that incredible insanity. How did everything go with the Chairman?"

"I snowed him. You're off the hook."

"Maybe I'm off his hook but not my own. I was seriously thinking of having myself committed this morning."

"What stopped you?"

"Well, I got involved in this patchouli synthesis and sort of forgot."

She laughed. "You don't have to worry. You're saved."

"You mean cured?"

"No, Blaise. Not any more than I'm cured of my blindness. But we're both saved because we're aware. We can cope now."

He nodded slowly but not happily.

"So what are you going to do today?" she asked cheerfully. "Struggle with patchouli?"

"No," he said gloomily. "I'm still in one hell of a shock. I think I'll take the day off."

"Perfect. Bring two dinners."

HOBSON'S CHOICE

This is a warning to accomplices like you, and me, and Addyer.

*Can you spare price of one cup coffee, honorable sir? I
am indigent organism which are hungering.*

By day, Addyer was a statistician. He concerned himself with
such matters as statistical tables, averages and dispersions, groups
that are not homogeneous, and random sampling. At night, Addyer
plunged into an elaborate escape fantasy divided into two parts.
Either he imagined himself moved back in time a hundred years
with a double armful of the *Encyclopaedia Britannica*, best-sellers, hit
plays, and gambling records; or else he imagined himself transported
forward in time a thousand years to the Golden Age of perfection.

There were other fantasies which Addyer entertained on odd
Thursdays, such as (by a fluke) becoming the only man left on earth
with a world of passionate beauties to fecundate; such as acquiring
the power of invisibility which would enable him to rob banks and
right wrongs with impunity; such as possessing the mysterious power
of working miracles.

Up to this point you and I and Addyer are identical. Where
we part company is in the fact that Addyer was a statistician.

Can you spare cost of one cup coffee, honorable miss?
For blessed charitability? I am beholden.

On Monday, Addyer rushed into his chief's office, waving a sheaf of papers. "Look here, Mr. Grande," Addyer sputtered. "I've found something fishy. Extremely fishy . . . In the statistical sense, that is."

"Oh, hell," Grande answered. "You're not supposed to be finding anything. We're in between statistics until the war's over."

"I was leafing through the Interior Department's reports. D'you know our population's up?"

"Not after the atom bomb it isn't," said Grande. "We've lost double what our birthrate can replace." He pointed out the window to the twenty-five-foot stub of the Washington Monument. "There's your documentation."

"But our population's up 3.0915 percent." Addyer displayed his figures. "What about that, Mr. Grande?"

"Must be a mistake somewhere," Grande muttered after a moment's inspection. "You'd better check."

"Yes, sir," said Addyer scurrying out of the office. "I knew you'd be interested, sir. You're the ideal statistician, sir." He was gone.

"Poop," said Grande and once again began computing the quantity of bored respirations left to him. It was his personalized anesthesia.

On Tuesday, Addyer discovered that there was no correlation between the mortality/birthrate ratio and the population increase. The war was multiplying mortality and reducing births; yet the population was minutely increasing. Addyer displayed his discovery to Grande, received a pat on the back, and went home to a new fantasy in which he woke up a million years in the future, learned the answer to the enigma, and decided to remain amid snow-capped mountains and snow-capped bosoms, safe under the aegis of a culture saner than Aureomycin.

On Wednesday, Addyer requisitioned the comptometer and file and ran a test check on Washington, D.C. To his dismay he discovered that the population of the former capital was down 0.0029 percent. This was distressing, and Addyer went home to escape into

a dream about Queen Victoria's Golden Age where he amazed and
confounded the world with his brilliant output of novels, plays, and
poetry, all cribbed from Shaw, Galsworthy, and Wilde.

*Can you spare price of one coffee, honorable sir? I am
distressed individual needful of chariting.*

On Thursday, Addyer tried another check, this time on the
city of Philadelphia. He discovered that Philadelphia's population
was up 0.0959 percent. Very encouraging. He tried a rundown on
Little Rock. Population up 1.1329 percent. He tested St. Louis.
Population up 2.0924 percent . . . and this despite the complete ex-
tinction of Jefferson County owing to one of those military mistakes
of an excessive nature.

"My God!" Addyer exclaimed, trembling with excitement.
"The closer I get to the center of the country, the greater the
increase. But it was the center of the country that took the heaviest
punishment in the buz-raid. What's the answer?"

That night he shuttled back and forth between the future and
the past in his ferment, and he was down at the shop by 7 A.M.
He put a twenty-four-hour claim on the compo and files. He followed up his hunch and he came up with a fantastic discovery
which he graphed in approved form. On the map of the remains
of the United States he drew concentric circles in colors illustrating
the areas of population increase. The red, orange, yellow, green,
and blue circles formed a perfect target around Finney County,
Kansas.

"Mr. Grande," Addyer shouted in a high statistical passion,
"Finney County has got to explain this."

"You go out there and get that explanation," Grande replied,
and Addyer departed.

"Poop," muttered Grande and began integrating his pulse rate
with his eye-blink.

*Can you spare price of one coffee, dearly madam? I am
starveling organism requiring nutritiousment.*

Now, travel in those days was hazardous. Addyer took ship to Charleston (there were no rail connections remaining in the North Atlantic states) and was wrecked off Hatteras by a rogue mine. He drifted in the icy waters for seventeen hours, muttering through his teeth: "Oh, Christ! If only I'd been born a hundred years ago." Apparently this form of prayer was potent. He was picked up by a navy sweeper and shipped to Charleston where he arrived just in time to acquire a subcritical radiation burn from a raid which fortunately left the railroad unharmed. He was treated for the burn from Charleston to Macon (change) from Birmingham to Memphis (bubonic plague) to Little Rock (polluted water) to Tulsa (fallout quarantine) to Kansas City (the O.K. Bus Co. Accepts No Liability for Lives Lost through Acts of War) to Lyonesse, Finney County, Kansas.

And there he was in Finney County with its great magma pits and scars and radiation streaks; whole farms blackened and razed; whole highways so blasted they looked like dotted lines; whole population 4-F. Clouds of soot and fallout neutralizers hung over Finney County by day, turning it into a Pittsburgh on a still afternoon. Auras of radiation glowed at night, highlighted by the blinking red warning beacons, turning the county into one of those overexposed night photographs, all blurred and cross-hatched by deadly slashes of light.

After a restless night in the Lyonesse Hotel, Addyer went over to the county seat for a check on their birth records. He was armed with the proper credentials, but the county seat was not armed with the statistics. That excessive military mistake again. It had extinguished the seat.

A little annoyed, Addyer marched off to the County Medical Association office. His idea was to poll the local doctors on births. There was an office and one attendant who had been a practical nurse. He informed Addyer that Finney County had lost its last doctor to the army eight months previous. Midwives might be the answer to the birth enigma but there was no record of midwives. Addyer would simply have to canvass from door to door, asking if any lady within practiced that ancient profession.

Further piqued, Addyer returned to the Lyonesse Hotel and wrote on a slip of tissue paper: HAVING DATA DIFFICULTIES. WILL

REPORT AS SOON AS INFORMATION AVAILABLE. He slipped the message into an aluminum capsule, attached it to his sole surviving carrier pigeon, and dispatched it to Washington with a prayer. Then he sat down at his window and brooded.

He was aroused by a curious sight. In the street below, the O.K. Bus Co. had just arrived from Kansas City. The old coach wheezed to a stop, opened its door with some difficulty and permitted a one-legged farmer to emerge. His burned face was freshly bandaged. Evidently this was a well-to-do burgess who could afford to travel for medical treatment. The bus backed up for the return trip to Kansas City and honked a warning horn. That was when the curious sight began.

From nowhere . . . absolutely nowhere . . . a horde of people appeared. They skipped from back alleys, from behind rubble piles; they popped out of stores, they filled the street. They were all jolly, healthy, brisk, happy. They laughed and chatted as they climbed into the bus. They looked like hikers and tourists, carrying knapsacks, carpetbags, box lunches, and even babies. In two minutes the bus was filled. It lurched off down the road, and as it disappeared Addyer heard happy singing break out and echo from the walls of rubble.

"I'll be damned," he said.

He hadn't heard spontaneous singing in over two years. He hadn't seen a carefree smile in over three years. He felt like a color-blind man who was seeing the full spectrum for the first time. It was uncanny. It was also a little blasphemous.

"Don't those people know there's a war on?" he asked himself.

And a little later: "They looked too healthy. Why aren't they in uniform?"

And last of all: "Who *were* they anyway?"

That night Addyer's fantasy was confused.

> *Can you spare price of one cup coffee, kindly sir? I am estrangered and faintly from hungering.*

The next morning Addyer arose early, hired a car at an exorbitant fee, found he could not buy any fuel at any price, and ultimately settled for a lame horse. He was allergic to horse dander

and suffered asthmatic tortures as he began his house-to-house canvass. He was discouraged when he returned to the Lyonesse Hotel
that afternoon. He was just in time to witness the departure of the
O.K. Bus Co.

Once again a horde of happy people appeared and boarded the
bus. Once again the bus hirpled off down the broken road. Once
again the joyous singing broke out.

"I *will* be damned," Addyer wheezed.

He dropped into the county surveyor's office for a large-scale
map of Finney County. It was his intent to plot the midwife cov-
erage in accepted statistical manner. There was a little difficulty
with the surveyor who was deaf, blind in one eye, and spectacleless
in the other. He could not read Addyer's credentials with any fac-
ulty or facility. As Addyer finally departed with the map, he said
to himself, "I think the old idiot thought I was a spy."

And later he muttered, "Spies?"

And just before bedtime: "Holy Moses! Maybe *that's* the answer
to *them.*"

That night he was Lincoln's secret agent, anticipating Lee's
every move, outwitting Jackson, Johnston, and Beauregard, foiling
John Wilkes Booth, and being elected President of the United
States by 1968.

The next day the O.K. Bus Co. carried off yet another load of
happy people.

And the next.

And the next.

"Four hundred tourists in five days," Addyer computed. "The
country's filled with espionage."

He began loafing around the streets trying to investigate these
joyous travelers. It was difficult. They were elusive before the bus
arrived. They had a friendly way of refusing to pass the time. The
locals of Lyonesse knew nothing about them and were not interested. Nobody was interested in much more than painful survival
these days. That was what made the singing obscene.

After seven days of cloak-and-dagger and seven days of counting, Addyer suddenly did the big take. "It adds up," he said. "Eighty
people a day leaving Lyonesse. Five hundred a week. Twenty-five
thousand a year. Maybe that's the answer to the population in-

crease." He spent fifty-five dollars on a telegram to Grande with no
more than a hope of delivery. The telegram read: "EUREKA: I
HAVE FOUND (IT)."

*Can you spare price of lone cup coffee, honorable ma-
dam? I am not tramp-handler but destitute life form.*

Addyer's opportunity came the next day. The O.K. Bus Co.
pulled in as usual. Another crowd assembled to board the bus, but
this time there were too many. Three people were refused passage.
They weren't in the least annoyed. They stepped back, waved energetically as the bus started, shouted instructions for future reun-
ions and then quietly turned and started off down the street.

Addyer was out of his hotel room like a shot. He followed the
trio down the main street, turned left after them onto Fourth Avenue, passed the ruined schoolhouse, passed the demolished tele-
phone building, passed the gutted library, railroad station,
Protestant church, Catholic church . . . and finally reached the out-
skirts of Lyonesse and then open country.

Here he had to be more cautious. It was difficult stalking the
spies with so much of the dusky road illuminated by warning lights.
He wasn't suicidal enough to think of hiding in radiation pits. He
hung back in an agony of indecision and was at last relieved to see
them turn off the broken road and enter the old Baker farmhouse.

"Ah-ha!" said Addyer.

He sat down at the edge of the road on the remnants of a
missile and asked himself: "Ah-ha what?" He could not answer, but
he knew where to find the answer. He waited until dusk deepened
to darkness and then slowly wormed his way forward toward the
farmhouse.

It was while he was creeping between the deadly radiation
glows and only occasionally butting his head against grave markers
that he first became aware of two figures in the night. They were
in the barnyard of the Baker place and were performing most peculiarly. One was tall and thin. A man. He stood stock-still, like a
lighthouse. Upon occasion he took a slow, stately step with infinite
caution and waved an arm in slow motion to the other figure. The

second was also a man. He was stocky and trotted jerkily back and forth.

As Addyer approached, he heard the tall man say: "Rooo booo fooo mooo hwaaa looo fooo."

Whereupon the trotter chattered, "Wd-nk-kd-ik-md-pd-ld-nk." Then they both laughed: the tall man like a locomotive, the trotter like a chipmunk. They turned. The trotter rocketed into the house. The tall man drifted in. And that was amazingly that.

"Oh-ho," said Addyer.

At that moment a pair of hands seized him and lifted him from the ground. Addyer's heart constricted. He had time for one convulsive spasm before something vague was pressed against his face. As he lost consciousness his last idiotic thought was of telescopes.

Can you spare price of solitary coffee for no-loafing unfortunate, honorable sir? Charity will blessings.

When Addyer awoke he was lying on a couch in a small whitewashed room. A gray-haired gentleman with heavy features was seated at a desk alongside the couch, busily ciphering on bits of paper. The desk was cluttered with what appeared to be intricate timetables. There was a small radio perched on one side.

"L-Listen . . ." Addyer began faintly.

"Just a minute, Mr. Addyer," the gentleman said pleasantly. He fiddled with the radio. A glow germinated in the middle of the room over a circular copper plate and coalesced into a girl. She was extremely nude and extremely attractive. She scurried to the desk, patted the gentleman's head with the speed of a pneumatic hammer. She laughed and chattered, "Wd-nk-tk-ik-lt-nk."

The gray-haired man smiled and pointed to the door. "Go outside and walk it off," he said. She turned and streaked through the door.

"It has something to do with temporal rates," the gentleman said to Addyer. "I don't understand it. When they come forward they've got accumulated momentum." He began ciphering again. "Why in the world did you have to come snooping, Mr. Addyer?"

"You're spies," Addyer said. "She was talking Chinese."

"Hardly. I'd say it was French. Early French. Middle fifteenth century."

"Middle fifteenth century!" Addyer exclaimed.

"That's what I'd say. You begin to acquire an ear for those stepped-up tempos. Just a minute, please."

He switched the radio on again. Another glow appeared and solidified into a nude man. He was stout, hairy, and lugubrious. With exasperating slowness he said, "Mooo fooo blooo wawww hawww pooo."

The gray-haired man pointed to the door. The stout man departed in slow motion.

"The way I see it," the gray-haired man continued conversationally, "when they come back they're swimming against the time current. That slows 'em down. When they come forward, they're swimming with the current. That speeds 'em up. Of course, in any case it doesn't last longer than a few minutes. It wears off."

"What?" Addyer said. "Time travel?"

"Yes. Of course."

"That thing . . ." Addyer pointed to the radio. "A time machine?"

"That's the idea. Roughly."

"But it's too small."

The gray-haired man laughed.

"What is this place anyway? What are you up to?"

"It's a funny thing," the gray-haired man said. "Everybody used to speculate about time travel. How it would be used for exploration, archaeology, historical, and social research, and so on. Nobody ever guessed what the real use would be. . . . Therapy."

"Therapy? You mean medical therapy?"

"That's right. Psychological therapy for the misfits who won't respond to any other cure. We let them emigrate. Escape. We've set up stations every quarter century. Stations like this."

"I don't understand."

"This is an immigration office."

"Oh, my God!" Addyer shot up from the couch. "Then you're the answer to the population increase. Yes? That's how I happened to notice it. Mortality's up so high and birth's down so low these days that your time-addition becomes significant. Yes?"

"Yes, Mr. Addyer."

"Thousands of you coming here. From where?"

"From the future, of course. Time travel wasn't developed until C/H 127. That's . . . oh, say, A.D. 2505 your chronology. We didn't set up our chain of stations until C/H 189."

"But those fast-moving ones. You said they came forward from the past."

"Oh, yes, but they're all from the future originally. They just decided they went too far back."

"Too far?"

The gray-haired man nodded and reflected. "It's amusing, the mistakes people will make. They become unrealistic when they read history. Lose contact with facts. Chap I knew . . . wouldn't be satisfied with anything less than Elizabethan times. 'Shakespeare,' he said. 'Good Queen Bess. Spanish Armada. Drake and Hawkins and Raleigh. Most virile period in history. The Golden Age. That's for me.' I couldn't talk sense into him, so we sent him back. Too bad."

"Well?" Addyer asked.

"Oh, he died in three weeks. Drank a glass of water. Typhoid."

"You didn't inoculate him? I mean, the army when it sends men overseas always . . ."

"Of course we did. Gave him all the immunization we could. But diseases evolve and change too. New strains develop. Old strains disappear. That's what causes pandemics. Evidently our shots wouldn't take against the Elizabethan typhoid. Excuse me. . . ."

Again the glow appeared. Another nude man appeared, chattered briefly and then whipped through the door. He almost collided with the nude girl who poked her head in, smiled and called in a curious accent, "Ie vous prie de me pardonner. Quy estoit cette gentilhomme?"

"I was right," the gray-haired man said. "That's Medieval French. They haven't spoken like that since Rabelais." To the girl he said, "Middle English, please. The American dialect."

"Oh, I'm sorry, Mr. Jelling. I get so damned fouled up with my linguistics. Fouled? Is that right? Or do they say . . ."

"Hey!" Addyer cried in anguish.

"They say it, but only in private these years. Not before strangers."

"Oh, yes. I remember. Who was that gentleman who just left?"

"Peters."

"From Athens?"

"That's right."

"Didn't like it, eh?"

"Not much. Seems the Peripatetics didn't have plumbing."

"Yes. You begin to hanker for a modern bathroom after a while. Where do I get some clothes . . . or don't they wear clothes this century?"

"No, that's a hundred years forward. Go see my wife. She's in the outfitting room in the barn. That's the big red building."

The tall lighthouse-man Addyer had first seen in the farmyard suddenly manifested himself behind the girl. He was now dressed and moving at normal speed. He stared at the girl; she stared at him. "Splem!" they both cried. They embraced and kissed shoulders.

"St'u my rock-ribbering rib-rockery to heart the hearts two," the man said.

"Heart's too, argal, too heart," the girl laughed.

"Eh? Then you st'u too."

They embraced again and left.

"What was that? Future talk?" Addyer asked. "Shorthand?"

"Shorthand?" Jelling exclaimed in a surprised tone. "Don't you know rhetoric when you hear it? That was thirtieth-century rhetoric, man. We don't talk anything else up there. Prosthesis, Diastole, Epergesis, Metabasis, Hendiadys . . . And we're all born scanning."

"You don't have to sound so stuck up," Addyer muttered enviously. "I could scan too if I tried."

"You'd find it damned inconvenient trying at your time of life."

"What difference would that make?"

"It would make a big difference," Jelling said, "because you'd find that living is the sum of conveniences. You might think plumbing is pretty unimportant compared to ancient Greek philosophers. Lots of people do. But the fact is, we already know the philosophy. After a while you get tired of seeing the great men and listening to them expound the material you already know. You begin to miss the conveniences and familiar patterns you used to take for granted."

"That," said Addyer, "is a superficial attitude."

"You think so? Try living in the past by candlelight, without central heating, without refrigeration, canned foods, elementary drugs . . . Or, futurewise, try living with Berganlicks, the Twenty-Two Commandments, duodecimal calendars and currency, or try speaking in meter, planning and scanning each sentence before you talk . . . and damned for a contemptible illiterate if you forget yourself and speak spontaneously in your own tongue."

"You're exaggerating," Addyer said. "I'll bet there are times where I could be very happy. I've thought about it for years, and I . . ."

"Tcha!" Jelling snorted. "The great illusion. Name one."

"The American Revolution."

"Pfui! No sanitation. No medicine. Cholera in Philadelphia. Malaria in New York. No anesthesia. The death penalty for hundreds of small crimes and petty infractions. None of the books and music you like best. None of the jobs or professions for which you've been trained. Try again."

"The Victorian Age."

"How are your teeth and eyes? In good shape? They'd better be. We can't send your inlays and spectacles back with you. How are your ethics? In bad shape? They'd better be or you'd starve in that cutthroat era. How do you feel about class distinctions? They were pretty strong in those days. What's your religion? You'd better not be a Jew or Catholic or Quaker or Moravian or any minority. What's your politics? If you're a reactionary today the same opinions would make you a dangerous radical a hundred years ago. I don't think you'd be happy."

"I'd be safe."

"Not unless you were rich; and we can't send money back. Only the flesh. No, Addyer, the poor died at the average age of forty in those days . . . worked out, worn out. Only the privileged survived, and you wouldn't be one of the privileged."

"Not with my superior knowledge?"

Jelling nodded wearily. "I knew *that* would come up sooner or later. What superior knowledge? Your hazy recollection of science and invention? Don't be a damned fool, Addyer. You enjoy your technology without the faintest idea of how it works."

"It wouldn't have to be hazy recollection. I could prepare."

"What, for instance?"

"Oh . . . say, the radio. I could make a fortune inventing the radio."

Jelling smiled. "You couldn't invent radio until you'd first invented the hundred allied technical discoveries that went into it. You'd have to create an entire new industrial world. You'd have to discover the vacuum rectifier and create an industry to manufacture it; the self-heterodyne circuit, the nonradiating neutrodyne receiver and so forth. You'd have to develop electric power production and transmission and alternating current. You'd have to—but why belabor the obvious? Could you invent internal combustion before the development of fuel oils?"

"My God!" Addyer groaned.

"And another thing," Jelling went on grimly. "I've been talking about technological tools, but language is a tool too; the tool of communication. Did you ever realize that all the studying you might do could never teach you how a language was really used centuries ago? Do you know how the Romans pronounced Latin? Do you know the Greek dialects? Could you learn to speak and think in Gaelic, seventeenth-century Flemish, Old Low German? Never. You'd be a deaf-mute."

"I never thought about it that way," Addyer said slowly.

"Escapists never do. All they're looking for is a vague excuse to run away."

"What about books? I could memorize a great book and . . ."

"And what? Go back far enough into the past to anticipate the real author? You'd be anticipating the public too. A book doesn't become great until the public's ready to understand it. It doesn't become profitable until the public's ready to buy it."

"What about going forward into the future?" Addyer asked.

"I've already told you. It's the same problem only in reverse. Could a medieval man survive in the twentieth century? Could he stay alive in street traffic? Drive cars? Speak the language? Think in the language? Adapt to the tempo, ideas, and coordinations you take for granted? Never. Could someone from the twenty-fifth century adapt to the thirtieth? Never."

"Well, then," Addyer said angrily, "if the past and future are so uncomfortable, what are those people traveling around for?"

"They're not traveling," Jelling said. "They're running."

"From what?"

"Their own time."

"Why?"

"They don't like it."

"Why not?"

"Do you like yours? Does any neurotic?"

"Where are they going?"

"Any place but where they belong. They keep looking for the Golden Age. Tramps! Time stiffs! Never satisfied. Always searching, shifting . . . bumming through the centuries. Pfui! Half the panhandlers you meet are probably time bums stuck in the wrong century."

"And those people coming here . . . they think *this* is a Golden Age?"

"They do."

"They're crazy," Addyer protested. "Have they seen the ruins? The radiation? The war? The anxiety? The hysteria?"

"Sure. That's what appeals to them. Don't ask me why. Think of it this way: you like the American Colonial period, yes?"

"Among others."

"Well, if you told Mr. George Washington the reasons why you liked his time, you'd probably be naming everything he hated about it."

"But that's not a fair comparison. This is the worst age in all history."

Jelling waved his hand. "That's how it looks to you. Everybody says that in every generation; but take my word for it, no matter when you live and how you live, there's always somebody else somewhere else who thinks you live in the Golden Age."

"Well, I'll be damned," Addyer said.

Jelling looked at him steadily for a moment. "You will be," he said sorrowfully. "I've got bad news for you, Addyer. We can't let you remain. You'll talk and make trouble, and our secret's got to be kept. We'll have to send you out one-way."

"I can talk wherever I go."

"But nobody'll pay attention to you outside your own time. You won't make sense. You'll be an eccentric . . . a lunatic . . . a foreigner . . . safe."

"What if I come back?"

"You won't be able to get back without a visa, and I'm not tattooing any visa on you. You won't be the first we've had to transport if that's any consolation to you. There was a Japanese, I remember . . ."

"Then you're going to send me somewhere in time? Permanently?"

"That's right. I'm really very sorry."

"To the future or the past?"

"You can take your choice. Think it over while you're getting undressed."

"You don't have to act so mournful," Addyer said. "It's a great adventure. A high adventure. It's something I've always dreamed."

"That's right. It's going to be wonderful."

"I could refuse," Addyer said nervously.

Jelling shook his head. "We'd only drug you and send you anyway. It might as well be your choice."

"It's a choice I'm delighted to make."

"Sure. That's the spirit, Addyer."

"Everybody says I was born a hundred years too soon."

"Everybody generally says that . . . unless they say you were born a hundred years too late."

"Some people say that too."

"Well, think it over. It's a permanent move. Which would you prefer . . . the phonetic future or the poetic past?"

Very slowly Addyer began to undress as he undressed each night when he began the prelude to his customary fantasy. But now his dreams were faced with fulfillment and the moment of decision terrified him. He was a little blue and rather unsteady on his legs when he stepped to the copper disk in the center of the floor. In answer to Jelling's inquiry he muttered his choice. Then he turned argent in the aura of an incandescent glow and disappeared from his time forever.

Where did he go? You know. I know. Addyer knows. Addyer traveled to the land of our pet fantasy. He escaped into the refuge that is our refuge, to the time of our dreams; and in practically no time at all he realized that he had in truth departed from the only time for himself.

Through the vistas of the years every age but our own seems glamorous and golden. We yearn for the yesterdays and tomorrows, never realizing that we are faced with Hobson's choice . . . that today, bitter or sweet, anxious or calm, is the only day for us. The dream of time is the traitor, and we are all accomplices to the betrayal of ourselves.

Can you spare price of one coffee, honorable sir? No, sir, I am not panhandling organism. I am starveling Japanese transient stranded in this somiserable year. Honorable sir! I beg in tears for holy charity. Will you donate to this destitute person one ticket to township of Lyonesse? I want to beg on knees for visa. I want to go back to year 1945 again. I want to be in Hiroshima again. I want to go home.

RAY BRADBURY

b. 1920

Ray Bradbury was born in Waukegan, Illinois, a town which also gave the world Jack Benny (and both these men have left their names on bits of the city's geography). When Bradbury was fourteen, the Great Depression sat heavily on the land. Jobs were scarce in the Midwest, and so Bradbury's father took the family to California in the hope of brighter prospects. Employment wasn't markedly easier in California, but there young Ray Bradbury found something that changed his life. He discovered, and entered, the world of science fiction fandom.

The people—mostly youngsters—who went out of their way to read science fiction in those days were a special breed, unlike the readers of any other kind of literature. They were a lot less passive. They habitually wrote letters to the editors of their magazines (every sf magazine contained a letter column, often the first thing those readers turned to when a new issue appeared). They sought out other like-minded readers, and they formed clubs—correspondence clubs for those in out of the way parts of the world, regular get-togethers in the flesh for those in communities large enough to support a fan population. The center of fannish activities in Los Angeles was the Los Angeles Science Fantasy Society (and still is; LASFS is still meeting regularly more than sixty years later). Young Ray immersed himself in the group. He joined it at seventeen, at nineteen began publishing his own science fiction fan magazine, *Futuria Fantasia*. He filled the fanzine with his own stories, but before long began sending them off to the professional magazines, collected his share of rejections and, in 1941, made his first sale. It was a collaboration with Henry Hasse, "Pendulum," and with it Ray was on his way.

Unusually for his generation of science fiction writers, Ray Bradbury was not a part of John Campbell's "Golden Age" of *Astounding*; Bradbury's poetic brand of sf was not to Campbell's taste. It was to everyone else's, though. His stories appeared in *Planet Stories, Thrilling Wonder Stories, Weird Tales*, and nearly every other magazine of science fiction or fantasy for the next half-dozen years. They were workmanlike shorts, appreciated by editors and enjoyed by readers, but it wasn't until 1946 that Bradbury published the story that lifted him out of the pack. The piece was called "The Million Year Picnic," and it turned out to be the first installment of his most famous work, *The Martian Chronicles*.

The Mars of Bradbury's *Chronicles* is not much like the one currently being explored by the real world's telescopes and space probes. Physically Bradbury's Mars is a lot like the American Midwest of his childhood, plus canals. Unlike the real Mars, it is inhabited, and its people have the capacity to change shape—conveniently making themselves look like the human colonists when they chose. As a book, *The Martian Chronicles* is indestructible. It has been continuously in print for forty years, has been filmed for TV, and translated into dozens of foreign languages.

By the time the book appeared Bradbury had begun to move out of the science fiction magazines, with his work appearing in such mass circulation slicks as *Collier's* and *The Saturday Evening Post*, big glossy weeklies which were the prestige markets of the time—with correspondingly fatter paychecks. In 1951 he returned to the science fiction magazine *Galaxy* with a novella called "The Fireman," a sort of tangential response to the flamboyant witch-hunts of Senator McCarthy; in the story, books have become forbidden, and the "Fireman," charged with the duty of seeking out and burning libraries, is himself a secret reader. Expanded to book length and published (and filmed) as *Fahrenheit 451*, it became Bradbury's other masterwork.

There is a curious subtext to Bradbury's work, evident in both *The Martian Chronicles* and *Fahrenheit 451*. By and large, science fiction writers celebrate technology. Ray Bradbury does not. In his stories the gadgets and machines of the future are dehumanizing. Virtue lies in the simpler, gentler times of his midwestern childhood. Bradbury himself is sufficiently hostile to technology that for many years (like that other Grand Master, Isaac Asimov) he refused to fly. Even more unusual, he may be the only Californian alive who declines to drive a car, for most of his life biking or taking taxis around the sprawling city of Los Angeles. (When he and I were walking along the streets of Century City some years ago, a sizable fraction of the cab drivers who drove past us waved greetings to Ray.)

Ray Bradbury was, however, Californian enough to become active in the film industry from early on, writing (or sharing writing of) such sci-fi films of the early 1950s as *The Beast from 20,000 Fathoms* and *It came from Outer Space*. In 1956 he collaborated with John Huston on a major project, the filming of one of the great classics of American literature, Herman Melville's *Moby Dick*. More recently he has had his own television series and has been deeply involved in creating images for the Walt Disney theme parks.

Almost from the beginning Bradbury's work explored areas of writing outside of science fiction, as shown in such collections and novels as *Dandelion Wine, Something Wicked This Way Comes*, and *The Illustrated Man*. After the 1950s he wrote little that was purely science fiction. Nevertheless for generations of Americans, who were learning the pleasures of reading from the flood of schoolbook texts which nearly unanimously included Bradbury stories, he represented their first encounter with science fiction.

Ray Bradbury is a unique voice, in science fiction and in the world, and he is indeed a Grand Master.

Recommended Reading
by Ray Bradbury

Fahrenheit 451
The Martian Chronicles
The Illustrated Man
Something Wicked This Way Comes
Dandelion Wine

THE CITY

The city waited twenty thousand years.

The planet moved through space and the flowers of the fields grew up and fell away, and still the city waited; and the rivers of the planet rose and waned and turned to dust. Still the city waited. The winds that had been young and wild grew old and serene, and the clouds of the sky that had been ripped and torn were left alone to drift in idle whitenesses. Still the city waited.

The city waited with its windows and its black obsidian walls and its sky towers and its unpennanted turrets, with its untrod streets and its untouched doorknobs, with not a scrap of paper or a fingerprint upon it. The city waited while the planet arced in space, following its orbit about a blue-white sun, and the seasons passed from ice to fire and back to ice and then to green fields and yellow summer meadows.

It was on a summer afternoon in the middle of the twenty-thousandth year that the city ceased waiting.

In the sky a rocket appeared.

The rocket soared over, turned, came back, and landed in the shale meadow fifty yards from the obsidian wall.

There were booted footsteps in the thin grass and calling voices from men within the rocket to men without.

"Ready?"

"All right, men. Careful! Into the city. Jensen, you and Hutch-inson patrol ahead. Keep a sharp eye."

The city opened secret nostrils in its black walls and a steady suction vent deep in the body of the city drew storms of air back through channels, through thistle filters and dust collectors, to a fine and tremblingly delicate series of coils and webs which glowed with silver light. Again and again the immense suctions occurred; again and again the odors from the meadow were borne upon warm winds into the city.

"Fire odor, the scent of a fallen meteor, hot metal. A ship has come from another world. The brass smell, the dusty fire smell of burned powder, sulphur and rocket brimstone."

This information, stamped on tapes which sprocketed into slots, slid down through yellow cogs into further machines.

Click-chakk-chakk-chakk.

A calculator made the sound of a metronome. Five, six, seven, eight, nine. Nine men! An instantaneous typewriter inked this message on tape which slithered and vanished.

Clickety-click-chakk-chakk.

The city awaited the soft tread of their rubberoid boots.

The great city nostrils dilated again.

The smell of butter. In the city air, from the stalking men, faintly, the aura which wafted to the great Nose broke down into memories of milk, cheese, ice cream, butter, the effluvia of a dairy economy.

Click-click.

"Careful, men!"

"Jones, get your gun out. Don't be a fool!"

"The city's dead; why worry?"

"You can't tell."

Now, at the barking talk, the Ears awoke. After centuries of listening to winds that blew small and faint, of hearing leaves strip from trees and grass grow softly in the time of melting snows, now the Ears oiled themselves in a self-lubrication, drew taut, great drums upon which the heartbeat of the invaders might pummel and thud delicately as the tremor of a gnat's wing. The Ears listened and the Nose siphoned up great chambers of odor.

The perspiration of frightened men arose. There were islands of sweat under their arms, and sweat in their hands as they held their guns.

The Nose sifted and worried this air, like a connoisseur busy with an ancient vintage.

Chikk-chikk-chakk-click.

Information rotated down on parallel check tapes. Perspiration; chlorides such-and-such percent; sulphates so-and-so; urea nitrogen, ammonia nitrogen. *thus:* creatinine, sugar, lactic acid, *there!*

Bells rang. Small totals jumped up.

The Nose whispered, expelling the tested air. The great Ears listened:

"I think we should go back to the rocket, Captain."

"I give the orders, Mr. Smith!"

"Yes, sir."

"You, up there! Patrol! *See* anything?"

"Nothing, sir. Looks like it's been dead a long time!"

"You see, Smith? Nothing to fear."

"I don't like it. I don't know why. You ever feel you've seen a place before? Well, this city's too familiar."

"Nonsense. This planetary system's billions of miles from Earth; we couldn't possibly've been here ever before. Ours is the only light-year rocket in existence."

"That's how I feel, anyway, sir. I think we should get out."

The footsteps faltered. There was only the sound of the intruder's breath on the still air.

The Ear heard and quickened. Rotors glided, liquids glittered in small creeks through valves and blowers. A formula and a concoction—one followed another. Moments later, responding to the summons of the Ear and Nose, through giant holes in the city walls a fresh vapor blew out over the invaders.

"Smell *that*, Smith? Ahh. Green grass. Ever smell anything better? By God, I just like to stand here and smell it."

Invisible chlorophyll blew among the standing men.

"*Ahh!*"

The footsteps continued.

"Nothing wrong with *that*, eh, Smith? Come on!"

The Ear and Nose relaxed a billionth of a fraction. The countermove had succeeded. The pawns were proceeding forward.

.   .   .

Now the cloudy Eyes of the city moved out of fog and mist.

"Captain, the windows!"

"What?"

"Those house windows, there! I saw them move!"

"*I* didn't see it."

"They shifted. They changed color. From dark to light."

"Look like ordinary square windows to me."

Blurred objects focused. In the mechanical ravines of the city oiled shafts plunged, balance wheels dipped over into green oil pools. The window frames flexed. The windows gleamed.

Below, in the street, walked two men, a patrol, followed, at a safe interval, by seven more. Their uniforms were white, their faces as pink as if they had been slapped; their eyes were blue. They walked upright, upon hind legs, carrying metal weapons. Their feet were booted. They were males, with eyes, ears, mouths, noses.

The windows trembled. The windows thinned. They dilated imperceptibly, like the irises of numberless eyes.

"I tell you, Captain, it's the windows!"

"Get along."

"I'm going back, sir."

"What?"

"I'm going back to the rocket."

"Mr. Smith!"

"I'm not falling into any trap!"

"Afraid of an empty city?"

The others laughed, uneasily.

"Go on, laugh!"

The street was stone-cobbled, each stone three inches wide, six inches long. With a move unrecognizable as such, the street settled. It weighed the invaders.

In a machine cellar a red wand touched a numeral: 178 pounds ... 210, 154, 201, 198—each man weighed, registered, and the record spooled down into a correlative darkness.

Now the city was fully awake!

Now the vents sucked and blew air, the tobacco odor from the invaders mouths, the green soap scent from their hands. Even their eyeballs had a delicate odor. The city detected it, and this information formed totals which scurried down to total other totals. The crystal windows glittered, the Ear tautened and skinned the drum of its hearing tight, tighter—all of the senses of the city swarming like a fall of unseen snow, counting the respiration and the dim hidden heartbeats of the men, listening, watching, tasting.

For the streets were like tongues, and where the men passed, the taste of their heels ebbed down through stone pores to be calculated on litmus. This chemical totality, so subtly collected, was appended to the now increasing sums waiting the final calculation among the whirling wheels and whispering spokes.

Footsteps. Running.

"Come back! Smith!"

"No, blast you!"

"Get him, men!"

Footsteps rushing.

A final test. The city, having listened, watched, tasted, felt, weighed, and balanced, must perform a final task.

A trap flung wide in the street. The captain, unseen by the others, running vanished.

Hung by his feet, a razor drawn across his throat, another down his chest, his carcass instantly emptied of its entrails, exposed upon a table under the street, in a hidden cell, the captain died. Great crystal microscopes stared at the red twines of muscle; bodiless fingers probed the still-pulsing heart. The flaps of his sliced skin were pinned to the table while hands shifted parts of his body like a quick and curious player of chess, using the red pawns and the red pieces.

Above on the street the men ran. Smith ran, men shouted. Smith shouted and below in this curious room blood flowed into capsules, was shaken, spun, shoved on smear slides under further microscopes, counts made, temperatures taken, heart cut in seventeen sections, liver and kidneys expertly halved. Brain was drilled and scooped from bone socket, nerves pulled forth like the dead wires of a switchboard, muscles plucked for elasticity, while in the electric subterrene of the city the Mind at last totaled out its grandest total and all of the machinery ground to a monstrous and momentary halt.

The total.

These are men. These are men from a far world, a certain planet, and they have certain eyes, certain ears, and they walk upon legs in a specified way and carry weapons and think and fight, and they have particular hearts and all such organs as are recorded from long ago.

Above, men ran down the street toward the rocket.

Smith ran.

The total.

These are our enemies. These are the ones we have waited for twenty thousand years to see again. These are the men upon whom we waited to visit revenge. Everything totals. These are the men of a planet called Earth, who declared war upon Taollan twenty thousand years ago, who kept us in slavery and ruined us and destroyed us with a great disease. Then they went off to live in another galaxy to escape that disease which they visited upon us after ransacking our world. They have forgotten that war and that time, and they have forgotten us. But we have not forgotten them. These are our enemies. This is certain. Our waiting is done.

"Smith, come back!"

Quickly. Upon the red table, with the spread-eagled captain's body empty, new hands began a flight of motion. Into the wet interior were placed organs of copper, brass, silver, aluminum, rubber, and silk; spiders spun gold web which was stung into the skin; a heart was attached, and into the skull case was fitted a platinum brain which hummed and fluttered small sparkles of blue fire, and the wires led down through the body to the arms and legs. In a moment the body was sewn tight, the incisions waxed, healed at neck and throat and about the skull—perfect, fresh, new.

The captain sat up and flexed his arms.

"Stop!"

On the street the captain reappeared, raised his gun, and fired.

Smith fell, a bullet in his heart.

The other men turned.

The captain ran to them.

"That fool! Afraid of a city!"

They looked at the body of Smith at their feet.

They looked at their captain, and their eyes widened and narrowed.

"Listen to me," said the captain. "I have something important to tell you."

Now the city, which had weighed and tasted and smelled them, which had used all its powers save one, prepared to use its final ability, the power of speech. It did not speak with the rage and hostility of its massed walls or towers, nor with the bulk of its cobbled avenues and fortresses of machinery. It spoke with the quiet voice of one man.

"I am no longer your captain," he said. "Nor am I a man."

The men moved back.

"I am the city," he said, and smiled.

"I've waited two hundred centuries," he said. "I've waited for the sons of the sons of the sons to return."

"Captain, sir!"

"Let me continue. Who built me? The city. The men who died built me. The old race who once lived here. The people whom the Earth Men left to die of a terrible disease, a form of leprosy with no cure. And the men of that old race, dreaming of the day when Earth Men might return, built this city, and the name of this city was and is Revenge, upon the Planet of Darkness, near the shore of the Sea of Centuries, by the Mountains of the Dead; all very poetic. This city was to be a balancing machine, a litmus, an antenna to test all future space travelers. In twenty thousand years only two other rockets landed here. One from a distant galaxy called Ennt, and the inhabitants of that craft were tested, weighed, found wanting, and let free, unscathed, from the city. As were the visitors in the second ship. But today! At long last, you've come! The revenge will be carried out to the last detail. Those men have been dead two hundred centuries, but they left a city here to welcome you."

"Captain, sir, you're not feeling well. Perhaps you'd better come back to the ship, sir."

The city trembled.

The pavements opened and the men fell, screaming. Falling, they saw bright razors flash to meet them!

Time passed. Soon came the call:

"Smith?"

"Here!"

"Jensen?"

"Here!"

"Jones, Hutchinson, Springer?"

"Here!" "Here!" "Here!"

They stood by the door of the rocket.

"We return to Earth immediately."

"Yes, sir!"

The incisions on their necks were invisible, as were their hidden brass hearts and silver organs and the fine golden wire of their nerves. There was a faint electric hum from their heads.

"On the double!"

Nine men hurried the golden bombs of disease culture into the rocket.

"These are to be dropped on Earth."

"Right, sir!"

The rocket valve slammed. The rocket jumped into the sky.

As the thunder faded, the city lay upon the summer meadow. Its glass eyes were dulled over. The Ear relaxed, the great nostril vents stopped, the streets no longer weighed or balanced, and the hidden machinery paused in its bath of oil.

In the sky the rocket dwindled.

Slowly, pleasurably, the city enjoyed the luxury of dying.

THE MILLION-YEAR PICNIC

Somehow the idea was brought up by Mom that perhaps the whole family would enjoy a fishing trip. But they weren't Mom's words; Timothy knew that. They were Dad's words, and Mom used them for him somehow.

Dad shuffled his feet in a clutter of Martian pebbles and agreed. So immediately there was a tumult and a shouting, and very quickly the camp was tucked into capsules and containers, Mom slipped into traveling jumpers and blouse, Dad stuffed his pipe full with trembling hands, his eyes on the Martian sky, and the three boys piled yelling into the motorboat, none of them really keeping an eye on Mom and Dad, except Timothy.

Dad pushed a stud. The water boat sent a humming sound up into the sky. The water shook back and the boat nosed ahead, and the family cried, "Hurrah!"

Timothy sat in the back of the boat with Dad, his small fingers atop Dad's hairy ones, watching the canal twist, leaving the crumbled place behind where they had landed in their small family rocket all the way from Earth. He remembered the night before they left Earth, the hustling and hurrying, the rocket that Dad had found somewhere, somehow, and the talk of a vacation on Mars. A long way to go for a vacation, but Timothy said nothing because of his younger brothers. They came to Mars and now, first thing, or so they said, they were going fishing.

Dad had a funny look in his eyes as the boat went up-canal. A look that Timothy couldn't figure. It was made of strong light and maybe a sort of relief. It made the deep wrinkles laugh instead of worry or cry.

So there went the cooling rocket, around a bend, gone.

"How far are we going?" Robert splashed his hand. It looked like a small crab jumping in the violent water.

Dad exhaled. "A million years."

"Gee," said Robert.

"Look, kids." Mother pointed one soft long arm. "There's a dead city."

They looked with fervent anticipation, and the dead city lay dead for them alone, drowsing in a hot silence of summer made on Mars by a Martian weatherman.

And Dad looked as if he was pleased that it was dead.

It was a futile spread of pink rocks sleeping on a rise of sand, a few tumbled pillars, one lonely shrine, and then the sweep of sand again. Nothing else for miles. A white desert around the canal and a blue desert over it.

Just then a bird flew up. Like a stone thrown across a blue pond, hitting, falling deep, and vanishing.

Dad got a frightened look when he saw it. "I thought it was a rocket."

Timothy looked at the deep ocean sky, trying to see Earth and the war and the ruined cities and the men killing each other since the day he was born. But he saw nothing. The war was as removed and far off as two flies battling to the death in the arch of a great high and silent cathedral. And just as senseless.

William Thomas wiped his forehead and felt the touch of his son's hand on his arm, like a young tarantula, thrilled. He beamed at his son. "How goes it, Timmy?"

"Fine, Dad."

Timothy hadn't quite figured out what was ticking inside the vast adult mechanism beside him. The man with the immense hawk nose, sunburnt, peeling—and the hot blue eyes like agate marbles you play with after school in summer back on Earth, and the long thick columnar legs in the loose riding breeches.

"What are you looking at so hard, Dad?"

"I was looking for Earthian logic, common sense, good government, peace, and responsibility."

"All that up there?"

"No. I didn't find it. It's not there any more. Maybe it'll never be there again. Maybe we fooled ourselves that it was ever there."

"Huh?"

"See the fish," said Dad, pointing.

There rose a soprano clamor from all three boys as they rocked the boat in arching their tender necks to see. They *oobed* and *abed*. A silver ring fish floated by them, undulating, and closing like an iris, instantly, around food particles, to assimilate them.

Dad looked at it. His voice was deep and quiet.

"Just like war. War swims along, sees food, contracts. A moment later—Earth is gone."

"William," said Mom.

"Sorry," said Dad.

They sat still and felt the canal water rush cool, swift, and glassy. The only sound was the motor hum, the glide of water, the sun expanding the air.

"When do we see the Martians?" cried Michael.

"Quite soon, perhaps," said Father. "Maybe tonight."

"Oh, but the Martians are a dead race now," said Mom.

"No, they're not. I'll show you some Martians, all right," Dad said presently.

Timothy scowled at that but said nothing. Everything was odd now. Vacations and fishing and looks between people.

The other boys were already engaged making shelves of their small hands and peering under them toward the seven-foot stone banks of the canal, watching for Martians.

"What do they look like?" demanded Michael.

"You'll know them when you see them." Dad sort of laughed, and Timothy saw a pulse beating time in his cheek.

Mother was slender and soft, with a woven plait of spun-gold hair over her head in a tiara, and eyes the color of the deep cool canal water where it ran in shadow, almost purple, with flecks of amber caught in it. You could see her thoughts swimming around in her eyes, like fish—some bright, some dark, some fast, quick, some slow and easy, and sometimes, like when she looked up where Earth was, being nothing but color and nothing else. She sat in the boat's prow, one hand resting on the side lip, the other on the lap of her dark blue breeches, and a line of sunburnt soft neck showing where her blouse opened like a white flower.

She kept looking ahead to see what was there, and, not being able to see it clearly enough, she looked backward toward her husband, and through his eyes, reflected then, she saw what was ahead; and since he added part of himself to this reflection, a determined firmness, her face relaxed and she accepted it and she turned back, knowing suddenly what to look for.

Timothy looked too. But all he saw was a straight pencil line of canal going violent through a wide shallow valley penned by low, eroded hills, and on until it fell over the sky's edge. And this canal went on and on, through cities that would have rattled like beetles in a dry skull if you shook them. A hundred or two hundred cities dreaming hot summer-day dreams and cool summer-night dreams . . .

They had come millions of miles for this outing—to fish. But there had been a gun on the rocket. This was a vacation. But why all the food, more than enough to last them years and years, left hidden back there near the rocket? Vacation. Just behind the veil of the vacation was not a soft face of laughter, but something hard and bony and perhaps terrifying. Timothy could not lift the veil, and the two other boys were busy being ten and eight years old, respectively.

"No Martians yet. Nuts." Robert put his V-shaped chin on his hands and glared at the canal.

Dad had brought an atomic radio along, strapped to his wrist. It functioned on an old-fashioned principle: you held it against the bones near your ear and it vibrated singing or talking to you. Dad listened to it now. His face looked like one of those fallen Martian cities, caved in, sucked dry, almost dead.

Then he gave it to Mom to listen. Her lips dropped open.

"What—" Timothy started to question, but never finished what he wished to say.

For at that moment there were two titanic, marrow-jolting explosions that grew upon themselves, followed by a half-dozen minor concussions.

Jerking his head up, Dad notched the boat speed higher immediately. The boat leaped and jounced and spanked. This shook Robert out of his funk and elicited yelps of frightened but ecstatic joy from Michael, who clung to Mom's legs and watched the water pour by his nose in a wet torrent.

Dad swerved the boat, cut speed, and ducked the craft into a little branch canal and under an ancient, crumbling stone wharf that smelled of crab flesh. The boat rammed the wharf hard enough to throw them all forward, but no one was hurt, and Dad was already twisted to see if the ripples on the canal were enough to map their route into hiding. Water lines went across, lapped the stones, and rippled back to meet each other, settling, to be dappled by the sun. It all went away.

Dad listened. So did everybody.

Dad's breathing echoed like fists beating against the cold wet wharf stones. In the shadow, Mom's cat eyes just watched Father for some clue to what next.

Dad relaxed and blew out a breath, laughing at himself.

"The rocket, of course. I'm getting jumpy. The rocket."

Michael said, "What happened, Dad, what happened?"

"Oh, we just blew up our rocket, is all," said Timothy, trying to sound matter-of-fact. "I've heard rockets blown up before. Ours just blew."

"Why did we blow up our rocket?" asked Michael. "Huh, Dad?"

"It's part of the game, silly!" said Timothy.

"A game!" Michael and Robert loved the word.

"Dad fixed it so it would blow up and no one'd know where we landed or went! In case they ever came looking, see?"

"Oh boy, a secret!"

"Scared by my own rocket," admitted Dad to Mom. "I am nervous. It's silly to think there'll ever *be* any more rockets. Except *one*, perhaps, if Edwards and his wife get through with *their* ship."

He put his tiny radio to his ear again. After two minutes he dropped his hand as you would drop a rag.

"It's over at last," he said to Mom. "The radio just went off the atomic beam. Every other world station's gone. They dwindled down to a couple in the last few years. Now the air's completely silent. It'll probably remain silent."

"For how long?" asked Robert.

"Maybe—your great-grandchildren will hear it again," said Dad. He just sat there, and the children were caught in the center of his awe and defeat and resignation and acceptance.

Finally he put the boat out into the canal again, and they continued in the direction in which they had originally started.

It was getting late. Already the sun was down the sky, and a series of dead cities lay ahead of them.

Dad talked very quietly and gently to his sons. Many times in the past he had been brisk, distant, removed from them, but now he patted them on the head with just a word and they felt it.

"Mike, pick a city."

"What, Dad?"

"Pick a city, Son. Any one of these cities we pass."

"All right," said Michael. "How do I pick?"

"Pick the one you like the most. You, too, Robert and Tim. Pick the city you like best."

"I want a city with Martians in it," said Michael.

"You'll have that," said Dad. "I promise." His lips were for the children, but his eyes were for Mom.

They passed six cities in twenty minutes. Dad didn't say anything more about the explosions; he seemed much more interested in having fun with his sons, keeping them happy, than anything else.

Michael liked the first city they passed, but this was vetoed because everyone doubted quick first judgments. The second city nobody liked. It was an Earth Man's settlement, built of wood and already rotting into sawdust. Timothy liked the third city because it was large. The fourth and fifth were too small and the sixth brought acclaim from everyone, including Mother, who joined in the Gees, Goshes, and Look-at-thats!

There were fifty or sixty huge structures still standing, streets were dusty but paved, and you could see one or two old centrifugal fountains still pulsing wetly in the plazas. That was the only life—water leaping in the late sunlight.

"This is the city," said everybody.

Steering the boat to a wharf, Dad jumped out.

"Here we are. This is ours. This is where we live from now on!"

"From now on?" Michael was incredulous. He stood up, looking, and then turned to blink back at where the rocket used to be. "What about the rocket? What about Minnesota?"

"Here," said Dad.

He touched the small radio to Michael's blond head. "Listen."

Michael listened.

"Nothing," he said.

"That's right. Nothing. Nothing at all any more. No more Minneapolis, no more rockets, no more Earth."

Michael considered the lethal revelation and began to sob little dry sobs.

"Wait a moment," said Dad the next instant. "I'm giving you a lot more in exchange, Mike!"

"What?" Michael held off the tears, curious, but quite ready to continue in case Dad's further revelation was as disconcerting as the original.

"I'm giving you this city, Mike. It's yours."

"Mine?"

"For you and Robert and Timothy, all three of you, to own for yourselves."

Timothy bounded from the boat. "Look, guys, all for us! All of that!" He was playing the game with Dad, playing it large and playing it well. Later, after it was all over and things had settled, he could go off by himself and cry for ten minutes. But now it was still a game, still a family outing, and the other kids must be kept playing.

Mike jumped out with Robert. They helped Mom.

"Be careful of your sister," said Dad, and nobody knew what he meant until later.

They hurried into the great pink-stoned city, whispering among themselves, because dead cities have a way of making you want to whisper, to watch the sun go down.

"In about five days," said Dad quietly, "I'll go back down to where our rocket was and collect the food hidden in the ruins there and bring it here; and I'll hunt for Bert Edwards and his wife and daughters there."

"Daughters?" asked Timothy. "How many?"

"Four."

"I can see that'll cause trouble later." Mom nodded slowly.

"Girls." Michael made a face like an ancient Martian stone image. "Girls."

"Are they coming in a rocket, too?"

"Yes. If they make it. Family rockets are made for travel to the Moon, not Mars. We were lucky we got through."

"Where did you get the rocket?" whispered Timothy, for the other boys were running ahead.

"I saved it. I saved it for twenty years, Tim. I had it hidden away, hoping I'd never have to use it. I suppose I should have given it to the government for the war, but I kept thinking about Mars. . . ."

"And a picnic!"

"Right. This is between you and me. When I saw everything was finishing on Earth, after I'd waited until the last moment, I packed us up. Bert Edwards had a ship hidden, too, but we decided it would be safer to take off separately, in case anyone tried to shoot us down."

"Why'd you blow up the rocket, Dad?"

"So we can't go back, ever. And so if any of those evil men ever come to Mars they won't know we're here."

"Is that why you look up all the time?"

"Yes, it's silly. They won't follow us, ever. They haven't anything to follow with. I'm being too careful, is all."

Michael came running back. "Is this really *our* city, Dad?"

"The whole darn planet belongs to us, kids. The whole darn planet."

They stood there, King of the Hill, Top of the Heap, Ruler of All They Surveyed, Unimpeachable Monarchs and Presidents, trying to understand what it meant to own a world and how big a world really was.

Night came quickly in the thin atmosphere, and Dad left them in the square by the pulsing fountain, went down to the boat, and came walking back carrying a stack of paper in his big hands.

He laid the papers in a clutter in an old courtyard and set them afire. To keep warm, they crouched around the blaze and laughed, and Timothy saw the little letters leap like frightened animals when the flames touched and engulfed them. The papers crinkled like an old man's skin, and the cremation surrounded innumerable words: "GOVERNMENT BONDS; Business Graph, 1999; Religious Prejudice: An Essay; The Science of Logistics; Problems of the Pan-American Unity; Stock Report for July 3, 1998; The War Digest . . ."

Dad had insisted on bringing these papers for this purpose. He sat there and fed them into the fire, one by one, with satisfaction, and told his children what it all meant.

"It's time I told you a few things. I don't suppose it was fair, keeping so much from you. I don't know if you'll understand, but I have to talk, even if only part of it gets over to you."

He dropped a leaf in the fire.

"I'm burning a way of life, just like that way of life is being burned clean of Earth right now. Forgive me if I talk like a politician. I am, after all, a former state governor, and I was honest and they hated me for it. Life on Earth never settled down to doing anything very good. Science ran too far ahead of us too quickly, and the people got lost in a mechanical wilderness, like children making over pretty things, gadgets, helicopters, rockets; emphasizing the wrong items, emphasizing machines instead of how to run the machines. Wars got bigger and bigger and finally killed Earth. That's what the silent radio means. That's what we ran away from.

"We were lucky. There aren't any more rockets left. It's time you knew this isn't a fishing trip at all. I put off telling you. Earth is gone. Interplanetary travel won't be back for centuries, maybe never. But that way of life proved itself wrong and strangled itself with its own hands. You're young. I'll tell you this again every day until it sinks in."

He paused to feed more papers to the fire.

"Now we're alone. We and a handful of others who'll land in a few days. Enough to start over. Enough to turn away from all that back on Earth and strike out on a new line—"

The fire leaped up to emphasize his talking. And then all the papers were gone except one. All the laws and beliefs of Earth were burnt into small hot ashes which soon would be carried off in a wind.

Timothy looked at the last thing that Dad tossed in the fire. It was a map of the World, and it wrinkled and distorted itself hotly and went—flimpf—and was gone like a warm, black butterfly. Timothy turned away.

"Now I'm going to show you the Martians," said Dad. "Come on, all of you. Here, Alice." He took her hand.

Michael was crying loudly, and Dad picked him up and carried him, and they walked down through the ruins toward the canal.

The canal. Where tomorrow or the next day their future wives would come up in a boat, small laughing girls now, with their father and mother.

The night came down around them, and there were stars. But Timothy couldn't find Earth. It had already set. That was something to think about.

A night bird called among the ruins as they walked. Dad said, "Your mother and I will try to teach you. Perhaps we'll fail. I hope not. We've had a good lot to see and learn from. We planned this trip years ago, before you were born. Even if there hadn't been a war we would have come to Mars, I think, to live and form our own standard of living. It would have been another century before Mars would have been really poisoned by the Earth civilization. Now, of course—"

They reached the canal. It was long and straight and cool and wet and reflective in the night.

"I've always wanted to see a Martian," said Michael. "Where are they, Dad? You promised."

"There they are," said Dad, and he shifted Michael on his shoulder and pointed straight down.

The Martians were there. Timothy began to shiver.

The Martians were there—in the canal—reflected in the water. Timothy and Michael and Robert and Mom and Dad.

The Martians stared back up at them for a long, long silent time from the rippling water. . . .

ALL SUMMER IN A DAY

Ready?"

"Ready."

"Now?"

"Soon."

"Do the scientists really know? Will it happen today, will it?"

"Look, look; see for yourself!"

The children pressed to each other like so many roses, so many weeds, intermixed, peering out for a look at the hidden sun.

It rained.

It had been raining for seven years; thousands upon thousands of days compounded and filled from one end to the other with rain, with the drum and gush of water, with the sweet crystal fall of showers and the concussion of storms so heavy they were tidal waves come over the islands. A thousand forests had been crushed under the rain and grown up a thousand times to be crushed again. And this was the way life was forever on the planet Venus, and this was the schoolroom of the children of the rocket men and women who had come to a raining world to set up civilization and live out their lives.

"It's stopping, it's stopping!'

"Yes, yes!"

Margot stood apart from them, from these children who could

never remember a time when there wasn't rain and rain and rain. They were all nine years old, and if there had been a day, seven years ago, when the sun came out for an hour and showed its face to the stunned world, they could not recall. Sometimes, at night, she heard them stir, in remembrance, and she knew they were dreaming and remembering gold or yellow crayon or a coin large enough to buy the world with. She knew they thought they remembered a warmness, like a blushing in the face, in the body, in the arms and legs and trembling hands. But then they always awoke to the tatting drum, the endless shaking down of clear bead necklaces upon the roof, the walk, the gardens, the forests, and their dreams were gone.

All day yesterday they had read in class about the sun. About how like a lemon it was, and how hot. And they had written small stories or essays or poems about it:

> I think the sun is a flower,
> That blooms for just one hour.

That was Margot's poem, read in a quiet voice in the still classroom while the rain was falling outside.

"Aw, you didn't write that!" protested one of the boys.

"I did," said Margot. "I did."

"William!" said the teacher.

But that was yesterday. Now the rain was slackening, and the children were crushed in the great thick windows.

"Where's teacher?"

"She'll be back."

"She'd better hurry, we'll miss it!"

They turned on themselves, like a feverish wheel, all tumbling spokes.

Margot stood alone. She was a very frail girl who looked as if she had been lost in the rain for years and the rain had washed out the blue from her eyes and the red from her mouth and the yellow from her hair. She was an old photograph dusted from an album, whitened away, and if she spoke at all her voice would be a ghost. Now she stood, separate, staring at the rain and the loud wet world beyond the huge glass.

"What're *you* looking at?" said William.

Margot said nothing.

"Speak when you're spoken to." He gave her a shove. But she did not move; rather she let herself be moved only by him and nothing else.

They edged away from her, they would not look at her. She felt them go away. And this was because she would play no games with them in the echoing tunnels of the underground city. If they tagged her and ran, she stood blinking after them and did not follow. When the class sang songs about happiness and life and games her lips barely moved. Only when they sang about the sun and the summer did her lips move as she watched the drenched windows.

And then, of course, the biggest crime of all was that she had come here only five years ago from Earth, and she remembered the sun and the way the sun was and the sky was when she was four in Ohio. And they, they had been on Venus all their lives, and they had been only two years old when last the sun came out and had long since forgotten the color and heat of it and the way it really was. But Margot remembered.

"It's like a penny," she said once, eyes closed.

"No, it's not!" the children cried.

"It's like a fire," she said, "in the stove."

"You're lying, you don't remember!" cried the children.

But she remembered and stood quietly apart from all of them and watched the patterning windows. And once, a month ago, she had refused to shower in the school shower rooms, had clutched her hands to her ears and over her head, screaming the water mustn't touch her head. So after that, dimly, dimly, she sensed it, she was different and they knew her difference and kept away.

There was talk that her father and mother were taking her back to Earth next year; it seemed vital to her that they do so, though it would mean the loss of thousands of dollars to her family. And so, the children hated her for all these reasons of big and little consequence. They hated her pale snow face, her waiting silence, her thinness, and her possible future.

"Get away!" The boy gave her another push. "What're you waiting for?"

Then, for the first time, she turned and looked at him. And what she was waiting for was in her eyes.

"Well, don't wait around here!" cried the boy savagely. "You won't see nothing!"

Her lips moved.

"Nothing!" he cried. "It was all a joke, wasn't it?" He turned to the other children. "Nothing's happening today. Is it?"

They all blinked at him and then, understanding, laughed and shook their heads. "Nothing, nothing!"

"Oh, but," Margot whispered, her eyes helpless. "But this is the day, the scientists predict, they say, they *know*, the sun . . ."

"All a joke!" said the boy, and seized her roughly. "Hey, everyone, let's put her in a closet before teacher comes!"

"No," said Margot, falling back.

They surged about her, caught her up and bore her, protesting, and then pleading, and then crying, back into a tunnel, a room, a closet, where they slammed and locked the door. They stood looking at the door and saw it tremble from her beating and throwing herself against it. They heard her muffled cries. Then, smiling, they turned and went out and back down the tunnel, just as the teacher arrived.

"Ready, children?" She glanced at her watch.

"Yes!" said everyone.

"Are we all here?"

"Yes!"

The rain slackened still more.

They crowded to the huge door.

The rain stopped.

It was as if, in the midst of a film concerning an avalanche, a tornado, a hurricane, a volcanic eruption, something had, first, gone wrong with the sound apparatus, thus muffling and finally cutting off all noise, all of the blasts and repercussions and thunders, and then, second, ripped the film from the projector and inserted in its place a peaceful tropical slide which did not move or tremor. The world ground to a standstill. The silence was so immense and unbelievable that you felt your ears had been stuffed or you had lost your hearing altogether. The children put their hands to their ears. They stood apart. The door slid back and the smell of the silent, waiting world came in to them.

The sun came out.

It was the color of flaming bronze and it was very large. And the sky around it was a blazing blue tile color. And the jungle burned with sunlight as the children, released from their spell, rushed out, yelling, into the springtime.

"Now, don't go too far," called the teacher after them. "You've only two hours, you know. You wouldn't want to get caught out!"

But they were running and turning their faces up to the sky and feeling the sun on their cheeks like a warm iron; they were taking off their jackets and letting the sun burn their arms.

"Oh, it's better than the sun lamps, isn't it?"

"Much, much better!"

They stopped running and stood in the great jungle that covered Venus, that grew and never stopped growing, tumultuously, even as you watched it. It was a nest of octopi, clustering up great arms of fleshlike weed, wavering, flowering in this brief spring. It was the color of rubber and ash, this jungle, from the many years without sun. It was the color of stones and white cheeses and ink, and it was the color of the moon.

The children lay out, laughing, on the jungle mattress, and heard it sigh and squeak under them, resilient and alive. They ran among the trees, they slipped and fell, they pushed each other, they played hide-and-seek and tag, but most of all they squinted at the sun until tears ran down their faces, they put their hands up to that yellowness and that amazing blueness and they breathed of the fresh, fresh air and listened and listened to the silence which suspended them in a blessed sea of no sound and no motion. They looked at everything and savored everything. Then, wildly, like animals escaped from their caves, they ran and ran in shouting circles. They ran for an hour and did not stop running.

And then—

In the midst of their running one of the girls wailed.

Everyone stopped.

The girl, standing in the open, held out her hand.

"Oh, look, look," she said, trembling.

They came slowly to look at her opened palm.

In the center of it, cupped and huge, was a single raindrop.

She began to cry, looking at it.

They glanced quietly at the sky.

"Oh. Oh."

A few cold drops fell on their noses and their cheeks and their mouths. The sun faded behind a stir of mist. A wind blew cool around them. They turned and started to walk back toward the underground house, their hands at their sides, their smiles vanishing away.

A boom of thunder startled them and like leaves before a new hurricane, they tumbled upon each other and ran. Lightning struck ten miles away, five miles away, a mile, a half mile. The sky darkened into midnight in a flash.

They stood in the doorway of the underground for a moment until it was raining hard. Then they closed the door and heard the gigantic sound of the rain falling in tons and avalanches, everywhere and forever.

"Will it be seven more years?"

"Yes. Seven."

Then one of them gave a little cry.

"Margot!"

"What?"

"She's still in the closet where we locked her."

"Margot."

They stood as if someone had driven them, like so many stakes, into the floor. They looked at each other and then looked away. They glanced out at the world that was raining now and raining and raining steadily. They could not meet each other's glances. Their faces were solemn and pale. They looked at their hands and feet, their faces down.

"Margot."

One of the girls said, "Well ... ?"

No one moved.

"Go on," whispered the girl.

They walked slowly down the hall in the sound of cold rain. They turned through the doorway to the room in the sound of the storm and thunder, lightning on their faces, blue and terrible. They walked over to the closet door slowly and stood by it.

Behind the closet door was only silence.

They unlocked the door, even more slowly, and let Margot out.

THERE WILL COME SOFT RAINS

In the living room the voice-clock sang, *Tick-tock, seven o'clock, time to get up, time to get up, seven o'clock!* as if it were afraid that nobody would. The morning house lay empty. The clock ticked on, repeating and repeating its sounds into the emptiness. *Seven-nine, breakfast time, seven-nine!*

In the kitchen the breakfast stove gave a hissing sigh and ejected from its warm interior eight pieces of perfectly browned toast, eight eggs sunnyside up, sixteen slices of bacon, two coffees, and two cool glasses of milk.

"Today is August 4, 2026," said a second voice from the kitchen ceiling, "in the city of Allendale, California." It repeated the date three times for memory's sake. "Today is Mr. Featherstone's birthday. Today is the anniversary of Tilita's marriage. Insurance is payable, as are the water, gas, and light bills."

Somewhere in the walls, relays clicked, memory tapes glided under electric eyes.

Eight-one, tick-tock, eight-one o'clock, off to school, off to work, run, run, eight-one! But no doors slammed, no carpets took the soft tread of rubber heels. It was raining outside. The weather box on the front door sang quietly: "Rain, rain, go away; rubbers, raincoats for today . . ." And the rain tapped on the empty house, echoing.

Outside, the garage chimed and lifted its door to reveal the waiting car. After a long wait the door swung down again.

At eight-thirty the eggs were shriveled and the toast was like stone. An aluminum wedge scraped them into the sink, where hot water whirled them down a metal throat which digested and flushed them away to the distant sea. The dirty dishes were dropped into a hot washer and emerged twinkling dry.

Nine-fifteen, sang the clock, *time to clean*.

Out of warrens in the wall, tiny robot mice darted. The rooms were acrawl with the small cleaning animals, all rubber and metal. They thudded against chairs, whirling their mustached runners, kneading the rug nap, sucking gently at hidden dust. Then, like mysterious invaders, they popped into their burrows. Their pink electric eyes faded. The house was clean.

Ten o'clock. The sun came out from behind the rain. The house stood alone in a city of rubble and ashes. This was the one house left standing. At night the ruined city gave off a radioactive glow which could be seen for miles.

Ten-fifteen. The garden sprinklers whirled up in golden founts, filling the soft morning air with scatterings of brightness. The water pelted windowpanes, running down the charred west side where the house had been burned evenly free of its white paint. The entire west face of the house was black, save for five places. Here the silhouette in paint of a man mowing a lawn. Here, as in a photograph, a woman bent to pick flowers. Still farther over, their images burned on wood in one titanic instant, a small boy, hands flung into the air; higher up, the image of a thrown ball, and opposite him a girl, hands raised to catch a ball which never came down.

The five spots of paint—the man, the woman, the children, the ball—remained. The rest was a thin charcoaled layer.

The gentle sprinkler rain filled the garden with falling light.

Until this day, how well the house had kept its peace. How carefully it had inquired, "Who goes there? What's the password?" and, getting no answer from lonely foxes and whining cats, it had shut up its windows and drawn shades in an old-maidenly preoccupation with self-protection which bordered on a mechanical paranoia.

It quivered at each sound, the house did. If a sparrow brushed a window, the shade snapped up. The bird, startled, flew off! No, not even a bird must touch the house!

The house was an altar with ten thousand attendants, big, small, servicing, attending, in choirs. But the gods had gone away, and the ritual of the religion continued senselessly, uselessly.

Twelve noon.

A dog whined, shivering, on the front porch.

The front door recognized the dog voice and opened. The dog, once huge and fleshy, but now gone to bone and covered with sores, moved in and through the house, tracking mud. Behind it whirred angry mice, angry at having to pick up mud, angry at inconvenience.

For not a leaf fragment blew under the door but what the wall panels flipped open and the copper scrap rats flashed swiftly out. The offending dust, hair, or paper, seized in miniature steel jaws, was raced back to the burrows. There, down tubes which fed into the cellar, it was dropped into the sighing vent of an incinerator which sat like evil Baal in a dark corner.

The dog ran upstairs, hysterically yelping to each door, at last realizing, as the house realized, that only silence was here.

It sniffed the air and scratched the kitchen door. Behind the door, the stove was making pancakes which filled the house with a rich baked odor and the scent of maple syrup.

The dog frothed at the mouth, lying at the door, sniffing, its eyes turned to fire. It ran wildly in circles, biting at its tail, spun in a frenzy, and died. It lay in the parlor for an hour.

Two o'clock, sang a voice.

Delicately sensing decay at last, the regiments of mice hummed out as softly as blown gray leaves in an electrical wind.

Two-fifteen.

The dog was gone.

In the cellar, the incinerator glowed suddenly and a whirl of sparks leaped up the chimney.

Two thirty-five.

Bridge tables sprouted from patio walls. Playing cards fluttered onto pads in a shower of pips. Martinis manifested on an oaken bench with egg-salad sandwiches. Music played.

But the tables were silent and the cards untouched.

At four o'clock the tables folded like great butterflies back through the paneled walls.

Four-thirty.

The nursery walls glowed.

Animals took shape: yellow giraffes, blue lions, pink antelopes, lilac panthers cavorting in crystal substance. The walls were glass. They looked out upon color and fantasy. Hidden films clocked through well-oiled sprockets, and the walls lived. The nursery floor was woven to resemble a crisp, cereal meadow. Over this ran aluminum roaches and iron crickets, and in the hot still air butterflies of delicate red tissue wavered among the sharp aromas of animal spoors! There was the sound like a great matted yellow hive of bees within a dark bellows, the lazy bumble of a purring lion. And there was the patter of okapi feet and the murmur of a fresh jungle rain, like other hoofs, falling upon the summer-starched grass. Now the walls dissolved into distances of parched weed, mile on mile, and warm endless sky. The animals drew away into thorn brakes and water holes.

It was the children's hour.

Five o'clock. The bath filled with clear hot water.

Six, seven, eight o'clock. The dinner dishes manipulated like magic tricks, and in the study a *click*. In the metal stand opposite the hearth where a fire now blazed up warmly, a cigar popped out, half an inch of soft gray ash on it, smoking, waiting.

Nine o'clock. The beds warmed their hidden circuits, for nights were cool here.

Nine-five. A voice spoke from the study ceiling:

"Mrs. McClellan, which poem would you like this evening?"

The house was silent.

The voice said at last, "Since you express no preference, I shall select a poem at random." Quiet music rose to back the voice. "Sara Teasdale. As I recall, your favorite. . . .

There will come soft rains and the smell of the ground,
And swallows circling with their shimmering sound;

And frogs in the pools singing at night,
And wild plum trees in tremulous white;

Robins will wear their feathery fire,
Whistling their whims on a low fence-wire;

And not one will know of the war, not one
Will care at last when it is done.

Not one would mind, neither bird nor tree,
If mankind perished utterly;

And Spring herself, when she woke at dawn
Would scarcely know that we were gone.

The fire burned on the stone hearth and the cigar fell away into a mound of quiet ash on its tray. The empty chairs faced each other between the silent walls, and the music played.

At ten o'clock the house began to die.

The wind blew. A falling tree bough crashed through the kitchen window. Cleaning solvent, bottled, shattered over the stove. The room was ablaze in an instant!

"Fire!" screamed a voice. The house lights flashed, water pumps shot water from the ceilings. But the solvent spread on the linoleum, licking, eating, under the kitchen door, while the voices took it up in chorus: "Fire, fire, fire!"

The house tried to save itself. Doors sprang tightly shut, but the windows were broken by the heat and the wind blew and sucked upon the fire.

The house gave ground as the fire in ten billion angry sparks moved with flaming ease from room to room and then up the stairs. While scurrying water rats squeaked from the walls, pistoled their water, and ran for more. And the wall sprays let down showers of mechanical rain.

But too late. Somewhere, sighing, a pump shrugged to a stop. The quenching rain ceased. The reserve water supply which had filled baths and washed dishes for many quiet days was gone.

The fire crackled up the stairs. It fed upon Picassos and Matisses in the upper halls, like delicacies, baking off the oily flesh, tenderly crisping the canvases into black shavings.

Now the fire lay in beds, stood in windows, changed the colors of drapes!

And then, reinforcements.

From attic trapdoors, blind robot faces peered down with faucet mouths gushing green chemical.

The fire backed off, as even an elephant must at the sight of a dead snake. Now there were twenty snakes whipping over the floor, killing the fire with a clear cold venom of green froth.

But the fire was clever. It had sent flame outside the house, up through the attic to the pumps there. An explosion! The attic brain which directed the pumps was shattered into bronze shrapnel on the beams.

The fire rushed back into every closet and felt of the clothes hung there.

The house shuddered, oak bone on bone, its bared skeleton cringing from the heat, its wire, its nerves revealed as if a surgeon had torn the skin off to let the red veins and capillaries quiver in the scalded air. Help, help! Fire! Run, run! Heat snapped mirrors like the first brittle winter ice. And the voices wailed, Fire, fire, run, run, like a tragic nursery rhyme, a dozen voices, high, low, like children dying in a forest, alone, alone. And the voices fading as the wires popped their sheathings like hot chestnuts. One, two, three, four, five voices died.

In the nursery the jungle burned. Blue lions roared, purple giraffes bounded off. The panthers ran in circles, changing color, and ten million animals, running before the fire, vanished off toward a distant steaming river. . . .

Ten more voices died. In the last instant under the fire avalanche, other choruses, oblivious, could be heard announcing the time, playing music, cutting the lawn by remote-control mower, or setting an umbrella frantically out and in, the slamming and opening front door, a thousand things happening, like a clock shop when each clock strikes the hour insanely before or after the other, a scene of maniac confusion, yet unity; singing, screaming, a few last cleaning mice darting bravely out to carry the horrid ashes away! And one voice, with sublime disregard for the situation, read poetry aloud in the fiery study, until all the films spools burned, until all the wires withered and the circuits cracked.

The fire burst the house and let it slam flat down, puffing out skirts of spark and smoke.

In the kitchen, an instant before the rain of fire and timber, the stove could be seen making breakfasts at a psychopathic rate, ten dozen eggs, six loaves of toast, twenty dozen bacon strips, which, eaten by fire, started the stove working again, hysterically hissing!

The crash. The attic smashing into kitchen and parlor. The parlor into cellar, cellar into subcellar. Deep freeze, armchair, film tapes, circuits, beds, and all like skeletons thrown in a cluttered mound deep under.

Smoke and silence. A great quantity of smoke.

Dawn showed faintly in the east. Among the ruins, one wall stood alone. Within the wall, a last voice said, over and over again and again, even as the sun rose to shine upon the heaped rubble and steam:

"Today is August 5, 2026, today is August 5, 2026, today is . . ."

THE AFFLUENCE OF DESPAIR

H ow come? How come we're one of the greatest nations in the world . . . and yet, there is this feeling of Doom? How come, while our president walks wounded, we ourselves jog along nicely, but . . . under a dark cloud that says something awful is about to happen? How come, with 500,000 immigrants a year yammering to flood in . . . we enjoy what could be described as The Affluence of Despair?

America today: We wonder how we look at this hour, what we feel this minute, what we're imagining now. So we switch the television on. How do we look in the 80 million-lensed TV eye on America the beautiful? Did you catch me last night confessing what I caught and what caught me?

Recall Starbuck's advice to mad Ahab? "Do not fear me, old man. Beware of thy self, my captain." America should beware of itself. Today, we are everywhere loving to be watched. My God, look, I am on Channel Nine! We do not suffer from totalitarian lunatics, but from the astonishing proliferation of our images. We perform for ourselves, not Big Brother. We have fallen in love with mirrors. Flash a camera and your merest broccoli-headed citizen morphs into Travolta or Madonna.

And all of it on local TV news, in 15-second disaster updates.

Breaking bones, breaking news, at 11. "Tell us, Mrs. Guiterrez, how's it feel with your son shotgunned minutes ago?"

We do not go to the theater, we *are* the theater. We have invaded the TV studios and run the country to mania on talking-head shows. We display our brilliance on "Jeopardy," forgetting that its factoids are 90% useless once you kill the set. We don't ask who Napoleon was but where he was buried. Or why he invaded Russia, but when.

A friend of mine bragged he had bought a dish that could cup, cull, and catch 200 channels raining across a moron sky. Hell, I said, you've just got a bigger windmill to catch more of nothing: O. J. blood here, House of Usher AIDS there, the Killing Fields of America's high roads, each car a glorious pyre to mindless speed. And in every front yard a Mrs. Guiterrez being questioned but watching the TV mirror to see how she plays.

Those epileptic souls at football, baseball, hockey matches, who frenzy for the TV camera—how to end their pantomimes? We the judges and jurors trying, damning or freeing the guilty, weighing topics we're unqualified to answer—how to cork this motor-mouth?

The problem is not necessarily with our national full-coverage news, which can be only mildly depressing. It is with the assault of the local TV paparazzi, who machine-gun you with decapitations, sexual harassments, gangster executions in 15-second explosions for the full half-hour. No attack army could survive that fusillade. Bullets, real and psychological, wound and kill.

So we must stand alert, ward off a central core despair, target our Panic of the Week Syndrome, guard against the local TV news séance. Every week, 52 weeks a year, they need a prime disaster focus to spin the garbage and glue the potato people to the tube.

Remember the Alar-poisoned apples that the dinner time news-bites claimed would destroy us, so they destroyed some part of the apple industry? Recall the poison cellar gas rising to asphyxiate your kids? Or those arsenic Peruvian grapes promising to strip our gears? Or the Three Mile Island nuclear meltdown where nothing melted, no injuries, no deaths? Panic for two weeks, make it three. Ratings up. Morale down.

What to do? Leave a message on your local station's machine, describing their stupidity. If you meet their news readers, tell them that they are overpaid and underbrained. Ask them if it would be too much trouble to air 20-second newsbites instead of 15-second flashes. Think of the extra enrichment!

Stop saying that these TV hookers are high-class thinkers. Ask them to give back their fortunes and hand us real news. Instead of treating them as Cinderellas, tell them they are ugly sisters whose lips spew not diamonds and emeralds but spiders, frogs and toads: Each time they open their mouths, they spoil the ecology.

We must speak to these confessors of our dark souls and tell them that their awful truths in awesome repetition end with the Big Lie. We are not as bad as they say we are, but we feel this despair because they have somehow won us over.

The bottom line is that if you stare like stunned deer in mid-road, blinded by the lights that rush to run you down, you must expect that 1,000 such nights will convince you that the end of the world is at hand, that America is bestial, and that suicide, murder, rape, and AIDS are our lot.

We have condemned ourselves. Now we must save ourselves. No one else can. Shut off the set. Write your local TV news people. Tell them to go to hell. Go sit on the lawn with friends.